PRAISE FOR *THE (*

"In this Southern Gothic love letter to the spookier side of New Orleans's storied past, Arden spins out a moody tale of magic and mystery . . . A thoroughly satisfying page-turner and a strong debut."
—*Publishers Weekly*, Starred Review

"Debut author Arden offers readers a full plate of Southern Gothic atmospherics and sparkling teen romance in a patiently crafted tale that will best reward careful readers . . . Satisfying teen entertainment but also a cathartic, uncompromising tribute to New Orleans."
—*Kirkus Reviews*

"A slow-burning novel in the tradition of Anne Rice."
—*Rue Morgue Magazine*

"A smart story with a surprising amount of emotional depth . . . in the grand tradition of *Buffy* and *The Lost Boys*."
—*IndieReader*

"Nothing short of a stunner . . . It's as if Arden took her life experiences within the Vieux Carre, assembled a few Hogwarts students as Avengers, channeled Magneto into Wednesday Adams, and drenched the process in Parisian detail."
—Examiner.com

"Eerie, magical, and gritty, getting into the grimy seams of New Orleans in the tradition of Anne Rice or Poppy Z Brite."
—*SP Reviews*

The Romeo Catchers

ALSO BY ALYS ARDEN

The Casquette Girls Series

The Casquette Girls

The Romeo Catchers

ALYS ARDEN

SKYSCAPE

SKYSCAPE

Published by Skyscape, New York

www.apub.com

Amazon, the Amazon logo, and Skyscape are trademarks of Amazon.com, Inc., or its affiliates.

ISBN-13: 9781503940000
ISBN-10: 1503940004

Cover illustration by Galen Dara

Cover design by Maeve Norton

Map illustration by Mystic Blue Signs

Chapter heading designs by Christy Zolty

Printed in the United States of America

To the generations of Medici, whose lives were more lush and enigmatic than the pages of fiction.

And to the Starman. You'll always be alive in Adele's world. RIP.

PART 1

The Secrets

My guiding principle is this: Guilt is never to be doubted.

Franz Kafka

CHAPTER 1
Brooklyn Boy

The water tastes like mudpies as it rushes my throat—a mix of dirt, oil, and unimaginably foul dregs turns my screams into garbles. My lungs jerk for air, but there's only more water to inhale. It fills my ears, dulling the sounds of branches snapping and porches cracking as the river smashes down the street. I kick wildly as the current swoops at my feet, pulling us deeper with each passing second. My fingertips break the surface, but waves roll into my chest, pummeling us back down, debris scraping my arms as I try to shield it away. I no longer hear her screams. One more breath of water will be the end.

Don't panic. Dominate. Panicking is not an option.

My feet thrash, searching for the street to push us back up to the top, but there's only water—below me, above me, filling my lungs like lava.

Fight the current, Isaac. Dominate.

But there's only water.

A gasp jerked me awake. My arms flailed as I dropped the five feet from the crappy mattress and crashed onto my hip on the stainless steel floor.

Turning on my back, I lay there in the darkness, heart racing, trying to catch my breath. *I'm not drowning. It was a dream.*

I moved my wrist close to my face and pushed away the swath of embroidered bracelets covering my watch: 0100 hours. Just like every other night.

Over the last four months, I'd lost count of the number of times I'd fallen out of the bed, but I still hadn't moved to the bottom bunk, despite my roommate having moved out to shack up with a nurse he'd met at a blood drive back in September.

I rolled onto my chest, pressed myself up, and then back down. "One." *Moving to the bottom bunk is admitting defeat.* "Two." *The nightmare winning.* "Three."

It will go away.

I used tricks to not think about the nightmare during the day—stuff the shrink had told me after my mom died. "Focus excess energy into a creative outlet," he'd advised. I sketched more hours of the day than not, and now I was doing metalwork in Mac's studio. *Check.* I pressed myself faster to the floor.

"Nine," I said into the darkness. "Ten."

"Engage in physical activity to relieve excess anxiety," he'd said. Work covered that. Plus the patrolling. And the training. *Check.* The burn moved up my arms into my shoulders as I pounded through ten more. I welcomed the pain; at least I was alive to feel it.

"Twenty."

Lastly, he'd always said, "Talk to someone about it."

It's just a stupid fucking dream—just stop thinking about it.

But that's the problem: it wasn't just a dream. It was a memory. My first day in New Orleans, or my second? Third? It all became a blur once the levees started breaking. There hadn't been nearly enough of us. Not enough muscles to pull people out, and not enough medics to patch people up. Not enough social workers for the kids or shelters for the animals. There weren't enough military to stop the looting or enough supplies for people in the convention center. There hadn't been enough of . . . anything.

Four months later, every time I slept, I drowned.

I always woke from the fall with raw lungs, as if I'd been choking on the water all over again. "Thirty."

Focus on things you can control. Things you can affect.

I thought about the roof I was nearly finished rebuilding with my crew. I thought about flying. I thought about all the places in New Orleans I wanted to sketch—all the sights burned into my memory. I thought about Adele, although I'm not sure how much control I had of that situation. I wished she were here right now. I'd tell her about the nightmare. "Forty."

Pfft. No, you wouldn't. "Forty-one."

I thought about losing her, and the push-ups went faster. *She picked you,* I reminded myself. Sometimes it didn't feel like it, with that asshat locked in the attic half a mile away.

I engaged my core, shifting some of the weight off my wrists. "Forty-six. Forty-seven."

Niccolò Medici.

"Fifty."

"Fifty-one." I pushed harder. *You have to be stronger.*

"Fifty-three. Fifty-four."

Quicker.

"Fifty-five."

Smarter.

"Fifty-six."

More in control.

"Fifty-seven."

If you're going to protect people.

"Fifty-eight. Fifty-nine. Sixty."

My arms shook just like they had in the floodwaters. *A million push-ups won't make you stronger than Mother Nature.* I slammed through ten more.

"Seventy."

And a million push-ups will never make you as strong as them.

When I got to eighty, I collapsed onto the floor and turned over, the stainless steel cool against my sweaty back.

The coven already defeated the Medici clan.

It was true, but I didn't need a crystal ball to know the fight wasn't over.

My back arched, and I sprang to my feet. Not exactly with the deftness of Bruce Lee, but a move I'd been practicing relentlessly. I'd have it down soon.

In autopilot mode, I stepped into my worn-down sneakers, pulled the laces, and ran out the door, down the hallway, and up the stairs as quietly as I could, until my breath was louder than my steps.

On the outer deck, I broke into a sprint. I knew exactly how many steps it was to the edge of the SS *Hope*, the shithole I called home— which I was quite certain was the gateway to Dante's inferno and one morning I would actually wake up in hell. *But it's fine.* Really. Half the population of New Orleans had it a lot worse.

One. Two. Three steps up the sidewall, and I kicked off the rail and leaped out into the darkness, the moon guiding my swan dive. *Hold it. Steady.* Warmth spread through my body in an explosion of prickles, and just before my head made contact with the water, I swooped back up.

Higher.

Higher.

Higher.

The wind zipped through my feathers. This was the way to stop thinking about the dream. To stop thinking about failed levees and water crashing over us. This was the way to feel close to my mom.

When I flew, everything felt coated in a thin layer of magic— somewhere in between real and celestial.

In the air, it was easy to realize I couldn't control everything. I could be sharper and faster, and I could perfect my swoops and dives, but I was still in the hands of Mother Nature, whose silent black sky dripped crystal stars above me—the flecks of light enough for my bird vision to see perfectly below. I caught the current and glided down the street, through the oak trees and the lingering protection spells on Esplanade Avenue.

Before I'd come down south, I thought I had everything figured out. It was just before my eighteenth birthday: I'd spend one last summer painting the faces of sticky-handed kids down at Coney Island, one last summer surfing the Rockaways with the guys from the neighborhood, and one last summer tumbling around Sherri Steinman's backseat before she returned to SVA and pretended I didn't exist. Then one more year at Stuyvesant before I broke my pop's heart and told him I wasn't going to Columbia, his alma mater, and instead was going to Parsons or Pratt to study fine art or maybe industrial design—that I hadn't quite decided. It'd taken half my summer cash just to pay all the application fees for both schools, so he wouldn't find out.

SAT, *check*. Early admissions application, *check*. Portfolio, *check*. International volunteer work, *check*. Essay on "The Importance of Street Art in Urban Development," bullshit extracurriculars, and good-enough grades. *Check. Check. Check.* Other than a million absences due to being dragged around by my pop's office, my record was perfect for art-school admittance officers.

But then the Storm hit and everything changed.

That's how we ended up in New Orleans . . . how I became a high school dropout and ended up living on a navy ship. And how I met the girl of my dreams. So, planning was for the birds. That's the other thing I hadn't planned for: being a witch.

I veered from the river and swooped over the Moonwalk, over the train tracks, and up over the amphitheater, which was my favorite place in the city. Adele had taken me there, not the night of our first kiss or anything like that—no, that was in a mold-infested Storm house, *moron, Isaac*. We'd been in the amphitheater the night Adele first showed me her magic. Before that we'd had a million secrets; now we didn't have any. Now I didn't keep anything from her.

Well, at least I tried not to. Really, really tried not to.

My wings tilted, and I made a wide turn onto Toulouse, cruising past Le Chat Noir, Mac's club. From the outside it looked completely shut, but if you felt for it, you could sense the vibrations coming from the back of the property. Then again, maybe it was just me? Most of my senses were amplified when I turned, or "transmuted," as Désirée called it. Sometimes I even felt like my brain worked better this way.

The magic was extraordinary, but new; sometimes it was still hard to fathom.

It was still hard to believe we pulled off Halloween night. Contained the vampires, and reinstated the curse our ancestors had cast three hundred years ago. *But what if the curse doesn't hold and they escape again?* Sometimes I think I'm stressed out more now than when they were on the loose, which was probably exactly what Niccolò Medici wanted.

Fucker.

And so, paranoia made the convent a regular part of my patrolling route. But not yet. After the club, it was always Vodou Pourvoyeur.

Only in New Orleans would the biggest political family in history also be the biggest witching family in town. *Actually, that makes perfect sense.* Just one meeting with Désirée's gran and her bags of bones, and you knew there was nothing to worry about at the shop, but I always did a full loop anyway, because Désirée and I were connected now, magically speaking. Dee loved to act blasé when it came to magic, anything to do with family tradition—which I could relate to: her family produced witches like mine produced military pilots, generation after generation, and there was no chance in hell I was going down that route—but Dee secretly loved it all. And if I knew her, she wasn't sleeping right now either. She'd probably been up all night working on finding our other coven members, one of our current points of disagreement.

I just didn't care about finding the other members. I was perfectly content with her and Adele and my Air powers. Plus, with only half a coven, we could never give the Medici what they wanted—we couldn't break our ancestor's curse.

I glided over the brick wall that surrounded the back of the Borges property. In the middle of the post-Storm-ravaged city of brown and gray and rust, the Borges courtyard was an oasis that rivaled the botanical gardens in Brooklyn. *Earth witches.*

Banana trees and elephant ears towered over the brick wall, while ferns and vines crawled over every inch, between blossoming flowers whose shades of marigold and plum made you feel like you were somewhere way more exotic than Louisiana. Part forest. Part jungle. All magical.

I loved the hidden sanctuary.

I flew into an herb bed whose perfectly symmetrical rows of Kelly-green basil leaves were far too large to not have been magically modified. I practiced swooping in and out, like it was my personal obstacle course.

"Infected," a voice said, startling me so abruptly I nearly crashed into an enlarged sunflower. Throughout my weeks of patrolling, no one had ever been in the courtyard at this hour.

"Crimes against . . ." Her voice petered out, but I recognized it—Désirée's gran, Ritha. Definitely not someone I wanted to think *I* was a trespasser, but instead of hightailing it out, I swooped low along the algae-coated, bricked path, curious about these murmurs of a crime.

"Not right. Not right," she muttered. "This town is not right . . ."

I dropped to the ground, hiding beneath blue flowers whose petals hung over me like blooming bells.

"Something's upsetting the balance."

I peered out between the drooping flowers to get a better look at the vine-entwined enclave in the garden where she sat. A single candle flame cast the shadows of ivy onto her headdress, which gleamed white in the dark night. A cement fountain of a horned creature obstructed my view of whoever she was speaking to. I hopped a few steps closer but still saw no one else.

"Not mundane crimes," she said.

My feathers pricked up, telling me to get the hell out, but crime convo was my catnip—birdnip—and kept me there against my better judgment.

"Everything is linked," she said, her head falling forward and then bobbing back up.

I hopped a few steps closer. *What's linked? The crime wave?*

"Supernatural. Ripples."

Are they talking about the vampires? Because that crime wave is over. You're welcome, Ritha.

I crept closer, trying to see who she was talking to. Ritha whipped my way, flinging her arm directly at me, and in an explosion of magic I was lying on the ground in human form, shielding my head as if to protect myself from supernatural shrapnel.

"Ripple. Ripple. Ripple!" she yelled.

When I looked up, there was no one else there—her eyes were completely white, as if rolled back in her head, and her finger was pointed at me.

"The magical ecosystem. Destroy the binding, and everything will unravel."

I stood up, her white-eyed, glossy gaze following me.

"Witch," she said, taking a step forward, causing me to take one back. *"Air witch."*

The way she said it suddenly made me feel like that was a bad thing.

"Ghost witch." Her mouth opened into a hiss, and I stumbled back, losing my footing. Before I could hit the ground, I took crow form again and conjured my own current to lift me into the sky faster than my wings could flap.

"Protect the binding, protect the magic . . . !" Her voice faded out under the sounds of my pounding pulse.

It took several blocks to regain my composure in flight, the air current pushing down beneath me at an unnatural speed thanks to my magical boost.

Next on my route usually came the abandoned brothel, but tonight I skipped it, feeling the need to put a little more distance between me and Ritha Borges.

What the hell was she talking about? Supernatural crime? Could more vamps have arrived in town? Or maybe I was just thinking about vampires because I'd arrived at the convent.

Ironically, the Catholic property was under the protection spells of *my* family, because Susannah Norwood Bowen had lived here in 1728— so it always got more than a flyby. I circled the perimeter, checking out each one of the window shutters, which were secured with a thousand antique nails and Adele's family magic, then I swooped over the roof and around the attic, where the vamps were trapped. The original four: Gabriel Medici; his two vamp-spawn, Lisette and Martine; and his sister, Giovanna. And, of course, the two bonus vamps we captured when we reinstated the curse, the biggest assholes of the lot: Emilio and Niccolò.

"Dammit!" I yelled, jerking back to human form about thirty seconds before I'd meant to, tumbling the last four feet to the roof.

I got up and shook it off, cursing all the more.

Stop letting that bloodsucking, leather-jacket-wearing asshole get under your skin.

I paced the length of the roof. Whenever I thought about Nicco, it was harder to control my magic, and nothing pissed me off more than losing control of my magic.

Nothing other than Nicco.

I paused, fishing a small metal object out of my wallet; I flipped it into the air with a casualness that contradicted the precious way I kept it hidden. With a quick whip, I caught it and continued to pace.

I flicked it up again, almost hoping a strong gust would take it away, relieving me of all responsibility. Of course, I didn't *really* wish for that; otherwise I'd have conjured up a gust and spun it all the way up to the Arctic.

I had no idea what it was, but Nicco must have given it to Adele on Halloween night before he threw her out the attic window, because she'd been holding it when I caught her. I was pretty sure she didn't remember ever having it.

It was just smaller than my palm and resembled origami made of folded metal—pewter, maybe? On the smooth side, three interlocking circles had been etched, each with a triangular peak, so they looked like three diamond rings. Something about it was romantic, which annoyed me even more. Leaving behind tokens had *not* been part of our plan. Then again, I don't think ending up in the attic had been part of Nicco's plan either. He must have known it was a possibility though if he'd thought ahead enough to bring this stupid thing. I had the sneaking suspicion that whatever it was, it was his ticket to getting out of the attic. His insurance plan.

Dammit.

The thought of Nicco being one step ahead pissed me off the most. I hated that he'd been the one to come up with the plan—that he'd insisted Adele would risk her own freedom to save everyone else. "If it comes down to it," he'd said, "I'll throw her to safety, and you have to catch her." Then he told me what he'd do to me if I failed to catch her.

He was right about needing the plan. Only, I can't imagine that me ending up with Adele, and with this *thing*, was exactly what he had in mind.

I swallowed a laugh. *It's not funny, Isaac.* I hated it. It was the only secret I had from her.

This stupid metal thing, and me and Nicco's plan on Halloween night.

I sat down, peering out over the French Quarter, legs dangling over the roof's edge, just like I'd done so many other nights. I squeezed the metal object in my palm until the corners pierced my skin.

Can you smell that blood, Nicco? I hope so. I hope it drives you nuts.

I flicked the metal origami up and watched it spin back into my hand—the prize waiting to be claimed. *Let him try.* If it weren't for the promise I made to the coven, I'd burn the whole convent down right now, vampires and all. I hated Niccolò Medici. And not just because he was a vampire—a killer. I hated him because he was in love with my girlfriend.

He'd never told me he was in love with Adele. In fact, he'd never really said much at all. But he must have known she'd close the seal after he threw her out the window. As far as I could see, there were only two possible explanations why Nicco would allow himself to be trapped. *Cursed.* The first was that he loved Adele, and he was willing to trade his life for hers. The second was that she was worth more to him alive than dead—so much so that he betrayed his family and trapped himself inside the coven's spell.

All so she could live.

Either way, he'd traded her martyrdom for his own—not that it was quite the same considering he was immortal but not exactly something you did for an acquaintance. *None of that matters now, because Adele thinks Nicco tried to kill her.*

I imagined him lying there in cold fury, judging me for not correcting Adele's mistake. Part of me knew he was right, but when she saw him as her potential killer, it was the first time she saw him for what he truly was.

A monster.

"I couldn't do it," I said into the darkness. "Sorry, Nicco. But you belong locked away."

Pushing away the guilt, I remembered the morning I'd tried to return the metal object to her. I knew it wasn't right to keep it, but then she kissed me—a kiss free of tears and elixirs—and I suddenly didn't care anymore if she knew the whole truth, just as long as she never saw Nicco again.

I should have been ecstatic, now that he was trapped for eternity, but I couldn't help thinking Niccolò Medici was the kind of guy who always had a backup plan.

My fingers crushed around the metal. *She doesn't owe him anything.* If the way to prevent him from reentering her life meant me being haunted by him forever through this origami thing, then so be it.

I could feel him beneath the roof. All of them. It was a hint of the same cold feeling I got when I neared a dead body on a recovery site. Death.

It made sense—you can't be a vampire without dying. Just like you can't be a vampire without being a monster.

I slipped it back into my wallet, ran the length of the convent roof, and jumped off. It was stupid and risky, and I'd never do it if it wasn't for the curfew, but it made me feel like I owned the streets of the French Quarter, and that they didn't.

I swooped back up and over the roofs. There was one more stop after the convent.

I always told myself I'd just check on her, but it never ended up that way. I circled Adele's house three times before landing on the second-story wrought-iron balcony across the street. If I stayed behind the potted plant, I was out of her sight line from the window. I think. She hated it when I perched across the street.

I knew she'd especially hate it tonight. She'd done her best to hide it all week, but I'd seen the ambivalence setting in. The wall she was putting up to prevent the pain from overwhelming her . . . Hopefully tomorrow would bring her some closure. My beak opened into a wide yawn, and I stretched my wings.

My perching wasn't about her; it was about me. I had to be at work in two hours, and when I slept this close to her, I never had the nightmare.

I wasn't stalking her; I was stalking sleep.

CHAPTER 2

The Corpse Whisperer

November 20th

"Stormy!" I yelled into the pitch black, my voice wobbling as my board rolled over the bumpy road. The first signs of morning had yet to light the sky, but I didn't have to worry about waking the residents—no one had returned to the Bywater post-Storm. There was nothing to come home to. Not yet, at least.

I held up my flashlight, which at this point felt like a natural extension of my arm. I was never anywhere without it. The gas lamps on houses became fewer and farther between when you left the Quarter heading east, until there were zilch in the destitute area, where my crew was rebuilding houses in the Lower Ninth.

"Stormy!" I yelled again, my eyes flicking back and forth to the ground, looking for potholes that could send me flying into the next state.

When I got to the train tracks, I hopped off and kicked the board into my hand. I'd attempted the jump a few times before, but it never ended well after I'd been up most of the night.

"Stormmmmy!"

Movement came from the decrepit porch of an abandoned house, and Stormy sprang out of a tire. *That's why she always smells like rubber.* "There you are, girl. Don't scare me like that."

She yapped, running down the stairs to me.

I bent down to pet her as she rubbed her head into my palm. "Do I have a treat for you today." I pulled a crumpled ball of tinfoil from my knapsack and removed the strip of bacon from it.

Her eyes widened, but she didn't go nuts like I expected.

"I saved this for you." I held the bacon close to her nose so she wouldn't bite my hand off when she smelled it.

But she just stared, as if confused.

"I know it's been a while since you've had table food, but really?"

I held it out for a couple more seconds, but she remained disinterested and then nudged at my other pocket.

"Fine, more for me," I said, and crammed it in my mouth. *Man, you know this place is screwed up when the dogs won't take bacon.*

I wondered if she was sick. I'd never be able to get her to a rescue shelter for a checkup. The last time I tried to take her somewhere was the only time she'd ever bitten me. She made it perfectly clear that she *did not* leave her hood.

She lit up as I pulled the old tennis ball out of my pocket. I hurled it, and she took off. I dropped my board and kicked off after her, just like every other morning on my way to work. She brought the ball back, and I threw it again, feeling the tightness in my arm after the night of flying.

I stretched my arm over my shoulder as my board bumped over the shitty road.

When I threw the ball again, an undeniable sound sent a chill ripping up my spine: a shotgun cocking. My board skidded out from under my feet, and my hands shot up. The flashlight crashed to the street.

"I'm just on my way to work!" I yelled, heart racing.

"Work?" came a voice from the house to my right. "Now, I know that's some bull."

Stormy ran back, jumping up on my legs, barking, not understanding why we stopped.

"There ain't no work around here, boy. You loot, we shoot."

"I'm not a looter!"

A beam of light shone my way, and I slowly turned toward the voice. All I could make out were two male silhouettes on the porch of a house that no longer had a front wall. One guy held a flashlight, the other a shotgun.

A breeze picked up, blowing the trash around my feet. "I'm a recovery worker! On my way to the site now."

He shined the flashlight directly at my face, and the guy next to him uncocked the gun.

Thank God. The wind around us gently subsided.

Stormy continued to yelp, but they didn't seem bothered by her. He turned the flashlight, illuminating his own face, and I got a better view of the wall-less room behind him. There were a couple of women and a bunch of kids sprawled out sleeping on the floor.

"When's someone gonna get to our street?" he asked.

"I—I don't know." I left out the part about the waiting list being epically longer than the approved funding. Instead I pulled a card out of my back pocket and approached the porch. "If you have the means, call this number and ask." I looked him straight in the eye, not wanting him to see the pity I felt for his family. My pity wasn't going to feed his kids.

"They ain't gonna tell me anything."

"Probably not. But that's the direct line to the director's office. Feel free to blow it up anyway."

There were no thank-yous and no good-byes; then again, there were no bullets fired either. I considered it a win.

And if I hustled, I wouldn't be late for work.

"Isaac!" a voice boomed from down the street. "You're late!" It was AJ, our crew captain.

"Sorry!" I yelled, running the last half block. I liked AJ because he didn't treat me like I was the boss's kid. "Trying not to get my head blown off. Looter-shooter!"

"Oh, good Lord, Isaac," said Betsy. "I *told* you Brett and I would pick you up on the way. It's *dan-ger-ous* around these parts. Especially before sunrise." Betsy's southern accent gave syllables so much separation they needed their own zip codes.

She was standing in the middle of the dark street with the rest of the crew, all getting their assignments. We had a system: AJ, Chase, and I ripped stuff out, and Jory, Betsy, and Brett hauled it out to the curb. There it would all sit for God only knows how long. There was no trash service up and running, because the government had yet to figure out where it would all go. Urban Crisis Management—or UCM, as my father referred to it—was on a fast track to nowhere sorting that kind of stuff out.

"Thanks, Bets, but it's fine."

"You make my prayers work in overdrive."

"And I appreciate it." I smiled. Betsy and her boyfriend, Brett, were Jesus fanatics from Florida, who proudly wore their abstinence on their fingers and liked nothing more than to preach.

"It's too early for God-squading," Jory said, stomping out a cigarette. He was a student at Tulane—at least he had been before the Storm. Philosophy major.

"He must believe and not doubt," Betsy recited, "because he who doubts is like a wave of the sea, blown and tossed by the wind."

"You know what I have faith in?" asked Chase, our resident adrenaline junkie. "I have faith in sledgehammers." He picked one up and handed it to Jory. Chase spent half the year as a smoke jumper, which meant he was partly insane. "I also have faith in crowbars," he continued, picking one up and handing it to me. "And I have faith in each and every one of you tearing the shit out of this house so we can rebuild it."

"Amen to that," I echoed, wrapping a bandana over my mouth and nose.

Everyone else did the same, and we ran to the residence. Since we were starting a new house, it was going to be a demolition kind of day. Dirty, disgusting work. I caught a glimpse of the X on the exterior as I hopped up the steps—it wasn't one of mine, although we weren't too far from the streets where my first-responder crew had worked the weeks after the Storm.

Jory and I stepped into the house at the same time—we both nearly vomited.

The running joke was, never eat breakfast before coming to work if you didn't like wasting food. There was more puking between recovery workers than sorority sisters. The Storm-stench was not something a person got used to.

My jaw clamped shut to prevent the vile smell of rot and death from rushing into my mouth, but when it hit my nostrils, I paused, bending over.

"He's going down!" Chase slapped my back as he sped past me. We had a routine whenever we started a new house. The pukers went back outside while the rest of us ran through holding our breath, opening all of the windows. If they didn't open, we broke them—anything to let the air flow in.

I choked back the vomit and pressed forward; lingering would only ensure that I wouldn't be able to suppress the next wave. I made it to a dining room window and jammed it open before vomiting up the bacon projectile-style. *Effing disgusting.*

I hung outside the window for a couple breaths, aggressively spitting. Shudders swept across my shoulders, and I broke a puke-sweat.

Before heading back inside, I grabbed a bottle of water from my knap-sack, gargled, then jammed a piece of gum in my mouth.

Headphones in, I blew through two Beastie Boys albums, ripping apart the upper level of the camelback house. Baseboards, crown molding, a wooden fireplace mantel, a bathroom floor three layers of linoleum deep. Nothing was salvageable; the house had been completely submerged all the way up to the roof. One more floorboard and this room would be done. Dirty sweat dripped off my face as I tried to yank out the board with the crowbar. It didn't want to come up.

"Chase," I yelled out the door, "I need the sledgehammer back!"

I pulled off the bandana and wiped my face. A breeze kicked in through the window. At first it felt good, but then it made me shiver beneath my sweat-soaked shirt.

Cold.

Too cold for today. Maybe even too cold for New Orleans. Debris rustled on the floor as the breeze traipsed around me and out the bedroom door. I followed it, and a sinking feeling followed me.

"Here," Chase said, meeting me in the hallway with the sledgehammer.

"Thanks." I took it and walked past him, down the stairs, not wanting to lose the breeze—the cold.

"There he goes," Betsy said, coming out of a bathroom, signing the cross as she joined us.

I entered the bedroom Jory was working in. "Oh no," he said as I walked straight past him to a door on the opposite side of the room.

When I turned the knob, it didn't open.

"It's swollen in the frame," he said. "I couldn't get it to budge."

I tried again, this time with more force, but the result wasn't any different. "Stay back," I said, and swung the blunt tool into the first hinge. The second swing smashed the next hinge, and then I jerked the door away from the frame. A black cloud whooshed out. Jory screamed louder than Betsy as we all dropped to the floor, covering our faces. Thousands of flies swarmed us, buzzing in our ears. I swatted at them with one hand, covering my nose and mouth with the other hand, and gagging as the true smell of death billowed out.

I didn't want to move forward, but I didn't dare look back; Betsy was already puking, and then someone else was too. Puking had a domino effect like that.

I crept closer to the door, holding the bandana over my face, my stomach muscles jerking uncontrollably. I peered into the dark room, which was no bigger than a walk-in closet. The walls were bright red, and a mirror hung at the rear, reflecting the light from the bedroom onto an altar below it. Mold had sprouted like mutant ferns, blanketing the scene: candles, twenty or thirty were on the table, some big, some small, all with hardened drips of wax frozen in time down the sides. Strands of beads hung on statues of the Virgin Mary next to conch shells and plastic flowers, all covered in gray, green, and black. Spots on spots on spots of mold covered the crucifixes and black-and-white photos that hung on the walls.

"What the . . . ," my voice trailed.

"A prayer room," Jory said from behind me, swatting away flies.

In the mirror's reflection, I saw the body on the floor. I tried not to imagine him kneeling at the altar, the water slowly rising around him. I tried not to think about what was going through his head when he gave up on trying to evacuate. *Was he old? Injured? Maybe he just wanted to die praying rather than out there on his own? Maybe he'd already found peace.*

The reflection moved. I gagged violently and kicked the door shut.

"Maggots," I said.

"The Corpse Whisperer strikes again!" Jory yelled.

"It's not funny," I choked.

"No, it's not funny. It's freakin' weird, dude. You find more dead bodies than Jessica Jones."

Behind us, AJ's two-way bleeped. "We got another floater," he said.

Someone on the other side would alert D-MORT, the FEMA-sponsored Disaster Mortuary Operational Response Team, which happened to be one of my pop's projects. They'd arrange the pickup. No one knew for sure—well, someone knew for sure—but it's been said that over eight thousand bodies had been processed in the facility. Of course, no one had bothered to define "processed." As far as I could tell it meant "checked in." Only a fraction of those had been identified. There was a website where people could report missing persons and answer a survey that begged for details: scars, tattoos, piercings, surgical histories. I even heard they were using facial recognition from Facebook photos. But for floaters with this level of decomposition, the only chance was dental records. Hopefully, being found inside a home would expedite his identification.

"Lord have mercy, Isaac," Betsy said. "Lord have mercy."

"You have some kind of predilection for the dead, kid?" AJ asked, pocketing the handheld radio. "What is that? Nine? Ten?"

"A baker's dozen," Jory answered.

He was right: I'd found thirteen bodies—with this crew. If you tallied all of the corpses from my first-responder days, the number was seventy-six. Seventy-six corpses. But they didn't need to know that. Holding the record for corpses recovered wasn't exactly something to brag about.

"You got some shit luck, kid," said AJ.

"Yeah . . ."

What was I supposed to tell them? That a breeze always seemed to enter the room and lead me to the dead body? *Oh, I just have this special relationship with the air—you know, because I'm a witch.*

What happened next always felt the weirdest: I shut the door, and we went back to work. The shock factor for everyone had worn away along with the hope that it would be the last one.

Three Wu-Tang records later, I let the crowbar drop to the ground. "Is there running water here?"

"I think so," Jory answered.

I ran upstairs to the master bathroom as we continued to yell back and forth.

"Don't drink it! Boil-water advisory!"

"I'm not an idiot!" Actually I was—I should have left an hour ago. Gone back home and showered. *Now you're going to be late. And disgusting, and covered in drywall dust and mold flakes.* I turned on the tub faucet. The pipes shook and sputtered until water gurgled out.

"Come on, come on," I mumbled, pulling off my shirt.

The water ran a color that wasn't brown but wasn't quite clear either.

"Good enough."

I splashed the water up my arms, carefully turning my face away, and then pulled a bar of soap from my bag and stuck my head under the faucet to rinse out my hair.

I emerged wearing a fresh set of clothes. Black clothes.

"Ya going to a funeral, boy?" AJ asked.

"I gotta leave early. See ya tomorrow."

"We're gonna pray for that floater's soul," Betsy said. "Me and Brett. Don't you worry about him, Isaac."

"Thanks, Bets!" I yelled, hopping down the porch. The sad truth was, I'd already stopped thinking about the dead body, because I was worried about someone else now. Adele.

I threw down my board but then turned back and ran up to the front door. I pulled a can of spray paint out of my knapsack, shook it quickly, and popped the cap. When the paint hissed out, I slashed out the *0* and painted a *1*.

RIP, Mr. Seventy-Six.

CHAPTER 3

Death by Mold

Breathe.

I smoothed my skirt. The metallic fabric was silky against my fingers. Even in the dark space, it gleamed, reflecting the light from the racks of melting candles. I sucked in a big breath. It didn't help. The mold-tinged air felt dank and cumbersome, too heavy for my lungs to push in and out.

Breathe, Adele.

Muted rays of sun shone through the stained-glass windows high above us, cutting through the dark room on a sharp diagonal. Even through my sunglasses, I could see all the dust and particles of God knows what else floating in the trail of light.

Father McKinley's voice droned on in the background.

Like the rest of the Ninth Ward, the church lacked electricity and was far from operational, but it was the closest one to St. Vincent's that wasn't a total hazard. I think we were still breaking a dozen different laws by occupying it, but who was going to stop us? The government hadn't officially condemned it, so that left it a free-for-all.

I imagined what the holy space had looked like with ten-plus feet of muddy river water flooded inside: The long wooden pews and the ceramic heads of religious icons bobbing between candle racks and collection boxes. Hymnbooks floating higher and higher to the heavens. A whole new meaning to the term "holy water."

A memory of Lisette Monvoisin throwing a saintly statue at Nicco whipped through my mind.

I was grateful for my sunglasses as I blinked it away, as if my eyelids were burying the memory back into my subconscious.

Everyone shifted as more latecomers squeezed into the already-crowded pews, until we were elbow to elbow. The bout of claustrophobia came back. Most of the vast church had been emptied—maybe by looters, maybe by the archdiocese—so I shouldn't have felt so trapped, but we were all crowded to one side. Tape blocked off the other half, where broken pews and dismantled confessional booths waited to be hauled off. The pile of trash glittered with the brightly colored glass that had shattered from the now-boarded frescos.

Jesus, how long is the priest going to talk? Was it absolutely necessary for this Mass to be inside given the circumstances?

Breathe.

I sat up straight and rolled my neck, flinching at the small pop.

On the next breath, I imagined thousands of microscopic mold spores flying into my nose, down my esophagus, and planting themselves inside my lungs. The seedlings germinated into cruciferous-like plants, and the bulbous vegetation grew into my throat until every bit of air was blocked from coming or going, choking my imaginary self to death.

I adjusted the collar of my black blouse, which was tied into a limp bow at my throat.

Just breathe, Adele. Stop thinking about mold.

Or death.

Death by mold.

I focused on the rack of candles next to the priest, trying to distract myself from having an anxious fit. I slowly squinted and released my eyelids, watching the flames change size. Warmth radiated from within my belly, and it took a full minute of playing with the fire to realize it wasn't just an optical illusion. The flames were actually growing taller.

A wave of panic came next, and one of the flames doubled in size. *Shit.*

With a quick glance that begged my father not to follow, I squeezed past him and slowly pushed through the rest of the people in the front pew. I tried to be light on my feet so as not to distract from the service, but my shoes on the marble floor made it altogether impossible. Heads turned as I hurried down the side aisle, and then a slice of light pierced the congregation as I opened the door just enough to slip outside.

Freedom.

For a moment I leaned against the heavy door, but then it wasn't enough; I needed more distance.

I bobbed down the marble steps, my feet pinching inside the pointy-toed shoes, and the gold lamé flouncing above my knees. Two thin layers of crinoline beneath the silky fabric gave the high-waisted skirt a slight flare. I didn't stop until my heels clicked the bricks of the residential Bywater street.

Almost four months after the Storm had touched ground, the neighborhood still looked exactly as it had the day my father and I drove in after the evacuation. The postapocalyptic-zombie vibe crept up with a vengeance.

A gentle scraping sound to my left pulled my attention—I whirled around. It was just an empty Coke can knocking down the street in the breeze. A mangy black cat emerged from underneath the wrecked porch of a house whose tennis-ball-colored paint job still managed to beam through the layer of grime left by the Storm. The cat lazily stretched its back. I wondered who'd lived in the house and where they were now.

The waterline was over my head, swallowing most of the one-story. Were they home when the levees broke? Did the water rush in all at once like a giant wave tunneling down the street? Or did it slowly rise, giving them the false hope that it might stop before it touched their toes . . . before it swept around their shins and soaked their clothes and chilled their bones? Before they climbed to the highest, driest spot in the house? Were they thinking that if they climbed high enough God would rescue them? Because, really, who drowns in an attic?

My eyes fixated on the numerals inside the orange spray-painted *X*.

0-1-0-0

The numbers sprayed in the bottom quadrant sank my heart.
Who drowns in an attic?
This person did, that's who.

The *0* meant there'd been no survivors found by the rescue crew, and the *1* meant a corpse had been. I wondered if they ever got a funeral, or just a label on a body-bag tag at the new city morgue. "D-MORT," as Isaac called it.

My hand moved to a tendril of hair, deftly twisting it between my fingers, and the Coke can skittered across the broken road, landing next to my shoe as if it had been well trained. It rattled in place. I kicked it hard and sent it skidding down the street.

"Chill out," I said, re-smoothing my skirt. The sun gleamed off the shiny gold fabric like brass.

Brass.

Notes squeezed out of a saxophone from a nearby street. The scales got louder and closer—someone warming up on their way here. The ground trembled underneath my feet. Tuba tremors.

A large, jolly-looking man rounded the corner with the enormous instrument wrapped around his body. His cheeks puffed up like a blowfish, and he gave me a sympathy nod as he walked past, the sun bouncing hard off the banged-up horn, which looked like it had recently been shined.

I squinted behind the dark, round lenses, which now felt like a part of my armor, shielding people from seeing my eyes and knowing my thoughts.

If people knew what I was thinking . . . what I had done.

Well, at least they'd stop looking at me with those *poor little girl* eyes.

I sighed and looked around, suddenly very aware that I was standing by myself in a crowd of people filtering out from the church.

Chatter came from every direction. Laughter. Whispers. Hoots and hollers. More instruments warmed up. A trumpet. A bass drum pounding. Cymbals clanking.

The more instruments that joined the warm-up, the louder the crowd became over them, like birds squawking and chirping. My pulse began to climb. *Chirp. Chirp.* More brass. More chirping. More metal. More vibrations.

Too much metal.

The vibrations traveled through my body, rippling through my bloodstream. I broke a sweat.

"This is so weird," a voice whispered close to my ear.

I twitched, but he didn't recoil from the rejection. Isaac.

His hand went to the small of my back, and I took a deep breath. I knew the gesture was supposed to be comforting, but it wasn't—not today.

And people kept doing it. The small of my back, my shoulder, my arms. If it wasn't Isaac, it was Sébastien or my dad or Ren. Even Detective Matthews had kissed my cheek. But I couldn't expect anything less. This was the South after all.

"The skirt came out amazing, by the way."

He was trying to distract me. "Thanks," I mumbled.

He ignored my attitude and slid his hand around my hip. My entire body tensed. I didn't mean for it to, but the fact that he was being so nice annoyed me. He'd been babying me since early yesterday . . .

I'd spent most of the day distracting myself by making the gold skirt. Instead of going to the café like he normally did after work, Isaac came over and sat on the floor against the wall in my bedroom, one leg outstretched and the other bent at the knee to rest his sketch pad. It took me most of the morning to draft the pattern pieces. Our eyes met only once—when he was switching knees and I was pulling out the fabric. I wasn't able to force another smile after that point. It was the gold fabric . . . I'd bought it in France.

When I'd spotted it through the small shop window in Paris, I'd nearly leaned off Émile-slash-Emilio's Vespa. His arm caught me as he came to a sudden stop.

"Don't do that, please. Your mother will kill me if anything happens to you," he'd said in French, his touch lingering, making me wonder if he was really the one who cared.

"Unlikely," I'd said, and smiled, running into the store.

On the ride back to my dormitory, I hugged the tissue-wrapped pillow of gold fabric so I didn't accidentally hug him. *I am such an idiot.*

The memory now made me shudder.

Of course, I couldn't think about Émile without thinking about Brigitte, and after that I was hardly able to look at Isaac, knowing I'd lied to him about what happened in the attic on Halloween.

About my mother being trapped inside.

About my mother being a vampire.

An omission of truth counts as a lie, right?

The guilt had gnawed my nerves ever since, especially as we'd promised each other no more secrets on that very evening. Before we'd gone out that night, I never got the chance to tell him or Désirée that Adeline had killed Giovanna Medici. So, naturally, when Isaac pushed an extra female vampire into the attic with Martine, he assumed she was Nicco's sister Giovanna.

And I hadn't corrected him. Yet.

"Breathe," he whispered, his forehead knocking the side of my head and his fingers pressing into my hip.

The music stopped. Mouths disengaged from conversation.

Short squeaks danced out of a solo clarinet, floating out over the crowd. The opening notes of the mournful hymn jabbed into my heart. I looked down at my chest, half expecting to see blood gushing out.

Isaac squeezed me tighter.

This is really it.

From behind us at the back of the crowd, a trombone blew. The long notes slid deeper and deeper until they felt like they were inside my stomach. I knew without looking that Alphonse Jones was playing that horn. A few measures later he was weaving through people, past us, with the satin sash of grand marshal across his chest. Back from Los Angeles for the occasion, or to meet with their insurance agent, or FEMA. I wished Brooke had come with him. I'd only spoken to her once since Halloween night—when she spilled the beans about being cast on the next season of *American Idol*, and how she'd be going dark while they were shooting, per her NDA.

I changed my mind about wishing she was here. *How would I explain all this to her?*

"I think that's my cue," Isaac said softly, in a way that sought my approval.

When I nodded, he kissed my cheek—the gesture broke through my numbness. Face burning, I darted a quick glance left and right to see if anyone had witnessed the PG-PDA.

No eyes were on me.

As Isaac walked away, he paused to stretch his arms. He must have been out flying last night. The hem of his black T-shirt lifted as he deepened the stretch, exposing his hip bone. I looked away, trying not to blush. After all his hours of manual labor, his black T-shirt and black jeans were now too tight, like most of the clothes he'd brought from New York. His work hours seemed to increase by the day. Isaac just couldn't *not* help people.

He looked strange in the dark clothing. That kind of ensemble was more reserved for Nicco. My gaze dropped to the ground.

More feet joined Isaac's tan work boots. My father's. Sébastien's.

"Pretty girls don't frown." The words came from lips that were now kissing my cheek. "Hold on to my parasol, *s'il vous plaît*?" Blanche pressed it into my hands and kept moving past me.

"Good thing I'm not a pretty girl," I mumbled.

He turned back around. "You betta be ready to dance!"

I forced a smile, only to feel like a grimacing clown, but then the back of his outfit made a genuine smile spread across my face. On the tails of his black tuxedo jacket were swirling appliqués of silver and iridescent sequins. They matched his purple satin shirt and signature glitter-swept lids.

Ren's boyfriend, Theis, brushed past me too, giving my shoulder a squeeze on the way. It felt awkward coming from the standoffish Scandinavian. More taps on the shoulders, and more kisses on my cheek: Chatham and Edgar Daure, with their three sons. Codi, who was closest to my age, lingered behind, pulling me into a hug. I hadn't seen him since before the Storm, at his going away party when he'd left for freshman year at U of A.

"This is seriously the weakest hug ever, Adele," he said, refusing to let go. I sighed, wrapping my arms tighter around him. He tightened too.

"Oh God," I said. "Don't do that. You're going to squeeze the tears out."

"Fine." He held the hug for one more second before joining the others at the casket. Along with some guys from the roasters, they all picked it up and lifted it to their shoulders.

There should have been two caskets, but resources were scarce thanks to the Storm. I didn't think Mémé and Pépé Michel would mind being crammed together for eternity. In fact, I couldn't imagine them wanting it any other way.

It had been three weeks since they'd died—*since Emilio had murdered them.* A long wait for a funeral, but their bodies had been held as part of the investigation. Really, I think the system was just utterly overwhelmed. There weren't enough cops back yet, let alone detectives, forensics, coroners. The rumor was there were still over five thousand unclaimed bodies from the Storm.

The funeral being delayed had somehow allowed me to put all my most overwhelming feelings on hold. I'd buried myself in schoolwork, in Kafka and Shakespeare. I'd spent too much time thinking about the way Isaac's rough hand felt in mine and making mental lists of all the places I wanted to show him when things improved—if things ever improved.

But over the last few days it had all started to crash around me: the guilt, the sadness, the loss, and the horror of their deaths.

And of the role I had played.

But it wasn't just the time lapse. The adrenaline from the battle with the Medici—the win—and the dark, phantasmal nature of it all had somehow superseded thinking about everything else. Our victory had overshadowed the fact that Emilio had killed two people I loved.

At least the Medici didn't get what they were after, whatever it was.

At the time, the win felt like we had redeemed everyone who'd died. *We* had won.

But what exactly had we won?

Your life, I reminded myself. *And Désirée's, and Isaac's. The lives of who knows how many other innocent people.*

More musicians joined the clarinet and trombone duo, and we followed behind the casket, walking in time with the mournful dirge. A lot of the local musicians had worked at the roasters when the cash from their horns wasn't enough, so there was no way they were letting Mémé and Pépé go without a proper send-off. Dozens of others followed behind us, waving white handkerchiefs, wearing Saints jerseys and three-piece suits and everything in between. Some were as old as Méme and Pépe; others were younger than me. A guy whose curls were so black they gleamed blue—or maybe it was the silver-sequined umbrella the lady next to him carried, reflecting the sky—drifted with the crowd; his enthralled look gave away his out-of-towner status.

Désirée stepped in line next to me with a huff.

"What's your issue?" I asked.

"Nothing . . ." She crossed her arms as her grandmother and parents walked past us with smiles and waves, photographer in tow.

Isaac glanced back. Despite carrying two dead people, he was still checking on me.

"Ugh," I whispered beneath the requiem. "I'm so glad the funeral is finally happening so people will stop looking at me like that."

Désirée raised an eyebrow.

"He's treating me like a delicate flower that's about to fall apart. I haven't even cried since *that* night."

"That's exactly why he's concerned." She pulled a flask from the waistband of her tight black pencil skirt and handed it to me.

"What's that supposed to mean?" I didn't even think about it before unscrewing the cap.

"*You* are a crier."

It was totally something Brooke would have said; my dry eyes went to the sky as my lips pinched the metal, and I knocked my head back. *Locked myself in an attic full of vengeful vampires, but I'm still known as the crier.*

The booze, minty instead of fiery, went down surprisingly easy. It was cool on my throat, which burned from . . . trying not to cry. Both the tingling aftertaste and the smile on Désirée's lips told me that the flask was *not* filled with alcohol.

I sniffed the remaining contents. "What did I just drink?"

"You're welcome."

"Dee!"

Note to self: do not consume anything from a Borges without first inquiring.

"Chill out." She yanked the flask back, took a swig, then offered it to me again. "It's just a little herbal refreshment to take the edge off the day. I figured you'd be freaking out."

Is this why Désirée is so placid all of the time? Swigs of enchanted herbs?

I reclaimed the flask and raised it to my lips. "Back to you. What were you in a tizzy about?"

"The Casquette Girls Coven descendant research has to pause for now. Not that you or Isaac care—neither of you have been helping me."

It's not that I didn't care about finding the rest of our coven members. It just wasn't a priority these days. I looked back at the casket.

"Sorry," she said with an expression that might have been sympathy.

"Why do you have to stop the search?" I asked, taking another sip.

"Gran found out about the coven."

Potion sprayed out of my lips. She yanked back the flask and stealthily tucked it into her blazer pocket before anyone saw.

"What do you mean she found out? Does she know about the curse? About what we *did*?"

"Relax. She doesn't know about anything else. She just knows we bound the coven, and she's *pissed*."

"Pissed about what?"

"That I joined another coven instead of the family's. We got into the fight to end all fights. Books were thrown. Jars exploded. A batch of fermenting seaweed got on everything. She even tried to make me break the coven's bond."

"*What?*"

"Don't worry. I didn't."

"Does that mean she knows about . . . me?"

"*Oui*, and Isaac. Although, I think she's always known you're witches. Obviously she doesn't have a problem with your magic, just as long as Borges aren't binding themselves to it. We're supposed to stick to our kind. You know, keep the magic line as strong as possible."

Jeanne dropped into step beside me, looking perfectly put together in Mémé's pearls and the black pantsuit I'd picked out for her. The loose braid I'd swept her long blond locks into was mostly intact. She extended her open palm toward Désirée in a way that made her look much older than her twenty years.

My stomach tightened. Only I would get busted for drinking when I'm not even drinking.

"What?" Désirée asked, as if clueless.

Jeanne further extended her arm. "I'll give it back."

Désirée shrugged and conceded the flask. "Drink at your own risk."

I wondered what *exactly* was in the herbal cocktail, or more precisely what spell she had used—and whether Jeanne, in her life, had ever drunk a sip of anything stronger than the tight-rolled leaves of China Gunpowder tea.

I guess we're about to find out.

As we continued to walk, she took a healthy swig, but before she swallowed, she swished it between her cheeks. "What is this? It's not alcohol."

"*Pfft.*" Désirée smiled. "Like you'd know, Little Miss Scientist."

I gave her a harsh look, but Jeanne was utterly unfazed by the jab.

"It's *Dr.* Little Miss Scientist," she answered, somehow still holding the liquid in her cheeks. "And that's exactly how I know there's nothing fermented in this solution." She gargled for a deeper investigation.

"Is she serious?"

"As a starved alligator." I fought the urge to smile.

Walking in between the two of them, my anxiety began to dissipate. Neither Jeanne nor Désirée could coddle me if their lives depended on it. Jeanne's empathy gene was buried deep beneath all of her genius—I was pretty sure she had to consciously remember simple social norms like greeting people when she walked into a room. And Désirée was, well . . . Désirée.

My gaze wandered to check on Isaac, which made me feel like a hypocrite.

Sometimes his New Yorkiness—his mouth—made him stand out, but now he totally looked like a fish out of water, surely the only person in the krewe who had never seen a casket dance. When he'd offered to help carry Mémé and Pépé, I wasn't sure if he was trying to be helpful or just trying to befriend Sébastien, or my father, who wasn't exactly thrilled about our sudden closeness. Either way, they weren't going to turn down his roof-repairing upper-body strength. As the rest of the guys began to casually shake with the beat, Isaac's awkwardness made my smile finally crack.

He has no idea what he's gotten himself into.

It was tradition at a New Orleans jazz funeral for the pallbearers to shake the casket on the way to the cemetery in order to give the deceased one last dance before they were locked away for eternity.

But Isaac didn't seem scared of our weird ways in New Orleans. He didn't seem to be scared of anything, actually.

The tempo picked up as the trumpets transitioned the band into a jazzier tune, and for a full street block, I watched him watch the others sway with the music, like trying to learn the moves from an aerobics instructor without tripping in the process. After another block, his body began to move naturally with the rhythm, and I found myself starting to wish he was back here with me.

Ren, Chatham, and the others carried the huge box like they had done it a hundred times before. Maybe they had.

I wondered if Isaac had carried his mother's casket at her funeral. *Do they play jazz at funerals in Brooklyn? Was it a small, intimate affair?*

My mother didn't get a funeral. No one had mourned for her. No one even knew that she'd died, other than me.

Except, of course, her killer.

And his *famiglia*.

Before my thoughts could spiral any deeper, a man turned around—the mayor—and offered his hand to Dee. "Y'all need to stop looking like someone died." A satin Zulu sash was tied across his chest.

Each Social Aid and Pleasure Club had their own marching krewe with their own colors, costumes, rituals, and funeral rites. The walking parade rolled to celebrate the joy of someone's life, rather than the ominous fact that it was over. The family, the casket bearers, the krewe, and the band made up the First Line, while the mourners-slash-celebrators, and really anyone in the neighborhood, formed the Second Line.

He pulled Désirée away. The staff photographer put a white handkerchief in her hand and followed behind them. Dee despised that guy and his camera clicks, and I couldn't blame her. I could tell she was trying to not give the photographer the shot, but when her father twisted her around, she cracked a smile.

Watching them dance made my senses wildly confused. My hips wanted to sway along with the brassy song as the band really got going, and my arms wanted to wave Blanche's umbrella above my head, but my brain told me that I should be overwhelmed with melancholy.

Dee danced back, grabbed my hand, and spun me around just as I crossed a pothole. I had to grind my heel into the rocky road to help balance the momentum to keep from falling. More and more people joined the parade behind us, until I was sure that everyone east of the Quarter who'd returned post-Storm had joined the Second Line. More singing, and more dancing, and more handkerchiefs waving high as paraders riled up.

At first it was only my shoulders moving side to side as I walked, but half a block later, Blanche's umbrella was open to the sky, getting the proper attention a purple bedazzled parasol deserved. My strut slid into a bounce, and the bounce, well that's what New Orleans dance is all about. Once you've hit the bounce, you're doomed. The world ceases to exist as the energy pushes through your muscles, making your body pop. When it occurs in the middle of the street with a large group of people, half of whom you've known since birth and half total strangers, well, it's something special.

I yelled to Jeanne. She shook her head fiercely, refusing to join me, but I grabbed her hand and twirled her until her blond braid spun. Désirée's potion coursed through my veins like a permission slip to smile.

Despite the occasion, and despite dancing through such a heavily devastated area, euphoria washed over me as the music pounded. The energy from the krewes was infectious, and for a few blocks I forgot why we were parading. A genuine giggle slipped from Jeanne's mouth, and I gave myself over to the zeal of the crowd.

If we didn't hold on to the spirit of the city, it would be like all of those people lost in the Storm had died in vain . . . if we didn't stay and rebuild, if we didn't shake the caskets and dance to the beats on the mispronounced French streets.

Mother Nature had taken our homes, our schools, our electricity, and even our people, but there's no way New Orleans would let her take our traditions.

The brass band banged on. I floated down the street in the euphoric bubble with the Pleasure Club krewes in their brightly colored jackets—magenta, tangerine, and teal—and their matching hats with towering feathers. The ladies of a club who all wore lime green twirled by, waving fans made of fuchsia feathers that looked like they were borrowed from a Las Vegas showgirl's dressing room. The explosion of color against the decrepit post-Storm Ninth Ward gray was impossible to process.

But I didn't want to process anymore; I just wanted to be.

And so I danced on, past sights that will haunt me forever. It wasn't the conditions of the streets or the spray-painted Xs—those I was getting used to. It was the evidence of returned life that now stood out so starkly.

We danced past a sign painted on an old sheet:

FUCK FEMA

And then another, which had been painted on the side of a half-demolished house:

LOOTERS WILL BE SHOT ON SIGHT!!

Then another:

STILL ALIVE

I hoped they were.

The landscape didn't seem to bother anyone else, for we were rolling and today was about Bertrand and Sabine Michel and giving them their last dance.

My quads burned, and my toes bordered on numb, but the color-me-lime-clad ladies were revving up for the end of the road. Or better said, getting down—because when buckjumping, the lower you got to the ground, the better.

A lady with cushy shoulders and an enormous fuchsia-feathered hat backed up against me, nearly making me topple. Doing anything else but joining her felt downright disrespectful. The tandem dance created an energy that defied public humiliation.

Her back supported mine, and mine hers, as we bounced and bounced, getting ever closer to the ground. The people around us clapped and shouted, and the band rang louder. I laughed, worrying that if we got any lower I wouldn't be able to get back up. But the adrenaline pushed me down. And then the music pulled me back up.

I let my weight press against her back so I didn't bounce away.

But then the euphoric bubble popped. The procession halted, and the music stopped. We had arrived at the cemetery.

CHAPTER 4

Never Trust a Vampire

The Second Line slowly walked underneath an iron archway that spelled out St. Vincent De Paul Cemetery No. 1, and the mood changed so suddenly, chills swept up my arms.

As the priest led our procession to Bertrand and Sabine's new home, a solo came from Alphonse Jones's horn, so somber and quiet I could hear the birds swooping above us. Michel had been carved into the mausoleum where Jeanne and Sébastien's parents already resided. I'd never given the idea of eternity much thought, but now its vastness sucked me in like a black hole.

They were gone *forever*.

The pallbearers set the casket down, and my father walked over to join me. He stretched his back. "I'm getting too old—"

I plowed into him like a child, my arms locking tightly around his chest, as I buried my face in his shoulder.

"Hey," he said, cupping the back of my head.

"I don't want you to die, Dad."

"Sweetheart, I'm not going to die. Well, not anytime soon."

"I don't want you to die ever."

"I guess you'll be accompanying me on more runs, then?"
I looked up with a meek smile.

He rested his arm around my shoulder and guided me to the front row. Jeanne and Sébastien filled the space on my other side, Dee and the Borges on his other side. Isaac filed behind us with Ren's crew and the Daures. I hoped neither of them had just witnessed the moment with my father; surely that was *crier* behavior. The rest of the crowd filled in, and the priest moved to the head of the closed casket.

I tried not to think about the level of decomposition hidden underneath the lid. I tried not to think about how much the casket looked like *les cassettes* stacked in the convent attic.

"May the souls of the faithful departed through the mercy of God rest in peace." Father McKinley's voice was the kind that made you believe things, like Ritha's, and as he spoke about life and about death, I was moved by his words . . . until he began to talk about forgiveness.

I will never *forgive Emilio for what he did. To Mémé and Pépé or to my mother.* My clammy palms clutched handfuls of my skirt. *Was it random when he killed her, or was it planned?* Had Nicco known he was going to do it? My chain rippled against my chest, along with the sun charm and Isaac's feather. I took a deep breath.

When Father McKinley finished, my father left my side to deliver the eulogy. He did his best to keep the speech lighthearted, starting out with a joke about Bertrand's "French hours" fitting perfectly into New Orleanian work culture. I caught sight of Ritha's expression—the one worn too often by New Orleanians lately—the *how did this senseless tragedy happen* look.

My pulse accelerated thinking about exactly how it had happened. *Ritha knows about the coven. She knows about my magic.* Another ripple of my necklace made chills jaunt down my spine.

Ritha looked down at the rosary woven between her fingers, then unthreaded the beads and held them in her palm. I felt my eyes go wide as I realized her beads were shaking too.

Relax, Adele. I turned back to my father as he finished with a comment about how he hoped Sabine had passed the recipe for her heavenly croissants on to me.

Jeanne and Sébastien got up and walked to the podium, leaving the two chairs on my other side empty too. I crossed and uncrossed my ankles, feeling all of the metal around me. I slid my hands underneath my legs. And then, just as the next wave of anxiety came, arms slid around my shoulders from behind and locked in place. I nearly jumped up, thinking that Isaac had lost his mind, but as the arms pressed, weighing me down, familiarity rushed me rather than anxiety.

"It's going to be okay," Codi whispered into my ear, just loud enough for me and no one else to hear, like he'd done when we were kids. "I've got you."

I nodded, my hand reaching for his arm, and I inhaled.

The twins took my father's place at the podium, and Codi's arms slipped away as my father sat back down and took my hand in his.

Tears came to Jeanne's eyes, but then she took a deep breath and sucked them back. Her words came out in her clear, strong voice. "What kind of monster preys on two innocent senior citizens? A pathetic coward." She got louder as she continued to lambast the unknown murderer. "Not only did you kill the only family we have left, but you ruined two cadavers that were supposed to be donated to science!"

Sébastien turned a bright shade of red and he cut her off. "We're just so thankful that Mémé and Pépé can finally rest in peace. *Merci* for coming, everyone."

They came back to their places, all four aquamarine eyes on me, and in the silence, Jeanne's words pounded into my head.

"Adele?" my father whispered, and his hand moved to my back.

Other than my pounding heart, every inch of my body felt paralyzed.

"It's okay if you don't want to . . ." His voice sounded distant.

"*Non. Ça va,*" I said, getting up. I tried to hold a neutral expression as I walked to the front.

I moved the sunglasses to the top of my head and tried to channel Brooke's fearlessness, but the guilt was overtaking me. I just knew everyone could see straight through my wide eyes into all of my memories.

All of my secrets.

Everyone in the crowd had the same *poor little girl* look of sympathy. A wave of undeservedness made me feel light-headed. I shifted my focus from the crowd to the casket.

You can do this, Adele. Pour Mémé et Pépé.

My first remark came out in perfect French, and I got a handful of recognition from the small Francophile contingency. After I translated the sentence, I took a pause for people to understand the joke, but all I got back were the same blank stares.

Ren's brow dipped in concern, and then so did Chatham's, and I realized I'd repeated the line in French. My gaze went back to Mémé and Pépé. I clutched my shaking hands together behind my back and tried a third time, but the words still came out in French. The warble in my voice made my face flush, and the flutters moved from my stomach to my lungs until they expanded so much I could barely breathe. The speech I'd written seemed so stupid now. *Lies.* Nicco had warned me that his family would retaliate, and I'd done nothing that night to protect anyone. This was the consequence.

Focus.

But I couldn't think. The multitude of brass instruments out in the crowd overwhelmed my senses. The only person who wasn't staring at me was Ritha. She was squinting at the casket. I squinted too, and that's when I realized the screws in the hinges were slowly turning—one was almost completely out. It *tinked* to the floor. She looked straight at me. The tremble in my hands mutated into a violent shake. Any second now the instruments would start to shake too.

"Désolée!" My voice cracked out the apology. *"Désolée!"* And then I bolted down the center aisle.

My father gripped Isaac's shoulder as I ran past. "Let her have some space."

Heads rippled as I hurried past the tombs. I had to escape the burning looks of sympathy. As I ran straight through the iron archway, it took all of my strength to keep the gate from slamming closed behind me.

I could barely feel my pinched toes as my shoes pounded the pavement.

Faster.

Faster.

The faster I ran, the easier it was to fight the tears.

By the time the NOSA campus was in sight, my chest felt like it was going to explode, and by the time I made it around the final building to the statue, I was panting.

I fell to the ground, the dead grass crunching under my lamé skirt, and leaned up against the metal figure. She was cool through my thin blouse. My toes pulsed with pain. I kicked off my shoes and raised my hands over my head, trying to catch my breath; when I looked up, I saw her. My mother. I still hadn't returned the mask to the statue.

Why did you come here, Adele? But I knew the answer. I always came here.

I just hadn't been back since Halloween night, when I discovered it was Brigitte beneath the carnival mask. The night I locked her in the convent attic, before the coven cast the slumbering spell—a spell that we weren't even certain worked. For all I knew my mother was dead.

Twice over.

45

Suddenly my safe space felt unfamiliar. Tainted. Undeserving. *What if I killed my mother for good?* I'd scorched her just before I locked the shutter—before Niccolò Medici hurled me out the third-story window. *Nicco let go of my hands.*

Sparks buzzed from my palms. I balled them into fists.

I was glad to have a wall of spells between us. I wanted to launch him into another dimension for betraying me. *For betraying us.*

"There was no *us!*" I screamed to no one. It was the millionth time I'd told myself the words. "There is something seriously wrong with your judgment of character, Adele. Forget about him!"

"Forget about her" was a mantra I'd been telling myself for the last twelve years in regard to my mother. Every year it got easier. I said the mantra on every birthday when she didn't call, every Mother's Day when I had no one to celebrate with, and every Christmas when it was just me and my dad, until she rarely crossed my mind. The only reminder of her was the sadness in my father's eyes.

Now that I knew she hadn't just abandoned us, per se, she was harder to forget. There were so many questions I wanted to ask her. I wanted to know what happened. I wanted to know if she really still cared about me. I wanted to apologize for hating her all these years.

The longer I sat under the statue, the more anxious I became, until suddenly I was squeezing my swollen feet into my shoes and walking the remaining blocks back to the French Quarter.

I told myself I was going home.

As I walked my thoughts remained on my father, who was surely freaking out by now. *Would he hate me if he knew what I did to my mother?*

Would he still love her if he knew she was a vampire? Should I still love her? I barely even remembered loving her as a human.

My pace quickened to a near jog. Again, I told myself I was going home.

I imagined myself opening the front door, running up to my bedroom, pulling off the constricting clothes, and flopping on my bed, crying. *Go home, Adele.* I imagined myself mourning for the Michels and for my mother.

But my feet disagreed. My heart knew I was lying to myself.

Go home, Adele.

Go.

Home.

The gate swung open, and I weaved my way through the overgrown hedges, panting and overwhelmed with guilt.

With each step I told myself to turn back, but then I found myself walking through the front door. I felt compelled to move fast—like I might change my mind if I slowed down. My feet screamed as I pounded the stairs, the skin having rubbed off in spots.

I wound up the staircase, passing the second floor, gaining speed up the steps to the next, and then I was standing in front of the giant padlock on the door that closed off the third floor—the door Nicco had broken when Gabe's strength had failed, when I thought we were on the same team.

My chest puffed up, struggling to regain breath.

When I touched the wooden door, the tinge of nostalgia mixed with guilt was like a bullet to the gut.

Which was worse: Locking up my mother for eternity, or not telling my father what I'd learned about her disappearance? Or knowing how many had died at the hands of these predators before I acted to stop it?

Or the fact that I still thought about Nicco?

You can't do this to the coven, Adele. Or to Adeline's coven. Do you really need a reminder of Medici retaliation on today of all days?

My stomach clenched as my fingers whipped across the padlock, ripping it away. The lock hit the ground, the loud thud echoing behind me as I hurried on while I still had the courage to do it.

Courage? You're delusional.

My eyes were slow to adjust to the dark hallway, and despite the lack of light, despite having only been inside the attic once, something guided me through the sea of objects in the storage room, as if I'd done it a thousand times. *Emotion? Intuition?* It certainly wasn't instinct, because my instincts screamed at me to turn around, asking me if I wanted to die. The darkness flooded around me like quicksand trying to prevent me from trudging closer.

Turn around, Adele.

The tingles started in my toes; I moved down the hallway as if magnetized. When I got to the small door, the tingle ripped up my spine. Goose bumps clutched the back of my head.

Don't do this. Go. Home.

The protection wards pulsed like a shield around the door, far stronger than the first time I'd managed to undo the locks.

Can I even break the slumbering spell on my own?

My hands shook as I brushed the series of intricate locks that lined the door. A giant, invisible fist pounded against my heart.

Thump-thump.

I pressed my cheek lightly against the wood. It was cool on my skin. Almost damp from the humidity.

No sound came from the other side. Perfect silence.

What are you expecting to hear? A tea party?

I remembered the excitement radiating from Gabriel as he'd stood behind me, waiting for me to undo the enchanted locks, and the anxiety that had radiated from Nicco. The memory of him was so strong I glanced behind just to make sure I was still alone.

Thump-thump.

My stomach clenched; I pressed my forehead against the door. *You were wrong about him, Adele.* And nothing had felt right since. Being wrong about him made my whole world feel slightly off-kilter, even more than when I'd found out he was a vampire, even more than when I found out that Isaac was the crow.

Isaac.

Thump-thump.

Thump-thump.

Isaac never had problems doing the right thing. Everything was so black and white for him. Good. Bad. Right. Wrong. All vampires were monsters.

What's wrong with me? Why do I want to open the door so badly? Was it love, or was it curiosity? Why did my mom help me escape? Could she really be completely horrible?

I grasped the door handle to keep my body from shaking. *Why did Nicco let go of my hands?* I slumped to my knees, fighting the tears.

Fighting myself.

Never trust a vampire.

Thump-thump.

CHAPTER 5

Casa Medici

I accidentally let the quill rest while thinking on the last stanza I wrote, and a stain of ink forms on the page. The porous parchment absorbs the glossy pigment until the blotch has grown from the size of a pebble to a ducat, encroaching on the nearest word, but instead of making an effort to stop it, I just stare at the letters about to be engulfed.

The words leap off the page, taunting me. The verse is so terrible, so shallow and meaningless, that even the ink is trying to absorb it back into nothingness. I want to tear the page from the sheaf of papers and shred it to a thousand pieces, but instead I force myself to read the words over and over in the hopes that I will discover what is wrong with the poem and see a way to bring to life the feeling I'm so desperately trying to convey. A thought even more melancholic crosses my mind: maybe I have not lived enough of life in my fourteen years to express anything worth reading.

"*Dannazione!* I don't deserve the attention of these words. *Sta venendo uno schifo . . .*"

The pile of crumbled papers on the floor only fuels my frustration. Everything in the room represents my year's worth of nothingness—a multitude of failed experiments to find my calling: An instrument used to view the stars, built by my tutor, sits next to the stone window. A smattering of scales, vials, and an apparatus for containing flames covers a table on the far side of the room. Two mandolas, a viola da gamba, and a flute lay on top of a litter of sketches and paintings on the floor. Despite having so many interests, I've yet to figure out my purpose in life.

Beauty versus reason has become my great struggle.

From my lips escapes a sigh so pitiful I become grateful for my solitude. No one should witness such an expression of lament, and especially not my brothers nor my sister, though sometimes I think she, unlike them, is capable of compassion.

By the time Emilio reached fourteen years, he had already killed a man in defense of our father and become a hero. It was four years ago, but I still remember the parade thrown in his honor as if it were yesterday. Now he is well on his way to being handed the key to the Florentine Guard. My heart tremors at the idea of Emilio having an arsenal of weapons at his disposal, but he has been primed since birth to become the best man to defend the city.

When Gabriel was fourteen, he became the youngest foreign diplomat in the history of Firenze, in all the kingdoms of Italia, and now he's a key ambassador in Roma, Milano, and Venezia—an integral part of the family business. I possess neither the brutality nor the charm necessary to join either of my brothers on their paths to greatness on the battlefield or in politics. However, it is not their qualities that I covet, but rather their confidence in knowing their own destinies, enabling them to hurl themselves forward.

And, of course, my sweet Giovanna, whose upcoming marriage is destined to create one of the greatest alliances in Florentine history. Perhaps greater than anything my brothers could achieve through negotiation or force.

I have no burning desire for greatness, and I seek neither the attention my brothers demand nor the acclamation they crave, but every day the giant clock sitting on my shoulders ticks louder in my ears, telling me that if I don't carve my own path, one will certainly be carved for me. And as my brothers are so keen to remind me, there are far worse things than the army or politics.

"Sword, coin, or cross," I mumble, dragging my fingers through my hair. I beg the spirit of our grandfather to guide me.

Scuffles come from the hallway, and my fingers rest on the dagger tucked at my waist.

"From here on out," a familiar voice says, "you will be a Medici. Do you understand the importance?"

"Father!" I cry, leaping to my feet. *But who is he speaking to?*

I hurry around the desk as he opens the door and comes through, his arms outstretched. He embraces me tightly. *"Figlio mio!"* he says with love, and kisses my cheeks.

"You have returned!"

"I hear you have been busy, Niccolò. Emilio tells me you have quite the talent for the written word. You must read us some of your poems after dinner."

My teeth sink into my lower lip as scenarios of fratricide run through my head. *"Sì, Padre,"* I reply through locked jaw.

"My son, let me introduce your cousin, León Medici, who has just arrived with me to Firenze."

Cousin? I turn to the stranger with suspicion.

He looks about my age. His features are handsome, and his hair sits in piles of dark-cypress-colored curls atop his head. His clothes are distinctly Italian—Florentine, even—but each piece seems too large, making me wonder if he was not the person they were intended for . . . like his birth name, apparently.

"You will treat him with the same fondness as your brothers," my father says. "You will share your tutoring sessions and then, shortly, go to Siena together for university—"

"University? How long will he be staying here?"

"You will spend the summer helping him master Italian—"

"Why, I beg, have I been assigned this task? I am very busy with"—I look around the room—"my experiments."

"Because you have a kind heart, Niccolò . . . and because, in time, I think you will find that the two of you have a lot in common. You will be able to . . . *learn* from each other."

"Learn? Learn what?"

"Plus, with your passion for the city, I know you'll make a Florentine out of him in no time." He embraces me again.

I grow impatient, knowing he is about to leave without giving me any real information on this *misterioso cugino*.

"Lend him some clothes until we can have some proper garments made," my father says. "Don't let your brothers beat him up too badly."

"Sì, Padre."

He says nothing more, just nods to the boy and walks out of the room, leaving me and *mio cugino* alone.

We gaze at one another, frowning.

"A Medici who doesn't know the ways of Florence?" I ask as I return behind my desk. I lean back in my chair, scrutinizing the boy, wondering if he's really my half brother. *My father's bastard.* I immediately feel defensive for my mother.

His eyes are a shade of blue almost as dark as a nighttime sky, nothing like the glassy, light green all four children of this house share. He has neither Gabriel's sharp chin nor Emilio's prominent nose, which has been broken so many times it now has a permanent crook.

"And what is so special about Florence, *cugino mio*?" León asks in perfect Italian, but with a hint of dialect I cannot place. "Is that what you spend your days writing about? The splendor of Tuscany?"

He reaches for my sonnet and begins dragging the paper across the desk with an interested eye, but I whip my dagger from its sheath and stab the page, straight in between two of his fingers.

Never breaking his gaze, I slowly drag the page back.

"You cut me," he says, bringing his finger to his mouth.

"*Sì*. Stay out of my things, or next time you will lose a finger."

"Of course, cousin," he says, seemingly unaffected by the threat.

He strolls around the room, taking in each detail with equal scrutiny and fascination, and I detect an aura of entitlement. It is well hidden beneath a lifetime of armor, but I recognize it.

"Who *are* you?" I ask, genuine curiosity overtaking my suspicion. "Where are you from?"

He picks up the viola da gamba and pulls the bow slowly across the strings. I expect him to stop after the dramatic display, but instead he whips it back across the strings into a melody that sounds distinctly Spanish—Catalonian maybe. He plays with both confidence and ease, his body moving jovially with the instrument.

He ends the tune with a slight bow and sets the instrument down. He glances over at my sonnet, which now contains a second blotch from the droplet of his blood. "You have your secrets," he says, his tone almost playful, "and I have mine."

I relax into the chair as he moves to pick up the mandola. Instead of plucking the strings, he flips the instrument over and pats the back of the gourd.

Thump-thump.

Again he slaps the hollow cavern with his hand.

Thump-thump.

The room starts to spin. Léon looks directly at me and begins to laugh.

No. This is not how it happened. León did not laugh at me.

His image blurs, and his voice grows distant, as if he's a mile away, but the drumbeat becomes louder. I hold my head, and my blurred vision becomes gray; the gray is swallowed into black. I blink, but there is only blinding darkness.

Thump-thump.

I cry out to León but hear nothing in return. I no longer hear even the sound of my own voice. The muscles in my throat move, but I get nothing back other than an all-encompassing, senses-destroying obsidian.

Thump-thump.

In the silence between the beats, the sound of water rushes like a river.

I am no longer fourteen.

I am no longer in Florence.

I am lying on my back in a very small space.

I command my fist to punch through the cassette, but I cannot move. It's as if my body is full of sand. I cannot even open my eyes.

Magic.

I cling to the moment of consciousness, now remembering it won't last long.

Thump-thump.

Thump-thump.

The pounds vibrate against my rib cage, rippling through my entire skeleton. The water rushes through me. Drowning me.

It's not water. It's blood.

It's not my heartbeat.

It's *her* heartbeat.

Thump-thump.

Thump-thump.

Adele must be close.

The phantom smile that spreads across my face feels more real than any previous smile from the past four centuries in which I had lived.

She's going to open the door.

CHAPTER 6

Breathe

No matter how many times I blinked awake, nothing came into focus—just darkness.

What the hell?

Then the more pressing question came: "Where am I?" A little ball of fire rose from my hand and hovered close to my face, illuminating my surroundings.

I sat up quickly as it all rushed back: the moldy church, my eulogy *en français.* The convent.

The light fizzled out, and the darkness returned.

I came to the convent. I'm in the attic.

My arm shot up, and I slapped around feeling the door. *The locks.* They were all still there. The door was sealed.

Of course they are. You didn't open the door.

I continued trying to ignore the dream, trying to ignore my memories of the boy with the poetry that . . . Nicco had written.

I dreamt of Nicco.

Blood rushed my cheeks, and I reveled in the invisibility of darkness. I'd been so adamant about not allowing myself to think about him, the fact that he'd entered my unconscious state felt like a violation. Maybe it had been a hallucination thanks to Désirée's herbal refreshment? Surely.

Why else would I dream of Nicco . . . as a human?

It was hard to even imagine such a thing now that I was awake. I did *not* want to think about Niccolò Medici being human, as a real person I'd trapped. It was hard enough trying to think of my mother as a vampire on the other side of the door. Trapped.

Halloween night was still so vivid in my mind: Martine and Lisette chained to the ceiling, Lisette hanging upside down like a bat, furious. My hand moved to the claw marks she'd left on my neck, and my mind drifted from the events of that night to a familiar fantasy where I quietly opened the door and tiptoed inside, careful not to wake any of the vampires from their unadulterated slumber. Lisette and Martine in the rafters and Gabriel on the floor against the wall, wrapped in chains, perhaps still spewing obscenities at me in his sleep. But Nicco, Emilio, and my mother would be uninhibited, sleeping where they'd dropped. I'd creep in past the Medici, take my mother under the arms, quietly drag her out, and then reseal the door.

Great plan, Adele. And then what would you do with your slumber-spelled, three-week-starved vampire mother?

People have solved bigger problems . . .

I turned my gaze toward the locks above me. The shroud of darkness suddenly scared me, like it could keep me unaccountable for my actions.

No one would see me do it.

She was *right* there. On the other side of the door.

No one knows she's in there, so no one would know if she's taken out.

"No," I whispered. "They're monsters, Adele. Go home."

Monsters.

My mother is right on the other side of this door. My mother is a monster.

57

The tears that had been caged all day nearly escaped. I locked her in there, and that made me feel like a monster—

"Adele!"

I froze as my name echoed down the hallway. *Shit. How did he—?*

"Adele!"

A flicker of artificial light came with the next shout, and I was made. Isaac's footsteps pounded down the hallway until the only thing separating us was a tidal wave of mortification.

"Jesus Christ, Adele." He fell beside me.

I shielded my face as the light struck my eyes.

"Are you okay?"

My heart sunk as the full extent of what I'd almost done registered—and even *worse*, Isaac had found me here, lying against the door of our sworn enemy. I pulled my knees into my chest, nodding. I didn't have to look up to know he was clamping his jaw shut.

"Are you okay?" he asked again.

I nodded. All I could do was stare silently at the floor.

"Then what are you *doing* here?"

The tears welled. *Just tell him, Adele. You swore no more secrets. Tell him about Brigitte. Tell him that you want to get her out—that you* need *to get her out. That you want him to help you and not hate her because she's a vampire.*

My chest burned, and when I opened my mouth to speak, nothing came out. No words. No air. I looked up at him.

My throat tightened, and my lungs contracted, but they didn't expand. I tried to suck in air through my nose, but it didn't go past my throat.

"Adele?"

Invisible chains wrapped themselves around my ribs, cinching the bones tighter around my lungs, just like the thick iron links I'd smacked around Gabriel, crushing his bones.

My hand slapped the wall behind me.

"Adele, breathe," Isaac said, but the fear in his eyes made my anxiety grow.

I tried to suck in more air, to no avail. The wheezing noise from my throat sounded just like the first time I'd had a panic attack—just after my mother left, at the playground on my first day of kindergarten. After that the doctor ordered me to carry an inhaler with me *everywhere*. My father had been so concerned about me being lax, he'd explained death to me. When I asked him if Mommy had stopped breathing and that's why she went away, he got teary and said, "No, Mommy is just visiting with *grand-mère*."

I hadn't used an inhaler in years, so I didn't carry them on me anymore. *This can't be happening. Not in front of Isaac.*

"Adele, look at me!"

The wheezing worsened; I clung to his wrist.

"Adele, you have to breathe."

I frantically pulled the bow from around my neck. I really wanted to rip the entire shirt off. The chains pulled tighter. I tugged at the high waistband of the skirt, dizziness dancing up my spine before I slumped to the floor.

After everything that'd happened—after we'd finally won—I was going to die next to the sealed attic, cracking from the pressure.

A chuckle that couldn't slip out of my mouth flung out of my eyes in the form of tears.

Whispering under his breath, Isaac yanked the hem of my blouse from my skirt.

"Do not close your eyes!" he yelled, grabbing my jaw with one hand. His other hand slipped beneath my shirt.

Spots appeared all around his head—pink, red, blue—as his rough hands slid over my stomach and unhooked the clasp on my bra. The ease of tension around my chest brought a second of relief. I attempted another gasp, which just resulted in a deathly choke. I thought if the panic attack didn't kill me, I'd actually die from mortification.

A moment later, his touch no longer induced panic. I was barely aware of what was going on . . . barely aware as his hand slid from my ribs to just underneath my breasts, or when he applied a small amount of pressure and the last bit of air deflated from my lungs. I felt my eyes roll back in my head, and I became weightless, like I was floating.

Like the first time we'd kissed, in the Tremé.

Only this time instead of floating with him, I was floating away from him. I didn't want to float away.

Pressure on my mouth pushed me back down to reality—to him.

Tingles. First in my throat and then crackling into my chest like icy Pop Rocks melting onto my inflamed lungs. Another cool burst entered my chest, like the inhaler steroids only without the icky medicinal taste. The air pushed my lungs open, raising my chest along with Isaac's resting hand. Just when I thought they might burst, I felt the air slowly begin to pull out, still icy against my scorched lungs.

He slowly breathed into my mouth again. On the third time, my eyes popped open.

"I'm okay," I choked, pushing him away and exhaling deeply. "I'm okay."

I raised myself up on one arm, my lungs remembering how to inflate and deflate on their own.

He sat back, nodding. I stared at him, no longer with embarrassment, but with disbelief, taking a moment to commit the tingle of his breath to memory.

His air was magical.

He was magical.

What's wrong with me? Why would I ever run away from him? Why would I ever hide anything from him?

I rolled over on my side so I could quickly hook my bra, my modesty returning with the oxygen flow to my brain. When I turned back, he was still just sitting there in shock, breathing heavily.

My words were soft: "I want to go home."

"Thank God," he said, part seasoned first responder, part freaked-out witch.

Before I could attempt to stand, he slipped his arms underneath me and scooped me into his chest. The tautness of his arms told me not to fight him on the lift.

"Aren't you tired after carrying the casket?"

"No."

The short reply made me wonder whether he was a little mad or off-the-charts mad that I'd come to the attic.

I considered lighting the wall sconces as we walked down the hall, but I wasn't ready for the look on his face.

He paused at the top of the stairs so I could relock the door.

"Are you going to put me down now?"

"No." He gripped me tighter.

"Ooookey dokey." I flicked my right hand, and the base of the padlock flew from the wooden floor and reattached itself to the hook with one quick jerk. "Done."

I tried not to be annoyed when he tested it; instead I hugged him tighter, resting my head against his neck.

He bounced down the wide, winding staircase, careful not to bump me on the banister. On the last set of stairs, he finally spoke: "For future reference . . . there are much easier ways to get me to cop a feel."

My face burned. "For future reference, we are never going to talk about this, or you will never cop another feel."

"Talk about what?"

I couldn't control my grin or my blushing, so I burrowed my face into his shoulder. *Could I be a bigger loser? The first time my boyfriend feels me up is to try to keep me from self-inflicted asphyxiation. If he is my boyfriend, that is . . . It's not like we've ever had* that *discussion.*

"And for the record, I barely touched your boobs."

"I know." I hugged him tighter, burying my face deeper into the crevice of his shoulder, which was tense to say the least.

He didn't let my feet touch the ground until we were halfway through the labyrinth of hedges in the garden, and by then it was me who wasn't ready to let go—I hung on to his neck, pulling him down until his lips touched mine.

For a split second, he hesitated, and that hesitation shook me. Isaac was always ready—to help someone, to stop a looter, to stop a monster—and he was *always* ready to kiss me. In that microsecond I realized how much I'd been taking him for granted, and I felt the emptiness of what it'd be like to lose him.

His hand cupped my cheek, keeping my face close to his. "You scared the shit out of me."

"I'm sorry." My voice was meek. I didn't know if he was referring to my running away or the panic attack or my coming to the attic. "I'm sorry," I repeated, peering directly into his eyes so I couldn't see the shutters behind him. All I wanted to see was him. "Please don't be mad."

"I'm not mad . . . I just wonder . . . what it's going to be like when you come to school here every day."

My stomach tensed. My father had enrolled me at Ursuline because he knew how much I hated Sacred Heart. That, plus the monumental difference in tuition costs and the proximity to our house, meant there was no way I was getting out of the transfer. I didn't know what to say.

I hooked a single finger into his and whispered, "Let's go."

And he walked me home, finger in finger.

When we got to my stoop, I unlocked the gate and turned back to him from the first step, closer to eye level. "Everything's going to be fine in January. Today just sucked with the funeral."

He nodded, but the crease in his brow did not smooth out.

"Ooooor you could enroll and finish your senior year in the vampire holding tank with me."

He gave me a limp smile. "Why, you embarrassed to be with a dropout?"

I shook my head, sliding my arms around his neck.

He pulled me closer, and my heart breathed a sigh of relief. Our lips brushed, and this time there was no hesitation when he kissed me. In that moment I was so thankful I hadn't opened the attic door. I pulled him closer and kissed him until he had to pause for air.

"Breathe," I whispered, with our heads together and my lips still smiling against his.

And he did.

CHAPTER 7

ASG

Metal on metal screeched from my father's studio. A grinder or a band saw.

He's not at work?

The ear slaughter got louder as I walked down the hall. Somehow my anxiety attack had brought on a new sense of calm—cathartic release, perhaps. Or maybe it was just the residual effect of Isaac's kisses.

The studio was open, which was rare; my father always kept the door closed as a courtesy, containing the screeching tools and harsh chemicals.

He's waiting for me to come home.

I grabbed a pair of earmuffs—he kept protective gear hanging in the hallway just outside the door—adjusted them to fit my head, and put on plastic eyewear before I went in. My father was a stickler for safety.

"Dad!" I yelled, waving my arm to get his attention.

"One second!" He turned off the saw. "Keep your muffs on!"

I nodded as he picked up a ball-peen hammer and slammed it into a large sheet of metal. He held up his hand, letting me know that he wasn't done.

It was too early in the process to guess at what he was making.

He whacked the metal again, the explosion of sound still intensely loud through the muffs.

Mac had two kinds of swings when it came to blacksmithing. The first had the careful precision of an artist; when he made those kinds of swings, you could almost see the end piece sitting in his head, each swing getting him one step closer. Other times, his pounding was more aggressive—yes, he was making art, but he was also working something out . . . something that had *nothing* to do with art. These were swings of the latter variety. A final swing squeezed a spark from the metal and a grunt from his throat. I could practically feel the reverberation through my fingertips.

He tossed aside the hammer.

Definitely of the latter variety. My father's love affair with metal really made me wonder sometimes . . .

"Are you okay?" he asked as I pulled off the goggles and earmuffs. "Where have you been?"

"Nowhere, really. I exhausted myself walking around and then got upset and fell asleep."

His eyebrow slanted.

"At the Borges'," I added. "Désirée's mom made me some tea; then Isaac found me and walked me home." *It was mostly true.* I tried to convince myself the lie was better than giving my dad a meltdown with "I fell asleep in an abandoned building."

"You didn't answer the question." He wiped his forehead with his sleeve. His eyes were heavy and a little pink, maybe from the air in the studio, more likely from going straight from a graveyard shift to the graveyard. "Are you okay?"

"My feet hurt," I said, but he just looked at me until I conceded. "I'm fine, Dad. I just . . . can't believe they're gone." I swallowed the lump in my throat. I wanted people to stop worrying about me.

"I can't either," he said, pulling a stool over and sitting down.

I looked at the pile of tools on the floor and back to him. "Dad, are *you* okay?" When was the last time someone asked him that?

"Yeah, sweetheart. I'm fine."

His stock answer was unconvincing. "You sure?"

"I'm sure. I'm just worried about you." He leaned down, picked the hammer back up, and flipped it around in his hand. "And . . . just a little surprised your mother didn't come to the funeral to support you, considering she's in town. That's all."

"Oh—" My breath caught short at the mention of my mother, and when he flipped the hammer again, it spun out of his hand and shot directly to my feet.

"Watch out!" He jumped up.

My feet danced out of the way. "I'm fine!"

"Jesus, I'm sorry. Did it nick you?"

I shook my head, scooped up the hammer, and handed it back to him. Frowning, he put it down safely on the tool bench.

"She surprised me," he continued without questioning the hammer's unnatural trajectory, thank God. "And I didn't think Brigitte could still surprise me."

It was so strange hearing him say her name. He usually only referred to her as "your mother." The one little word humanized her more than all the good things he'd ever told me about her—things that had fallen on angsty ears.

"I *know*, Adele, that you're not going to believe me, because you were too young to remember your mom before she left, but it's just not something she would do. I even left her a message with the details. I *knew* she'd want to be there for you, but . . . I guess I don't know her at all anymore. It's so hard to accept that she's a different person now."

I stood there, stunned, the lump swelling in my throat. *Literally a different person.*

"She called me," I said.

"What?" His back straightened.

"She called me and told me how much she wished she could have been there." Tears rose, but I fought them back down. "She was on a plane back to France when you left the message. Émile was supposed to call me to say they were leaving New Orleans sooner than expected. She was furious when she found out he hadn't . . ."

"Her *assistant* was supposed to tell you she was leaving?" His head shook in disappointment—and that headshake was the worst thing my father had ever said about my mother. I wished I'd left out the part about Émile. I hadn't thought fast enough.

"It's okay, Dad. Émile and I were friends in Paris."

"It's not, Adele. It's not okay."

I was pretty sure he knew I was lying, but he didn't push it. I was also pretty sure he knew I was doing it to spare his feelings—there was no other reason I'd have ever covered for Brigitte's irresponsibility in the past. He had no idea of the real level of lying I'd sunk to.

"I'm sorry, sweetheart, I shouldn't say anything to you about it."

"Dad, it's okay. I'm not a kid anymore."

His arm went around my shoulder. "You'll always be my kid."

"One day I'll be your adult."

"Not a chance." He gave me a squeeze and then walked me to the stairs. As he told me good night, the distance in his eyes killed me. It was obvious he was still thinking about Brigitte. None of it made sense to him, from the moment when she'd just packed up and dumped us for her native France. I hated how the lack of closure made it impossible for him to move on. And I hated lying to him, and not just about Mom—about everything.

Most of all, I hated that we had secrets now.

I climbed the stairs to my room, wondering if he would ever learn the truth about Brigitte Dupré Le Moyne.

I didn't bother turning on the lights. All I cared about was removing the restricting clothing. I kicked off my shoes, immediate relief washing over me as my toes spread out. I hurled the mutilated pantyhose directly into the garbage can. *Not salvageable.*

Sweatpants, a T-shirt, and a washed face, and I went straight for my bed.

Alone in the darkness, under the security of my duvet, I continued to think about Brigitte.

My dad was right. This *wasn't* okay. None of it was.

The tears released: slow trickles down the sides of my face.

My mother is dead.

My mother is a vampire who murdered two students, and I locked her in an attic for eternity.

That was the moment I decided I had to know everything. Not just everything that had happened to her—all of it. The magic. The coven. The feud.

Getting answers to why the Medici were after Adeline, the Count, and now me was the only way I'd ever get her out. It was also the moment I decided: *I have to save my mother.*

Whatever they were after, I needed it. It was the only thing they seemed to care about. Nicco was willing to kill me for it, which meant it could be a bargaining chip.

My mother wasn't a part of their family. She was a part of our family—the Saint-Germains. And I was going to get her back.

But I couldn't just charge into the attic. If I broke the seal, we'd be right back where we'd started, with the Medici still half-cursed and wholly pissed, and Gabe and crew stuck in the Quarter. They'd retaliate by killing people until we broke the rest of the curse, which we couldn't do unless we found the other descendants. Besides, giving them what they wanted didn't exactly work for me either. They'd just go back out into the world, feed on people, and turn other innocents—other people's mothers—into vampires too.

No, opening the attic was out of the question. The Medici were monsters who belonged caged.

But my mom isn't a Medici. She tried to save me that night, even against Emilio's orders. *She's not a monster. She's just caught in the crosshairs of this ridiculous family feud.* There had to be a way to get her out.

I scanned my memories for missed clues: every interaction I'd had with Emilio in France, everything Ritha had ever told me about magic, every word of Adeline's. But no matter where my thoughts started, they always ended up in the one place I was always trying to avoid: *Nicco.*

Why had he been after the Saint-Germains in 1728? And why was he still after the Count? Why had he pretended to care about me?

My eyes watered again, but this time I sat up. I refused to cry over Nicco. How had I ever been so stupid to think he was on my side, that he'd betray his family for me?

Family.

Adeline wouldn't let them have her dad, and I wasn't going to let them have my mom.

A slow creak came from beside the bed, almost as if in response to the intensity of my thoughts.

I turned my head as the closet door creaked open wider.

I'd been ignoring Adeline ever since that night. I had an implicit love for her, but Adeline Saint-Germain had caused me nothing but trouble since the moment I'd discovered her. Now it felt like she was in the room with me.

I slid out of bed into the darkness, heart pounding. Things were different now.

Now I was ready for trouble.

I tiptoed inside the little closet room, which I'd cleaned out as a distraction from the funeral. Only the two antique steamer trunks remained and the darkness and silence, and the remnant smell of the vanilla candle I'd burned trying to cover up the must. A slither of moonlight slipped through a muck-stained window, providing just enough light to guide me to Adeline's floorboard.

I knelt down, and the door swung closed behind me, shutting me in the tiny room. I took a deep breath, pushed out any claustrophobic feelings, and looked up at the decaying string. It was attached to a little strand of ball 'n' chain, hanging from the Edison bulb. I envisioned the chain pulling down.

Click.

Beneath the muted light, the floorboards, old and worn, all looked the same, but they weren't. I raised my hand over the wood, and the nails began to shake. The magical tingling, the sensation of supernatural energy, crept from my fingertips into my hands and then my arms, until the nails wriggled out and popped up into my palms. I gently put them aside and did the same with the nails in the adjacent floorboard.

Wedging my fingers between the loose wood, I popped the boards out, feeling a rush of excitement when I saw the metal underneath. It was cool to the touch but radiated magical energy. *Her magic . . . Saint-Germain magic.*

Our magic.

My hands hovered over Adeline's safe. I'd done this twice before, but it wasn't as simple as turning on the light or opening the door. *Focus, Adele.* My hands shook, feeling polarized against the metal beneath them, like two repelling magnets.

"Come on, steady," I said, rising on my knees. *"Come on."*

The metal rippled.

"Almost there . . ."

I gasped as it morphed, parting ways like water. As fast as I could, I reached in and grabbed her things, still afraid of the magic, as if the safe might simply close up and cut off my hand.

My fingers were spared, but the safe did close quicker than it had opened, like it didn't want me to renege and shove everything back in.

Clutching Adeline's necklace and diary, and my journal with the French translation, I scooted away from the hole until my back knocked against one of the trunks. I sat there under the moonlit window, slowing my breath, my thumb rubbing the opalescent stone on the medallion. I hadn't worn it since the night we sealed the attic.

It had started out a simple necklace: a gift from the Count to his daughter. The initials *ASG* were etched onto the silver disc in a delicate calligraphy, but were now mostly covered by a silver star. Now that I thought about it, I wondered if it had ever really been so simple. The more puzzle pieces I put together, the more I understood that nothing about Adeline or her father was ever simple. On her journey across the Atlantic, Adeline had pressed the giant opal—formerly of the eye socket of a pirate captain—into the other side of the medallion to serve as a reminder of just how dangerous the Medici were. And that was something I needed to remember now.

I slipped the medallion back onto my chain where it belonged, next to my father's sun and Isaac's feather. It was hard to believe I'd ever taken it off, but at the time I'd just wanted to bury it all. I wanted to believe we were finished with the Medici.

I hadn't yet processed my mother coming back into my life.

I'd only found half of the medallion in our attic; Brigitte had sent the other half back from France with me. *Did she know what it was? Had she been trying to help me, even back then?*

That meant she'd helped me twice—consciously or not. *Now it's my turn to help her.*

And so, I needed to know everything about the enemies I'd inherited. But everyone who had answers about the past was locked in the attic.

The only thing I had to turn to now was . . . magic.

We have *to put the rest of the coven together.*

Together we could figure out a way to save my mother. I pictured myself calling a cabal and telling Dee and Isaac everything, finding the other descendants, and sorting all of this out. My nerves ate away at the image like hungry rats until it was gone. It was too risky. I'd tell them after we found the other members.

I took Adeline's things back to my room, tossed them on the bed, and grabbed my phone.

Adele	**6:29 p.m.**	We need to find the rest of the descendants.
Désirée	**6:29 p.m.**	Thank God. What brought on this revelation?
Adele	**6:30 p.m.**	I guess the funeral put things into perspective. Priorities.
Désirée	**6:30 p.m.**	Great, now u just have to convince Isaac that putting together the coven is a worthwhile cause.
Adele	**6:30 p.m.**	Why me?
Désirée	**6:31 p.m.**	Please...
Adele	**6:31 p.m.**	Ok. I'm sure it won't be that hard. Right? He's obsessed w everything magic.
Désirée	**6:31 p.m.**	I'm burning a candle for u.

Just thinking about asking Isaac to help with breaking the curse, even if indirectly, made my heart race, especially after today.

I opened the leather cover of Adeline's diary and turned the first few pages until her handwriting, with all its flourishes and exotic French phrases, appeared. I used to think the dry, aged pages were too precious to handle, that the diary should be in a museum, not in my possession; but now I suspected it was magically indestructible, like Adeline's spirit. Every piece of the puzzle I'd found so far—every artifact, person, curse, and mystery—had always connected back to Adeline. All roads led back to the Saint-Germains.

To the Count.

Why were the Medici so obsessed with him? Any person who held so much power over the Medici made me insatiably curious. But most importantly, *how the hell is the Count still alive?* Emilio seemed to think it was plausible when I tricked him Halloween night.

After leafing through some of the pages at random, I turned back to the first page.

And so, back to the beginning, I went.

3 mars 1728

Le voyage a commencé, Papa. Nous avons été à bord du SS Gironde, sous le commandement du capitaine Vauberci . . .

And I read and read, until I was dreaming about Parisian salons, and bubbly wine . . . and Monsieur Cartier.

CHAPTER 8

Street Smart

I reached out for the bed frame and caught myself, but my arm jerked so hard in its socket, I wished I'd crashed to the floor.

Fucking dream.

My phone blinked 01:46 hours. I didn't try to convince myself to go back to sleep—after finding Adele at the convent earlier, I didn't know how I'd fallen asleep in the first place. I stepped straight into my shoes, not bothering to grab a shirt from the pile on the floor as I ran out of the room.

What the hell was she doing there?

I leaped off the deck, but tonight being in the air wasn't enough to bring me any serenity. No, tonight, if there was trouble to be had, I would find it.

I swooped past Le Chat and contemplated stopping in for a beer. *Don't push your luck with Mac.* He was just starting to seem kind of okay with me dating his daughter. Instead I picked up an air current that carried me over the rooftops. Getting a bird's-eye view high above the roosting city was one of my favorite things about flying. Although, according to Adele, the Quarter never roosted before the Storm.

I rode the updraft peacefully, until the strike of shattering glass echoed down the street.

Looters.

Post-Storm looting really got me hotheaded. Raiding a Walmart because your family needed food was totally acceptable in my book, especially after such epic institutional failure, but stealing from someone else whose life had already been ruined by the Storm was not okay.

I dipped off in the direction of the sound. Another smash of glass led me straight to a three-story Creole town house on Royal Street. The mint-green paintwork had taken a beating in the Storm, revealing the red brick beneath it. The long shutters, a much darker green, were all closed. I soared past the gallery on the second level. Scrolling brackets of ironwork framed the outside sitting area, curling and looping so intricately with the vines and ferns it was hard to tell where the metal ended and the foliage began.

Another crash came from the upper level, and I swooped over the gated alley to the back, scoping for their entry point, the first-responder protocol automatically stringing through my head: Observe. Adapt. Dominate—OAD.

Observe.

The mammoth trash pile in the driveway spread down the entire side of the house, which meant the owners must have returned post-Storm. If the place was as gutted as the trash pile indicated, my guess was that they weren't currently living here.

At the back of the house flames flickered in gas lamps hanging on either side of the entrance, illuminating a broken glass pane in the door. *Bingo.*

Another crash came from inside, and that was enough for me.

Adapt.

I dropped down to the ground, regained human form, and opened the door.

The room was made of mostly windows, which I'm sure at one time had been a lovely spot to sit—wicker chair rocking, sipping the kind of iced tea that made your teeth rot out—but now it was furnitureless and the floor had been ripped out. The flames from the outside gas lamps shone through the windows revealing tall piles of stuff: salvaged furniture, rolled-up rugs, ladders, and boxes of power tools. It all cast dark shadows on the walls. I didn't like it—there were too many large, bulky things for someone to hide behind.

I instinctually reached for my flashlight, but I didn't have my knapsack—I didn't even have a shirt on. I walked through with caution . . . peering into every shadow created by the moonlight pouring in from the windows.

The rooms became emptier the deeper I went, and a twinge of freshly applied drywall mud pervaded the air. Ladders and paintbrushes waited for workers to return. Sheets of plastic hung from the ceiling, gently rippling as I walked by. I lost all light as I moved farther into the interior of the house. My pulse thumped, waiting for someone to jump out.

Then I froze—footsteps briskly moved across the room overhead. I hurried, light on my feet through the dark hall, heading straight for a winding staircase.

I silently ascended to the next floor, listening for the intruder. The second floor seemed like it hadn't sustained any storm damage, and all the unboarded windows allowed me enough light to move faster. I entered the first bedroom, adrenaline pumping through my veins. *Clear.*

Another crash came, followed by an explosion of smashing glass and laughter. *What an asshole.* The sounds grew louder. I was getting closer. I slipped from bedroom to bedroom and back out into the L-shaped hallway that overlooked the first floor, until there was only one more door left.

There's nowhere else to hide.

I slipped through. Unlike the other rooms upstairs, which had all been sleeping quarters, this was an office, full of antiques. A regal desk with a tufted-leather chair sat in front of inset bookcases, and the room was decorated with fancy-looking rugs and statues—but there was no sign of intruders.

Shiny wooden pocket doors led to an adjoined room, which I guessed would be the street-facing room with the balcony I'd seen on Royal. I stepped toward them and paused.

A crash came from behind the sliding door. Then another, more violent. Something being hurled against a wall?

A peal of laughter floated out.

Dominate.

I grabbed a statue of a waistcoated rabbit holding a pocket watch off an end table, slipped inside the doors, and crept in, keeping close to the wall so no one could sneak up behind me.

A haze of moonlight shone through the long windows on the left wall, pouring over the enormous fireplace. The remains of vases, clocks, and tchotchkes were shattered over the marble floor in front of the hearth, and . . . a tiny figure? A wave of chills swept over my naked shoulder blades.

A little girl with long, stringy black ringlets, wearing a dingy white dress, stood with her back to me, facing the fireplace, whose mantel was empty except for an enormous mirror. She was surrounded by glittering glass, and had one arm extended into the moonlight, as if holding something out, but there was nothing in her hand.

Broken porcelain crunched underneath my feet, and she glanced back over her shoulder. Her eyes popped wide. She straightened up and dropped her arm to her side, her fingers still curled as if she was squeezing an invisible ball.

What is she doing? Playing a game?

"I didn't mean to scare you," I said, setting down the rabbit on the floor.

"You're not my brother." The tone in her voice sent the hairs on the back of my neck straight up.

She was as pale as a person with a pulse could be.

"Is your brother here too?" I asked. *Maybe he was the vandal?*

She nodded slowly, but her cold little stare never let up, as if warning me not to mess with her.

She began to tremble.

"Hey," I said, trying to be comforting, keeping my distance. "Are you okay?" *Is there such a thing as a kid-bloodsucker?*

Her fingers slowly tightened into a fist, her arms tensing and expression hardening. Then she released a huge breath. "Drat!" she yelled, looking angrily at me, like I'd just spoiled her tea party.

She's not a vamp, you moron; she's just a kid. A very weird kid.

"Stina!" a guy cried from another room, his footsteps drawing rapidly closer. "Celestina, where are you?"

He swung through the doorway but stopped short when he saw me, his ecstatic expression dissipating. His eyes slanted at me, then moved to her. "Stina, are you okay?"

I became acutely aware I was just standing there shirtless with a little girl. "I was just out running and heard something."

"Isn't it a bit late to be . . . running?" The guy looked only a few years older than me. He was as pale as the girl and shared her dark, curly hair. His white button-down shirt hung loosely over dark jeans. Also dingy. "Do you often go *running* after curfew?" he probed, taking a step toward me.

"Do you often break into people's houses at two o'clock in the morning?" I snapped. "I mean, assuming this isn't your place."

He sighed. "We used to live in one even more grand, before everything went to complete and total hell. Right, Celestina?"

"I'm hungry."

"I know, love." He held out his hand. Her eyes were such a dark shade of blue that, with her pale skin, she appeared dollish. "Things won't always be like this . . . We'll come out on top again, that I can promise you."

As she walked over and took his hand, I felt like shit. There were people in need all over the state, and I knew better than to jump to conclusions. I also knew that if I was homeless and the city was half-abandoned, I wouldn't squat in the shittiest house on the block when there were places like this.

"Come on, sweetheart, maybe we'll find something to eat next door." They walked to the door.

"Wait," I said, again thinking about how cold it was outside and the little girl.

"Do not try to stop me," the guy said. "I will make you regret it."

"No. It's none of my business. You stay. I'll go."

He nodded appreciation, and the little girl smiled—both creepy and cute at the same time.

I glided around the Borges and over to the convent, my feathers prickling, making me aware of how weirdly unsettled I felt. I didn't know if it was the funeral, finding Adele at the convent, or the strange squatter.

All of the above.

I circled the attic, flying even closer to the shutters than usual, making sure there wasn't so much as a rattle coming from inside. But tonight it wasn't enough to put me at ease. Instead of going straight for the roof like I normally did, I investigated the entire property, looking for unlocked doors or windows. When I couldn't find any, I had no choice but to go down one of the chimneys, which I hated doing because it was dirty and there were usually decaying rats, but when you spent your days fixing houses, vandalizing didn't come easy.

I held my breath and dove in, hoping not to lose too many feathers on the way down.

In a half tumble, half roll, I burst out of the fireplace onto the wooden floor, turning back into my human self, coughing out soot.

After pausing to brush myself off, I ran up the stairs to the third floor. I wasn't sure what I was expecting to find, but the padlock was intact, exactly how we'd left it earlier. I gave it a tug, and breathed a sigh of relief.

I imagined Adele coming here, unlocking the door with a swoop of her fingers, moving down the hall, and closing the distance between her and Nicco.

She stopped at the final door, Isaac.

"But why did she come here in the first place?" I yelled, smacking the wooden door.

Breathing heavily, I backed away. I hated this place.

No, I just hated *him*. No, I hated vampires. All of them.

I swooped back onto Royal Street, and a familiar voice sung out, loud and jovial like a pirate, singing the kind of song that everyone knew the words to but no one knew the name of. Each line slurred more than the one before because, also like a pirate, an unmarked bottle of booze hung from his left hand—the moonshine he and Mac were bootlegging. Ren was a giant man, but his knees were getting closer to the sidewalk with every step.

He shouldn't be so wasted out on the streets at this hour. The thought made me feel as old as my pop, but then again crime in the city hadn't actually downturned much since we captured the Medici.

As I debated whether I should walk him home to the Marigny, he collapsed.

"*Ren!*" I glided down with the current, nearly biting the pavement when I dropped beside him. "Ren, what's wrong?"

"Alessandro?" he asked as his eyes rolled back in his head *Exorcist*-style.

"Whoa, buddy, stay with me."

"Alessandro, is that you?"

"Ren, it's Isaac. Did you take something?"

"Bbbbbrrrbbb," his lips blew out like a baby's. "If there was something in this city to take, you think I'd be drinking this shite?"

He brought the bottle to his mouth, missed, and poured moonshine all over his face. He shot up into a sitting position and clocked me with a right hook.

"Fuck, Ren!"

I backed away, still cursing, and he looked down at his own fist, massaging it as if it had taken him by as much surprise as it had me.

"Hey, it's the Yankee!"

He tried but couldn't stand on his own, so I offered him a hand and pulled him up.

"Sorry about that, sonny."

I tried to reply, but my vision was still spinning, making it difficult to articulate words.

"How's Adele? Mac warming up to you yet?"

I rubbed my jaw and spit blood on the ground, trying to figure out if it was my lip or tongue. Both felt numb. When I looked back up, Ren's hands were coming for my chest, and he knocked me back down to the ground.

"What's your problem, Ren?" I snapped, baffled, as I pushed myself away. When he continued toward me, I jumped up, not wanting to have to take a swing back at one of the French Quarter's most beloved characters.

He lunged, but this time I was ready—he might have been bigger, but he was on another planet. I grabbed his arm and jerked it behind his back. His knees buckled, and for a flash I thought it wasn't just a drunken stupor and that he was going to try to flip me.

"Dude!" I yelled. "Have you lost it?"

A flash of blue and red responded, along with a quick *blurp* of siren.

"Back away," a cop said through a speaker.

Eff this. The cop can take him home.

As the car door opened, I released Ren's arm and took off.

Before either of them could look my way, I was already two stories up, gliding toward the moon.

CHAPTER 9

Supernatural Sensation

November 25th

Head in my hands, elbows on the counter at Café Orléans, I read Adeline's second-to-last journal entry four times, as if there might be some kind of hidden code beneath the words and I just wasn't getting it. Really I was procrastinating broaching the coven-speak with Isaac. In a weird way the incident at the attic had brought us closer, and I didn't want to spoil it. So I'd told myself I had until I finished reading the journal—because technically I was doing coven research—then I had to suck it up and ask him to join the cause. I'd managed to stretch my reading out for nearly a week already.

I just wished I had a better reason to tell him than "because."

A gentle breeze came through the open door. The temperature had dropped; a storm was coming. I took a sip of my chamomile tea, trying to ignore the Wolfman's replacement DJ droning in the background.

"The chief of police is imploring people to stay off the streets at night and to obey the mayor's mandatory curfew. Police response is still slow. NOPD is operating at thirty percent, and the crime rate is outpacing them like a Formula One at the dog track."

I debated switching it off, but a quick glance at Isaac sitting at the corner table told me he was listening—busy sketching—but also listening intently, judging by the stern furrow in his brow. He was *obsessed* with the city's crime reports.

"The body was called in by Gentilly neighbor Lori Broussard, who we got a hold of earlier today." The radio crackled as the woman spoke. "When I found him, I didn't know dat was Mr. O'Keefe! His body was so white, I thought it was one of those washed up Storm-corpses people been talking 'bout. But I guess dat's what happens when you dead. White. *White.* Looked like he been dead foreva, but I know dat ain't true 'cause I just saw 'em Tuesday. He was going to help his daughter get that damn blue tarp stay up on her roof."

The DJ cut back in. "Based on the police statement, the victim's home showed signs of breaking and entering, looters, most likely. The deceased is survived by two daughters."

You know the world's gone mad when your first thought after hearing about a murder is *Thank God it wasn't the vampires I accidentally let loose.* The sad truth was, New Orleanians had been killing each other since long before the Medici had showed up to town, and now that the vampire problem was taken care of, we were back to the regularly scheduled human-on-human crime, which was less frightening for some reason but far more depressing.

I looked up at Isaac and caught him glancing at me as he sketched. I playfully rolled my eyes, shaking my head.

"Busted," he said, smiling.

I hated it when he sketched me, but he was so good, I was finding it impossible to ask him to stop.

He closed his sketch pad and started packing his bag; my heart sank a little. The café used to be my second home, but now I hated being alone here.

"You're leaving?"

"I'm meeting Chase over at the Moonwalk to train."

"Like you need more training . . ."

"Did you hear the same crime report that I just heard?"

"Nothing new." I was far more desensitized to the city's crime than Isaac was.

"I mean, I can stay if you need—"

"No, I'm fine. Go run obstacle courses with Chase, or whatever it is the two of you do."

"One of these days I'm going to drag you along."

I snickered. "Yeah, right, maybe me *and* Dee."

"You laugh, but it will happen—just wait. You'll both be able to throw a stake from a hundred feet."

My back stiffened. "You guys practice throwing stakes? You *told* Chase—?"

"Relax." He walked up to the counter. "We don't train with stakes. We train with footballs and rope and bricks and branches and whatever else is lying around. It's not like we can go to the gym."

I certainly didn't need to ask what, or *who*, was in Isaac's head for target practice. He tried to play it off, but he'd been on edge ever since the day he found me in the attic. But just as we promised, we didn't talk about it.

"Adele." His tone was suddenly more serious. "If they ever get out of the attic, I'm going to be ready."

"Isaac, I'm not going to open the—"

"I'm going to be more prepared, that's all I'm saying. We all need to be." He leaned over the counter onto his elbows.

I gently brushed the hair from his cheek, careful not to touch the bruised area near his eye. "Your shiner's almost gone. I still can't believe Ren hit you."

He shook his head but didn't respond. His eyes were glued to my right cheek, where the thin white line stretched up to my eye—the scar left by his claw. He'd only stopped apologizing after I forced him to, but sometimes his eyes still said: *I can't believe I did this to you.*

I leaned over the counter and softly touched my lips to his, ending the silent exchange. As I lingered in the moment, I could feel his thoughts slip away, and my insides turned to goo.

Thunder cracked outside, and I broke the kiss with a smile. "Rain. Looks like you can't train with Chase and will have to stay." I thumbed through the embroidery thread bracelets that covered his left wrist—the mismatched colors and patterns a stark difference to his great-grandfather's military watch hidden beneath them. I loved it all mixed together.

He curled his fingers, touching my wrist. I tried not to smile. "Yeah, right, this is a guy who willingly jumps out of planes into wildfires. He'd never let me live it down."

Those were the words he said, but he wasn't exactly running for the door anymore. My eyes flicked to the journal next to our elbows and I remembered my mission.

"I was thinking . . ." My pulse accelerated so quickly I lost my words.

He slipped his hands into mine. "You were thinking . . . that you want to come throw stakes?" I knew he was joking, but still, the comment made me retract further.

"What is it?" He squeezed my hands.

Oh God, Adele, just ask him. He's obsessed with his magic; he should want the coven's power to grow. To find the other descendants.

But the image of him throwing stakes overtook me. "Um . . . while you're out training, could I . . . borrow Susannah's sketchbook?"

His hands broke away. I knew it was ridiculous to ask him to leave his most precious magic in my possession, but it was the first thing that popped in my head. He slung his knapsack on the counter and pulled out the leather-bound book.

"Of course you can." He leaned over the counter and kissed my cheek. "I trust you."

"Merci beaucoup," I said, kind of surprised. I would have been a bit more Gollum-like with Adeline's diary. For a second I was glad for its French so no one would ever ask to borrow it.

He smiled. "You're up to something." His eyes dropped to the medallion hanging against my chest—right next to his feather. "And I like it."

"Have fun staking imaginary vampires."

"Oh, I will. I'll call you later."

I nodded, a bit stunned, and watched him walk out the open door. Isaac trusted me so much that he was willing to loan me his family's grimoire, and without so much as a question about my sudden interest again in all things magic. Yet here I was speaking in half-truths to him. I had to find a way to tell him about Brigitte. I didn't want there to be any secrets between us. I was already struggling enough keeping things from my father.

". . . and that brings the crime rate up to—"

I snapped off the radio.

No more, for God's sake.

In the silence, I pulled his grimoire into my chest and hung on to his presence. I knew it would only take a few seconds for the sadness to creep in like a low-lying fog and permeate every pore of my being. The little corner café used to feel like an extension of Mémé and Pépé's living room, but now when I was here, the guilt poured over me like wet cement. It was inescapable. Not that I didn't try, hiding in the pages of fictional tragedies—I looked at the stack of assigned school books on the counter. I should have been reading them right now, but every spare second of headspace I had was consumed with my mission to help my mother.

I turned back to Adeline's diary.

Not only had the pages not given me any new answers this time around, they hadn't even given me a direction. No rabbit hole to jump down. No bread-crumb trail to follow. I could recite the pages by heart—in two languages—which was not something I could say about my half-written lit essay sitting under the pile of books.

Adeline seemed just as mystified in 1728 as to why the Medici were after our family as I was now. The only thing crystal clear was that their vendetta had started long before Adeline locked Gabe in the attic, killing Giovanna in the process. I trembled at the thought of the Medici brothers ever finding out it was Adeline who'd killed Giovanna. *Like they didn't hate my family enough.*

"But why did they want your father so badly, Adeline?" I opened her diary, scanning the pages once more. *Why didn't Nicco make it onto the ship with the rest of his siblings?*

Adeline hadn't allowed herself to be vamp-zapped, but he could have easily found a more innocent *fille à la cassette* to trick into passage like Gabe had done after Cosette denied him. *What made Nicco miss the boat?* Nothing seemed more important to Nicco than catching the Count. *Does that mean he got a better lead?*

I flipped open my notes titled **Théories du Complot–Le Comte de Saint-Germain**, which was only fitting because at this point, anything I came up with could only be considered a conspiracy.

I tried to look at everything from the Medici point of view, because thinking like a Saint-Germain was clearly getting me nowhere. *What could spark a family feud that would span centuries? Why are they so desperate to kill the Count?*

I remembered the disgust in Nicco's voice and the cold look in his eyes whenever I uttered the words "Saint-Germain" in his presence. It still made me shiver. *What's the worst thing someone could have done to Nicco? Killed him? Murdered him? Turned him into a vampire?*

Is the Count a vampire?

It was the only reasonable explanation for how he might still be alive centuries later. *But he can't be a vampire—the Count is a witch.* In 1728, Adeline wrote that they shared the same powers. He couldn't be both a witch and a vampire . . . Lisette had lost her magic when she was turned.

As I scribbled out a series of dates to cross-reference, another huge crack of thunder came from outside, and this time the rain poured down with it. The perfect backdrop as my thoughts danced into a dark corner of my imagination—macabre, uninhibited dancing that took my thoughts to family members slain, fortunes stolen, and lovers lost. Because every time I read over my notes, I kept coming back to three things: family, money, and love.

Outside, loud footsteps smacked into the already-forming puddles. I felt the prick of supernatural energy as the footsteps squelched into the entrance and paused. I finished writing my sentence as I said, "NOLA rain too much for you and Chase after all?"

"Excuse me?" asked an unfamiliar voice. I quickly looked up.

A guy with sopping black hair stepped up to the counter.

"Sorry!" I closed the book. "I thought you were someone else."

"Please don't be sorry. I'm the one who just tracked rain all over your café." He glanced back at the trail of water, which somehow seemed like it could have naturally been a part of his industrial look. A little black rain cloud hovering over his head would have perfectly matched his black boots and jeans that had been worn to death, and a blue T-shirt so drenched it looked black too.

"*Pfft*. Please, it's New Orleans," I said, throwing him a clean hand towel. I stretched out my fingers against my palms. Whatever I'd felt when he'd walked in was gone now. Still I remained cautious.

"Thanks." He wiped off his face and ran the hand towel through his black curls, which also might have been dyed with a tint of blue.

"What can I get you?"

"Uh." He looked at my tea, and then his eyes looked past me in a way that I'd grown familiar with. He didn't have any money. "I'm okay. I was hoping the bookstore next door was open. I heard the owner is a dealer of antiquities and has an amazing collection of rare books."

"He does. And he'll talk your ear off if you let him."

"I'd be okay with that."

I laughed. "Yeah, me too. So you're in the market for rare books?"

"Um . . . well, I also heard that sometimes he gives away old paperbacks when he runs out of space. The library doesn't look like it's reopening anytime soon."

"Mr. Mauer hasn't been around too much these days. His house was wiped."

"That's too bad. Then I guess I won't be getting my fix of old-book smell anytime soon."

I sighed, grabbing a mug. "Arcadian has a really good old-book smell too."

His gaze wandered to my stack on the counter.

As I turned to pump coffee into the mug, the tingling feeling blinked back. It was faint, but it was there—I was sure of it. I looked over my shoulder, wishing I hadn't left Adeline's and Susannah's books out in the open. I so rarely had customers these days, I'd become lax.

"Are you into family feuds?" I asked.

"Excuse me?"

"You know, vendettas to the death, lovers to long-lost siblings, tumbling monarchies, self-fulfilling prophecies. That sort of thing."

He leaned on the counter, an intense look of intrigue on his face. "Who *are* you?" he asked.

I set the coffee down. "Considering you're the one who walked into my café, I think the question is, who are *you*?"

"I asked first."

I pulled two thin paperbacks from the stack, tossed him the copies of *Macbeth* and *Oedipus Rex*, and mentally crossed my arms. "A girl writing an essay comparing and contrasting family values."

"Ah." He picked up *Oedipus*. "Well, that one didn't end well for anyone."

"Understatement of the year. Feel free to read it with your coffee." I slid the mug to him. "On the house."

"That's very kind of you."

I passed him the sugar. "Welcome to the South," I said, because there was something about him that made it clear he wasn't from around here. I didn't need magic to know it, just my years of growing up in the Quarter tourist filter.

"Callis," he said, holding out his hand.

When our palms touched, the feeling came back tenfold. "Adele," I said, and he peered at me with the same intrigue-slash-caution I was feeling.

We released our hands, and once again the feeling blinked out. He traded *Oedipus* for *Macbeth* and took the corner table in the window where Isaac always sat. I shamelessly watched him as he took a sip of the coffee and turned to the first page.

A storm gust rushed into the café's open door, and a wave of shivers jaunted up my arms. The perpetual humidity made the chill in New Orleans's winters organ rattling, but shutting the doors would drop the number of customers from a few to zilch. *Screw it. It's too cold today.* Before I could get off the stool, the door swung closed. *Shit.*

The guy looked up to the door and then back to me.

"Cross breeze," I said. "Happens all the time."

He looked to a back door that led to the courtyard. It was closed.

I shrugged, trying to play it off. "Or a poltergeist. It's an old building."

The corner of his mouth turned up. "Let's just hope it's a friendly ghost."

"Yeah," I said, struggling to make my laugh sound natural.

He went back to the book. *Crisis averted.*

I tucked Adeline's and Susannah's books under the counter for safekeeping and pulled out a large woolly sweater. It was the color of

Christmas trees and hung down to my thighs, completely covering my pale pink babydoll dress when I slipped it on.

Unlike the pervasive undercurrent of danger I always felt around the vampires, any weirdness I'd sensed—or thought I'd sensed—around the book-loving stranger had evaporated. He remained so quiet in the corner reading Shakespeare that it was easy to forget he was there. He didn't seem particularly interested in me—no stolen glances or inquiries about my past. In fact, he faced the rainy window.

After a while, I refilled his coffee and came back to my stool.

I wrapped my hands into the cuffs of the sweater and buried my face into the cable-knit. I wasn't sure there was anything that could rid the wool of the lingering Shalimar, which Mémé had drenched herself in every morning, noon, and night. I used to find the scent too pungent, but now it reminded me of her wrinkly hands and her warm kitchen and her Édith Piaf records.

I hugged myself tighter into the sweater and could feel the tears coming as I stared at the back corner, where their slain bodies had grown cold, waiting to be discovered. I hoped they'd been unconscious before they died. I hoped one of them hadn't been forced to watch the other die first, which seemed so much worse than death itself.

Was Emilio that cruel?

A spark squeezed from my fist.

I sucked in a big breath, floated my phone over to the speaker, and soon Ziggy Stardust was dancing through the air like waves of glittering cupcakes.

CHAPTER 10

An Offer Refused

Near the end of the album, the café door opened. I blinked away the tears—not even the Spiders from Mars were enough to pull me through this one.

"Hello, Miss Addie!"

I turned toward the entrance. Chatham Daure, a regular and a family friend, was shaking an umbrella in the doorway. I hadn't seen him since the funeral.

"Hey, Mr. Daure!" *Is that a cat on his shoulder?*

"Cold enough for ya?" he asked.

"Organ rattling." I rubbed my hands together as the cat stood and stretched. Part of me wanted to think this was weird, but the rest of me knew this was just the Daures.

"Don't worry," he said, "when Monday rolls around, we'll be back to T-shirts."

Chatham Daure made weather predictions with unwavering certainty, in just the same way everyone in his family spoke about the future: like they were reading from invisible scrolls that hung down from the heavens. Just like his mother, and his mother's mother had been, Chatham was the owner of the Bottom of the Cup Tearoom, the oldest-running psychic shop in the country. It was just across the way on Royal Street, right next to Touchdown Jesus, where the Wolfman's body had been dumped.

Other than two tiny gold hoops in his left ear, Chatham always looked straitlaced in his thin wire-rimmed glasses and collection of pastel polo shirts. I guess they can't all be as kooky as Ritha Borges—although today at least he had complemented his preppy attire with the cat.

The guy in the corner, who was still reading *Macbeth*, looked up.

Chatham set his crescent-handled moon mug on the counter for me. "Glad to know your pa's raising you right." He nodded up to the speaker.

"Oh yeah, Mac has a total man crush on Bowie."

"I know many people in the Quarter who'd be jealous of Bowie, then."

"Gross." I slid over the navy-blue moon mug. The inside was covered in stars, and the words WORLD FAMOUS BOTTOM OF THE CUP TEAROOM whirled. The mugs were kind of cheesy—the kind of merch the shop made specifically to sell to tourists—but I liked them. I liked that they were still the same as they'd always been. There was a phase of my childhood when I drank out of nothing but "the moon."

Chatham's sons—Caleb, Cameron, and Codi—spanned the years in between me and the twins. We'd all grown up together, French Quarter Rats, and thick as thieves. I was the youngest, and at ten became the last kid standing when Codi transferred to a private school for junior high. The twins, of course, were already at Tulane by then. Now all the Daure boys were at colleges spread across the South, and I only talked to them on holidays when they came in for café au lait and croissants. Or funerals, apparently.

I tried to smile as I grabbed the crescent handle, but Chatham touched my hand, making me pause. "We miss them too, baby . . ."

I nodded and quickly turned to fill his coffee.

Pumping the medium roast, I glanced back. His expression was grim as he slowly walked around the room. The cat jumped down, as if to investigate with him.

"It's cold in here," Chatham muttered, maybe to me, maybe to himself. Maybe to the cat. "I don't know if that will be going away come Monday." He shook his head. "No. Definitely not."

"Well, this should warm you up." I slid out the sugar and nondairy creamer.

The cat came around the counter to meet me, threading between my legs and rubbing its head firmly against my ankles.

"And who are you?" I scooped him up to the counter, which broke, like, ten health-code violations, but none of that seemed to matter post-Storm. "You're beautiful."

He purred a barely audible purr and rubbed his head against my hand.

Chatham shook his head, smiling. "Meet Onyx, the newest addition to the Daure household. He popped up just post-Storm, but he's the kind of creature that makes himself so quickly at home, you feel like he's been around forever."

"So soft." I stroked its back all the way up to its tail.

Chatham picked up the canister of sugar and poured a long stream into his moon. "How are you doing, Adele?"

"I'm fine . . . I mean, all things considered."

"Your aura begs to differ."

I laughed.

"It's not good for your soul, Addie. All of this sadness."

"My soul can handle it. It's just hard being *here*." I braced myself for a Hallmark line about eternal peace. But he didn't go there.

"At least they're together," he said. "Not even death could take Bertrand and Sabine from each other."

For a heart's flicker, I felt a little lighter.

"Adele, I don't want to overstep here, but I have an idea. One that I think would be good for both you *and* your soul."

"Like chicken soup?"

"I'm serious. All I can afford is minimum wage, but I think you'll find spending time at Bottom of the Cup to be . . . beneficial in other ways. It will do you good to get some space from this place—from Bertrand and Sabine."

"You talk about them like they're still here."

"For you, they are."

"You must be the only shop in town actually hiring right now."

"It's a precarious position to be in, no doubt, always booming in times of calamity: hurricanes, terrorist attacks, Y2K, years of the rapture. Times that leave people looking for answers for the monstrous and unexplainable." Onyx jumped onto Chatham's shoulder, settling around his neck like a stole.

"What do you think, Adele?" He looked around the nearly empty café. "I'm sure they could spare you. At least until the city is back up and running."

"Oh no, I couldn't."

"Okay, ten dollars per hour! Mac's taught you well."

I shook my head.

"Come on, you're already well versed in tea."

"I'm not leaving," I nearly shouted, unable to stop myself from getting overly defensive. The guy looked over to us from the corner, and I felt my cheeks flush.

Chatham took my hand. "I didn't mean to upset you. I understand, sweetheart."

"I'm—I'm not upset. I'm sorry. I just can't leave."

Luckily the conversation halted when Ren walked through the door: "Just the man I wanted to see!" he boomed, four poncho-clad people in tow. Pre-Storm the number would have been closer to thirty, but now the eight people in the café felt like a party.

Happy for the interruption, I started pulling mugs down. There was no way I could abandon this place. It just felt *wrong*. We'd only just buried Mémé and Pépé, for God's sake. The spoon on my saucer flung itself to the floor on the other side of the counter.

Breathe, Adele.

Chatham bent down to get it, looking at me as he set it back on the counter.

"This gentleman," Ren said to his tour group, "is the proprietor of the world-famous Bottom of the Cup Tearoom, famous not only for its tarot cards and palm readings, but for being one of the most haunted digs in the world. Grab a cup of chicory from this fine young lady, and then hurry back to the front of the café to hear the story of the strongest specter in the Vieux Carré."

Whispers buzzed through the group as they dispersed—Ren had that effect on people.

He slapped Chatham on the shoulder. I slid him a mug of coffee, and like clockwork, he reached for the flask in his brocade jacket, but before he could spin off the lid, I reached over and grabbed it from him. "I don't think so!"

They both looked over to me.

"Excuse me, young lady, since when do you care how I take my coffee?"

"Since you gave Isaac a black eye." My voice rose louder than I intended, causing everyone to look our way, including the booklover.

"Oh," he mumbled. "Would you really call it a black eye?"

My arms crossed.

"She's right," Chatham said, extending his palm for the flask. "You need to lay off the bottle." I handed it to him.

"I really don't think *this* is the best time to turn over a new leaf. How ever will I cope with my FEMA caseworker, my insurance agent, the seven people crashing on our living room floor, or the people running this damn town?"

They continued the conversation as I handed mugs of coffee to the others.

"Have you been doing the meditation routine I taught you?" Chatham asked.

"*Pfft.*" Ren twisted his mustache.

"Well, you should. Your chakras are all aflutter."

"Regarding my chakras . . . I have a few questions for the cards."

"You know where to find me," Chatham said as I passed the sugar to the tourists.

"*Oui. Oui.* All right, folks." Ren called the group to the front, and they settled at the window table at the opposite corner of the booklover.

Ren always told Julie's story in the café rather than the tearoom, because Chatham thought that letting the tourist groups into the shop en masse messed up the energy. I think it was his polite way of telling Ren he was too loud. I'd heard the story a million times, but I poured myself a cup of coffee, refilled Chatham's, and we both settled in to listen.

"Now, if you've found yourself a nonbeliever thus far," Ren said, "Chatham Daure here can corroborate this next one, him being one of the leading specter experts in the world."

"I don't know about all that," Chatham said, laughing, "but you do learn a thing or two growing up on Royal Street."

"And that's where we'll start. *Rue Royal.*" Ren pointed out the window to the cross street. "Home to more ghosts than any other street in New Orleans. I've already told you about Perrin, the photographer, and of poor Alessandro's balcony dive, but the best is to come.

"First let me bring you back to antebellum New Orleans: We were America's third-largest city, a booming cosmopolis with a newly minted railroad and shipping canal that brought both rivermen from the North and Latinos from the South. This was post–Haitian Revolution and pre–Civil War. With so much frontier still to be explored, the hope of prosperity bloomed bigger blossoms than the magnolia trees. We were American on paper, Catholic on Sundays, French Creole by cultural *société*, and everything in between by blood. And while French culture might have been more progressive than most of Americana, it was still a time where race, class, and your daddy's last name ruled. Interracial marriage wasn't an option, legally speaking, which made for an unusual period in New Orleans, because people were already so . . . blended. And so, a life of *plaçage* was totally normal in La Nouvelle-Orléans.

"In Creole New Orleans, there was an entire hierarchy based on the amount of black versus white in your family tree. Julie Metoyer was an octoroon, meaning she was one-eighth black and seven-eighths white, so the hue of her skin was probably not too different than Miss Adele's over there. Also, like Miss Adele, she was one of the most beautiful girls in the French Quarter."

I looked at Chatham and rolled my eyes, which made him laugh. Onyx jumped onto the counter and rested next to me.

"Julie was sophisticated and educated, and eventually she caught the eye of Jean-Paul Vacherie, son of one of the wealthiest planters in all of Louisiana. His wealth, surname, handsome looks, and European education made him one of the most eligible bachelors with society's daughters of La Nouvelle-Orléans. But none of that mattered to Jean-Paul after the very first time he saw Julie walking under a parasol in the Vieux Carré. He wasted no time making arrangements with her mother to formally meet Julie at one of the quadroon balls.

"And so they met and danced and flirted and danced some more. And it's said that Jean-Paul and Julie never spent a night apart. Because of her lineage, Jean-Paul courted Julie like any heart-strummed Frenchman would: as the law and society would dictate. Instead of asking her mother for Julie's hand in marriage, he negotiated contracts covering everything from the Royal Street town house he'd provide, to the support for any children she should bear, and what they would be willed upon the unfortunate event of his death. And with that, Julie formally entered into a life of *plaçage*.

"For a while this sufficed, for anything can seem perfect in lovers' paradise."

I scanned the room as Ren took a sip of coffee. I could tell that the booklover was listening to the story with bemusement, even though he was staring down at *Macbeth*.

"Jean-Paul was ruled by his heart, but his father only tolerated his philanderous arrangement for the length of carnival season. When Lent began, Jean-Paul was expected back upriver at the family plantation. Over the next two years, he gave up Julie for weeks at a time, sneaking down for weekends here and there. It was only during carnival season that he was able to stay, and they were able to truly live like man and wife. So Julie's role at their Royal Street home remained full-time, and Jean-Paul's part-time; after all, he was still expected to marry. A *white* woman."

One of the tourists snickered. "The French have always loved to have their cake and eat it too . . ."

"And here in New Orleans, they could," Ren said. "Jean-Paul was truly, madly in love with Julie, and she with him, but marrying her was out of the question. They'd be banned from society and run out of town, forgoing his wealth and reputation or possibly worse. But Julie didn't care about any of that; she only cared about Jean-Paul, and she held on to the dream that one day they'd run away to a foreign land where no one knew who she was and would not give a second look to her pale skin and straight hair, and they could marry in peace.

"Two years later, Julie still held on to that dream, but she'd grown weary of being just Jean-Paul's *placée*. Even though she was the third generation of freed people in her family, she'd never felt so trapped. She was chained by the inequalities of society, and deeply saddened that the family business was more important to her lover than she was.

"One February night during a particularly cold carnival season, Jean-Paul was entertaining some bachelor friends in the parlor, which is now the Bottom of the Cup storefront. The men were smoking pipes and drinking bourbon and playing cards. Around midnight, as per usual, Jean-Paul went to the third floor to check on his love. Instead of sleeping, she was laid across their bed, weeping. She pleaded the same case she always did: 'If you love me, Jean-Paul, you'll marry me, *mon amour!*'

"Jean-Paul was already quite tipsy and didn't want to fight, so he asked her in a fashion that he took to be jest, 'How much do you love me?'

"Her tears stopped long enough to listen to his proposal.

"'Do you love me more than you hate the cold?' he teased, kissing her. 'Strip off all of your clothes and spend the night on the roof. Then I will marry you tomorrow!'

"Julie dried her tears, and he kissed her some more, and then went back downstairs to his card game. His friends were the kind who didn't know when enough was enough, and so they stayed until the last drop of bourbon was gone, and then the brandy too—by the end of the night, Jean-Paul could hardly see his cards, they were so blurry. After he finally ushered everyone out, he didn't even make it past the couch.

"The next morning, he stumbled up the stairs, longing for the comfort of his bed and his beloved in his arms. Halfway up, he noticed a chill in the air but didn't become alarmed until he arrived in their room and Julie was nowhere to be seen. The last embers had burned out in the fireplace, the bed was still made from the day before, and the window was open, letting in the February air.

"Julie's dress fluttered toward him from the open shutter like a lacy ghost. 'No!' he cried. *Julie, ma vie!*

"He sprang out the window and up onto the roof, yelling her name, but the poor girl didn't answer, nor would she ever again call out to her lover. Never in a million years did Jean-Paul think she would do such a silly thing, but never did a *plaçee* love a Creole boy like Julie loved Jean-Paul.

"He found her body, naked just like he had asked, but now her skin was a hue of dusty blue, and a light frost clung to her hair. Jean-Paul had killed his love. Well, Mother Nature had, but he blamed himself and none other.

"In a bizarre twist of fate, less than six months later, his body was found in the bed he'd shared with Julie. The coroner said Jean-Paul died of natural causes, but at such a young age of twenty-six, it remained a mystery to his family, although not to the residents of the French Quarter. Those who knew him best said that Jean-Paul died of a broken heart."

Ren paused as his audience let out loud huffs and sighs and rounds of *"Poor Julie!"* Then they all clapped. Chatham and I joined in, as did the guy in the corner, whose leather cuffs and silver-ringed fingers made him look like he could easily fit into Ren's crowd.

"Merci, merci beaucoup," Ren said, bowing at the waist.

For another few minutes he answered questions, and they all commented on the horrors of antebellum society. I refilled their mugs while Chatham answered questions about his family home. One of the women in the group had asked him how to contact a ghost, and he crossed his arms, indicating that he was about to give her a carefully considered answer. I was sure he'd been asked the question a thousand times in his life.

"Making contact with the unseen can be complicated. People often assume that ghosts in specter form want interaction with the living, simply because they are still hanging around in the natural world, but I can tell you this is almost never the case. Unless you have a very good reason for making contact, I would advise that you *don't*. If a ghost has a message for you, they will find a way to deliver it . . . if you are open to the signs."

"What if the ghost has already crossed over?"

Something in Chatham's demeanor changed. His smile got bigger, but his arms crossed tighter. "Breaking through to the other side is an activity reserved for the *truly* gifted. Ghosts of the natural world are nearly impossible to catch, but once they've crossed over, well then it's a task that should absolutely be left to the professionals. Or your priest." He winked.

She smiled and thanked him.

"Now that we've caffeinated," Ren said, "it's time to go across the street to the Bourbon Orleans Hotel, where the steps of little ghost children are said to patter the hallway."

Chills bumped up my arms—no matter how many times I heard it, there was still something freaky about ghost children.

Ren ushered the group out, turning back to wave to me and yell to Chatham, "See you soon! Start shuffling the cards!"

Chatham nodded. "Well, Miss Addie, send my love to your pa, and please do keep my offer in mind. The door at Bottom of the Cup is always open for the young and gifted Adele Le Moyne."

"Thanks, Mr. Daure."

I nodded, and he walked out the door, moon in hand, cat on neck, umbrella overhead.

The booklover jumped up. "Thank you so much for the coffee, miss. And the fiction."

"Anytime . . ." My voice faded as he ran out the door.

"Excuse me, sir!" he yelled to Chatham, who stopped, and held the umbrella over the guy as they spoke.

I walked over to the table to retrieve the book and the mug, and through the window I watched them walk off together toward the tearoom.

Maybe he's a psychic? I laughed and went back to my spot.

I took a sip of my café au faux lait—I was actually getting used to the taste of the powdered milk; Mémé and Pépé would be appalled. I pulled out Susannah's sketchbook and opened it up.

It wasn't like I hadn't seen Isaac's grimoire a few times before, but there was something more intimate about it now, as I was flipping through the pages alone, listening to the rain pounding onto the street outside. The first part of the book was filled with more words than draw-ings, and the handwritten, antiquated English was almost as difficult to read as the Old French in Adeline's. Accompanying the long paragraphs were a multitude of diagrams, charts, and mathematical equations.

In the next part of the book, the handwriting changed and her draw-ings and watercolors of Bermudian beaches began. Clearly magic wasn't the only talent Isaac had inherited from his father's side. As I turned the page to the next sunset-drenched spell, Sébastien came through the back door, with a twenty-pound bag of coffee beans slung over his shoulder.

"Good Lord, has someone answered my prayers about not wanting to be alone in here today?" I said.

He dropped the beans on the counter. "What do you mean? You've been working here by yourself since you were twelve."

"Oh, I just meant . . . it's been different since—never mind."

"Adele, how many times do I have to tell you not to stay here out of obligation."

"I'm not staying out of obligation. It's my job."

"You're not being paid."

"Business will come back eventually."

"But—"

"This is not up for discussion, Sébastien. Jesus, are you and Chatham Daure conspiring to get me out of here?"

"Hé!" He grabbed my hand. "You know that we want you here forever. I just want you to remember, it's always your choice."

"I choose to stay," I mumbled in French.

"Super, mon petit chou. Un café s'il te plaît."

I smiled and made him a coffee as he asked me about my last precal test, which he'd helped me study for.

"B-plus, thanks to you!"

His nose scrunched. *"B?"* But before he could make me feel like an underachiever, his expression changed. "Oh!" He pulled a newspaper out of the messenger bag slung over his back. "I brought this for you in case you want another copy."

For the last few weeks, the *Times-Pic* had been printing a few sheets every couple days, but this was a thick newspaper. As he unfolded it on the counter and smoothed it out, I realized it was yesterday's *New York Times*.

"Why would I already have a copy of the *New York Times*?"

"Because your boyfriend's on the front page?"

My forehead crinkled as I bent over the paper. The feature article was about the Storm—lambasting the Army Corp of Engineers, citing new evidence that proved they had known for years about how weak the levees were. Just from skimming, I could tell it attacked everyone at all levels of government, including both Isaac's and Désirée's fathers.

Sébastien's finger tapped the photo, pulling my attention from the article.

"Holy . . ." The expletive tapered off as I looked closer at the picture.

It wasn't an aerial shot, but it'd been taken at a high angle—the perfect vantage to capture the giant tunnel of water rushing down St. Claude. A little girl was being held above the wave by the taut arms of a boy breaking the surface, mouth open in a giant O, gasping for air. A boy who, even with water pouring down his face, was very distinctly Isaac.

The caption underneath said: "Unknown hero nearly drowns saving NOLA girl amid levee breach."

"Did he ever tell you about it?" Sébastien asked.

"No . . . I mean, he's talked about being a first responder, but nothing like this."

I was stunned. It was the kind of photo that made you burst into tears—not because of the devastation it depicted, but because of the humanity. It was the kind of photo that stopped your heart. The kind that would be taught in university art classes and would make lesser photographers give up their craft.

"The photographer won a Pulitzer," Sébastien said. "For breaking-news reporting."

"Whoa."

"I think your new boyfriend deserves free coffee for life."

"I think you're right . . . but he's not my boyfriend." It seemed like a really big word to just throw around without it being official.

"Adele, I'm no subject matter expert, but he's here every day, and when he's not, the two of you are always texting. And . . . I saw you kissing last week."

My cheeks flushed.

"I'm pretty sure 'boyfriend' is exactly what he is. Boyfriend and hero, according to the *Times*." He kissed my cheeks good-bye. *"Au revoir."*

"Au revoir . . ." I looked back at the paper, mesmerized by the photo. "Hero, definitely," I mumbled to myself. I pulled out my phone, wanting to ask him about it, but what text message could possibly be appropriate for the questions this photo made me want to ask?

I stared at him and the little girl and thought about us rescuing my mom—even if he was currently at target practice. I picked up my phone and punched out a message.

Adele	4:03 p.m.	What do u say to a second training session tonight?
Isaac	4:03 p.m.	Are you coming on to me, Adele Le Moyne?
Adele	4:03 p.m.	That depends. But I was thinking more of the magical variety.
Isaac	4:04 p.m.	Oh, it will be magical.

I smiled, shaking my head, glad now that the café was empty.

Adele	4:04 p.m.	I'll tell Dee.

I paused, waiting for the inevitable three-way joke, but he didn't go there.

Isaac	4:05 p.m.	I knew u were up to something. See u tonight. <3

CHAPTER 11
Voodoo Soup

Raindrops plopped onto the umbrella overhead, but the downpour had reduced to a calming shower, so I took my time walking to Vodou Pourvoyeur. I tilted the umbrella back slightly as the teacup-shaped storefront sign at Bottom of the Cup came into view. From afar, the bay window beneath it appeared dingy, but if you got close, you could see the glass was just dark like smoky quartz, helping conceal the pasts, presents, and futures of the Daures' clientele.

When I reached the window, I paused and pressed my nose to the glass despite already knowing what the shop looked like inside: we'd played there a lot as kids, and not much had changed since then, maybe not even since the 1920s when the tearoom first opened.

There was a box on the marble mantel that I loved. It had a glass window and a red-tufted cushion, upon which sat a crown. Not the fancy tiara kind with a million jewels like the Mardi Gras queens wore, but more like a wreath of metal garland. Mrs. Philomena, the Daure matriarch, had once told me that it was her great-grandmother's wedding crown. I thought that meant surely her great-grandmother had been a princess back home in Germany.

I moved on down the street, hurrying under the gray clouds, thinking about the day the box had been seared into my memory. I'd been seven at the time. We were playing hide-and-seek, only "it" was a crystal ball and we gave each other cryptic clues until it was found, kind of like I Spy. When it was my turn to be the hider, I dragged a chair to the mantel, careful not to make a sound, and even more carefully placed the crystal ball in the center of the crown on the little tufted pillow. Knowing the ball could be seen through the glass window made me think I was so clever, hiding it in plain sight. I called the others back into the room and gave them the first clue: "The crystal ball sleeps on a pillow."

I could still remember the suspense as Caleb, Cameron, and Codi ran to the bay window and turned over all the cushions . . . How I threaded the hem of my dress through my fingers, anxiously waiting for one of them to step near the fireplace and see it.

As their grubby hands pillaged the room, turning over each and every thing—and in a psychic shop nearly a hundred years old, that was a lot of things—I never once looked at the box, having previously learned it was the quickest way to give away your hiding spot. Instead I focused on an antique gilded birdcage that hung from a stand in the corner by the clerk's counter.

And that's why I couldn't tell you how, in the middle of the game, the box tipped on its side, and the crystal ball fell to the brick floor with a loud clank and rolled directly to the shoes of Madame Morgana, who was standing in the hall doorway unannounced.

Madame Morgana, whose real name was Debra Swanson, was the scariest of all the psychics and infamous all around town. A medium whose reputation for communicating with the dead, along with her wardrobe, preceded her. She always looked like she'd stepped straight out of a closet from 1984—layers of iridescent chiffon and taffeta, one on top of the other, that matched the sparkles in her blue and purple eyeshadows. Her bottom was big and round and barely fit on the chair, and her ego hardly fit in the little booth where she read cards for tourists. She equally compared herself to Cyndi Lauper and Nostradamus and rarely spoke about anything but herself, unless she was complaining.

She complained about her back, or headaches, or being cold—even under all those layers of synthetic fabric. She hated noise, and for this reason she hated children. So when Madame Morgana picked up the crystal ball, panic set into my chest. She'd already warned us not to disturb her trance that day, "or else."

I saw the chip before she did—I scanned the floor, heart racing, and there it was: a chunk of the crystal ball, lying on the brick.

She didn't yell like I thought she would; instead, she walked straight to me with three long steps and slapped my cheek, eliciting yells from all the Daure kids.

She dropped the crystal ball into my palm. "You'll have twelve years' bad luck, you little fool!"

To my seven-year-old self, there'd never been a face so scary—and I'd grown up a couple blocks off Bourbon.

Caleb and Cam took off running down the hall, shouting for their grandmother, but Codi marched up to her and yelled, "No, she won't, you old hag!" He slammed his foot down on hers.

As she grabbed his shoulder, I stood there in shock, the broken crystal ball weighing down my hand, guiltily wondering how I could possibly have worse luck than I already had. My mother had already left us, and then horror struck me: Would my father leave me now too? I began to cry.

"How dare you strike a child in *my* house!" Mrs. Philomena shouted, hurrying into the room. "*Get out.* You are no longer welcome here. *Get out. Get out!*"

Mrs. Philly held her hand out toward the front door, which— I swear—through my tears I saw open by itself, and then Madame Morgana stumbled forward, protesting all the way to the curb.

The door slammed shut, and Mrs. Philomena walked to the window and flipped around the sign that said **Psychic Wanted**.

She turned around all smiles. "How about some cookies?" she asked, rubbing my back as I brushed away the tears, embarrassed to cry in front of the boys.

The Daure kids stood with arms crossed and smug smiles. Mrs. Philly hugged me and told me not to worry, and to keep the crystal ball because I'd marked it and that made it even more special. She made us Blue Eyes tea, which was my favorite because it brewed pink, and she opened a tin of vanilla butter ring cookies.

As everyone slurped their tea and munched shortbread from around their fingers, I kept wondering how the box had tipped in the first place. I knew I'd placed it securely on the mantel. Mrs. Philly never questioned me about it, and on the scale of trouble the Daure kids got into, the incident was quickly forgotten.

Now, thinking back on it, I knew.

It *was* my fault the little box tipped.

I hustled the last block, the rain plopping harder on the umbrella.

There were more cars parked on Désirée's block than usual—and by "usual" I meant post-Storm usual. Pre-Storm the street would have been bumper to bumper, with others slowly circling, waiting for someone to leave.

The sign hanging above the stoop was a simple wood carving: a curvy line wriggled underneath the words *Vodou Pourvoyeur* like a snake. If it wasn't for the sign, you'd probably walk past the shop altogether—a former shotgun house. Its long shutters were closed, and there were no other indicators it was a place of business, like posted store hours or decals showing they took Visa and MasterCard. I guess the people who were meant to be here knew to look for it. A pile of fried chicken bones was strewn on the sidewalk. I didn't know why, but I knew enough about the Borges to know that nothing here was random.

I shook out my umbrella, silenced my phone, and gently shut the door behind me, always feeling like I might be disrupting something important when I entered the shop. The atmosphere felt very particular, as if great care had gone into crafting it.

A lampshade made of strands of lavender and violet beads that glowed like amethyst droplets cast the front part of the room in a pool of lilac. Even though the store wasn't designed to be a tourist trap, the front rooms were full of things that might tickle their fancy: colorful candles guaranteed to bring you luck or love, gris-gris bags for protection, drums made of animal hides, bundles of sage and lavender, crystal skulls made up of thousands of tiny glass beads that glowed amber. Sometimes I wondered if all the tourist stuff was just a front, like a mafia-owned laundromat, except instead of crime it hid otherworldly happenings.

In the back corner, a tall lamp with a shade of woven bamboo shone a warm spotlight onto the altar devoted to a Loa named Erzulie. Désirée said Loa were kind of like spirits in Voodoo—the invisible ones, intermediaries between people and the supreme Bon Dieu. Small altars were constructed throughout the house, each one with different artworks and offerings for the chosen Loa. But then in the very back, behind a magenta velvet curtain, was the Borges ancestral altar, which was my favorite, because it was like a miniature museum dedicated to the witches in Désirée's family line. On one side of it hung the painting of the original Casquette Girls Coven, and on the other was a portrait of Marassa Makandal, the original Voodoo queen of New Orleans— Adeline Saint-Germain's most trusted confidant.

The curiosities became curiouser as I walked through each room— snakeskins, racks of necklaces ranging from leather fringe to fish bone to iridescent abalone. It was still difficult not to stop and look around, because every time I walked through the room I saw something new, like the two baskets on the floor with handmade signs, one that said *Chicken Feet* and the other *Bat Wings*. They were bookended with baskets of incense sticks and lime-green candles.

Yep. Totally normal.

A cat stepped out from behind an enormous tribal mask that rested against a drum. It looked up at me with keen interest. I stared back into its slate-gray eyes, and then it turned away disinterested. *Definitely related to Dee.*

I stepped into the room of Voodoo dolls, which had just as much diversity as the French Quarter residents themselves, and felt both joyfully artistic because of their wave of color and creepily serious by nature of their purpose. A waist-high doll made of crude burlap and straw with threaded *X*s for eyes seemed to stare at me as I walked past. My eyes fell to a group of pocket-size dolls wearing metallic pink sequins and rainbow-colored glitter, and it wasn't long before it felt like they were looking up at me too. I hurried along.

In the back room, the fireplace was ablaze, its reflection flickering on the glass jars of herbs, spices, oils, and salts that covered all four walls. Désirée was behind the wooden counter.

"Hey," she said, looking up for only a second.

"Hey, what are you . . ." My voice fizzled as she moved from behind the counter, motioning for me to follow her to the wall of shelves on my left.

She climbed up the rolling ladder and began handing me jars. Désirée wasn't exactly a chatterbox, but this was low energy even for her; her silence beckoned silence, so I didn't say anything, just continued to pass the jars back to the counter. In the void, noises filtered down from upstairs. Feet shuffling. Voices murmuring.

Hearing the movement and energy upstairs made me *feel* the quiet down here. It was the kind of quiet always followed by trouble.

Something was up.

The vibe was kind of like walking into the courtyard of the "not-in-operation" Le Chat Noir. Everything looked dark and shut down, but if you paused, you could feel the beats of music pulsing through the walls. Those beats told you that you weren't important enough to know what was going on, much less gain entry. Right now, the party was going on upstairs, and I was pretty sure Désirée wasn't invited.

"What's that all about?" I asked, tilting my head toward the ceiling.

Désirée climbed down from the ladder and went back behind the counter. "My gran's Saturday-night circle." Her tone was near bitter. She uncorked three of the bottles, and each let out a different color plume of dust: one white, one gold, and one baby blue. "They don't usually *all* meet here this time of year, which means something is going on."

"What kind of something?"

"Something of the magical variety, presumably. Gran kicked me out of the room in front of everyone."

"Ouch."

"She said I 'lost all privileges' when I joined a 'mixed-magic coven.'" Désirée flicked the lid of a jar so quickly it flew off, clanking to the floor. "But we're about to find out what they're up to."

I whipped the lid up into my palm. "Oh Lord." A sinking feeling told me that this was a *bad* idea. "Are you sure you've thought this through?"

She pulled a cauldron out from under the counter and set up her little portable spell-cooking station between us. "Fire," she said, and opened Marassa Makandal's large leather-bound grimoire.

When I didn't immediately comply, she looked directly at me. "Be useful, or go away."

"Okay, jeez." I flicked my gaze to the cauldron, igniting a flame underneath it, and then tried to bring the convo back to the coven search. "So, Dee, have you made any progress with the descendants?"

"Shhhh," she hissed, and pushed a pile of assorted dried herbs my way.

I grabbed a mortar and pestle made of dark granite. She took them back and replaced it with a set made of jade.

"Green is for edibles. The black one, nonedibles."

"Nonedibles?"

"Stones, brick, metals . . . or plant and animal material that's poisonous."

"Right." I laughed as I ground the herbs, thinking about the difference between the Le Moyne and the Borges household safety measures.

When the herbs started to resemble a powder, she took the mortar. "Grab a fistful of dried indigo," she said, adding the herbal powder pinch by pinch to the cauldron.

I turned to the wall and scanned over the labels. If they were in any kind of order, it eluded me.

"On the floor. Third basket from the door," she added in a way that indicated haste.

The basket contained long stalks with tiny shriveled flowers ranging from purple to black. When I returned to the counter, she was covering the sides of the cauldron with long banana-plant leaves.

"Break off the flower heads and throw them in. They're just for color—to help us direct the magic." She stirred the pot, while removing a black feather bookmark from the crease of Marassa's grimoire, and turned the page. The wooden spoon continued to stir itself as she scanned the spell with both hands.

"Okay, got it," she said to herself, laying her palms out to me on either side of the cauldron, which meant whatever she was about to do was complex and she wanted the power of two.

My pulse picked up, but I trusted Désirée as she read words from the antique tome about parting ways—*just enough to let sound seep through.*

Smoke billowed from the pot, purples and blues, accumulating into a beautiful little cloud that hovered at eye level. She used the banana leaves to fan the cloud straight up and then took my hands again, and we continued the chant three more times.

The cloud crawled across the ceiling, slowly and with intent, and then it stopped about four feet to my right. Désirée pushed the cauldron station over so we stayed directly underneath it.

"Come on," she said. "I know this will work."

The cloud seeped into the ceiling, creating a purple spot about the size of grapefruit, and a smile crossed Désirée's face. "It found the most porous place to penetrate."

"Penetrate what, Désirée? I know you aren't referring to just the ceiling."

She lowered her voice to a whisper. "I found a spell that lets me break down organic matter and move it at a molecular level."

I suddenly felt like I was talking to Jeanne or Sébastien.

"But it will only hold as long as the spell is active."

"Why would we want—?"

She drew a finger over her lips and looked up. The purple stain on the ceiling dissipated until it was barely noticeable—just a blurry wooden blotch.

The noises upstairs gradually became louder, seeping through the spot where the spell had thinned out the layers of ceiling and floor above us, but the words weren't comprehendible; they warbled in and out, nothing more than *wah, wah, wahs.*

"Dammit!" Désirée whispered. "I forgot about the privacy spells they always cast at the beginning of the night."

I couldn't tell if she was truly annoyed by this or enthralled to rise to the challenge. She walked to a waist-high barrel on the rear wall and grabbed a handful of the largest fava beans I'd ever seen. She dumped them in the pot along with a fistful of bay leaves and a fistful of rocks.

I bopped between total fascination and feeling like a bump on a log who couldn't offer assistance. "What are those rocks—?"

"Shhhh!"

She whispered words, waving her hand over the pot, and the smoke formed again. This time, instead of a cloud, the blues and purples and blacks twisted into each other, forming a thick smoky braid, which she pulled out of the pot like taffy and then guided it up to the ceiling until it connected with the spot, linking the ceiling to the cauldron. She whispered:

Écoute et répète. Listen and speak.

Écoute et répète. Tell us the words we seek.

And then the contents in the cauldron complied. The rocks rose to the top, joining the bay leaves and the beans, defying the laws of physics. The pot rattled and the water bubbled as everything swirled at the surface.

Dee continued to chant, and the potion ingredients began to move in different directions, fighting against the swirling water—the rocks zigged and the bay leaves zagged and the beans scattered about.

She leaned over the configuration, and a smile spread across her face. "It's working!"

As if Désirée ever thought something she was trying for the first time might not work.

She pulled me around the counter for a closer look. In rock and bean and leaf, a word was spelled out in the pot: **DISRUPTION**. By the time I'd finished reading it, a second one had appeared: **SPIRIT**.

"What. The. Hell?" I asked.

"Spycasting, level two." She looked up, and I realized the words in the pot were being spoken upstairs.

A third floated under our noses: **WORLD**.

More beans and rocks formed into letters until a coherent configuration of words appeared, stacked like Voodoo alphabet soup.

A

DISRUPTION

TO SPIRIT WORLD

"Disruption?" Désirée asked the brew. "What kind of disruption?"

I looked at her blankly and whispered, "Out of all the words floating here, 'disruption' is the one you're most curious about?"

Désirée held out her hand, indicating quiet. Her eyes slowly lifted to the ceiling, and I realized the house was now pin-droppingly silent.

Nothing stirred.

Nothing but a single creak from the ceiling at the front of the room. Then another. Someone was slowly walking across the room above us, and the creaks didn't stop until they were right over our heads—right above the magical blur in the ceiling.

We craned our necks up, and suddenly I was gargling a torrent of water.

"Gran!" Désirée screamed as we jumped away, not before getting soaked.

The water continued to pour straight through the ceiling into the cauldron, splashing away the message and breaking the smoke braid.

"Désirée Borges!" Ritha shouted from above. "How *dare* you spy-cast on a private gathering!"

The tone in her voice scared me to next Sunday, but as per usual, Désirée didn't seem fazed.

"A private gathering in my own house!" she yelled back up through the hole in the ceiling, which seemed to be growing.

Feet shuffled upstairs. Wiping water from my face, I shriveled back, not wanting to get any more tangled in this family drama than I already was.

"What is communicated in our gatherings is *private* information—information you are no longer privy to! You cast aside your family's coven, you cast aside your privileges."

"My privileges come with my blood, not my coven!"

"You're going to get nothing but trouble mixing magic with those two, child. You will learn the hard way. *Heed my words.*"

I shrank back farther, wondering if Ritha realized I was standing next to Désirée. *What trouble?*

"Not any more trouble than what comes with being my father's daughter!"

Ritha's tone flattened: "You want to act like a child, Désirée, then go outside and play like a child. And don't come back until after dawn, when our coven business is complete. Our *family* has traveled far so we can meet in full."

"Fine!" Désirée yanked a large leather satchel from under the counter and started grabbing things: herbs, salts, knives, and candles.

Was she grabbing at random or with purpose? Something told me the latter.

She stuffed a jumble of multicolored silk scarves into her satchel and followed them with some hastily selected vials of oils and a set of scales.

Pushing my wet hair aside, I looked up at the hole, sensing the energy above us firing up, making me feel like I was about to be in the middle of a spell-flinging family war.

"Désirée Nanette Borges, don't you take that book out of this house!"

I looked back at Désirée, who was sliding the enormous grimoire into the satchel.

Ritha had passed it down to Désirée, telling her it was the oldest book of magic in New Orleans. She was only partially right: it was *one* of the oldest grimoires in New Orleans. Ritha didn't know that the

Norwood family book of magic had come to town. I tightened my bag on my shoulder.

Voices bickered upstairs: "You gave her the book, Ritha. It's hers now. You can't control her."

"I told you she was too young to have something so important in her possession. Now look what she's done!"

"Another coven with the Makandal grimoire? A disgrace."

Ugh, how hard would it be to slip out of here unnoticed?

"Oh, quiet, all of you," a familiar voice snapped. Désirée's mother, Ana Marie. "The grimoire is Désirée's destiny. There's nothing you or this coven can do to stop that."

"Désirée!" Ritha yelled down again. The spot in the ceiling was changing from blurry to semitransparent, the molecules spreading so thin they were forming a hole. "You *cannot* take that book off these protected grounds."

Apparently Désirée was done talking. She glanced up at the ceiling with a look that said, *Watch me.* And then she took off for the front door, me following right behind her.

I glanced back over my shoulder in time to see Ritha Borges *jump down* through the hole in the ceiling like a spry little ninja.

"Dee!"

Footsteps stomped down the stairs. Without a hair out of place, Désirée pulled the front door, but it only opened a few inches before jerking out of her fingers and slamming shut. When I looked back, Ritha wasn't chasing us like I'd expected. She was standing among the Voodoo dolls with her arm extended out toward us—toward the door.

Désirée stood back. "Open the door, Adele."

"Um . . . your gran is—"

"Open the damn door, Adele!"

In my head, I whipped it open, but the door didn't replicate the motion. "It won't—"

"Focus," she mumbled, starting to jitter.

Her grandmother yelled again, just as her aunts reached the bottom of the stairs and charged forward.

I whipped my hands through the air, and this time the door flung open, this time the entire handle, the deadbolt, and all of the locks unbolted and flung out with it, crashing to the floor.

And then, in a blur of motion and magic, the door shut behind us, and we were on the other side: me, Désirée, and Marassa's grimoire. The door remained closed as long as I wanted the hinges to.

"Come on," Désirée said, pulling me forward.

As we crossed the Borges property line, energy buzzed through my veins—the kind that could only be produced by rule breaking. I half expected a sorceress alarm to trip and magically drag us back inside, but no such thing occurred. Outside, the streets were just like any other night.

Well, any other night in the French Quarter.

Désirée was too dignified to break into a run, so we just walked— very, very quickly.

How did I get wrapped into this?

I didn't even have that many family members to argue with, much less fling spells with. The only things my *grand-mère* was ever disappointed over were my choices of clothing *et mon accent français*. I'd never even gotten the chance to have fights with my mother, and the biggest fight my dad and I had ever gotten in was over sending me to boarding school, most of which had been over the phone and had involved a lot of crying on my part.

Other than her brow and lips being tauter than usual, this just seemed like any other day to Dee.

"So where do we go now?" I asked, my damp clothes making me shiver. "Or are we just going to wander the night with your homemade witch lab?"

"I don't know . . . Your house, I guess?"

Désirée Borges wanting to come to my house induced a mild wave of panic. I'd gone to great lengths to hide all of this from my father; brewing potions and practicing spells at home wasn't going to help conceal my magical life. I racked my brain for another spot.

We were most protected in the Quarter, and wherever we went had to be private. *Really* private. With enough room to practice without me burning it down or Isaac blowing the roof off.

I turned to her. "It's technically illegal, but I have an idea . . ."

CHAPTER 12
Location, Location, Location

A twelve-foot-high wrought-iron gate bordered the property, although if it weren't for the spiky posts sticking out from the top, you'd think it was just a wall of dead ivy. As the clouds passed away from the moon, the mammoth mansion shone with decrepit enchantment.

"I can't believe I didn't think of this," said Désirée.

The brothel was a lot more dilapidated than I remembered it, like it might fall on our heads upon entry. "Maybe this wasn't such a good idea," I said.

"No. This is good." The wall of dead leaves rippled when she spoke, as if in agreement. "Very good." And then the dead-looking tendrils shrank back, slithering through each other like snakes, revealing the gate door.

Désirée turned to me. "I didn't—"

The sound of metal sliding against metal cut her off, followed by the loud clank of the lock dropping. The wrought-iron gate creaked open just enough for us to walk through.

"Neither did I."

It was hard to feel like trespassers when the house itself seemed so eager for us to enter. We walked through the gate, pausing to look back when it clanked closed behind us. The thick brown vines slipped back into place, and it appeared once again like it hadn't been disturbed in centuries.

Flames slowly flickered to life in the gas lamps, lighting the brick footpath to the front door.

As we approached, sprinkles of supernatural energy tap-danced over my shoulders. I wondered if the sensation was a product of the old coven's protection spells, or if it was the invisibility shield we'd discovered the last time we were here—the one that had kept us hidden while Nicco fed on Theis right in front of our eyes.

"Remind me to test the limits of the invisibility spell," Désirée said, pulling the thought out of my head. "It's so badass . . ."

Way to go, Cosette. It only takes a miracle to impress Désirée Nanette Borges.

Ren had said there were only four original French buildings left in the Quarter that had survived the great fires of the eighteenth century. It could be no coincidence that three out of four of them had turned out to be places where the Casquette Girls Coven members had resided.

Moving vines, welcoming doors, and invisibility spells. *What more proof do we need that this place is also a part of our coven's history?*

This house had to be connected to Cosette Monvoisin. Ren had also said the house used to be a brothel once upon a time. According to Adeline's diary, Cosette got kicked out of the convent dormitory for indecent behavior. I hated to make assumptions, buuut she *was* able to control the hearts of men.

Excitement bubbled in my belly at the prospect of finding a clue to who Cosette's descendant was. Our next coven member.

Stairs ran up both sides of the once-lavish porch that sat on top of a raised basement, and the supernatural sensation became stronger as we climbed up. Four tall windows ran floor to ceiling on either side of the door. They'd been designed to catch a cross breeze through the mansion, the air-conditioning of the time, but now they were all boarded up and had been since long before the Storm.

A transom fanned out like a seashell over the door, which began to shake as we stood there—the magic struggling to push it open against decades of rust and filth and humidity-swollen wood.

When was it last opened?

Désirée and I glided our hands through the air, giving it a boost—her magic moving the wood and mine the metal. The door groaned open, splitting a blanket of cobwebs that covered the inside and startling a family of birds nesting in the foyer chandelier. As the sounds of their flapping wings faded into the house, my fingertips brushed the scar on the side of my face. But I wasn't scared.

I couldn't wait to call Isaac.

This was it. We were home.

A flame rose from my palm as Désirée and I lingered in the foyer. The fact that we were breaking and entering was only a distant hum in the back of my head—constantly present but easy to ignore. I was more focused on the sounds of scurrying claws. *Mice.* I shuddered.

Of course there'd be mice. *What did you expect to find in an old, abandoned mansion? Mermaids?*

The foyer forked into three different directions: straight ahead was a wide hallway that went all the way to the back door to create a cross-breeze tunnel through the house, splitting the ground level in half. The other two led to parlors.

I bobbed my hand, bouncing the flame shoulder-height, and there it hovered like a loyal pet, waiting to guide the way.

"Right or left?" Désirée asked, shining her phone at each doorway.

The flame floated to the parlor on the left.

It's just a house, I told myself as we followed. *A witch's house.*

A witch whose descendant we need to find.

123

The prospect burned out any fear, and I felt like I was walking into a gothic French dream. I gently pushed the flame around the dark room, letting it vacillate just long enough to get a good look.

The fifteen-foot-high ceiling had a grandiose medallion in the center from which hung a massive chandelier. The crystals must have once sparkled like diamonds, but now they were spun so tightly with cobwebs and bird nests that the fixture looked like a black cloud floating above the room. Layers of crown molding and millwork connected the walls to the ceiling like delicate, ornate puzzle pieces and reminded me of *ma grand-mère's* estate in Paris. I wondered how long it would take for her to get suspicious of my mother's whereabouts and show up on our porch one day. The thought terrified me. Luckily, my grandmother *loathes* America.

The floorboards creaked underfoot as we moved through the room. Dried leaves were piled in the corners, and the striped wallpaper on the lower half of the walls had been scratched by an assortment of claws.

The house had clearly been abandoned for decades, but it wasn't a time capsule from the eighteenth century either. The details in architecture might have been, and the tufted chairs and gilded, framed paintings of Parisian theatre scenes, but the tea cart Désirée was investigating had a glass shelf held by brass that curled into geometric patterns, which were distinctly art deco.

I walked to her side as she lifted a bottle from the cart and swirled it around.

"That's sure to bring a buzz that would rival the Green Faerie's," I said.

"Yeah, or kill you."

We moved on, each of us sliding one of the pocket doors that led to the next room. The flame dove ahead, but I held my hand out, calling it back. I bounced it up in the air, and it burst, fracturing off into a dozen smaller fireballs.

"You're getting pretty good at that," Désirée said.

"Merci beaucoup."

The tiny fireballs swarmed around the room, shedding light on thousands of books. Shelves and shelves of classics—science, history, philosophy. I pulled a few out and pushed them back in. None were any newer than 1940. Despite the tickle in my nose, I breathed in the overwhelming sent of leather, canvas, and parchment.

"Talk about old-book smell," I said, remembering the guy at the café this afternoon. I pulled a copy of *Henry V* from the shelf, and a cloud of dust puffed into my face. A sneeze burst out of my mouth, and the lights blinked out.

Something scurried across the dark room, and Désirée shrieked. When I reignited the flames, she was standing on the couch. I turned so she didn't see me laughing as she climbed down.

"Soooooo," I said, looking at an old map of the Vieux Carré hanging on the wall. "Are we going to talk about what happened back at the shop? What did Ritha mean when she said that you'll get nothing but trouble *mixing magic* with those two?"

She let out an enormous sigh. "The Borges are a *preserved*-magic family."

"Meaning?" I sent the light swarm into the next room. We followed side by side.

"Preserved-magic families have kept their magic lines pure throughout the centuries and never mixed in other base Elemental abilities."

The next room was an office. Faded wallpaper curled from the walls, and piles of leaves collected against the baseboards.

Dee leaned against a large wooden desk. "Witches are encouraged to master many traditions of magic, but at the end of the day, our family circle is still made up of only our inherent Elemental magic. According to my gran, there are very few of us preserved-magic families left in the world."

I walked past a typewriter and couldn't resist pressing one of the round keys to see if it still worked. The carriage released with a loud zing.

"Jesus, Adele," Désirée said, clutching her chest.

We moved on to the back corner of the house. The two exterior walls were made up of rows and rows of small panes of glass, now so murky I couldn't see through them. Brown plants sprawled across the windows and up the staircase that led to the second floor, forever frozen in place by death. I could imagine myself here in better days, curled up with a book in hand, cat in lap. The sun shining on my face, making it impossible to read more than ten pages at a time before daydreams stole me away to lands yet undiscovered.

I was officially in love with the room.

Rather than taking the staircase to the second floor, we crossed the hallway into the other side of the house.

"So everyone in your family has the Elemental magic Earth?" I asked, lighting the wall sconces with a glance around the room.

This corner room mirrored the one we'd just left, with the windows and the staircase, but it had a table and chairs and, in another lifetime, might have been a perfect breakfast nook.

"Everyone in my family with magic does, certainly everyone bound into the coven. It's so stupid—it's like magicism!"

I motioned for silence.

"What?" she asked.

"Shhh . . . !" My heart thumped. I could have sworn I heard something.

Creeeeeaaaaak.

There it was again. Directly above us.

Désirée stepped closer to my side. Another creak from above, and we craned our necks up.

"That is *not* a rat," I whispered.

With a slow exhale, the lanterns extinguished, and the flame hovering at my shoulder shriveled to a wisp of smoke. I motioned for her to hide behind the door, and I dropped to the floor and crawled underneath the table, sliding the chair in place behind me.

The creaks, now with the distinct sound of slow-moving footsteps, were coming down the staircase.

I held my breath as a figure came into view: a guy in a hoodie. It was impossible to make out much more in the dark. He paused, sniffing the air, probably catching the lingering scent of smoke.

Something went skittering across the floor with a series of squeaks, and he grabbed a vase from the mantel before realizing it was just a mouse. His shoulders relaxed, but he didn't put the vase down as he crossed the room.

I turned underneath the table, trying to feel for metal, but it was difficult to sense anything over the pounding of my pulse.

A loud creak came from the doorway where Désirée was hiding, a hinge in desperate need of oil. He shot toward the sound, raising the vase to strike, his hoodie slipping off, revealing his tiny, dirty-blond ponytail.

"No!" I yelled.

He spun toward me. "Adele, what the—?" The door cracked into the back of his skull, the vase smashed to the floor, and he stumbled forward, cursing.

I scrambled out from under the table and grabbed his wrists, knowing his knee-jerk reaction would be to turn and swing at his attacker. "Isaac, relax! It's just Dee!"

"Oops," she mumbled, coming out of the corner.

"Help me!" I said as Isaac started to lean heavily on me.

She pulled out a chair, and I toppled him onto the cushion, but the old wood collapsed beneath him and sent him to the floor.

"Jesus!" He swatted my arms away as I tried to help him up. "Get off!"

I backed away. "Sorry! I was just trying to help." My hand whipped in a circular motion, and all of the lanterns flickered to life.

"I know . . ." He pulled himself up, woozily reaching for another chair, testing its integrity before sitting. "I'm sorry," he said, clutching his head.

I pulled away his hand—it was covered in blood. "Jesus, Désirée!"

She made an apologetic face and shrugged. "He was about to hit me with that vase." She pointed to the pile of ceramic on the floor.

I pushed his hair aside to inspect his scalp.

"I'm fine. It's just a surface wound."

I leaned around his shoulder. "Because you can see the back of your head?"

"Let me see," Désirée said, nudging me aside. "Grab my bag from the counter."

"You're right," she said to him as I fetched her witch supplies. "It's a shallow cut."

"No shit. It's not the first time I've cracked my head open."

"And if there's anything certain in this world, it won't be the last."

He grunted.

She held back his hair with one hand and fished around in her bag with the other, all the while rambling on about how it was his own fault, which was her way of apologizing, because if she really didn't care, she would have moved on immediately. Finally, she produced a small glass bottle and popped the cork with her teeth. Without warning, she poured the contents onto his scalp. Isaac sprang up, his head nearly clocking her chin.

"What the witchy hell was that?" he yelled, coming to my side, as if I was going to protect him from her.

"You're such a ninny." She held out the unmarked bottle for us to see. "It's a homemade antiseptic. Don't want it to get infected, right?"

"You carry around a homemade antiseptic?" I asked.

"I don't like germs."

I laughed. "It's New Orleans."

"Exactly," she said, "it's a cesspool." And then she was laughing too.

Isaac, however, was not as amused. "Oh, this is *sooooo* funny . . ."

My giggles abruptly stopped. "Wait a second." I looked at him. "What are you even doing here?"

He rolled his neck. "I was looking for you."

"Why would you ever think to look *here*?" My tone slanted with suspicion.

He smiled. "Simple. I put a tracking app on your phone."

"You *what*?"

He was only able to hold the deadpan expression long enough for Désirée's arms to cross before he laughed. When neither of us responded, waiting for the real explanation, his laughter trailed off into an awkward throat clear. "What kind of idiot do you take me for? I used a location spell."

"Someone's been practicing their magic," Désirée said.

"What kind of location spell?" I asked.

"An incantation from Susannah's sketchbook. All you need are the magic words, and . . ." He opened his bag and pulled out the copy of *The Shining* I'd lent him. "A possession belonging to the person you're trying to find."

"One of my faves," I said of the tattered paperback, courtesy of Mr. Mauer at an age when I was far too young for King.

Désirée looked at him with something like approval. "Nice. Though now I'm wondering how effective the invisibility spell is if magic can get through it—"

"Don't worry, it didn't reveal you—even *with* my location spell."

"Then how did you find us?"

"The spell showed Adele on the map at the Voodoo shop, but as I headed there, you started moving down the street on the map—which was freakin' cool."

"You could have just called me like a normal person, you know?"

"You could have just answered your phone like a normal person, *you know?*"

I pulled my phone out of my bag: *3 missed calls: Isaac Thompson.*

Plus, three messages:

Isaac	6:17 p.m.	You off work yet??
Isaac	6:40 p.m.	Are we still training to-night?
Isaac	7:15 p.m.	I'm heading to Dee's.

"Oh, sorry. We were . . . held up."

"Excuse me," Désirée said. "Location spell. Finish."

"Right—you were moving down the street and then boom. You disappeared. Gone from the grid. At first I figured the spell crapped out; I was doing it from memory, since Adele has my grimoire, but for kicks I walked to the point on the map where you disappeared, and what do you know, I was right in front of the brothel. The invisibility spell. I flew over the gate and through a broken transom on the third floor."

He looked back and forth between us. "Now, I think the *real* question is . . . what are the two of you doing here? I thought breaking and entering was more my thing?"

"Note to self," Désirée said, "look into shielding against location spells."

"I wasn't doing anything weird!"

"I'm not worried about you. I don't like any old witch with a location spell being able to track us."

"Since when do we need to worry about other witches? Now, vamps, on the other hand, I don't want them sniffing us out."

"They're locked away, Isaac," I said, trying not to sound annoyed.

"They can't be the only six vampires in the world, Adele."

Dee's hands went squarely to her hips. "I don't care if they have bloodlust or magiclust, privacy is a key component to being a witch."

"Good point," said Isaac. "I don't like the idea of anyone being able to track us either."

I was pretty sure he thought Dee was speaking obtusely, but I assumed she meant hiding from her family.

"That's why we're here," I said when Dee offered him no further explanation. "We got kicked out of the shop."

"Whoa. You set something on fire?"

"No!" I smacked his arm.

"Gran caught us spycasting on her coven's circle and went all Wicked Witch of the West on us."

"Spycasting?"

Désirée let out a loud sigh and hopped off the counter. "It's a long story. I want to see more of the house."

As we explored the other side of the mansion—through a kitchen, a dining room that sat eighteen, a ballroom, and a double parlor, where we decided to camp out—Désirée went on a diatribe explaining her grandmother's obsession with keeping their family's magic line strictly inside the *family* coven. The parlor's baby-blue ceiling and navy-blue velvety damask wallpaper felt ethereally sea nymph and Versailles at the same time. I investigated the fireplace as they both sat on the couch.

"I'm the chosen one to take over after Gran," she said, "but does anyone ever ask me what I want?"

When it seemed reasonably safe, I lit the hearth with magical flames and then took a seat on the floor next to Isaac's legs. As he listened to her go on about the Borges, I slipped my hands into his backpack to find his sketchbook. I knew he was watching me in his periphery. When I leaned up and slid away the pencil from its permanent place behind his ear, he glanced at me, trying not to smile.

I settled back on the floor, propped against the couch, and opened the sketchbook to a new page, feeling a little warm and fuzzy, like I always did around the two of them and talks of magic. But it wasn't just the conversation. Isaac would twist someone's wrist for messing with his sketchbook, one of the few material possessions he cared about—that and his grandfather's watch—and I loved that he didn't twist mine.

CHAPTER 13
Magic vs. Mundane

Despite magic talk being one of my favorite things, it grew harder to pay attention to Dee with Adele pressed next to my leg, sliding my pencil over a fresh page in my sketchbook. I don't know when we slipped into this level of personal-space invasion, but I liked it.

Désirée's voice grew louder until she was fuming, comparing the idea of preserved-magic families to everything from incest to hate groups. I glanced at Adele's array of mismatched circles; as she began to shade them, they quickly became bubbles. Adele tensed up when we had to draw still lifes, but when it was something from her head, her fingers flew across the page. I couldn't imagine what it would've been like to grow up with Mac as a father. My pop didn't hate art; he just acted like it didn't exist, because it had been my mom's thing. For him, art died with her, no matter how much it meant to me.

"Hello?" Désirée said.

"Sorry." I turned back to her and asked a question to show I was paying attention. "So, what about other witches outside of your family with the same base magic? Would she have freaked if you'd joined a non-Borges all-Earth coven?"

"That would have been a lesser sin than consorting with a mixed-magic coven. Or a Symbios—or worse, an Aether."

"Dee, I don't know what the hell you're talking about."

Adele silently shook against the couch, laughing.

"Certain elements are more symbiotic with each other. Earth goes with Water, and Air goes with Fire."

Air and Fire? Hmm.

"The fifth element, Aether, is more like a wild card; it's symbiotic with *all* of the other elements. So Aether witches are seen as weaker to the rest of the witching community—that they're flippant, hard to trust, always moving on to the new shiniest thing."

"Cosette Monvoisin was an Aether," Adele said without looking up from the sketch—her wisps of smoke were so good they looked like they were floating off the page. "And she was fiercely loyal."

"As far as we know she abandoned the coven," said Dee.

"Mourning her triplet sisters who died because the coven wasn't strong enough to fight the Medici without casualties!"

"Yeah," I chimed in. "And it seems disrespectful to call her a deserter in her own house—if this is her house."

Adele turned around with a raised eyebrow.

"What? We still need proof."

"Whatever," Désirée said. "I'm not judging. I'm just saying that Aethers are the least respected in the witch world, and if I'd joined an Aether coven, my gran might have actually killed me."

"So we're a mutt coven?" I asked.

"I prefer to see it as highly curated. La crème de la crème. All my gran can see is that I'm breaking family tradition. But Marassa Makandal joined a mixed-magic coven in 1728, and to this day she's been the strongest witch in our family line. So really, I'm just going back to our roots. If Marassa can do it, I can do it."

She'd clearly given this a lot of thought, which wasn't surprising. Désirée might come across as indifferent, but if you paid attention, you'd know she made every decision with diamond-cut precision—like the way she let slang slip into her carefully articulated speech, letting you know that she was born into the elite but was firmly grounded in the real world. Cool and calculated, just like her legacy political family.

"I get why witches would stick together," I said, "but who cares if everyone's magic isn't the same? I mean, it's *magic*. It's all effing awesome."

"Witches are supposedly at their peak when they bond elementally—in life and in magic—which is why historically most witch power couples always match up element to element. For covens, there's an old belief that group magic is diluted by bringing in new Elementals. Of course, the biggest fear for any witch is diminishing magic or—Goddess forbid—losing it. So in theory, preserved-magic families are always at peak strength after centuries of purity."

"But the three of us are stronger together," Adele said.

"Yeah, stronger together than we are individually, but who's to know your magic wouldn't be infinitely stronger if you joined an all-Fire coven."

My pulse skipped imagining Adele with a different group of witches.

"I guess we'll never know," she said, smiling back at us, and then continued the sketch, which was starting to look like a bubbling cauldron.

"According to all the witch history my cousins and I endured growing up, back in the Old World, magical families went to extreme lengths, even rearing spies from birth, to infiltrate other covens to steal their secrets. Witches burned other covens' grimoires, breaking their bonds. Powers tumbled. People stopped mixing."

"So your gran thinks we're infiltrators?" Adele asked, turning around again. "We're the kids from the wrong side of the track?"

I laughed.

"Or does she think we kidnapped you and your magic? Magical world-domination agenda?"

"I'm sure it's more like lost witchlings without direction or proper magical upbringing," Dee replied.

Adele looked up at me. "We *are* the kids from the wrong side of the track!"

I pulled her up onto my lap, my arms circling her waist. She immediately tensed. It was a big move in front of Dee. Maybe too big.

I loosened up a little in case she wanted to move away, but she didn't; she even relaxed a bit, trying to be casual, as if I might have just pulled any girl onto my lap, which I thought was funny. "Then why doesn't Ritha just, like, adopt us?" she asked. "She could be our magical godmother?"

"That's what I thought was happening," Dee said. "But something changed. Clearly. And now I'm stuck on the outside. At first I thought it was just her exerting authority, or being paranoid about family secrets, which I can understand. It's taken *centuries* to perfect the magic in our grimoire, but it's not like I'd just do magic with any bozo off the street!"

My arm tightened around Adele's waist. "Aw, she loves us . . . even though we're street urchins."

"Someone get it on vid—" Adele started to say, but then Désirée stood and both legs on our side of the sofa snapped, and we toppled onto the floor.

"Dee!" Adele yelled. "That's an antique!"

Dee smiled slyly, and she mended the wood.

Adele resumed her place on the floor and picked up the sketchbook again. I climbed back to my seat next to Dee. "If you're so hell-bent on rebelling from the family coven, then why were you spying on their circle?"

"Because." She nearly snorted. "Something is up, and they won't tell me anything! Gran's paranoid about my friends, our coven, and us looking for any other witches in town. It's like she wants to build this magical cage around me so I can't interact with anyone other than Earth witches."

"Did you get any intel?"

As Dee began to explain how the spycasting spell worked, Adele's hand moved furiously against the page, finishing the sketch. And then just as Dee went on about a smoke braid, Adele flipped the illustration around to me. Floating on the surface of the bubbling cauldron's potion were letters spelled out by its ingredients:

A

DISRUPTION

TO SPIRIT WORLD

"What the hell does that mean?" I asked.

"No clue," Désirée said.

"Maybe we need to get a Ouija board," said Adele.

"I have one."

"Of course you do."

As they jokingly batted back and forth, I fixated on the last line. "Spirit world? There's really a spirit world?"

"Of course there's a spirit world," Désirée said, as if it were a place she visited every Sunday afternoon for high tea.

"The spirit world, the magical world, and the natural world are all connected—or more like layered. If something bad happened in the spirit world, it could cause a ripple effect everywhere else."

"The magical ecosystem . . . ," I said, my voice tapering off as I remembered that night in the Borges courtyard.

"Yes, exactly. That's what my gran always calls it."

"That's where I heard it."

Désirée smoothed her hair. "Excuse me?"

"Last week I was flying around in the middle of the night, patrolling for looters, and I heard someone in your courtyard, so I went down to check it out. It was just your gran—like in a trance or something."

Désirée's eyes grew wide. "You interrupted Gran when she was talking to the Loa?"

"I didn't interrupt! At least I don't think I did."

"What was she saying?"

"Nothing really. Most of it sounded like mumbles about the crime rate. About something not being right in this town."

"And you're *just now* telling us this?"

"What's there to tell? Everyone's always grumbling about the crime rate."

"But she didn't see you?"

"Well . . . she saw me, but I don't know if she *saw* me. She called me a witch. An Air witch." I shrugged, leaving out the part where she'd called me a *ghost witch*, because it freaked me out.

Désirée muttered to herself.

"Disruption to spirit world," Adele said. "It's so ominous."

Dee folded her legs beneath her. "So that's why all the Borges coven members have been popping into town. Usually the family coven only meets in full once a year, maybe twice, on St. John's Eve or Ganga-Bois, but not randomly."

Adele twisted around, draped her arms over my knees, and softly smiled. Magical excitement tingled from her fingertips through my jeans where her hands pressed. "Speaking of coven members . . ."

"What? I'm totally committed to the coven." I shifted the position of my legs, moving her before the feeling got *too* exciting.

"I'm glad to hear you say that"—she got up and sat on the couch next to me—"because we need to find the rest of our coven members."

"What?" My arms crossed. "Why?"

"We're a mutt coven. We might as well reap the benefits of diversified magic. How cool would it be to have a Water witch and an Aether?"

She turned to Dee. "Plus, we can prove to your gran that you did *not* join the wrong coven."

"Exactly, more coven members equal more knowledge, and knowledge equals power. And more power is always a good thing in the witching world."

They both looked at me.

I popped my knuckles. I was definitely into my magic reaching its full potential, but that piece of origami metal also burned a hole in my pocket, never letting me forget about the attic. Nicco. The curse. I couldn't let it ever be broken.

Adele's back shot straight up. "Wait, I have a condition."

She has a condition? Dee and I both looked to her.

"We—we can't tell the other witches about the curse, or the convent. Nothing about Halloween night."

"Why wouldn't we tell them about the curse?" Désirée asked. "It's part of their magical legacy."

"We can't tell them, because we don't know anything about these people." Nervousness poured out with her words. "What if they don't think the slumbering spell is a strong-enough punishment?"

"*Or* what if they're vampire sympathizers?" I said, really starting to wonder where Adele was coming from with this.

"Either way," she said, "it's not a risk we can take. Our secrets need to be earned, not doled out to witches with the right surname."

"Bringing new witches into the circle under false pretense won't bode well for our collective magic," Désirée said. "Covens are about perfect loyalty and trust."

"We can't tell them!" Adele shouted, drawing both of our gazes again. She quickly composed herself. "What we did—locking the Medici in an attic to essentially starve to death—it's a multitude of felonies."

"Felonies are against *humans*, Adele," I snapped. "Those things are *vampires*." Disgust filled the room with that single word.

Adele sank back deeper into her corner of the couch.

I leaned back too, my hands on my head. "But still . . . it's a good point. I'm eighteen; I don't need cops sniffing around us."

"So, we're all in agreement," Désirée said, holding her hand out in front of me. "We're going to find the other two descendants, then, assuming they aren't psychopaths, bind them into the circle. Later, whenever we collectively deem it appropriate, we fill them in on the past."

We piled our hands on top of Dee's, and a pact was made.

"*Laissez les bon temps rouler,*" she said, standing up. "I'm going to get my things."

As Adele and I sat there alone in awkward silence, her mouth began to curve upward.

"What are you so smiley about?"

She looked at me. "The coven. Doing magic together again."

I nodded, but uneasiness washed over me.

"We're on the same side, Isaac." She scooted next to me and touched my arm. "I want to put the coven together, but not at the expense of losing you."

I pulled her closer, our faces nearly touching. "You're not going to lose me."

"Isaac, we'll be stronger as five—stronger *against our enemies.*"

Her words made my heart pound, but when her lips pressed into mine, I could feel that she meant it. And when the kiss deepened, I could feel how much she wanted this—the coven—and suddenly it became more important to me too.

Taking a breath, she pulled my hand from her face but kept it in hers. "If you're not in, I'm not in."

"I'm in," I said, but this time I meant it.

Her smile made me smile, and our energies felt balanced again.

She quickly kissed me one last time and scooted away as Désirée came back into the room.

"I think it's time we break in this place," Dee said, resting her grimoire on the table along with a rolled canvas.

"You swiped the painting?" Adele asked, visibly excited.

Désirée walked to the marble fireplace and held the canvas up against the wall to the left. "Of course I swiped the painting." She looked over her shoulder to Adele. "Would you like to do the honors?"

We both stood, and Adele's hand slowly scanned the room. A pile of leaves in the far corner crinkled, and four small pieces of rusty metal rose into the air: two nails, one key, and an unidentifiable scrap. "That'll do," she said, and with a flick of her wrist, they all whizzed past Dee's head.

Dee exhaled loudly, letting go of the painting, which was now secured to the wall at each corner. "You're getting good at that too."

"Merci beaucoup." Adele walked over to the painting.

With that one little mark, it felt like we belonged here. I could see the future weeks unfurling. I could see the magic and the rituals. I could see myself kissing Adele in every single room. I was almost glad for the Borges family spat if that's how we ended up here.

I walked behind them and leaned an arm on each of their shoulders, looking at the painting.

"The original mixed-magic coven," Adele said. "I think Susannah painted it."

The swirls of purple mixed into the sky told me one thing: "She definitely did." And any coven that Susannah had been a part of was something I wanted a part of.

"So whose descendent do we try to identify first?" Dee asked. "Cosette's or Morning Star's?"

"Cosette!" Adele said, as if she'd been waiting for eternity for this moment. She kind of had—she's the one who dragged us here weeks ago, insisting the property was linked to our ancestor's coven.

"It seems only fitting," I said.

"Plus," Dee added, "Morning Star is bound to have even less of a paper trail than my former-slave ancestor."

"Paper trail . . . ," said Adele. "Maybe we could break into the Historic Center and look up the property records of this address? Tax records? Inheritance records? Or censuses?"

"That's not the worst idea," said Dee.

"I love how quickly you've both warmed up to petty crime as a solution to our magical dilemma."

"It's not like we're going to steal anything." Désirée tapped her chin like she was actually considering it.

"I don't think intent matters to cops when it comes to suspected burglary."

"My dad's the mayor, and yours is the director of FEMA."

"Director?" Adele asked me.

I didn't like talking about my pop, or FEMA. In the current postdisaster disarray, it typically led to names being called and punches being thrown. Everyone in the city had a different opinion over who was to blame for all of the injustices.

In my silence, Désirée answered for me: "Black was canned a week ago. They just haven't announced it to the press yet, so everyone's just pretending like Norwood isn't in charge now. As if he hadn't already taken over weeks ago."

Adele gave me a look that asked why she was the last to know.

I shrugged. "She's the mayor's daughter. She knows things. Can we get back to the dilemma at hand? The magical one?"

Adele turned back to the painting, contemplating. "It's not just the curse that binds them together." Excitement built in her voice, and I knew she had an idea. I also knew whatever she was about to say wasn't going to make sense immediately, because her head got ahead of her words when she was excited. "It's the *magic*." She looked at me. "You're right. It's a magical dilemma. I keep wanting to look for answers in the pages of books, but the answers have got to be in the *magic*, not in the *mundane.* Dee, when you wanted to spy on your gran, you could have just pressed your ear to the door like a normal person, but you didn't. And Isaac, when you wanted to find me, you could have just called—"

"I did. Like, fifty times—"

"Whatever. The point is, we're witches. We have other means to find these people."

"Isaac, how exactly does the location spell work?" Désirée asked.

"You need a map, a talisman, and something that belongs to the person."

"A talisman?" Adele asked.

"An object with some kind of magical charge," said Dee. "What did you use?"

I pulled the feather from the pages of my sketchbook.

"One of yours?" she asked.

"Obviously not." The feather was old and was a deep-red color, not black.

"Holy . . . Is that Susannah Bowen's?" Adele asked, which made me smile.

"I found it pressed in her grimoire."

Désirée took it from my hand. "Well, that's quite a talisman." She turned it over, examining it.

"I'll be right back," Adele said, walking out.

From a nearby room, something scraped across the floor. Adele returned with a large wooden frame, which she set down on the rug in front of the fireplace. It was a map—an antique map.

"Le Vieux Carré de La Nouvelle-Orléans, Capitale de la Louisiane en 1728," she said, reading the inscription at the bottom. "It's old, so some of the street names aren't the same, but we can figure it out."

"Assuming the descendant even lives in the Quarter," said Dee.

"Well, we have to start somewhere."

"Okay," I said. "But we still don't have any of their possessions."

"We might," said Adele, causing Dee's brow to rise. "Ritha said that magic is hereditary, and we know that spells pass down from one witch to the next, so maybe their magical possessions are automatically inherited by their descendants as well?"

Dee perked up. "So one of the casquette girls' old things might lead us straight to her descendant, the new rightful owner."

"Exactly!"

"But we don't have any of their ancestors' things either," I said.

"We're in Cosette Monvoisin's house, for God's sake!" Adele was so excited she was practically screaming. "Let's find something!"

"I'll check the first floor," Désirée said.

"Second!" chimed Adele.

"I guess that means I'm on top."

"Just grab anything that looks like it might have belonged to an eighteenth-century, bright-blond, brothel-bopping Aether," said Dee. "And be back here in thirty."

The upper level was cold and creepy. Damp winter air poured in through the broken transom, making the heavy drapes, weighed down with dust, ripple in the breeze. I shined my flashlight down the hallway.

Door after door and hallway after hallway led to small rooms not made for much else than sleeping . . . or brotheling.

Some of them had small pieces of furniture, some had an odd pair of shoes or a jacket. The one I was peering into had nothing but a lonely crucifix on the wall, which was a little too *Amityville* for my taste. I turned my flashlight beam away from it. The first sign of a tilting cross and I was out of here.

The last door at the end of the main hallway was different than all the others. An illustration had been carved into the wood: a forest scene where three naked, long-haired girls danced under the moonlight with a plethora of fairy-tale-looking animals watching on in delight. "Masterful" hardly began to describe the detail.

My fingers traced over one of the girls. Her mischievous smile made me desperately want to know what she was thinking. This piece was something that should have been in a museum, not in an abandoned, decaying mansion.

I pushed the brass handle down and swung the door open, suddenly much more interested in this treasure hunt.

My mood instantly deflated. The door wasn't at all representative of the room itself, and if it had been at one time, it showed no signs of it now.

Unlike the other rooms, this one was enormous, running the entire width of the house. It was mostly empty, with bare walls and bare floors. Windows lined the exterior wall, and rusty metal cots were stacked haphazardly against the interior wall. Even in their prime, there was unlikely ever anything inviting about them. They looked more utilitarian, like they belonged on the SS *Hope*, only a hundred years ago. Maybe this place had seen less risqué days in another life—a hospital or an orphanage or something?

A rat ran the length of the floor, tiny toenails clicking against the floorboards. It wasn't that I liked rats by any stretch, but they didn't scare me—the whole bird thing gave me a new respect for all tiny creatures.

I followed as it squeezed under a door. A supply closet, I deduced, pulling out a few of the shelved boxes to peek inside: plastic gloves melted together into a mound of yellowing rubber, metal syringes that were so old they had glass tubes, forceps, tongs, scalpels, and loads of other metal instruments whose last-century medical purpose frightened me. They probably didn't have any significance, but I pocketed a couple so I didn't return empty-handed.

When I exited the closet, I stopped suddenly, as if I'd run into a wall—an invisible wall of cold. I tried to move around it, but it moved too, as if not wanting me to pass.

My pulse spiked as I felt a touch against my chest—gentle, but icy through my T-shirt, the opposite of Adele's warm, magical touch. Again I tried to move away from it, but then it pressed against me with so much force I went flying backward to the floor, sliding back into the closet, crashing into the shelves. Boxes came tumbling over me. Wings flapped frantically—a bird that must have been roosting in one of them flew away, its nest spilling onto the floor. A glint caught my eye.

I fumbled for my flashlight, scooped up the nest, and examined it under the light.

There was something buried inside the funnel of twigs and gum wrappers and cigarette butts, all of which made me immediately hate people. I pinched a bead and pulled as gently as I could, trying not to destroy the habitat of nature and litter. A necklace came out, a strand of pearls, and in the center a tarnished heart.

It went into my pocket with the other things, and I headed for the stairs.

When I got to the second floor, instead of continuing all the way down, I peeled off into the darkness, weaving through the bedrooms and parlors, each lavish in a Miss Havisham kind of way.

Where is she?

My eye caught the flutter of her pale pink dress as she entered at the opposite end of the room, her gaze fixed on a painting on the far wall—I hurried the last few steps.

"Hey," I whispered behind her, grabbing her arm.

Her eyes flicked to mine as I pulled her straight into a kiss. When she smiled against my lips, the tension eased in my shoulders, after worrying for a second that the move was too forceful.

The scarf she was holding slunk to the floor as her hands crawled around my neck and she kissed me back. Two steps forward for me, backward for her, and she was against the wall and I was against her.

"We can't," she said. "We—have—to find—"

"It can wait two minu—"

She pulled my mouth back to hers. *Or five.*

Something was different about the way she touched me. Infectious excitement transferred from her fingertips, and for the first time I became *excited* about finding the other descendants—despite the risk of the attic being opened—if it made her this happy.

Just as my hands began to travel up from her waist, electronic dings on my phone sounded. Instead of stopping, the alarm just made the kisses more aggressive, as if just a few more seconds would be enough.

With an almost-groan, I pulled away. "Time's up," I whispered in her ear, with heavier breath and tighter pants than when we'd started. In a poof, I took crow form and flew out the door.

Because nothing save magic was going to get me to walk away from kissing her.

Downstairs in the double parlor we'd dubbed the "blue room," Désirée was already preparing for the spell. Our things had been moved to the side, and pillows now surrounded the map. Incense burned from an oyster shell, herbs floated in a bowl of water, and candles awaited Adele's flame. There was a small pile of objects next to one of the pillows, including an antique globe, a sharp ivory letter opener, a lace blanket or shawl, or something, and a stack of sheet music that had seen better days.

"She was a musician, right?" I asked, sitting on the floor. "Cosette?"

"Yeah, tutor to the queen, if I remember correctly."

"She was," Adele said from the doorway, holding a round hatbox brimming with objects. Her hair was a little tousled from where my fingers had run through it, making me want to pull her into my lap. "There were so many cool things up there, I wanted to take them all."

Of course she did. Adele loved old things.

She knelt by the map and laid down each item as if it was precious. I knew she was purposefully trying not to look at me so she wouldn't blush. Adding my loot to the pile, I brushed my hand against hers, just so I could see the tiny smile spread across her lips.

They settled on the pillows, and I opened my grimoire to the location-spell page: an island scene, presumably Susannah's home in Bermuda, but then again, who knew how long she'd spent on that pirate ship and how many beaches she'd seen. The drawing was one of my favorites: a cave in the bottom-right corner, dark but surrounded by glistening pools of water and rock formations baking in the sunlight.

I wonder if we've ever been to any of the same places in the Caribbean? Seen any of the same shorelines?

The greens in the water bled into blues, which bled into the pinks and purples in the sun-setting sky, over which her words scrolled. Watercolor wasn't a medium I'd given much thought to before, but seeing how much Susannah seemed to love it had made me start to love it too.

Dee placed the first object, a jeweled brooch from Adele's collection, into the center of the circle. We joined hands, and flames grew from the candles. Palms in palms, I said the words out loud, inserting our intention.

The owner of this object we must find.

Through streets and streams we will wind.

The Monvoisins were once three,

The owner of this object, reveal her to me.

Let this map be our guide,

So she can no longer hide.

They joined on the second repetition, and the feather stood on its point. A wave of energy rushed the room, sweeping across our shoulders, bringing volume to our voices, but that was it—four more verses, and it never moved again.

"The brooch wasn't hers," I said as the feather rested back on its side.

The result was no different when we repeated the spell on the globe.

We went through the rest of their objects until our throats were dry and our palms sweaty. Disappointment crept over both of them.

Dee started to lean back.

I fished the necklace out of the pocket of my jeans. "My turn!"

"What is it?" asked Adele.

I dropped it into her palm. "It's a necklace, like Désirée's bracelet."

Dee scoffed. "*This*," she said of the thick silver chain around her wrist, "is Tiffany."

"Whatever," I said. "They both have hearts."

The necklace began to vibrate in Adele's hand, and then the heart opened up, revealing a compartment with a salve inside.

"Lipstick?" I asked.

She brought it to her nose. "Perfume, I think."

"Don't touch that," said Dee. "In case it's not *just* perfume. We are in a witch's house after all."

Adele snapped it closed. "Noted."

She gently set it next to the oyster shell with the incense, and we joined hands again.

Before we finished the first lines of the chant, a loud boom exploded and everything went completely dark. Our hands gripped tighter as we repeated the lines. Two tiny flames rose from the candles in front of each of Adele's knees. Her smile spread, and the flames grew.

I followed her gaze to the middle of the map—Susannah's feather was standing upright on the tip. In the center of Jackson Square.

The words flowed from our lips, and the feather began to shake. It felt like the whole room did.

Then the feather slid directly in front of the cathedral.

Adele's hand squeezed mine so tight I thought she might snap the little bones in her fingers. The chant turned over, and the feather jerked down Chartres Street, toward Esplanade Avenue, and then there was another boom and the candles blew out again, the darkness cloaking the location.

Our hands released.

Adele relit all the wicks in the room, of which there were plenty, and we hovered over the map. The feather was lying back down, but the tip was resting on a *very* particular place. Chartres Street at the corner of Ursuline.

"The convent?" Adele whispered. "That can't be right."

We all sat back.

"We must have done something wrong," said Dee.

The speed at which my pulse raced didn't make me think we'd done anything wrong, but we did the spell three more times to satisfy Désirée's perfectionist tendencies.

After the third repetition, Adele sat back. "No more. I think I know what's throwing it off."

Dee and I both looked up.

"Vampires. Or one vampire, to be exact. Lisette Monvoisin."

"Ugh! Do you think that's possible?" asked Dee. It was the first time she'd ever asked our opinion on something magical.

"I—I don't know," said Adele. "Lisette's not a witch anymore, but she's not exactly dead either. Maybe somehow she's muddling the magic, making the spell think *she's* the next ancestor and blocking us from getting to the magical descendant?"

"Makes sense," Dee said. "Unfortunately."

"One more reason to burn the attic," I said, only half joking. Neither of them laughed.

Adele stood up and walked to the other side of the room.

I quietly sighed, got up, and followed her to the sliding pocket doors. She'd paused at the archway, looking up at the carving in the center—various pieces of fruit, surrounding a pineapple.

"*L'ananas,*" she said. "A symbol of welcome. They were given to plantation guests upon arrival, but if you ever came back to your room and found a second pineapple, you knew you'd overstayed your welcome." She looked back at me. "Southern passive-aggressiveness at its finest."

"Man, you know some random things." And she did—especially about New Orleans—and every strange fact she knew dripped with her love for the city.

"I wish I knew how to find our next descendant."

I squeezed her shoulder. "We'll find him."

"Him?"

"He's a guy; I can feel it."

She laughed. "Okay, Madame Morgana."

"Who's Madame Morgana?"

"Just someone I used to know."

Because kids who grew up in New Orleans knew people named Madame Morgana, and by sixteen were old enough to not know them anymore.

She leaned her head back onto my shoulder, and my hand slid around her waist. "You know I was just joking back there."

"*Oui.*"

"Then why does it bother you?"

Her head turned slightly so she could see me. "I don't know. I'm just scared you're going to do something stupid one day."

"Me do something stupid?" My fingers began poking her ribs, and I pulled her closer so I could use both hands.

"Noooooooo!" She hated being tickled, but I loved hearing her laugh. Unable to get away, she buckled, laughing in protest and pulling me down to the floor with her.

I loved hearing her laugh, but I hated that I was now thinking about the attic. I hated wondering if Adele was thinking about the attic too. I wanted to know if every time she thought about the attic, she thought about Nicco . . . like I did.

CHAPTER 14
Marked

"We never saw stars before the Storm," Adele said, all of us gazing up at the twinkling sky. "Too many lights in the Quarter."

And then we were back to a much-needed silence after all the chanting and all the magic. The three of us were lying on the thick edge of an enormous fountain, the centerpiece of the garden, in the vine-covered courtyard. Adele and I head to head, Désirée lying on the other side of the circle, doing deep breathing exercises so that she didn't spontaneously combust after all the failed magic.

The fountain had three life-size girls in the center, all with long flowing hair, just like on the door upstairs, dancing, hands to the sky. I could imagine how angelic they'd look under the moonlight with the water spraying out from the top, dripping down over their bodies like rain. But now they were coated in algae and draped with moss, their toes dipped in black rainwater, like they'd been dancing in a storm of torment. There was still something beautiful about the natural decay in comparison to the blunt destruction reaped by the Storm at the sites I worked on every day.

I tilted my head away from them, nearly knocking Adele's. Despite all of the failed spellwork, excitement bloomed from her cheeks as she tapped out a message on her phone. I raised an eyebrow.

"Telling my dad that I'm sleeping at Dee's so we don't have to stress about the curfew."

She smiled, and I wanted to kiss her.

Adele hadn't been particularly interested in magic ever since the incident in the attic, and at first I didn't mind. It had given us the chance to hang out like normal people; plus, the less we talked about magic, the less we talked about vampires, and the less we talked about vampires, the less we fought. I'd been hoping, though, that she'd snap out of it after the funeral, because now that I'd been practicing so much on my own, there was nothing that I wanted more than to do magic with her.

Well, almost nothing . . .

And now she was rosy cheeked and lying to Mac so she could stay and do coven things.

"What?" she asked.

"Nothing."

I'm definitely not wondering how hard it would be to sneak you on board the ship after curfew.

"We didn't smudge the house," Désirée's voice floated over to us. Adele shrugged when I looked at her in confusion. "No wonder the spell failed. Jesus." Dee's tone hardened. "If Gran was here, she'd kick me out all over again—"

"Dee," Adele said. *"Explique, s'il te plaît."*

"We didn't cleanse the space of any unwanted hexes, jinxes, or otherwise negative energy. I can't believe I let us do magic in here without a proper smudging. I'll pick up the supplies tomorrow. No more magic until then."

I didn't care if it was cleansed or uncleansed, I was quickly falling in love with this house after four months of living in a stainless steel box. We'd only been here for a few hours, and it was already feeling like ours.

Désirée shot straight up, causing us both to sit up.

"I want to do a séance. Contact the other side—find out what's going on with the spirit world."

"Uh, Dee, you just said no more magic until further notice," I reminded her.

"*Pfft.* We're not going to do the séance in the house." She got up and headed toward the back door. "I'm going to get my stuff."

"Then where?"

"The cemetery, obviously."

Adele and I both turned to each other with the same *is she serious* look.

I couldn't tell if the little orbs of light floating around us helped or if the shadows they created just made things creepier. Adele pushed the fireballs ahead, lighting the way through the rows of mausoleums, most of which looked about as old as the city.

Dee and Adele both seemed totally comfortable walking through the graveyard in the middle of the night. Although one could hardly call it a graveyard, because there was no *yard*, just brick pathways between rows and rows of mausoleums, because people in New Orleans were buried above ground. I, on the other hand, was not into this. The air felt thicker and damper the deeper we went, until my bones felt like they were shivering under my skin. "Alert" hardly described my senses as we walked through the rows of the dead.

Suck it up, Isaac.

A loud metallic creak split the air, sending goose pimples through my flesh. It was just the gate of a rusted iron fence in front of one of the mausoleums, swinging in the breeze. Rock and shell crunched under our feet as we moved ahead; I tried not to think about bones.

The mausoleums got bigger and bigger until they looked like miniature houses, guarded by cherubs and weeping angels and iron crosses. Some had glass windows so crusted with dust and grime you'd hardly know it was glass. A few appeared to have been tended to post-Storm— one had stained glass that reflected rainbow flecks when we walked past it with Adele's fire, some were whitewashed, and one even had fresh flowers laid out in front. But many others were crumbling, or were not much more than piles of bricks.

The only constant was the greenish-black line that ran across everything about chest high—the mark that showed exactly where the floodwater had sat before they were able to pump it out. We were still within walking distance from the brothel, but a few blocks outside of the Quarter. Just outside of the protection spell's border.

"Jesus!" Adele yelped, stumbling backward into my chest.

"What?" I held her steady.

She directed the swarm of flames to the left of her feet. They hummed like fireflies over the broken lid of a breached coffin. "That is so not okay," she said as she flicked a flame closer to the ground. She squeaked when it illuminated a skull sticking out of the smashed lid.

"It's just a bone," Désirée said. She knelt, gently pushed the skull back into the coffin, and repositioned the lid as best she could. Then, as if it were just another day in the park, she reached into her bag and pulled out the bottle of homemade antiseptic and spritzed her hands, sending vanilla notes wafting into the foggy air.

We moved on, but Adele hung back, her wide eyes not unnoticed by me.

"What's wrong?"

She shook her head. "Nothing."

I wrapped my fingers into hers, hoping she'd tell me whatever it was.

"Halloween night . . . Minette's . . . skeleton was in one of the cassettes. Lisette hurled her sister's skull into my stomach while we were fighting."

"Jesus." I pulled her close and walked her away from the coffin.

We followed Désirée between two mausoleums at the end of a row, to a patch of green in the back corner of the cemetery. The corner walls were covered with rows of oven tombs.

"This should be good," Désirée said, setting her bag down. "Adele, candles. Isaac, salt circle."

We both went to work.

A few minutes later the three of us were sitting in a circle surrounded by salt and unlit white candles. Dee laid a silk scarf in the middle and then a flat piece of slate she'd scavenged. She handed us each a little pouch made of burgundy velvet. Mine was about four times bigger than the gris-gris but just as light as a sack of air, even though it was stuffed full.

"Cup your stones," she said. "Get them warm in your hands. Exchange your energy with them."

What?

I poured the contents of the pouch into my hand: black stones, so light they felt like nothing.

"Lava stone," Dee said.

"Pyrite?" Adele asked, holding up glittering chunks of gold.

"Yes. And Jade for me." Dee lifted up a palm of green stones before setting them aside so she could empty two more pouches. "Moonstone and rose quartz for our missing sisters."

"Or brothers," I added.

"Dream on," she said, and placed her three piles of rocks in the middle of the circle. Adele and I did the same with ours and watched with wonder as she poured something that smelled like rum from a flask into a tin cup, placed it on a saucer, then unscrewed a fancy-looking thermos. "Sorry ancestors," she said as she poured the coffee into a porcelain cup. "It's from this morning. Adele will bring you a freshly brewed pot next time." She ripped open four packets of artificial sweet-ener and poured them into a shell. "And real sugar."

I looked at Adele and mouthed, *Next time?*

She shrugged. "Are we doing a séance, or having a tea party?"

Adele joked when she was nervous. When Désirée didn't give her the death stare, it made me wonder if she was nervous too, not an emo-tion I'd ever seen Désirée Borges exhibit.

"Dee, what exactly are we doing?" I asked.

Désirée opened Marassa's grimoire on her lap. "I figure the best chance we have for success is contacting someone from my ancestral line."

"Why is that?" I asked.

"Because we're surrounded by them."

In one whoosh, all of the candles around us lit up. We looked to Adele, who shrugged unapologetically.

In the light, I could read the names on the mausoleums behind us. Many were etched BORGES, and the older-looking mausoleums had names like PARRISH, GLAPION, and ROCHE. Knowing we were sur-rounded by the skulls and bones of Désirée's entire family line somehow made everything feel much more intense.

"Now it's just figuring out how far back to go," said Dee.

"How do we do that?" I asked.

"I'm not totally sure."

"So we're just going to cruise around your ancestral spirit graveyard and see who shows up?"

"Pretty much. That's what the offerings are for." She added some cookies on a plate. They looked lumpy and homemade, but ten times better than the Hooah! bars I'd been eating for the last five months. She held out her hands, and we all joined together.

Papa Legba, ouvrez la porte.

Papa Legba, ouvrez la porte, open the door.

I shut my eyes, listening to her repeat the chant. Désirée's energy always changed when she wanted us to join in. You could feel it through her palms—like the magic was pulsing from her pores. It came in a wave: the cue, the squeeze. Adele and I joined in, and we repeated the chant three times.

Open the door to the other side. Be our guide.

A connection to my ancestors, I seek.

So that I may get a peek

Into the havoc that may have been wreaked.

Papa Legba, open the door.

As we chanted, the temperature dropped, not in one quick plunge, but with every line it got just enough colder to notice. Adele's hand pulsed warmer in my palm.

"Holy sh . . ." Désirée's voice trailed.

I opened my eyes and understood why.

The stones were floating, some just inches above the ground, others at shoulder level. A smile spread over Désirée's face as she poked a piece of lava stone that had begun to float too far away. It moved back into the circle.

"Told you I have a Ouija board," she said to Adele, then squeezed our hands and refocused on her chanting. The stones rose higher, as if pulled up by invisible strings.

A breeze rushed around the circle, unnaturally cold.

Our arms rippled as the wind whipped under them and over them. Désirée's hand tightened in mine, and mine tightened around Adele's, as the stones rattled against each other. The chant got faster, and then, as the two of us continued the chant, Désirée called out, "Is anyone there?"

The stones moved around, and my pulse began to pound.

Désirée rose slightly off her seat. "Is someone there?"

The stones moved again, clumping together in specific formations.

When she asked the question a third time, they dropped to the ground, falling into a pattern in front of Désirée. It was a three-letter word:

OUI

She squeezed my hand tighter. "Are we related by blood?"

The rocks rose again, shifting formations, and fell down again, spelling out the same word.

OUI

"Can you tell us your name?"

MARA

Désirée got so jittery, I thought she was going to launch herself into the sky. "Marassa? Marassa Makandal?"

OUI

She regained her composure. "Marassa, is everything okay in your world?"

This time the rocks shot up quickly and immediately fell back to the ground.

NON

Before Désirée could get the next question out, the rocks shot up and down again.

NON NON NON NON

They rose, scattered, and fell again.

AIDEZ-MOI

Désirée's head whipped to Adele for translation.
"Um. *Help me.*"
"You need help?" Désirée asked. "Are you in danger?"

NON

"Who is in danger? Who needs help?"

PROTÉGEZ LA

Cold fingers slipped up my neck. I whipped around. There was no one there, but as soon as I faced forward, there it was again, slipping over my neck and down my chest—a hand so cold it felt like it had slid right through the thick hoodie fabric and was against my skin. *"Isaac,"* a voice said close to my neck.

The breeze curled around my stiffening spine. *"Isaac . . ."*

"Protégez la," another voice whispered directly into my left ear, making me jolt away, but a new voice whispered my name into my right, and then more whispers came from behind. *"Protégez la. Protégez la. Protégez la."*

Neither Adele nor Désirée seem bothered at the slightest by the whispers and stayed focused on the stones as they rearranged themselves once more, banging themselves down just in case the message wasn't clear.

PROTÉGEZ LA

The stones floated up again.

"Protégez la, Isaac. Protégez la. Protégez la. Isaac. Isaac. Protégez la." Our eyes rose and our necks craned as the voices floated high above our heads. Our hands still clasped in one another's, the chant still slipped from our lips. The breeze picked up all around us, sending Adele's hair whipping back. Voices—hundreds all around us, whispering the same thing over and over. Adele didn't look frightened, but I was, and I wanted to stop. I wanted her to make it— *"Stop!"* I yelled.

The cloud of stones exploded, and I yanked Adele into my lap, folding myself over her as the stones whipped past us, pelting against mausoleums, statues, and the wall of oven tombs.

In the next moments, still bent over her back, and with my eyes tightly closed, everything felt starkly calm—other than Adele's racing heart pounding against me.

Quiet but cold. A lingering cold.

Adele pushed us both up, her hair a bit wild from the wind, but not a strand of Désirée's was out of place. I don't think she'd even flinched.

We stood up slowly, looking around.

"Dammit," Désirée said. "We were so close! What did it mean?"

"Protect her," Adele said. "*Protégez la*, protect her."

"Protect who?" Désirée asked. "That can't be it. What does it *mean*?"

Still breathing hard, I rested my hands on the back of my head. For some reason, controlling the wind and turning into a bird was a lot easier for me to deal with than talking to dead people.

"What the?" Adele asked, getting up, looking out to the mausoleums. The stones hadn't dropped to the ground: they were all floating against the targets they'd hit, like little glints of shine and shimmer. The pyrite especially gleamed against the monochromatic palate of tombs.

She walked over to a floating moonstone. When she touched it, it didn't move. She pushed it harder, and it stayed resting against the *A* in NANETTE BORGES.

Dee got up and walked over to another stone, and then another, but neither of them could get a stone to budge. Adele moved quicker, with a peculiar look on her face.

I knew that expression. She had an idea or had figured something out. Normally I loved that look, but now I was feeling the cold in my bones, and I just sat there watching both of them, as if in a state of paralysis.

Adele ran back to me, grabbed the pen from behind my front pocket, and hurried back to the tomb wall. She glanced up and jotted things down on her arm. Désirée caught on and began running to the different stones, yelling back and forth to her, but I didn't move.

I was cold. I shuddered. Something wasn't right.

"Isaac . . . ," a voice said.

I whipped around.

"Protégez la . . ." The words slipped over my ear, making chills tear through my flesh.

"Stop it!" I yelled.

"Isaac . . . ," she said again. *"Ga-ga-gho . . . witch."* She sounded farther away but somehow more clear. *"Ghost witch."*

"Isaac!" her voice sounded different now. "Isaac!"

My eyes shot open. It was Adele's voice. Both her and Désirée were leaning over me. I was lying on the ground. Adele's hand was in mine. They were both yelling my name, shaking my shoulders. I sat up, embarrassed, kind of not caring. Still cold. My lips were still moving—muttering. "An-n-n-imaran-nimarumpraedatoranimarmanimarum."

"Isaac!" Adele yelled.

I stopped and blinked a few times.

"It worked. It worked! You were talking to her!" Désirée pounced on me, her arms around my neck, knocking me back down to the ground. "Could you see her? What did she look like? Why did she appear to you and not me?"

I pushed her off onto the grass next to me and sat up again.

"I want to see her! She's my grand-witch!"

Adele sank back on her knees, inhaling hard. *Are you okay?* she mouthed.

I nodded quickly. "Cool your jets," I said to Dee, balling my fists to stop them from shaking. "I didn't see anything."

Adele got up and went back to the stones. I was glad—I didn't want her to see that my hands were still shaking.

"What did she say?"

I looked back to Dee. "I don't know. That the spirit world is in trouble. She kept calling me a . . . ghost witch. Just like your gran did that night she was in the trance."

"Ghost witch? You failed to mention that earlier."

"Did I?"

"What else?"

"I don't know. That's all I heard—what I remember." Adele came back, and I shook it off.

She slid the pen back into my pocket and held out her arm—a list of names. Some of the letters were distinctly bolder than the others.

NAnette Borges
AngeLie Borges
MathiLde Roche

Soulie Henri
VictOire Parrish
Foucher MoUnier
Albert MiLon
RoSe Fortier

WILLIAM THIERRY
HENRIETTE ROCHE
JEAN-BAPTISTE MILON
EULALIE HENRI

ORY BORGES
FAVRE DAQUIN
HENRI FORTIER
FRANCOIS PICOT
MAZANT E DAQUIN
ZAMORA THIERRY

"Those are the letters the stones hit," Adele said. "That's one hell of a planchette, Désirée Borges."

"'All souls will suffer,'" Désirée read out loud. "Well, that's ominous, as per usual."

Adele touched my hand. "You're freezing."

"Yeah," I said, standing. I pulled her up with me, then both of us offered a hand to Désirée.

"Isaac," Adele said, her eyes growing wide.

"What? What's wrong?"

"You're . . . glowing."

A faint light was shining through the sleeve of my hoodie. "What the eff?" I ripped up my sleeve, and on my arm, glowing icy silver, was a triangle with a line through its peak. "What the hell?"

"*Whoa,*" said Dee, which was not exactly the reaction I wanted from her. From Dee you always wanted the exact matter-of-fact explanation when something weird was happening.

"Does it hurt?" Adele asked.

"No. It just kind of . . . tingles." The glow faded away, but we all just stood there staring at my arm.

"Well at least it's gone now," said Dee.

"What do you mean 'gone'?" The glow was gone, but in its place was the exact same shape, just now with thin black lines.

"What do *you* mean?" she asked.

"I mean, there is a giant triangle on my arm!"

Adele looked at me, concern on her face. "Isaac, there's nothing there."

My pulse sped. "You seriously can't see it?"

They both shook their heads.

"What the fuck?" I stared back at the symbol. I knew the mark. It was carved into the bottom corner of Susannah's grimoire, my grimoire—the alchemical symbol for Air.

Désirée sprawled out on the parlor floor with Marassa's grimoire and an assortment of Voodoo accoutrements, on a quest to discover why a magical mark would appear on a witch.

Adele lit the fireplace and sat next to me on the floor, our backs against the sofa. I pulled off my hoodie, wanting the warmth of the fire on my skin, and she took my left arm in her hands, turning it to the inside.

"Are you sure you can't see it?" I whispered, almost hesitant to ask. Her head shook.

I took her finger and traced it over the black line as she continued to shake her head. She traced it again from memory, sending a wave of chills up my arm, her bright blue eyes locked with mine. She rested her head on my shoulder, and we both stared out into the fire, her fingers unconsciously tracing the symbol until my skin felt a little numb.

In the comfort of the parlor and out of the dead zone, I wasn't even sure if I was opposed to the mark. I wasn't opposed to ink, and I couldn't really think of anything more badass than magical ink. But if it was magical, why couldn't they see it? They're witches. We're bound together, for Christ's sake. *Why can't they see it?*

"We'll figure it out," Adele whispered, and softly pressed her lips to my cheek.

She got up and stepped over me toward a regal-looking chair to the right of the couch. It had carved lion's feet and was the color of the periwinkle that grew in the abandoned, overgrown lots back home. She draped herself across the chair, legs dangling over one of the arms.

Her fingers played with the chain around her neck as she quickly got lost in Adeline's diary. The feather I'd sculpted clinked against her medallion when she moved. I was glad to see her wearing Adeline's talisman again.

I pulled out my sketch pad and uncapped my pen, trying not to stare at my arm too much as I drew.

It was clear that the mansion was to become coven HQ, and that the blue room was to become the epicenter. It felt like home. Which I'd almost forgotten was a thing.

"Isaac," Adele whispered from the velvet chair, "are you still awake?"

"Yeah."

I looked up from the couch just in time to see her grab her bag and walk out of the room into the adjacent parlor. I wasn't sure if that was my cue to follow her, but I certainly made it my cue.

As she lit the candles on the mantel, I slid the pocket doors closed as quietly as I could, hoping that we had the same idea. When she pulled me next to her on the paisley couch, my hopes raised higher.

"I've been waiting for Désirée to fall asleep so I could ask you something."

"Okay." I pulled her closer. Whatever it was, she seemed to be getting more timid by the second.

"You know you can tell me anything, right?"

"Um . . . yeah?" I wondered if I'd done something wrong.

"Like, things that happened in the past that you may not have been comfortable telling me about." She touched my hand. "Pretending that it didn't happen won't make it go away."

She remembers. She remembers the token, and she wants it back. I stood up and paced to the fireplace. *So this is why she wants to get the rest of the coven together. To break the curse. To let him out.* "How did you find out?"

"Sébastien told me."

"Sébastien? How does he know?"

"This is New Orleans, not Mars, Isaac. We get the *New York Times*."

"The *New York Times*?"

She leaned into her bag and pulled out the paper. "You really haven't seen this?"

I sat back down next to her, taking the paper from her hands.

And just like that, my nightmare became real.

That postapocalyptic day collided with my current reality, and a rush of deep resentment and rage washed over me. "That *fucking* fuck," I spat, my fingers crumpling the edges of the newspaper. *Unknown hero?*

Adele said something about the photo, and I sprang up, back to the fireplace. I couldn't even look at her. Anxiety rushed my chest, choking me, pummeling me like the water had, and suddenly I was drowning again, and those little fingers were slipping out of my grasp. My eyes blinked wet. *Stop being a pussy. You can't cry in front of Adele.*

My fingers rattled against the marble mantel.

But she's not supposed to know about that day. She'd never be able to count on me. She'd never be able to look at me.

"So it is you?" Her hand touched my shoulder.

I pushed right through it, walking back to the couch. "I don't want to talk about it." Elbows on knees, my head went to my clammy palms. "It's nothing." My foot tapped the floor.

"It doesn't seem like nothing."

I didn't say anything. I didn't look up. But then she was sitting next to me and her hand was on my back. "You saved a little girl."

"I'm gonna kill that fucking photographer."

"Isaac. *What happened?*"

"I don't want to talk about it." In a flash I saw everything collapsing, the fight we were about to have, the fraud she'd think I was, and how she'd never speak to me again. But I yelled at her anyway: "I don't want to talk about it!"

A moment of silence went by. She just stared back at me with her wide blue eyes. Eyes I never wanted to hurt or disappoint.

Eyes that didn't waver. "Okay," she said, resting her hand on my shoulder.

I realized I was shaking—not shivers, but violent tremors.

"Okay," she said again, nodding. She scooted behind me, her hand sliding to my chest, pushing me down to the pillows. And then we were lying there on the couch, her head on my shoulder and her arm wrapped around me.

"Okay," she said, one more time, and that was it.

As we lay there, her heart raced against my chest. I'd scared her, and I hated that. Not that she'd shown any outward sign of being frightened, but that bothered me too. I liked all of her emotions. I liked that she wasn't cold and unrufflable like Désirée.

I'd *never* snapped like that before.

She'd just caught me so off guard. I'd planned to tell her one day, when I was ready, but right now I wasn't even ready to bring it to the forefront of my consciousness. I'd always imagined the conversation being private and intimate between just her and me, and she'd understand. And she'd somehow make it better. Make the nightmare stop. It wouldn't be on the cover of the *Times* for the entire world to judge . . . to call me a hero.

Fuck.

And then she curled up closer and held on to me tighter, and if there was ever any doubt that I loved this girl, it was gone forever.

All the flames flickered out when she drifted off . . . a beautiful harmony of consciousness and magic. The deeper into sleep she fell, the more she curled into my chest.

I don't know when I fell asleep, but I know that I didn't have the nightmare with her tucked beneath my arm, and I didn't care that my sleep was brief, because I woke up to her thumb rubbing my arm, and to her wanting to kiss me nearly until my alarm went off. And I certainly didn't care that today at work was going to be brutal because of it.

PART 2

The Unseen

By the pricking of my thumbs,

Something wicked this way comes.

William Shakespeare, *Macbeth*

CHAPTER 15

Blue-Tent City

January 2nd

The radio program hummed in the background as I wiped the tables down, the deluge of crime reports, water-boil advisories, and economic statistics: a constant reminder of the police-like state we were living in.

"The National Guard, in conjunction with the NOPD, has apprehended the prime suspect in the O'Keefe homicide."

With a quick flick of my eyes, I turned up the volume.

"Simon Fuller: thirty-three-year-old black male. Resident of the Lower Ninth Ward."

I stuffed the edge of the rag into the back pocket of my jeans and felt something crinkle—I pulled out a folded coffee filter. *How the—?* But then I saw the ink peeking through. Isaac must have slipped it into my pocket when he stopped in this morning.

I unfolded the thin paper to reveal the sketch. Two pairs of legs, the river and the sunset beyond. *New Year's Eve.* Or I guess I should say New Year's Morning.

After the party at Le Chat, we'd stayed up all night to watch the sun rise. He was sitting against a tree, my back against his chest, his sketch pad propped up against my knees. As the sun rose, the moment was so perfect we tried to capture it on paper. Both of us furiously sketched it out on the same page as the sky became more and more orange.

I don't think either of us wanted the night to end—and we were both a little buzzed from sneaking champagne—so he drew a figure breaking the water's surface, a dolphin, as if, in the Mississippi. I decided the dolphin's friend was a Pegasus, flying over the ferry boat, and soon the page was filled with water nymphs and Loch Ness monsters and backstroking unicorns until the sun was so magnificent in the sky we had to set the drawing aside. With our hoodies over our heads and his arms curled around me, we watched the first morning of the new year roll in together. And now it was immortalized on a coffee filter.

I swear he had some kind of special memory power for detail. It was all there, in a perfect blend of kitsch and beauty. I smiled, folding it back up. I'd always thought the butterflies were supposed to come in the very beginning, in a big knee-melting, heart-gushing, warm and fuzzy rush, but the more I got to know Isaac, the more he made my stomach cartwheel.

It had been over a month since the night I'd asked him about the newspaper article. Since then, there'd been handmade Christmas presents and midnight New Year's Eve kisses and spills off his skateboard, and amid it all, Isaac Norwood Thompson had become my boyfriend.

We never had a discussion; it just kind of happened sometime between our metalwork lessons, joint spellwork, and falling asleep too many times together on the couch after talking all night, and subsequently freaking my dad out when he got home from work, because he didn't know whether kicking an eighteen-year-old kid out onto the curfew-silent, crime-ridden streets or letting him stay was the right thing to do.

I showed Isaac the city, and he sketched most of it. He told me about Pratt and Prospect Park and the difference between Yankees and Mets fans. And that a schmear was the cream cheese paired with a bagel. That he could legally fly a plane! And about how his mom had died of breast cancer and how his dad, who he called Pop, had done nothing but work ever since. He said he didn't mind because all his pop cared about was making things better for people. I'd yet to meet his father, but I guess I now knew where Isaac got his selflessness.

We talked about everything, but we never talked about that night at the brothel and his picture in the paper.

I'd woken up alone that morning. He'd already gone off to work without waking me, but he'd left a sketch on the mantel, right next to the painting of the original coven. It was of me, him, and Dee sitting on the brothel porch.

The newspaper was gone, but of course I managed to get another copy. I didn't tell him that, or that there'd been a follow-up article trying to solve the identity of the mystery hero—the guy won the Pulitzer, so people were starting to obsess over the photo.

Every day I thought about bringing it up, but then I remembered the way his pulse had raced against my chest, how scared it had made him. And Isaac wasn't scared of anything, for better or for worse. The Storm had affected everyone in different ways, New Yorkers not excluded.

He'll tell me about it one day. Who am I to push the subject?

I, who clammed up anytime he asked me about Paris. I wanted to know what had happened to him the day the levees broke, but not pushing him somehow made me feel better about not telling him the whole truth about my mother.

I'll tell him about Brigitte one day.

But not until I figured out how to help her. Because I didn't want to lose her, and I didn't want to lose him, and the only thing Isaac didn't have a shred of compassion for was vampires. I knew that if I could just find a way to save her—so he could meet her and see her as more than a faceless monster in an attic, he would see her as my mother.

"It's pathetic," the radio DJ said. "Nothing has been released in terms of motive, and the suspect had no prior criminal record. His two small children have been taken into police custody, at the time of arrest, 'At least they'll get some food now,' a bystander heard him saying. Pathetic. People. Pathetic!"

I wondered how long a vampire could go without eating before they lost control of their bloodlust. I fantasized about it being a really big number. Months. Years, even. After all, Gabe, Lisette, and Martine had been locked away for nearly three centuries. Brigitte had been in the attic for nine weeks. Every morning I woke up wondering if I would be too late, and every evening I went to sleep wondering if I would ever figure out a way to save her. Each day I stressed out about it a little more, and each day I learned to push it down deeper inside. She was enduring the attic to save me. I could endure keeping her secret to save her.

I ran the rag under hot water until all of the coffee grounds came clean.

Despite not needing the inventory, Sébastien had refilled all of the jars on the wall with coffee beans, for which I was grateful because it brought back the intoxicating smell to the little corner café. Those little signs of familiarity were the things I gripped on to on the days when everything felt so different. The smell of chicory, the sound of Ren's voice on the street, telling the story of Delphine LaLaurie for the eight millionth time.

Some changes happened so gradually you didn't even notice when the abnormal took over. You got used to eating meals that came exclusively from cans and dehydrated bags, and to carrying scarves around with you in case you found yourself surrounded by mold, and to boiling water before drinking it. You got used to the electricity only working sometimes, and to the blinking lights that indicated the overwhelmed grid had crashed again. And you got used to all the blue tarps on roofs.

The city was covered in them.

The more people that came back, the more blue tarps went up. We all should have bought stock in blue plastic.

Government-issued trailers popped up on lawns for people who no longer had housing. They weren't much more than white boxes on concrete blocks, and the joke around town was that FEMA required you to have a house with working electricity and running water to be eligible for one. The circular logic was pissing people off endlessly, and, I assumed, making Norwood Thompson's life a nightmare.

If Brooke and her parents had stayed in the city, they'd be living in one of those trailers while fighting day and night with their insurance company. I guess Alphonse and Klara were right about their family being better off in L.A. I'd had one phone call with Brooke—which was really made up of ten phone calls because the reception kept dropping. She was having the time of her life shooting the reality show, and I was happy for her. *I know she'll win; she always does.* I mostly told her about Isaac, because there was certainly nothing else in my life I could tell her about, other than the bleak state of the city. For her it was still shocking; for us it was just . . . life.

Five months after the Storm had soused the city, no real progress had been made other than finally pumping the water out. Life had become more about trying to adjust to the insanity rather than improving it, and along the way everything became normal: the missions for generator gas, your dad illegally running a bar and moonshine business, moving metal objects with your mind—all just another day. As was your new best friend being the heir to a Voodoo priestess and your boyfriend being able to turn into a crow.

But whether the city was moving forward or not, we went on with our lives. Isaac's crew fixed our back wall (paid in moonshine), and I taught him how to properly make a roux, and he even worked some of the shifts at the café—for free—because I refused to let it close down. Without being asked, he repaired the kitchen door and hauled crates of illegal booze from Ren's to the bar for my dad. Mac doubled our grocery supply. I think my dad approved of him even before I did. Like I said, the abnormal had become normal.

"Does anyone care about this city?" the DJ asked. "The president? The governor? What about you, Mayor Borges? How are you choosing which people get help? And how much to give them, and when? I guess some things never change, not even at the end of the world."

During the holiday break, between work and family things, the three of us spent our remaining moments at Madam Monvoisin's brothel, which had become a part of our lives just as seamlessly as the magic had. It effortlessly became routine like a new school year did: strange and shiny at first, but almost immediately the everyday. It became our headquarters—our sanctuary from Storm life.

The mansion was dilapidated and without certain amenities, but it had been like that for a long time, which was somehow different for us than if the Storm had taken it down. And with the invisibility spells enabling us to practice magic so freely, the non-amenities were soon fixed one by one with magical solutions—that and Isaac's recovery-worker skills.

And it all became normal too. Well, the new normal.

Mastering our elements. Practicing new spells. Looking for answers about Isaac's mark, which we still couldn't see, but he insisted was there. Isaac refused to do any more séances, and Dee refused to ask her gran about the mark. Needless to say, the list of questions was piling up alarmingly faster than the list of answers.

We spent hours drying herbs, grinding rocks of pink Himalayan salt, and brewing potions, all the while trying to guess what had happened to Adeline and our ancestors postdiary—what kind of lives they'd had. I made an insane timeline with everything we knew about them and the Medici, covering the walls of the little closet room where Adeline's safe was hidden beneath the floor. I even broke into the New Orleans Historical Society and scoured everything they had from the years 1725 to 1750, from tax records to property records to books on historical French architecture to the history of prostitution in the Vieux Carré, but we were no closer to coven members, and no closer to helping Brigitte. And I was certainly no further along finding anything about the Count.

To top it all off, school started back tomorrow, and with the completion of my Sacred Heart exams, my records had transferred from *the* Academy to Ursuline Academy. The only person more nervous than me about it was Isaac.

Not that he'd said anything, but I could tell.

"Is it actually possible that the crime in the city is worse post-Storm than pre-Storm?" the DJ ranted. "Where does the buck stop when it comes to protecting your family after the establishment fails? If you have electricity and if you have telephone service, give ole Bobby a buzz . . . My question to you listeners is this: Is this city making monsters?"

CHAPTER 16
Morning Star

I came straight from the café, the first to arrive at the brothel, and was curled onto the couch, lost in a chapter on Jelly Roll Morton getting his start playing piano in the Storyville bordellos.

A hell of a job for a teenage boy.

While I was gaining an affection for nineteenth-century prostitutes, I wasn't getting any clues that would bring me closer to Cosette's descendant. There wasn't a single, solitary mention of our brothel, as either a business or a residence, in any of the books over the years. It was as if this *magnifique manoir* that had miraculously been spared by every major fire just didn't exist. I wondered if its off-book status had been achieved with bribes or by magic. I'd say in New Orleans there was a fifty-fifty chance. "You are good, Cosette. You are good."

"You know what they say about people who talk to themselves?" Désirée asked, walking in, Isaac in tow.

"That they're geniuses?" I replied, not looking up.

Isaac plopped down next to me, and Désirée went straight to the floor at the coffee table, where her cauldron rested on a portable hearth Isaac had built her.

He pulled the book from my hands. "Still obsessed with hooker fashion?"

"I'm obsessed with these tights," I said, pointing to a picture of a girl who probably wasn't much older than me. She was tawdrily looking at a glass of rye, wearing nothing but a shawl tied toga-style at her right shoulder and black-and-white, vertical-striped tights.

"*Très carnaval,*" he said.

"I know. I love the stripes."

Désirée cleared her throat. "Have you found anything of actual use? *Remember?* Coven members?"

"She's in a mood," Isaac said. "Try not to act too excited when she tells you her news."

"What news?" I looked at Dee.

She ripped apart a bunch of dandelion stalks.

"Hey, what did those herbs do to you?"

She ripped more flowers apart.

"Stop torturing those plants! Wasn't it you who said that all of our intention goes into a spell?" When she still didn't respond, I looked at Isaac.

"Daddy Mayor is in a lot of heat right now with the press, and his publicity team thinks some changes should be made to the Borges household, so the family seems more *relatable*. You know: Morgan spending free time with Habitat, rebuilding poor people's houses. Ana Marie hosting blood drives."

"Uh-huh."

"And Dee . . . gets to change schools."

"*Pfft.* Join the club," I said as she continued to throw things into her pot. "Ursuline will be my fourth school this year, and it's only January. What uptown prepfest was lucky enough to be added to the press release?"

When Dee didn't answer, Isaac said, "Your downtown prepfest."

"*What?*" I sprang up from the couch. "This is amazing!"

"This is not amazing," Dee said. "It's not the plan. The plan is Sacred Heart Preparatory Academy, Oxford, Yale Law, Congress, the Whi—"

"You're coming to school with me?" I dropped to the floor and flung my arms around her shoulders. Her back stiffened. "We'll be just like Adeline and Marassa. I mean, only with no-more-slavery-everyone-has-equal-rights."

"Give me your gris-gris." She held out her hand.

"You can't take back my gris-gris just because I hugged you."

"Both of you."

I slapped my chest, but it was too late. The ribbon untied itself behind my neck and floated into her hand.

"Dee. What comes after Congress?" asked Isaac, willingly handing over his gris-gris.

"The White House, obviously. First female black president."

"You're not going to become the first female black president," I said. She scowled at me, and I slid my arm around her shoulders. "You're going to be the first female black *witch* president."

"Yes, I am."

"I can't believe this is actually happening," I said as she untied the little pouches. "You're really coming with me to the Vampire Catacomb Academy?"

She added a pebble-size stone and sprig of rosemary to each. "Could you try not to be so happy about the dismantling of my future?" She paused, whispered a few words as she retied the bags, and then handed them back to each of us. "Now they should shield your location, should any witches get any magical ideas."

"Dee, it's an offshoot of Ursuline Academy uptown—not exactly slumming it." I slipped the gris-gris back around my neck and tucked it underneath my fuzzy peach sweater.

"It's not part of the plan."

"I'll hold your hand tomorrow."

"I'm glad you're transferring," Isaac said, his eyes on his foot, which was anxiously tapping the floor.

"Why do you care where my education is cultivated?" she asked.

"Because someone will be there with Adele . . ."

"Hey, I'm a pro at transferring schools."

His foot stopped tapping, and he looked up at us. "In case she gets any ideas about breaking the seals."

"What?" I whispered.

"That's a pretty dickish thing to say," Désirée said.

"If Dee's going to spend Monday through Friday there, she deserves to know that you're a possible risk."

My heart felt like it was actually ripped from my chest.

She turned to me. "What is he talking about?"

I barely heard the question as my chest cavity—an open, gaping hole—bled out onto the floor.

"The day of the funeral . . . Adele went to the convent. I found her right outside the attic door."

I looked at Isaac. "You. *Asshole.*"

"Adeeeele?" Dee asked, but my gaze didn't break from his.

A wave of heat rushed through me so strong, it lifted me up.

He crossed his arms. "I'm sorry, I'm doing this for your own good. For the coven's protection."

"No, Isaac," I said, my gaze still unwavering, sparks squeezing from my fists. "You're not doing it for me; you're doing it for *you.* For your own protection."

Désirée turned to me. "It's true? Have you forgotten that the Medici *murdered* Bertrand and Sabine?"

The words felt like daggers lodging between my ribs.

Isaac started to backpedal. "Adele, I'm sorry—"

I turned and walked away, muttering what I really thought about him in French. There was an explosion behind me. Metal hitting glass.

"Shit!" Désirée yelled. "Go stop her before she burns the house down!"

But he didn't. Even Isaac knew better than to come near me.

I'm going to kill him, I thought, walking around and around the endless loops of bricked paths in the backyard, shedding my sweater and fanning out my T-shirt—exposing as much skin as possible to the damp January air. Emotions sizzled out of my pores in waves of steam.

I can't believe Isaac sold me out! I can't believe Désirée knows.

I'd suspected that Isaac was nervous about me going to the school at the convent, but this was low. *Low.*

I circled the triplets' fountain, squeezing my fists. And then turned around and circled it again. If the water wasn't so putrid, I'd have jumped in, anything to cool down my magic-induced body heat.

Breathe, Adele.

I sat on the ledge, the chill from the bricks seeping through my jeans as I stared at the water, focusing on pulling the damp air into my lungs.

This surpasses Isaac's New York abrasiveness.

A small fish broke the surface of the water and dove back through the algae. *How is it surviving in that muck?* Maybe the water had magical properties, like everything else here seemed to have? Maybe our last coven member would be a Water witch? Maybe she'd be able to fix the fountain.

A wave of chills swept over me, and I broke into a sweat, breaking the magic fever.

My chest continued to shake. *Relax, Adele.* Then I realized it wasn't *me* shaking. It was the gentle hum of the medallion. I cupped the talisman in my palm.

It was warm, and it vibrated, kind of like that day in the Tremé when it led me to Brooke's star. Adeline's star. Morning . . . Star.

I jumped up, flipping the necklace over.

The eight-pointed star that nearly covered Adeline's initials had been a gift from Morning Star, the final witch in Adeline's coven. I hovered my right hand over the medallion, and the star slowly turned counterclockwise. And just as easy as it had attached that day I'd found it in the Tremé, it twisted off.

I ran back up to the house.

Even though I'd rather have died than go back into the blue room, I lifted my chin and walked into the parlor.

Isaac looked up, hopeful.

I ignored him, grabbed the framed map from the wall, and set it on the rug in front of the fireplace. "I have a lead on the next coven member."

"Give it up," Désirée said. "I'm not doing the locator spell again."

"Fine, don't."

"Cosette's objects always point to the convent. It's a dead end."

"I'm not looking for Cosette."

She turned to me.

"What do you mean?" Isaac asked.

I held out the star with two fingers, keeping my focus squarely on Dee. "It used to belong to Morning Star's family. Maybe the connection is still there? Maybe we can get to her descendant through it?"

"Nice," said Isaac. "Let's do it."

I knew he was attempting the path to reconciliation, but I refused to look at him.

Désirée joined the circle, only looking at Isaac.

"Well, this energy should make for a great spell," I muttered.

They both ignored me but opened their palms, and we linked hands. When Isaac squeezed, I didn't squeeze back.

This time I was the one who started the chant, altering the words to suit Morning Star.

On the third line, the feather slowly lifted onto its point, standing in the center of Jackson Square, just like it always did. The air in the room, which had felt heavy when we started, now felt weightless, and we continued the chant as if we all might rise from the floor. The map began to vibrate. So did the mirror above the fireplace, and then Désirée's cauldron on the table. The chant turned over twice more, and this time, instead of turning down Chartres, the feather zipped straight through the cathedral, through St. Anthony's Garden and onto Royal Street, sending a rip of energy up my spine. It paused at the corner of Orleans, right in front of the café. We all leaned in. I reflexively squeezed their hands as we chanted the verse, over and over. *Come on.*

In one swooping jerk it skidded a couple inches toward the Marigny and stopped. The energy halted; the room stilled. The spell was over.

Désirée and I leaned closer. "The Rodrigue Studio is on that corner," she said. "And next to that is . . . ?"

My voice was soft. "The Bottom of the Cup Tearoom."

The Daures? One of their customers, maybe? There was always a mélange of mystical types in and out of their doors.

"The place that offered you a job?" Isaac asked.

I nodded. "Yeah, old family friends."

"Looks like someone has a new job," Désirée said, making it sound more like a command than a suggestion, which I didn't like. "Congratulations." She smirked her uptown smirk and turned her back to me, returning to her herbs, now with a gentler, more poised touch. Good ole Dee, cool as an ice cube.

"Do you . . . Do you want to go over there with me?" I asked her.

She plugged in her earbuds. Even though she wanted nothing more than to put the rest of this coven together, it seemed her peevishness at me superseded that.

"I'll go with you," Isaac said.

A disgusted huff expelled from my throat.

CHAPTER 17

Broken Moons

Adele's feet moved down the sidewalk faster than her usual southern tortoise, which still wasn't as quick as my usual New York hare.

I wanted to ask her if she was going to take the job—I knew how sensitive she was about the café staying open—but her posture gave me pause. She'd stuffed her hands into her pockets, as if to ensure that I wouldn't be able to hold one . . . or maybe it was so she didn't accidentally throw a fireball at me.

I touched her arm, she jerked it away, and I instantly regretted everything I'd said back at the brothel. I knew she had this intense guilt over what we did on Halloween night, even if she wouldn't admit it. *Why can't I get her to see that it's misplaced? That she didn't do anything wrong? That they're monsters!* I'd just thought, if she knew Désirée was watching, she wouldn't feel tempted to unlock the door . . . and maybe wouldn't be so guilt ridden and anxious. Now that sounded stupid even in my head. And now I'd started World War Three with the coven.

You're an effing dumbass.

I definitely hadn't intended to start a fight between her and Désirée, especially not the night before their first day of school, where they'd soon be reading Shakespeare under the same roof as that douche-pire and his family. And I sure as hell hadn't wanted to make her this mad at me.

I looked her way. Her jaw was tightly clenched.

Don't do anything. Don't say anything. Just let her cool off.

"So, what's the plan?" I asked, as if I had some disease that physically made words come out of my mouth.

"I don't know. Walk in and ask if anyone's a witch? Or if any of them are descendants of a Native American princess? Or I just give up on Mémé *et* Pépé and their American dream and take the job."

"Hey," I said, pulling her arm.

She stopped but didn't look at me.

"You're *not* giving up on them. I know I didn't know them, but I'm sure they'd want you to be happy, Adele. And being in that place all the time does *not* make you happy."

Her eyes didn't lift from the ground, but she didn't lash out at me either. It felt like a small win. Not wanting to push my luck, I didn't say anything else. My hand went to her back, which stiffened, and we continued to walk.

World Famous

Bottom of the Cup Tearoom

EST. 1929

New Orleans

Psychic Readings

Rust dripped from the blue metal sign, which was shaped like a teacup and saucer and looked retro enough to be in a signage museum. Adele pushed the door open and went ahead without so much as a glance in my direction.

The feeling hit as soon as we crossed the threshold—kind of like when Adele took me to Vodou Pourvoyeur for the first time. Although, the Voodoo shop always felt earthy and warm; this place felt dark and frigid. Not in a scary way, just . . . mystical. A chill swept up my neck as I closed the door behind us.

I rubbed my arms as we passed round black-and-white café tables that were carved like zodiac circles and approached the glass counter, which stretched the width of the shop. Behind it a dark corridor led deep into the back of the house like a tunnel.

An emo-looking guy behind the counter spoke to Adele as we approached. "Clearly we're destined to know each other."

"Ha," she said warmly, "did you ever make it to Arcadian?"

"I did, and you were right: they have stellar old-book smell."

Based on their conversation, it was hard to tell how well they knew each other.

He glanced over her shoulder at me. "And with the barista—the nightwatcher," he said in a tone that made me unsure whether it was friendly or not.

The nightwatcher?

"You two know each other?" Adele asked me.

As I tried to place him, a black cat slowly walked across the glass counter. It rubbed its head on Adele's arm and then jumped up to her shoulder. She didn't even flinch. "Onyx," she said as the cat stretched across her shoulders, getting comfortable.

The guy watched Adele with intense curiosity, and I watched him even more intensely.

"The big brother!" I said, suddenly remembering the Royal Street town house—it had been over a month since that night. I was glad he'd found a job.

Although, the gainful employment had done nothing for the sickly hue of his face. Not that he looked frail—he looked like he could hold his own, and he had the kind of stare that let me know he was keenly aware of everything going on around him, like all the guys I knew back home who spent too much time on the streets. I didn't automatically like him because of it, but it begged a natural sense of respect.

He held out his hand. "Callis."

"Isaac Thompson." His hand was as cold as the room was, but the shake was solid.

Adele turned to me, as if waiting for an explanation.

My eyes bopped between them. "We, uh, met on the street one night . . . after curfew," I said, not wanting to give away his—hopefully former—squatter status.

"It appears that we're both late-night soul-searchers," said Callis, who seemed to appreciate me not calling him out.

She looked at me, her eyebrow raised.

Without words, I tried to convey, *I'll tell you the whole story as soon as we get out of here.*

"Yeah." I laughed. "I'm a pretty hardcore insomniac. How's your sister?"

That got me an even higher raised eyebrow from Adele.

"Great," Callis said. "Now that we've taken up legitimate residence here on Royal Street and have regular meals—"

The tin shelf behind him tipped from the wall so suddenly that there was only enough time for him to jump out of the way as stacks of moon-shaped mugs crashed to the brick floor, along with the shelf.

"Not again," Callis said, bending down to the floor.

We leaned over the counter as he picked up a broken crescent handle.

"This will surely be the one to get me fired."

I whipped to Adele, who scowled and shrugged.

Accidents tended to follow wherever Adele went. Désirée claimed it was because Adele was so emotional, but I had a feeling it was more complicated than that. I spent far more time practicing than Adele did. Something about it all—the magic, the monsters—seemed to take Adele a little longer to believe. *Accept.*

Movement came from the far end of the dark corridor: a young woman, peeking out of a doorway, covering her mouth as if trying not to laugh. But then a man stepped into the hallway, and she disappeared back behind a curtain.

"What was *that*?" he asked, heading our way, kimono billowing behind him.

At the doorway, his hands went straight to his hips, and a smile beamed across his face when he saw Adele. "I knew you'd come today."

Other than the kimono, he looked like just your average guy. Jeans. Mint-green polo, tucked in. Trimmed beard. It was an odd combo, but nothing close to the strangest thing I'd seen on Royal Street, which wasn't even one of the weirder streets of the French Quarter.

Smiling, Adele shook her head with a playful eye roll. "Hi, Mr. Daure."

He leaned over the counter and gripped both of our hands. "And this must be the beau?"

"Is that what your crystal ball told you?" she asked, still playful.

"No, your dad."

Her cheeks went pink, but her tone was cool as she glanced my way. "He's something like that." She didn't even introduce me.

Shit.

The man smiled at me in a way that offered a mutual understanding—sympathy, even. "Chatham Daure," he said. "Pleased to make your acquaintance."

"Isaac Thompson, and likewise."

More handshaking. More obligatory introduction questions. I swear, Adele Le Moyne had more fatherly figures than any girl I'd ever known. Sometimes I felt like I couldn't hold her hand on the street without some guy looking at me funny. Like every dude within a twelve-block radius was in Mac's biker-slash-drag-queen-slash-psychic mafia. And I was pretty sure she had no clue.

He turned back to Adele. "So does this mean you're ready to give the cards a shuffle?"

"*Pfft*. You know I can't read tarot cards."

"No, *you* know you can't read tarot cards. I know you can. What about tea leaves?"

Her head cocked to the side.

"Palms? Crystal balls?"

She smiled.

"Okay, bones! I know you've been hanging out over at the Borges."

"I'll stick to reading books, *merci*. But maybe Isaac should try? His friends call him the Corpse Whisperer."

Before my mouth could gape, another man walked in from the corridor, wearing a matching kimono, tied at the waist. "How morbid," he said. He leaned on Chatham and, in an accent that was southern but not New Orleans, introduced himself as "the other Mr. Daure," and I don't think he meant brother.

"Very morbid," chimed Callis, standing up with a handful of salvaged mugs. He turned to stack them on the back counter but then froze, his gaze locked on my arm. He recovered quickly and carried on stacking.

What the hell was that? I tried to shuffle my sleeve down without drawing attention to it.

"He sees dead people," Adele said.

My back stiffened.

Her face turned to mine, and it very clearly said, *How do you like your secrets being told?* And I felt like a total asshole.

Both Mr. Daures leaned on the counter, eyes on me, nodding as if with understanding.

"Um . . . I . . ."

"Literally," she added. "Dead bodies. He's a recovery worker."

No one laughed or smiled, because it wasn't funny, and she hadn't intended it to be.

"It's not a glamorous job," I said.

They all continued to nod.

Adele began to babble awkwardly, trying to change the subject. I knew she regretted saying it. She wasn't good at being mean.

Mr. Daure number two took my hand and flipped it over, gently stroking my palm. I think he had on some kind of eyeshadow that made his eyelids shimmer. It was barely noticeable unless the light caught it. As he continued to map out my calluses, I became paranoid that he could see everything about my future and thought it wasn't good enough for Adele. But then he looked up at me with a smile that seemed genuine, although sometimes it was hard to tell in the South.

"You're going to fit right in here, Isaac," he said.

That's a good thing . . . right?

"So, Addie," Chatham said, "can you start tomorrow? That's why you're here, isn't it?"

"Um, well, yes, but it looks like you already hired someone." She looked at Callis in a way that implied she would never take his job.

"Didn't I say there's always room for you here, Adele?"

She smiled.

"Plus, you already know Callis. He'll show you the ropes, and you can teach him all about the locals as they trickle back to town." He winked.

"We don't *know* each other. We met once."

"It was a rainy afternoon," Callis said with a slight dramatic flair that fit well with the atmosphere in the shop. "Full of family feuds, poltergeists, and tragic love affairs."

Adele smiled, apparently understanding whatever he was talking about—I had no clue.

"All right," she said. "It's a deal."

"*Shoot.* Welcome to the family," said Chatham, "or should I say, welcome back to the family, darling? It's been so long."

Mr. Daure number two practically pulled her across the counter into a hug, and as all the southerners got caught up in their smiling, another man emerged from a room into the hallway. He slowly made

Alys Arden

his way down the long corridor but stopped a few feet back in the dark hall. His hair was silver and swept behind his ear, and he leaned onto a thick carved stick that had a stringed feather dangling from the top.

"Addie Le Moyne." His voice was gentle yet billowed authority. Everyone looked back. "Don't do it," he said.

"Don't take the job?" she asked.

"Papa!" Chatham said.

He ignored everyone else, speaking directly to Adele. "Don't open the attic, Addie."

What the fuck?

Everyone looked at her to see if she knew what he was talking about. Everyone but me. I knew exactly what he meant.

"Um . . . o-o-kay, Papa Olsin," she stuttered.

"Don't open the attic," he said again.

She stepped against me, and her hand slipped into mine. She didn't say anything else and the old man just stood there in the shadows, shaking his head.

"You'll regret it," he said.

Her fingers crushed mine, and mine tightened around hers. I wanted to grab this guy from the hallway and shake out everything he knew. *What the hell does he know?*

She looked up at me. "I don't know what he's talking about."

"Oh, honey," said Daure number two. "Don't let that ole queen shake ya. But in the meantime, stay clear of attics. You know Papa when he gets his knickers in a twist."

"We . . . we don't even have an attic anymore. It's my bedroom now."

The two Mr. Daures looked at her lovingly, like maybe she didn't get what he was trying to tell her now but one day she'd figure it out.

Oh, she knows, I wanted to tell them.

In the lingering silence, an ambient rush of waterfalls and chirping birds piped through the speakers.

194

Adele shifted her weight.

Finally, Callis cleared his throat. "Isaac, do you think your boss would take one more on his crew? I love it here, but I could double up."

"Yeah, probably," I said, nodding.

I let go of Adele's hand, grabbed a pen and business card from the counter, and scribbled down an address. "Come talk to AJ tomorrow morning. Four thirty. He hates it when people are late."

I turned back to Adele, focusing all of my energy on keeping my expression neutral rather than staring daggers at her. "We should go."

"What the hell?" I yelled as soon as we turned the street corner. I paced ahead, then turned back around. "What the hell, Adele? You're going to open the attic?"

She folded her arms across her chest. "You cannot be *serious?*"

"How does that guy even know about the attic? Maybe I was right to tell Désirée about your little field trip! Maybe I should warn everyone in the entire administration that their lives are in danger?"

"You believe that old quack? You don't even know him!"

"Maybe you should try believing a little more! Maybe then the attic would never have been opened in the first place! Maybe you'd be further along with your magic!" Before I even finished the words, I regretted saying them. I'd gone too far.

She didn't say anything, but if looks could kill, I'd be fried.

I wanted to take it back—to apologize—and she stood there a moment, as if giving me the chance to, but I didn't. I was too pissed off.

"Believe whatever you want, Isaac. Clearly you don't believe in me."

"Adele." I tried to grab her arm as she walked past me, but she yanked it away, hurrying along.

"Adele, I'm sor—"

She turned around, waiting for it, and for some God-only-knows reason, my apology morphed into a question instead: "Is that really why you want to put the coven together? To open the attic? To save Nicco?"

She shook her head. "I'm not the one obsessed with the attic, Isaac. You are. *You're* obsessed with Nicco. Not me."

CHAPTER 18
Floating Kisses

The tip of my pencil snapped on the paper.

Instead of sharpening it, I set the sketch pad aside and pulled out a crate of wood scraps from underneath the bottom bunk—pieces I'd salvaged over the last couple weeks.

I chose a stick and flipped it in my hand a couple times, deciding which end would be best to work on, and then started whittling with a knife Mac had loaned me.

Hours had gone by since we left the tearoom, and I was still just as angry. I'd run five miles—all the way to *the bridge* and back. I'd done push-ups. Curl-ups on the bar in the doorway. Sit-ups. Had a hot shower. Then a cold shower. Nothing was helping. No matter what activity I forced myself into, all I thought about were the things I'd said to Adele.

Worse, like a reel stuck on repeat, I kept imagining her opening the attic, letting him out.

I pressed my thumb against the tip of the stake and, with very little pressure, drew blood. Sharp enough. I thought about the amount of strength it would actually take to force it through something. *Someone.*

My stake collection was no different than Désirée upgrading the invisibility spell at the brothel or enhancing our gris-gris. I just wanted to be prepared.

Failing to plan is planning to fail, as my pop would say.

I tossed it back into the crate with the others and grabbed another scrap of wood.

Six fresh stakes later, the stainless steel room smelled of cedar, and I was still thinking about Nicco. I dropped the knife into the crate and lay back on the bottom bunk, trying to think about Adele instead.

I liked all of our firsts. First text. First date. First kiss. First art lesson. First . . . other things. But I *did not* like our first real fight.

This. Sucks.

I pushed aside the threaded bracelets covering my watch. It was after one. I had to be up in three hours for work. With a sigh, I moved to the top bunk and grabbed the copy of *The Shining* from under the pillow. If Jack Torrance couldn't take my mind off Adele, nothing could. Even if it was Adele's book.

The water twists, turning us.

Her arms are so tight around my neck, I can barely breathe, but the only thing I fear more than the water is her losing her grip. My head breaks the surface, and I gasp so hard I suck in a mouthful of water along with the air.

"Don't let go!" I choke out as a wave crashes over us again, pushing us faster down the street. My left hand clutches her left ankle as her little body clings around my back. We pummel past a truck, my right hand slapping for it as we bounce against the metal. But it's too slippery. Just before the water sweeps us out of reach, I grab on to the tailgate, and we jerk to a stop. My fingers refuse to let go. With one last burst of strength, I haul us up, one foot digging into the bumper, and fling us up into the bed of the truck.

"It's okay," I say, sloshing through the water on all fours. "It's okay."

I stand up, the little girl still on my back, and lean on the cabin. The truck bobs up and down with the waves. Her knees feel permanently lodged into my ribs.

Wheezing, I try to suck in big breaths. I pry her arms from around my neck and let her drop down to the watery truck bed, the need for air suddenly outweighing everything else.

She clings to my leg, screaming, and her fear ripples through me. Still panting, and my arms still like jelly, I lift her back up, but I can't comfort her. I can only hold her, gripping the top of the truck cabin as I choke up brown water.

The truck rocks back and forth, waves sloshing over the sides.

The big rushing waves are over, but now the water is slowly rising. In every direction, there's floodwater for miles—in between the rows of houses and shops and trees and floating cars. A gash bleeds steadily down my arm. A dog barks nearby, and I move to the side of the truck, searching for her in the debris. The high-pitched yelps grow closer, and the little girl in my arms screams louder, just one word, over and over again.

"Jade! Jade!"

Gasping. Choking. Drowning.

No—falling.

Shit.

I grabbed on to the edge of the bed, managing to get one foot on the floor before crashing down, my chest pounding, lungs gasping. The cool stainless steel frame in my hand felt like the edge of the truck.

I exhaled loudly, heart racing. *It was more than four months ago, Isaac. Get a grip.*

I checked my phone, not that I thought Adele would've responded in the middle of the night.

My last three messages stared back at me. Read, but unresponded to.

Isaac	23:13	Please, just talk to me so I can apologize.
Isaac	0:17	If I could write a spell that would let me start the day over, I'd do everything differently, I swear.
Isaac	0:45	I'll fix this, I promise. Sweet dreams.

I grabbed a towel from a hook on the wall, wiped away the nightmare sweats, and stretched a plain white shirt over my head. There was no point in getting back into the bed. The chance of falling asleep again was already slim, thanks to drowning little girls slipping from my arms in my nightmares. With the fight now on my mind as well, there was no chance in hell. I hated that bed. I hated this little metal box.

And for the first time since I'd been in New Orleans, I missed home. Home in Brooklyn, where my mattress didn't poke into my back, and where hissing steam from the radiator made everything warm and hummed me to sleep. I swung my arms, which were still sore from the anger workout.

The anger had been replaced with regret, and now that I was thinking more clearly, I just wanted to go back in time and punch that psychic in the nose, and not yell at Adele.

The worst part was that I was still worried about what he'd said—about her opening the attic. I laughed out loud, rubbing my face. Only a dope wrecks the best thing in the world because of a stranger's crazy predictions. *Christ.*

I wedged into my sneakers and pulled my wool cap over my head. There was only one girl who would still want to see me at this hour, and I didn't feel bad about waking her up. She could sleep all day.

In the pitch-black park, I hurled the ball as far as I could, and Stormy bolted off after it. I was glad she could see it, because I sure as shit couldn't.

She raced back, gleefully bouncing up and down, ball in mouth, like she was playing in some white-picket-fenced, sunshine-drenched, petunia-filled yard. In reality, she was just a lonely, mangy-furred mutt in a condemned neighborhood. She playfully tried to keep the ball from me, but I grabbed it from her mouth and threw it again.

My phone vibrated in my pocket—I pulled it out so fast I nearly dropped it.

I sighed when I saw the name. Désirée. *I swear, that girl never sleeps either.*

Dee	**02:07**	I still think we should just go back to the cemetery and ask Marassa about ur mark.

The message was only to me, not the group. *Not a good sign.* The only things Dee and I ever texted about were logistics for a meet-up, or political news—keeping the other informed of tidbits heard about our pops, like each other's personal *HuffPo*'s. Magic, and pretty much everything else, was reserved for the group chat.

Great, now I've ruined the coven.

I slipped the phone back into my pocket without responding and pulled the wool cap farther down my head, covering my ears. *And Adele is never going to speak to me again, so, Nicco wins. Even trapped in an attic and unconscious, Nicco wins.*

Stormy brought the ball back. I threw it again and then sat on a scraggly patch of grass, trying to imagine what the park would have looked like before the Storm. Metal pilings stuck out of a sad plot of Astroturf covered in mud. Clearly it had been some kind of playground before, but now it was just a hazard. The trees were dead and the grass was dead, all drowned in the Storm. Springs of green weeds, like little breaths of Mother Nature, popped up here and there in between all of the trash—the rotten clothes, books, toys, and random belongings that had floated away from people's homes forever. A Monopoly board was wedged into a nearby tree like an axe, and the rusted frame of an overturned car lay where a slide might have been in another lifetime.

Stormy got in my face, sniffing and licking, her mood unaffected by the destitution.

"Adele's going to come around, right girl?" I pushed her down, but it only riled her up more; she thought it was a game. "She can't stay mad at me forever, can she?"

Her head bent to the ground, and a low growl rumbled from her throat, building to an aggressive yap.

I laughed. "Don't worry, girl, there's room in my life for the two of you."

But she growled again, followed by a string of high-pitched barks directed over my shoulder.

Snickers burst out from behind me, and I sprang up, twisting around.

"You escape from Charity during the Storm or sumthin?" said a girl whose enormous gold hoop earrings bobbed when she spoke.

The two guys with her laughed. One was skinny and the other fat with a black bandana tied into a band around his bald head. Stormy barked even louder.

"Shhhhh," I said, trying to calm her down.

When I glanced back up, the barrel of a baseball bat was only inches from my face. The fat guy glared down its length. "Whuddyou say to me?"

"What? I was talking to the dog."

"You calling my girl a dog?"

"Come on, man," I said, "don't be a dick. I don't want any trouble."

Stormy went full on at the big one, growling and barking. I lunged for her just as he brought the bat down over my shoulder, missing me entirely. It smashed the ground, kicking up dirt. I scooped Stormy up and took off running to the park entrance, all three of them coming after me. I could have sped ahead easily if Stormy wasn't twisting around in my arms, barking and trying to jump away to attack.

I flicked a tiny gust, inconspicuous enough, and the park fence swung open as we tore through. Out on the dark street, I hauled ass. Glancing back over my shoulder, I saw the skinny one grab the bat and charge ahead of the others. I just needed to gain a long-enough lead so I could duck around a corner and take crow form.

A slew of profanity and threats came from my pursuer, who was now swinging the bat over his head. "Now you're screwed!"

When I faced forward, glints of the chain-link fence came into view—it was at least fifteen feet high. *Fuck.*

Instinct was to launch myself at it full speed. I knew I could climb it faster and get away. I doubt he'd even bother. But that wasn't an option. There was no way I was leaving Stormy behind.

My sneakers slid on the gravel as I turned on my heel and sprinted back the way I came, toward the guy. The other two were not far behind him, catching up. He swung the bat, but I dodged it and peeled off into an alley.

"That's another dead end, genius!" yelled the girl.

"Stormy, you better be ready to book it," I said, releasing her onto the ground. As soon as her toes hit the street, my wings were spreading into the air, and I was flapping higher, to the back of the alley. I made one long swoop around a dumpster and zoomed back the way we came. Stormy charged along beneath me, right past the thugs.

"Where'd he go?" the girl yelled.

A crash came, which I could only presume was the bat smashing into the metal dumpster.

A part of me wanted to blow them into the river, but instead I pulled up a gust and rode the current away, flying low enough for Stormy to follow.

She ran below me all the way to the train tracks, but then, as usual, she stopped. I'd hoped that maybe she'd follow me this time, since I was in animal form, but that girl wasn't going to leave the Bywater any more than the Mets were going to win the World Series.

By the time I sailed into the Quarter, the adrenaline spike was starting to crash and I was entering 0300 hour exhaustion, but I flew past the convent, past the Voodoo shop, and Mac's bar, which was still secretly bumping, and then past the brothel. I made the complete rounds, only to feel justified swooping down her street. If I checked on her too—it was just routine.

You're not staying, I told myself.

But then my claws touched the cool iron, wrapping around the balcony rail across the street, and I could *see* her. Tonight the shade and the curtain were drawn open at the window near the piano, and her head was on the sill, nestled into her arms. A tea light, with a tiny flame, was next to her face. I took a mental shot of the image, as it begged to be immortalized on a page in my sketchbook.

I soared across the street and landed on the window ledge, the flutter of my feathers causing her to stir. She sat up with sleepy eyes and reached for the window, raising it halfway.

She's letting me in.

Pulse thumping, I hopped through and swooped down to the ground. Never in my life had I been scared to turn back into human form, but in that moment I was.

I felt every second of it as I grew taller and her gaze moved up to meet mine, all of her attention on me as she stood in the moonlight, barefoot and bare legged, in a T-shirt so perfectly thin I could see the curve of her waist and her bare breasts through it.

I didn't know where to look, and suddenly I couldn't remember all the things I wanted to say, and—

"I was trying to wait up for you," she said.

My gaze finally met hers. "What do you mean?" I wanted to move closer, to touch her waist, but wasn't sure if she wanted me to.

"Isaac, I know that you always perch on the balcony across the street around two. You're late."

"Oh . . ." My throat went dry. "Not the greatest night." Her eyes were puffy—she'd been crying, and that made my voice crack. "I'm *so* sorry, Adele." I forgot to think, and I touched her arm. "I'm so, so sorry."

She leaned in, letting me pull her close; she just stood there, not exactly reciprocating but letting me hold her against my chest.

"I don't know what I was thinking telling Dee about the attic. Please, *please* don't think you can't trust me. You can, I swear."

I held her a bit tighter and stroked her hair.

"Actually . . . I do know what I was thinking . . . I can't stop imagining you around the attic all the time at school, the convent becoming more and more familiar, like a second home, where he's so close to you and I'm not." I couldn't believe I'd said it out loud—that I admitted it to her.

She broke away, just enough to look up at me. "Do you really believe I'm going to open the attic to save Nicco?"

"No . . ."

"Because *you* didn't stop me from opening the attic that day. I stopped myself. And I'm not going to let you punish me for something I didn't even do."

"I'm not trying to punish you—I know I wasn't the one who stopped you." I wrapped my arms around her again, and she rested her head on my shoulder. "I don't think you're going to open the attic to save him."

I don't know what I believed about the attic, but I believed in her, and I needed her to know that.

Her voice was small when she finally spoke. "Do you really think I'm bad at magic?"

"Jesus, no." *Fucking moron, Isaac. What were you thinking?* "You're awesome at magic. Your magic kicks my magic's ass."

"Yeah, right," she scoffed.

"If you want to know a secret—and if you ever tell Dee I said this, I'll lie and deny it—I think your natural magical ability drives her nuts."

"You're so full of it. You guys are *insanely* better than me."

"Yeah, because we practice *all* the time." I pulled her away and looked her in the eye so she could see how much I meant it. "You don't even need to practice. You just *are* good."

She blushed. It was true, even if she didn't want to admit it. And that's one of the reasons she's so incredible—she hadn't even noticed that she's better than us in any way. She smiled, and I knew she was considering it.

My hand slipped underneath her jaw, and I kissed her, softly, my lips barely touching hers. It was only when she kissed me back that the piano-size anvil lifted from my shoulders.

Her hands moved up my chest, her nose bumping mine. "I . . . I don't want to fight."

"Me neither." The words came out a whisper, but I meant it more than anything. Her arms circled around my neck, and I kissed her less gently, reaching one arm out behind her to shut her window.

"Wait!" She broke away, tensing up. "You can't stay the night."

"Oh . . . I thought. It's just . . . it's so late." I kissed her again. "It's after three . . ."

And even though she kissed me back, I could feel her pulling away, so I stopped. I tightened my arms but rested my forehead against hers. "What's the difference? I have to be at work in a couple hours."

She smirked. "You cannot stay the night if you want to be my boyfriend for more than the next couple of hours."

When the subsequent pause became too long, she looked up, catching me. "Why are you so smiley?"

"That's the first time you've ever called me your boyfriend." I buried my face beneath her hair, my lips brushing her neck, embarrassed for her to see how much it pleased me.

"No, it's not," she barely managed to say as I let each kiss linger.

"It most definitely is." My lips nipped her earlobe, and her body pressed deeper into mine. When my arms slid around her, accidentally hiking the thin T-shirt up over her stomach, she didn't seem to care about tugging it down.

She pulled my face back to hers and kissed me with a need that I wanted to feel forever.

I told myself that the next time I felt the need to mouth off about the attic, I'd remember the flowery taste of chamomile tea on her lips, and the scent of the sophisticated French perfume that always lingered in her hair, and the way her Fire-magic fingers tingled against my skin.

How I wanted her more than I knew I could.

I slowly pulled in a draft through the window until the posters on her walls lightly rustled around us.

"Oh my God!" Her arms locked around my neck, gripping me tight as the air whirled, taking us up.

"Just relax," I whispered. "I've got you." Her heart raced against my chest through that perfectly thin T-shirt. "I'll never let you fall."

She nodded and relaxed, letting my magic support some of her weight. I kissed her softly, and as she became more confident in the air, she kissed me more passionately, tightening her arms and pulling herself closer. As my hands roamed over her hips, her back arched, and I kissed her harder, all several feet above the floor in a swirl of air and magic.

I'd never let her go.

CHAPTER 19

The Corpse Whisperer Strikes Again

January 3rd

"Isaac . . . ?"

My nose was cold.

"Isaac?"

I snapped awake. A figure, dark against the winter sky, stepped back, as if I might have a physical reaction to being woken up. Callis. *Smart guy.*

"Hey," I said, blinking my phone on: 0425 hours.

I'd only been asleep for twenty-one minutes, but it felt like I was coming out of a deep hibernation.

After having to book it out of Adele's window when Mac came home earlier than usual, I'd gone home to change but hadn't dared to sit on my bed out of fear of falling asleep and not waking up. So I came straight to the house we were starting today and must have crashed out on the porch.

"Rough night?" Callis asked.

"Started out that way. Got better." I knew I was smiling too hard as I rubbed my eyes, but I was way too tired to stop it.

"Nice," he said, sitting next to me on the step, lightly hitting my shoulder. Some kind of universal bro-code of approval.

Not *getting-laid* nice, I wanted to say, but I didn't. I mean, he was going to be working with my girlfriend; he didn't need to know about her private life. I adjusted the wool cap to cover my ears, feeling strangely territorial.

"I hear we got fresh blood this morning?" a voice boomed.

We walked down to the street. "AJ, meet Callis. Callis, AJ."

As they shook hands, I stretched, trying to wake up. I hoped the dark would work in Callis's favor, and that AJ wouldn't see how sickly he looked. Although, I didn't think Habitat or FEMA would turn anyone down; they were so desperate for able bodies.

"You ever lifted a hammer?" AJ asked.

"I've got some experience with electrical, but I'm guessing that won't come in too handy right now."

"If you can spell electrical, that's more experience than some of the kids I've got. Shadow Isaac today. Then hang around afterwards to fill out paperwork."

The rest of the crew rolled up together in Brett's truck. Chase and Jory jumped out of the bed before the engine was cut.

After I introduced Callis, Betsy volunteered to unload the tools, which she often did to avoid "the run." I didn't blame her. The run was always the worst on day one, and this one was fresh.

Fresh like a zombie.

I pulled the bandana from my pocket and almost offered it to Callis, but my stomach twitched at the thought of what was about to come. *Everyone has to learn the hard way.* Not that a square of fabric really did anything for you on day one. Nothing could shield you from the smell of the putrid rot.

I tied it around my face, looking at the house, more like a Victorian mansion. It was the last one on a block we'd been working on for weeks; it sat on the end, facing out toward the river.

"If you puke," Jory said to Callis, "vacate the house so it doesn't start a chain reaction." He slapped his back and ran for the door.

"What?"

"Godspeed," I said, and took off running with others.

I glanced at the *X* on the exterior as we stepped inside:

8-18 / #41 / 0 / 0

Searched on August 18th by crew 41. No people, animals, or bodies were found.

Six steps in, my hands went to my knees, and the coughs came in waves of three. The key was not to linger, even when your body rejected pressing forward. I clamped my jaw shut. It became mind over matter as I forced myself deeper into the smell of decomposition, the odors so thick I could almost feel them on my fingertips and taste them on my tongue. An amuse-bouche of molding textiles, mildewing drywall, and rotting rugs.

The hardest part always came right after the first wave of gagging— I pushed through the near-puking fit and made a mad dash for a window on the other side of the room. I didn't want to seem like a wuss on Callis's first day.

I forced the window up, splintering the wood. A glance behind as I jammed it open showed me that Callis only made it a few feet inside the door. Props to him, though; most firsties don't make it in without running straight back out. *And he's not even puking yet. We've never had a first timer who didn't puke.*

He ran over and shoved his head out the window next to mine, and we sucked up the damp winter air from the courtyard.

"You can thank me later," I said.

"I—I am thankful. At least it's a job."

I didn't puke, and neither did he. He twitched and coughed and made a teeny gagging sound, but he didn't puke, and nothing could have impressed the team more. He was officially one of us.

AJ and Chase took the bottom floor, where the water had sat the longest. Betsy and Brett took the second floor, which would be the easiest as far as damage went. That left me, Callis, and Jory on the top floor, where most of the damage was due to half the roof being blown off.

I was extra careful as I tore things away, trying to preserve as much as possible. The house seemed like it had been a beauty in its day.

Callis did everything exactly as I showed him. I could tell he didn't want to mess up this gig; at the rate he was going, he had nothing to worry about.

The dim, shadowy house reminded me of the night we first met, and how weird his sister had looked . . . as pale as a vampire.

I glanced over at him as we worked side by side in the master bedroom, prying the last of the molding from the back wall.

What if he didn't throw up because *he doesn't need to eat?*

Once the unsettling idea was in my head, I couldn't focus on anything else.

Callis removed the last of the baseboards and picked up a sledgehammer. I stepped back as he began ripping the plaster away.

Could there be new vampires in town? The crime rate in the city was still astronomical after all. *What if I just put my entire crew's lives in danger? And Adele's too?*

I waited until Jory left for a smoke, then jammed my hand over the sharp edge of a piece of cracked molding. "Dammit!"

"Are you okay?" Callis yelled over the sound of power tools below us.

This was a stupid idea, Isaac. I squatted and squeezed my hand. The blood dripped to the floor.

Too late now.

His head turned my way, and our eyes locked, the sledgehammer still in his right hand. I lifted the cuff of my jeans, ready to yank the stake from my boot.

"You're bleeding," he said, stepping toward me. My back stiffened, but then he moved past me to a dresser. He opened and shut a few drawers and then removed a ball of socks. "I'm sure they can spare a pair," he said, pulling them apart.

He wrapped one sock around my hand, tying it tight. "You might want to get some disinfectant on that, pronto. This place is like a petri dish of disease."

"Yeah," I said, sucking in a big breath of air.

For the next few hours, Callis, Jory, and I carefully attacked bedroom after bedroom, the three of us synced in a destructive dance that left us each covered in sweat and plaster dust and mold specks.

I worked until I couldn't stand the itchy feeling from the insulation anymore; then I grabbed my knapsack and headed for the bathroom.

The room was narrow and dark except for a bright trail of sunlight from the single window at the far end, above the toilet. It was just enough to see the coating of destruction dust covering everything: the tiled floor, the bathtub, and even the pale-pink shower curtain. It was inescapable.

I pulled off my wool cap, shook out my hair, and turned on the faucet to let the water run clean while I retrieved the bar of soap and towel from my bag.

The sink turned black as I washed the grime off my arms and neck. I carefully splashed my face. It would be unfortunate to survive drowning in a levee breach, countless looter scuffles, and a vampire attack, only to bite it from a microscopic, brain-eating amoeba living in the Louisiana water supply.

As I dried off, I glanced in the mirror and froze. Letters were smudged into the thin layer of dust.

ANIMARUM
PRAEDATOR

A chill kissed the wet droplets resting on the back of my neck. I shook it off. Jory's musings, no doubt. I nearly yelled to him about it, but I lacked the energy for whatever philosophical rant he was on thanks to this week's lesson on Nietzsche.

I stuffed the damp towel back into my bag, glancing at the words one more time. My sweat-soaked T-shirt suddenly felt chilled.

"*Isaac.*" A quick whisper passed my ear.

"Funny, Jory."

The temperature dropped again.

"*Isaac . . .*" The sound of my name tickled over the back of my neck. I whirled around. There was no one else in the room.

What the hell?

I hurried back out into the master bedroom, trying to wipe the look of fear from my face.

"Lunch break?" Jory asked, and tossed me a PB&J.

I caught it and tossed it back. "No, thanks."

"*Isaac . . .*" I swatted at my right ear, as if I could knock it away.

A draft, noticeably warmer, blew open the curtains and funneled directly toward me, blowing away the sound, wrapping around me like a protective blanket.

An odd sensation pulsed underneath my skin at my wrist, like little lightning bolts. I pushed up my sleeve, but the mark didn't look any different. I turned and headed for the stairs.

"There he goes!" Jory said to Callis. "Let's go."

"Go where?" Callis asked as they both quickly caught up.

I took the stairs fast, and so did they.

"Oh Lord," Betsy chimed as I landed on the second floor. She followed behind as I crossed the hall to the next set of stairs. "That boy is special, I tell ya. He talks to angels."

"How do you know they're not demons?" Jory asked.

I took the steps faster—I had to catch up with the cold.

"Oh Jesus," AJ said when I got downstairs to the living room, where all the wall beams were now exposed.

I looked back through a cloud of plaster dust. He and Chase were putting down their tools.

I made the turns like the house was my own. Down a hall, through a kitchen full of blown-out windows that overlooked a backyard full of bricks and ivy. Glass crunched underneath my feet as I crossed to the back door.

The sun grew brighter as I pushed past banana-tree leaves and overgrown ferns, fearing I'd lost it.

The whisper whipped behind me. *"Protégez la."*

I glanced over my shoulder, felt the cement edge under my foot, and teetered, arms flailing, over the edge of a pool so thick with algae and plant sludge that it looked solid. There was no time to do anything but hold my breath before I submerged in toxic-looking slime.

"I've got you!" Callis grabbed my collar and pulled me so hard I fell backward onto the bricks, scraping my palms.

Now at ground level, I saw her.

Spirals of greenish-blond hair floated around her head like a halo. Her skin was stained with algae, and her light-blue dress ballooned at the surface of the water.

Footsteps shuffled behind us, and Betsy was already muttering prayers under her breath. I didn't have to turn around to know Brett was making the sign of the cross.

Callis stared at the body, shocked but completely silent. He looked at me, and then back to the body, and then back to me.

"Welcome to the crew," I said.

"I guess Adele was serious when she said your friends call you the Corpse Whisperer."

I didn't say anything else.

He offered his hand and pulled me to my feet. "How often does this happen?"

"Too often," I said, suppressing a wave of nausea. I shielded my eyes as a cloud shifted and the sun beat down on the pond. The girl's shiny black shoes, just breaking the surface of the green water, glistened. I frowned. "But this one is different. Look at those shoes . . . There's no way that girl's been in there since the Storm."

AJ's two-way bleeped. "You might want to get NOPD down here for this one," he said, confirming my suspicions. This was no Storm victim. I thought about the thugs last night, about all the recent crime reports, and about Adele and Dee walking around the Quarter alone. We weren't that far away.

When I turned back to Callis, he was staring at my left arm. "Something wrong?" I asked.

"No . . ." His eyes slid down to my wound; the bandage had fallen off sometime in the ordeal. "How's your hand?"

My stare hardened. "Just another day at the office." There was something about the way he was looking at me that I didn't like.

He turned to the body like he was trying to swallow a smile and then looked back at me. "I'm sorry if I seem excitable. It's just that I've mostly been hanging out with a nine-year-old for the past couple months."

Suddenly we were back to that night at the hotel, and I felt like I was unnecessarily intimidating him.

I grabbed his shoulder. "Man, I'm going to have to get you out of the house more often."

"That's exactly what I was thinking." He smiled.

By the time D-MORT arrived and then left—claiming that crime scenes weren't their protocol—most of the crew had already packed up and left. Only AJ and I had stuck around waiting. And Callis was filling out his paperwork.

I sat on a brick step near the pool of algae sludge. Even though it was ridiculous, I felt the need to watch over her—*protégez la*. I could barely even pronounce the two words, but they'd been seared into my memory the night of the séance. I imagined Adele floating face-first in the pool. *Protect her.*

Protect who?

I thought about that psychic and the attic. "You'll regret it," he'd said to Adele. *Protégez la. Protect Adele?*

"AJ, where y'at?"

When I looked up, I saw Detective Matthews entering the court-yard. NOPD was finally here, which turned out to mean just Detective Matthews and his partner.

They rolled out the yellow tape and fished the girl out with the same stick they used to scoop leaves from the pool, because they had no idea how long it'd take forensics to arrive. They zipped and catalogued her and left the body bag at the side of the pool, next to a cement cherub riding a water-spitting dolphin.

And then that was all I could take. I had to get the hell out of there.

I hurried upstairs to the third-floor bedroom, grabbed my bag, and started back down. When I got to the second floor, Callis was coming out of a room with a bounce in his step.

My old grief counselor's voice ticked in my head: *Everyone handles tragedy differently.*

I hooked my arm around his shoulder as we went to the last set of stairs. "I think you must have been a coroner in another lifetime. Or a mortician or something. I've never seen someone so chill after finding a dead body."

"Maybe," he said with a sly smile. "I'm not sure how much I believe in other lifetimes." He turned to me. "And I owe you a thanks, Isaac, for giving me a chance. I think you'll find that we're not so different, you and I."

"No worries," I said, trying to imagine myself wearing black nail polish.

When we got to the bottom, he headed to the front door. "Job number two calls."

I nodded, and he was out. I did one last loop back to tell AJ I was bouncing.

The courtyard was now swarming. More cops, National Guard. The woman from D-MORT was back, arguing with one of the detectives about who was responsible for taking the body.

"What the hell is going on in this city?" AJ asked Detective Matthews, who he'd cornered near the pool. AJ was a retired Miami cop, so he was used to both crime scenes and storms. He still worked the beat some nights as a reserve; he liked to feel involved.

Matthews shrugged, the exhaustion showing on his face. "This new crime wave is like nothing I've ever seen before. Record violent-crime arrests in the last two months. No profiles . . . The only pattern seems to be the number of first-time offenders—it's mind-blowing. People got nothing to lose."

"Any progress on the Leecher?" AJ asked. I hung back a sec, waiting for the answer.

"No new victims in over two months. Not enough resources to keep on cold cases."

Leecher was the name the media gave the post-Storm "serial killer." I was too tired to not roll my eyes. I butted in. "See you tomorrow, AJ."

Matthews caught my eye. "You the one who found this body?"

"No, the whole crew was here." That wasn't exactly true, but Robbie Lombardo, one of my guys back in Brooklyn, always said never drop your name near a cop.

"You look familiar," he said, taking a step closer.

I shrugged.

"Aren't you the guy who's been hanging around Mac's daughter?"

"So?"

"You kids have some kind of thing for dead bodies?"

"You look familiar too. From Mac's bar?" On more than one occasion, I'd helped Mac carry him to a bed in a back room after one too many moonshines. I wouldn't normally be so brazen with a cop, but this one got on my nerves. I hadn't forgotten how quickly he'd suspected Adele of *homicide* at the Wolfman's crime scene last fall.

His stare hardened, and I knew I was about to get the "You better treat her good or else" speech for the millionth time.

"Watch out for that one," he said, instead. "I've been a cop for a long time, and something tells me she's not all that she seems. Like her ma."

My arms crossed. *What the hell is that supposed to mean?*

"Maybe that's what I like about her." I lifted my arm overhead as if to stretch, and a breeze whipped through, spattering the algae-infested sludge from the pool all over the detective's suit.

"Messy job," I said, trying not to smirk as he swore up and down the length of the pool.

When I stepped out the front door, the paparazzi were there waiting like vultures. One jerkoff was scaling a pole to the gallery. *Fucking media.*

"Private property," I said, and yanked his ankle.

He fell back down, but I caught him by the collar.

"All right!" he said, putting his hands in the air.

Chill out, Isaac, before he puts his camera in your face.

I walked away, threw down my board, and kicked off, thinking about asshole reporters, and asshole detectives—*what the hell had he meant about Adele's mom?*—but mostly I thought about dead bodies as I rolled down the shitty road.

I pushed off a few more times and fabricated an air current to give me an extra boost.

After I'd found the first few corpses on site, I thought I just had really bad luck. We all knew that every time we started a new home, finding a body was a possibility. I knew firsthand that the priority for first responders had been people who were still in need of rescue, not the dead.

Then I realized that a gentle breeze always swept through a house just before I found a corpse. At first I'd just assumed it was my Air magic, but now I realized there were other factors guiding me to the dead bodies as if I were following the threads of invisible cobwebs.

Like the cold.

And now there were the whispers—at the cemetery and again today at the house.

Something had whispered my name . . .

CHAPTER 20

Vampire Catacomb Academy

I stood on the street across from the convent, overlooking the imposing concrete wall into Medici territory. *Why did I get here so early?* Especially considering how much I'd been dreading the first day of school.

But the longer I'd sat at my vanity in my polyester uniform, the more nervous I'd become, so I ripped the Band-Aid off and walked straight here. Now I wished I'd gone to the café first instead.

Because now I was standing in the exact spot I'd stood calling 9-1-1 to report the man with the blue eyes' body.

Right before I accidentally broke the enchanted seal.

Even now, the metal pulled me—not in a way that was tempting, but with a slight tingle of energy, making me acutely aware that I had some kind of connection to it.

I tried to ignore it, instead focusing on how swollen my lips felt, and how the skin on my neck felt a tiny bit raw from Isaac's unshaven face. The slight sensation gave him an ever-presence, instantly making me feel calmer about walking into this place.

I was surprised by how much the fight with Isaac had affected me, and equally surprised by how eager I'd been to let it all go. I think I'd been waiting for it. Deep down, I knew he'd been a ticking time bomb ever since that day at the attic. In a way it felt good to have one less secret out there in the world. Brigitte's was enough for me.

Now, to just patch up things with Dee.

"Is that Adele Le Moyne?" a familiar voice called out. "My favorite downtown girl?"

I turned to the right. A dusty-haired, bronze-skinned boy was walking toward me from the parking lot.

"Thurston Gregory Van der Veer the third," I said. "My favorite socialite. Fancy running into you here."

We hugged. Annabelle wasn't here to kill me for it, and none of her little shark-swarming minions were here to spy.

This was a step down for a Van der Veer, but I knew he hated going to Sacred Heart as much as I did. Thurston might have lived in one of the biggest mansions on Audubon Place—a cul-de-sac off St. Charles so exclusive I'd never been so privileged as to drive down it—but before the Storm he'd gone to Holy Cross, an old prep school in the Lower Ninth now decimated. Who knew why he went to school so far from uptown; probably something to do with his family's fraternity traditions . . . I was also pretty sure there was one other reason he wanted out of Sacred Heart, and that reason was approaching us now.

"Hey, Adele," Georgie said. He kissed me on the cheek and nodded casually to Thurston.

They avoided each other's gaze, but I could tell they were both beaming from the inside and doing their best to hide it.

"Yo, lab partner!"

We turned toward Esplanade to find another familiar face approaching: Tyrelle Laurent, physics curve popper, one of my fellow displaced juniors, and probably the only person who I think hated the Academy more than I did. Despite him being the heir to one of music's biggest hip-hop fortunes (which also spanned fashion, liquor, and sports teams), I don't think his nouveau-riche-ness was very *accepted* by some of the other kids. Last semester, uptown, Tyrelle would have walked past me for consorting with the establishment elite, but today his outward smile was as big as Georgie's inside smile.

We hugged. The three of them did some kind of bro-bump, and it was clear that things were officially different. It was all so high school normal it almost felt weird.

Then the son of a rapper, the sons of oil tycoons, and the daughter of a bartender crossed the street to the convent together like old friends. And the strangest part was I didn't even wonder, *Whose life is this?* It was mine. Things were going to be different downtown. How could they not?

As we walked through the open gate, I felt it shake with magic. Was it excitement for my return? Susannah Bowen's protection spells? Or was it just my nerves starting to rattle as I entered a new world beneath the vampires?

Looking around the garden, I joked, "Did they bring over the land-scaper from the Academy?"

The boys laughed.

The formerly Storm-ravaged, junglelike labyrinth was now a maze of perfectly sculpted hedges and weed-free brick paths. I'd never been here pre-Storm, so I'd never seen how beautiful the garden could look. A mix of palm trees and banana plants framed the edges of the yard, and in the corner where the main building met the church was an elaborate iron gazebo that caged a giant bell with swirling metalwork—my dad would have loved it.

The ever-present Norwood family magic made me feel like Susannah's spirit was here wandering the school grounds with me. I liked not feeling alone, like someone was watching. Not that I was plan-ning on doing anything stupid, but I'd scared myself that day I came to the attic. Not that I'd ever admit that to Isaac.

There was something ironic about the convent being Nicco's place of eternal slumber and also so strongly bound to Isaac's family magic. I wondered if Isaac hated that or got off on it. *Both, probably.*

A giant white cross topped the center roof gable, and a series of French and Louisiana State flags hung from the pulpit-like balcony above the entrance. Between them was a hand-painted banner that read, **WELCOME STUDENTS**.

My eyes crept up to the shutters, and the lingering memory of yesterday's unsolicited psychic reading made my heart skip.

Control, Adele. You are in control of your powers. Not the other way around.

I hustled inside with the boys.

A red rope hung across the old winding staircase—the route to the attic—indicating it was off-limits. *Symbolic, much?* I almost wondered if Isaac had come this morning and planted it.

The stairs were empty, but the hallways were full of kids. The property, which hadn't functioned as a school since the 1930s, was now full of lonely, wandering teens in mismatched uniforms, hoping to see someone in a familiar plaid. The school had mandated we all wear uniforms, but as a sign of welcoming and compassion, they hadn't demanded specific Ursuline threads. The parents of the new crop of students were the kind who could afford to send their kids to Catholic school but who were also now living in FEMA trailers, trying to figure out how to get their insurance settlements, not how to get new uniform cardigans monogrammed in the post-Storm city.

We walked straight through the hall to another set of doors that led to the backyard, which was also freshly landscaped and looked even more gorgeous than the front. Palm trees and banana-plant leaves hid the bordering concrete wall. Citrus trees filled the spaces between the buildings, dangling lemons, oranges, and limes from branches, despite it being the dead of winter. Combined, it all created a bizarre sense of privacy, a hidden oasis in the middle of the Quarter—the exact opposite feeling I usually got when thinking about the convent and its curses, vampires, and bloody battles. Now I could picture the cloistered nuns in prayer and service, finding a peaceful way of life despite being two blocks from Bourbon.

"Over here," Thurston said, leading us to a patch of grass so green it got me wondering about Susannah's magic, and her love of plants.

He plopped down in the middle of an arc of white marble statues that gleamed blindingly in the morning sun. Their hands were folded in prayer, their chins slightly turned up.

Thurston pulled me down next to him. We'd arrived.

A girl I didn't recognize walked over, but we were wearing the same plaid skirt. I smiled, and she joined us, tension vaporizing from her shoulders—her worry that she wouldn't know anyone and would have to eat lunch by herself, that she'd be the "new girl loser." Basically, the worry that she'd be *me*. Or maybe it was the old me?

With a thankful smile, she dove straight into the conversation Thurston, Tyrelle, and Georgie were having about an upcoming Saints game; I gazed around the yard. Two by two and then by threes and fours, people matched themselves up, plaid to plaid. Kids that might never have spoken to each other at their previous schools were now hugging, and the strays found each other with awkward waves and shy hellos, but with the same look of relief, to have found *someone*.

I was in a mutt coven, and now I was at a mutt school.

Heads turned toward the entrance—my back tensed as Désirée walked into the courtyard, kicking up whispers about the mayor being her father and a couple of low wolf whistles from an obnoxious group of guys near the door.

Suddenly every cold look or harsh thing she'd ever said to me echoed in my head, out of fear that we were about to be back there.

Should I have even sat here with her friends, knowing she's mad at me? Did I just make a bitch-move without even realizing it?

Just as the anxiety rushed me, the rules of high school social hierarchy relieved it. Her long legs strode straight to the group, whose hellos she hardly acknowledged, and she sat down next to me just like we hadn't gotten into an epic fight yesterday. Because this was her place and her group and her plaid, and this was where she was meant to be.

"Hey." Her tone was despondent, but it didn't feel cold or bitchy. It just felt like Dee.

"Hey . . ." The silence became awkward, surely more for me than her. My words rushed out. "I'm sorry about yesterday. I'm sorry about everything. Most of all . . ." I took a breath and slowed down. "I'm sorry for not telling you."

"I know," she said, and lowered her voice. "Did you take the job?"

"Yeah." And with that, I knew the fight was done. "I'm starting this afternoon."

"You have to call me, stat. You're going to find this descendent, Adele."

"Thanks for having so much faith in me."

"I have faith in magic. The location spell."

"Right."

Her gaze went up to the roof, to one of the shuttered windows protruding from the attic.

"I'm not going to open the freaking attic."

"I know. I just hate that he knew and I didn't."

That was the *last* thing I expected to hear her say. "Désirée Nanette Borges, are you jealous of Isaac?"

"Maybe. He's like the gross older brother I never wanted."

"He's not gross." I had to restrain myself from laughing at her melodrama, and then so did she.

She cracked a smile. "Fine. We can keep him."

"Merci beaucoup."

"I just didn't think *we* had any secrets," she added.

Then I got it. She wasn't pissed that I didn't tell her about the attic; she was pissed that I'd never told her about me and Isaac. Everything about this scenario felt like a dream—that I even had a boyfriend in the first place, and that Désirée Borges cared about it.

"Dee, I'll be sure to tell you evvvvvvery single thing in the future."

"Ew. No. Refer to previous brother comment, please." She looked at me, finally. "You know, sometimes you surprise me, Adele. I really thought you were going to end up with the dark and broody one. Not that Isaac doesn't have that sullen-artist-in-the-corner thing down, but compared to Nicco Medici, he's a sunburst."

My smile became more nervous than I wanted it to be, and I knew she noticed, but then Thurston asked me a question about Drew Brees. I had no idea what he was talking about, but Dee, surprisingly—and yet, not surprisingly, because she's Dee—rattled off something about record yardage.

For ten more glorious minutes I felt like my life was going to be different. That school was going to be different. I didn't think about vampires, or dead mothers, or magic, or witches. We were swapping schedules, and talking about what we did over Christmas break, and debunking Storm horror stories. Thurston confirmed that it was *not* a rumor that his neighborhood association had hired Blackwater to patrol his street with helicopters a mere twenty-four hours after the Storm. As the rest of us were giving him shit, a new voice arose, and all of the rays of happiness crashed at once. I didn't need to look up for confirmation, because the look on Georgie's face told me everything.

Thurston swallowed his shock like a pro, quickly stood to greet his girlfriend, and then lied for all of us. "And I didn't think this morning could get any better. What are you doing here, Annabelle?"

Everyone looked up with smiles that had taken years to perfect. Smiles that hid every shred of emotion and replaced them with the truth as society dictated.

"What can I say, babe," she said. "I got spoiled having you around."

He leaned down and kissed her—a move I couldn't imagine ever doing in the middle of the schoolyard, or even in front of all of our friends.

Tyrelle looked at me, the only one willing to outwardly show how much this sucked. I smoothed my skirt. Order had been restored.

Annabelle took a seat in the circle, underneath Thurston's arm, as if we'd been saving it for her the whole time.

Désirée was the only one with the guts to actually say something about it. "Annabelle Lee Drake willfully giving up her place at Sacred Heart Prep? The next thing we know she'll be renouncing her position in the Comus junior court and giving away her cotillion Vera."

"Dream on, Dee." Annabelle peeled herself away from Thurston and crawled between us. "I'm not heartless. You're my bestie, and if you and Thurston have to suffer out the rest of the year here, I can do it too. And then we'll all be at Vanderbilt before we know it. Well, most of us will," she added, looking directly at Tyrelle. Her tone had an edge that I would have thought a little too overt for Annabelle.

He got up to leave.

"No, Ty, don't go," she said. And then to everyone's shock, but mostly his, I think, he sat back down.

I hate her.

She smiled at him, pleased as punch, and took my schedule from my hand. "Adele, we have second period together. History. Yay for quality time. We should really spend this semester getting to know each other better. You're one of *us* now."

I took the little card back, staring down at the words, instantly dreading second block. I got up, lifting my bag.

"That's the thing, Annabelle. I'm not."

I walked away.

Alone.

As I entered civics, a familiar voice nearly made my stern frown dissolve.

"Seeing you in that uniform is so weird," said Veronica Bergeron, one of my former classmates from NOSA. Johnnie West, another familiar NOSA face, was sitting on her desk.

"Tell me about it," I said.

They both laughed. We hadn't really been friends, but now I found myself hugging both of them.

"Did you manage to get a mentorship?" Veronica asked. "Or do you have to stay in this prepfest all day?"

"Kind of. It's with my dad . . ."

"We're both at the Marigny Opera House. The place hasn't been condemned, but it needs to be gutted. We're basically free manual labor for the semester."

The bell rang, and my shoulders relaxed as our teacher walked in: a petite woman in a white blouse, navy-blue skirt, and matching habit. A large silver cross hung from a chain around her neck.

"Welcome to civics. I'm Sister Carla. In this class we're going to examine the structures of different types of government, not fight over the decisions made by the poor excuse of an administration currently in office. I encourage open debate but will not tolerate disrespect."

We all looked at each other. Even the nuns downtown were badass.

When the bell rang, I crossed the hall to history class and took a seat by the window.

As my fellow juniors trickled into the room, I doodled in my notebook—fantasizing about dropping out of school and working with Isaac. A girl in brown-and-gold plaid sat next to me. More seats filled.

I felt Annabelle's energy as soon as she walked in the room.

She came straight toward me, smile beaming. I held her gaze so I didn't seem intimidated. Her perfect auburn hair held perfect

Hollywood finger waves. I'd been so jittery about the convent, I'm not sure I'd even brushed my hair this morning before I tied it up into a bun.

"Hey! Where'd you get off to earlier?" Annabelle asked as she, *of course*, took the seat behind me.

I prepared myself for backlash after the incident in the quad, but then I remembered this was Annabelle, and her MO was to kill you softly like a boiling frog.

"I have something for you," she said.

Before I could turn around, a metal chain was slipping across my neck.

She clicked it shut and adjusted the clasp to the center. I didn't have to look down to know a flat silver heart was resting against my throat—her whole clique back at Sacred Heart wore them. *Tiffany*. The thick links felt heavy, especially compared to the thin chain that held my charms. I envisioned her choking me with it from behind.

"Every girl needs a little love in her daily wardrobe."

Everyone in the room was looking at us like it was the kindest, coolest thing they'd ever witnessed. But it felt like the opposite, like she'd just branded me—that she'd claimed me as one of hers. This was her letting me know that she was going to run this school. Downtown or not.

"*Merci beaucoup*, Annabelle," I said, sinking into my seat, the tips of my fingers on the heart. What she didn't realize was that I couldn't be bought off with silver like Judas Iscariot, even if it was Tiffany. "*C'est beau. J'aime.*"

"*Avec plaisir,*" she responded sweetly. And it absolutely was her pleasure. "We should hang out after school today."

"Oh, I have to work. Maybe some other time." *Like never.*

"I'll come by the café."

"Actually." I turned around. "I'm starting a new job. Isaac's covering my shift at the café." He'd offered as part of his apology last night because he knew how much it meant to me.

"Well maybe this weekend, then. We should plan a party."

As the second bell rang, a man in a houndstooth vest and mustard-colored corduroys walked into the classroom. I'd never been so happy to see a teacher. He set his satchel on the desk up front and pulled his glasses from the top of his head, wiping them clean as he spoke.

"This is a remarkable time, people. Look around at your neighbors."

Our eyes moved to each other, not wanting to move our heads in case he was being rhetorical.

"*Look* around," he said, and we did, as he huffed on his glasses and wiped them some more. "Remember this moment, because we are living in a time of historical significance. Of epic calamity! When Mother Nature will go down in history, and when the magnitude of government failure will go down with her. Academics will write theses, book deals will be inked, films will be shot, and records will be recorded. And *you* are the witnesses. So look around the room right now and remember this moment, because in ten, twenty, thirty years, someone will still be asking how you were able to live through this humanity-testing time."

Finally satisfied with the state of his lenses, he put the glasses on and looked out to us.

"Graham Noah. World history. Louisiana history. Gentilly. Formerly of Brother Martin High School. And who are you?" He looked straight at a girl in the front row.

"Uh, Miranda Jackson. Lakeview. Formerly of Mount Carmel. We just got a FEMA trailer last week."

"Welcome, Miranda."

And then he did this horrible thing where he went around the room making every single person introduce themselves. I quickly did the math. Thirty-two students. I sat back.

On any other day I would have been genuinely interested in where everyone came from and how their part of the city had fared, but the cloud nine from the almost-best-first-day-ever had crashed, and now the sleepless night was catching up. On the plus side, I was now too tired to care about Annabelle and whatever she was up to anymore.

I yawned, covering my face from Mr. Noah, but my eyes watered, giving me away.

The sleepiness also broke whatever subconscious barrier was keeping me from thinking about how only the second story and some enchanted nails separated me from my undead mother and her clan, most of whom—*all* of whom—would be trying to kill me if not for a sleeping spell. I tried to focus on my classmates so my mind didn't spiral to a dark place.

"Mike Ferguson," one of them said. "Mid-City. Warren Easton."

They were right upstairs. My mom . . .

And Nicco.

I looked out the window into the garden, where I would have plummeted to my death if Isaac hadn't caught me that night.

Even though I'd ended up with the bruises to prove it, it was still hard to believe that Nicco had thrown me out the window.

The voices droned on in the background. "Sarah Flores. The Tremé. Ben Franklin."

My eyes fluttered.

CHAPTER 21

Sword, Cross, or Coin

My feet dance forward, pushing León backward as our rapiers clank together in a familiar joust. The blades are sharp, but our moves are playful, mine far more aggressive than his, pushing him to swing at me harder as we cross the interior courtyard, the song of metal echoing up the arching stone walls of the palazzo to the sky. I spin and take a swing, changing the direction of the blade. He is just fast enough to catch it with his own, but I repeat the move thrice more, each time gaining momentum, our blades clanging with more force. By the fifth advance, he is close to the wall and has lost the full range of his swing. When his sword catches mine, there is nothing he can do but block. I push harder, waiting for him to buckle under the weight of the blades. After the last year, I know that León is a worthy adversary, but I have long suspected he holds back when sparring with me—a true sign that he isn't a Medici.

Maybe he isn't my father's bastard after all.

But then, much to my delight, with a bout of sheer strength, he pushes my sword off. This can only mean one thing: *Giovanna.*

Suddenly my feet are dancing backward, and I am the one deflecting his swings.

As our weapons clang and clank, I glance around and spot her on the mezzanine, draped over the stone balcony, her head resting in her palm, her bosom displayed on the ledge. "Aha!" I say to him.

León keeps his eyes on me just as he always does when my sister is near, which torments her, I'm sure, but pleases me. My tutors claim León to be one of the brightest pupils they've ever known, which I cannot deny, but he is an absolute fool if he thinks I fail to catch his stolen glances when my back is turned. It makes me smile, because I love him and I love my sister, and I love that this unrequited love now makes the fight more worthy of the exercise.

He takes a swoop at my middle, trying to tear my shirt.

"Finally," I say as I parry his swing, his blade sliding the length of mine until it slams into the cross hilt. Both of our swings become faster, and we dance across the courtyard under my sister's gaze.

I am quite certain León will never do anything about Giovanna—his natural abstemiousness, also not a Medicean trait—for he is not a worthy match for Giovanna Simona Medici, who is so beautiful she was betrothed first at thirteen, and then, after the marriage contract was lost in a duel to a rat-faced Neapolitan prince, betrothed a second time at sixteen. Her marriage will mean more for the family than all of Gabriel's diplomatic efforts and all of Emilio's battlefield conquests, but it is a subject matter that, when discussed among three Medici brothers, can result in the kind of murderous plots that start wars between kingdoms.

Regardless, it is a situation that will never end up in León's favor. Emilio would rather have his head than see Giovanna marry beneath her position, even if that means our darling jewel of a sister ends up in the bed of a rat-faced bastard who is rumored to be suffering so severely from the Great Pox that he is unable to leave Naples. I pray, for the sake of my sister, that the disease takes him soon, leaving her with another dead betrothed.

We all have our duty to bring greatness to the Medici name and to Florence, but I hate how Giovanna is traded to the highest bidder, though she is not the only one expected to advance the family fortune via marriage. My father has been trying to convince Gabriel to propose to an Austrian princess for the past year. It is most certainly the reason Gabriel constantly travels, not to visit her, but to avoid our father. Gabriel would travel to the earth's edge if it meant shirking the marriage bed.

León's eyes give away his next move, making it easy for me to parry. Giovanna laughs girlishly as we increase the tempo. Although she is barely a year older than me, the girlish way she poses herself is the most playful I've seen her in ages, which makes my lips curl into a smile. Charming, *sì*; cunning, *sì*; but "playful" is not a word I would have ever associated with Giovanna, until this moment.

I tap the tip of his sword away but make no move to counterattack, letting his blows grow stronger with his momentum.

"You're not fooling anyone, Niccolò!" Giovanna yells. "You're letting him win!"

"Mi dispiace, fratello," I say to León with a sympathetic look, and I return his strike with a quick riposte—the undercut is so sharp he loses his grip and his rapier goes flying across the stone floor.

"Bravo, fratellino! Bravo!" a familiar voice cheers from the sideline, whilst someone else claps slowly.

"Gabriel! Emilio!" Giovanna yells, springing up. She runs to the stairs, her shoes leaving a trail of echoing clicks as she descends. "You have finally arrived!"

She jumps into Gabriel's arms first, but she lingers for longer in Emilio's as she speaks. "All of us here at the same time. This brings me so much joy. It feels like my birthday rather than Niccolò's!" She kisses his cheek over and over.

Emilio embraces her with a tenderness he shows toward no other living creature. Giovanna is our jewel, but for Emilio, she is especially precious, the one person who brings out the slivers of humanity buried deep within his soul. One of our parents must be an angel to have borne a creature that could work such divine magic upon him.

"Brother!" I hug Gabriel with near equal enthusiasm. "You've stayed away from Florence for far too long."

"Never have words been more true, little brother."

Gabriel greets León in a fraternal way, but Emilio only nods at him as he sets Giovanna back onto the floor.

"Tanti auguri, fratellino," Emilio says to me, stepping close and pulling me in. His embraces feel like moves learned on the battlefield. He then wraps his arms around my head and says into my ear, "Now let's see how you'd fair in a real fight." He kisses my jaw and throws me backward. An onlooker might have thought he was being playful, but a swordsman who heard the way the metal hisses out of his sheath would know he wasn't.

I draw my rapier and ground my stance, knowing Emilio is always serious when weaponry is involved. We all have the scars to prove it.

"Else how would we test this beauty?" He tosses me a bundle of leather.

Within the hide is a dagger of the finest craftsmanship I have ever seen.

"Happy birthday, Niccolò."

Before I can respond, his rapier crashes into mine, and I am barely able to position the gift in my left hand before we are swinging four blades. A look of victory already glows on his face, and it is not unearned. I have never beaten Emilio in my fifteen years. Very few have.

Luckily for me, one of those who had defeated him has been training me for the last three years—every time he comes home to give Father reports.

Emilio would rather fall on his rapier than admit that Gabriel is his equal when it comes to wielding the sword. Emilio's reputation on the battlefield precedes him so far and wide that only the master swordsmen of Florence know how worthy of an opponent Gabriel is—except of course for me and Father. Gabriel's lackadaisical attitude toward war and weaponry makes him appear the lesser fighter. This works to everyone's advantage, for it leaves Emilio's ego unthreatened and catches Gabriel's opponents off guard. No man has been challenged to more duels of honor than Gabriel Medici, but because his swing is as sharp as his wit, no man has won as many either. Nor has any bed seen more victory celebrations, and this is a fact no one in Florence—perhaps no one in all of Tuscany—would dispute.

Clank. Clank. Clank.

My sword moves fast, blocking each of his advances. Despite being on the defense, my feet plant firmly with each step back. This is always the most difficult part of fighting Emilio: he charges without fear and without mercy, so getting into a position of offense requires equal commitment to the fight.

But no one knows him better than Gabriel after their years of training together, and I feel the rhythm of his swings just as Gabriel has taught me, just as we have practiced a hundred times. I count them off in my head, and on his next strike, I increase my pace by a hair and catch his blade higher. With our arms overhead, Emilio's chest is open to my dagger. After only a second's strain, he pushes down hard, breaking my parry, forcing my blade back into submission. My feet step backward even faster than before while fire dances in Emilio's eyes.

Gabriel steps closer. As do Giovanna and León.

I can almost hear Gabriel in my head: *You have two hands, Niccolò. Use them always. In battle. In bed.*

Clank. Clank. Clank.

This time I don't count, and I don't think—I just feel. When I pull back my blade, I thrust my dagger in its place, blocking his sword, holding on as he tries to crush my weaker wrist. It is all I need. My rapier hisses through the air to him.

He stumbles back and tries to parry with his dagger, but off balance, he misses. I lunge again, carefully planning where each swing will force his feet. Two more quick steps move him in front of a small gargoyle. This time the kiss of my blade knocks him into the little stone monster and sends him to the ground. I think we are in equal shock when the tip of my rapier meets his throat.

He grunts.

"Un miracolo," I say, sheathing my sword, wondering if Emilio was simply caught off guard by how much I'd grown since the last time we'd fought. *"Grazie, fratello,"* I say, moving the dagger in front of my face. "If it can beat you, it is the most exquisite gift I've ever received."

"Glad to know it will be put to better use than I expected."

Still catching my breath, I offer my hand to help him stand. He reaches up with a quick blur of motion, and I hear Gabriel yell before I feel the dirt hit my eyes. A swift kick to the back of my legs knocks me to the ground, and suddenly our positions are reversed. Emilio stands over me, his blade at my throat, eyes twinkling.

"Never trust a Medici," he says, thoroughly pleased with himself. He sheathes his sword as I turn on my side, coughing and spitting mud.

"Sei un bastardo, Emilio!" Gabriel yells. "It's his birthday!"

León fetches me some water from the fountain while Giovanna kneels beside me, tending to me like I am a child, which makes matters even more humiliating. *I should have seen it coming.*

"Emilio!" she scolds him. "You don't have to win every single time."

"Sì, sister, I do."

"But at what cost?"

"At any cost. You are all too soft on him. So is Father. He's *weak* because of it."

My dagger whizzes past his head, slicing his ear, silencing him, and causing all heads to flip my way.

"I—I'm sorry. I didn't mean to!" In truth, it was such a fit of fury, I couldn't even recall the dagger leaving my hand. *How could you be so reckless, Niccolò!*

Sometimes I worry that Emilio and I aren't so different after all.

Gabriel and León step in front of me, as if in preparation for his retaliation.

Emilio pushes them aside. "*That's* more like it, brother!" He clasps my hand. "Let the festivities begin!" He pulls me up, tousles my hair, and for once I am glad for Emilio's polarizing personality. "Gabriel hasn't even given you his gift yet."

"A birthday hat for the birthday boy," Gabriel says, pulling a red cap from his cloak and flicking it open. Before I can get a good look at the garment, he is tucking my hair underneath it and everyone is laughing; even León is shaking his head.

"Oh, Niccolò," Giovanna says. "My beautiful brother. You'll be the youngest pope in the history of the Vatican, an accomplishment greater than *our* achievements combined."

I snatch the cap from my head, now recognizing the crimson. "How did you even come by this vestment? It's property of the Church. It's *sacred.*"

"Now it's property of the Medici," Gabriel says, smiling his infamous smile.

"Gabriel!" Giovanna turns to him. "You stole a hat from a cardinal?"

"Not exactly," Emilio answers for him. "His favorite courtesan did."

"Gabriel!" she yells, as if she is too innocent for the thought, but we all know better than that. "It never ceases to amaze me the things women will do for you."

Emilio smirks. "Oh, sister, you have no idea."

"There is a simple way to avoid your path to priesthood, Niccolò," says Gabriel. "Come on tour with me, and I will show you all the secrets of Medici investment."

"Or come to the battleground with me," Emilio chimes, "once Father lets me lead the palace guard."

"I'll find my own path, *grazie.*"

"Just think, Niccolò," Emilio continues, sliding his arm around my neck. "When you're a cardinal, you can have your own private quarters at the bordello, where Gabriel's whores can steal your vestments."

"I am *not* interested in the priesthood; I am interested in medicine, and in anatomy. In the human spirit."

"*Perfetto,*" Gabriel says. "Your anatomy lessons are going to start tonight."

Emilio snickers.

"*Cosa?*"

"You're fifteen, Nicco. It's time you become a man."

"No," Giovanna says, catching on before I do.

Emilio pulls my dagger from the wall. "Sword," he says, then stuffs the hat back on my head. "Cross." Lastly, he takes my hand and drops a pouch of ducats into it. "*And coin.* You're going to need these tonight. Try not to fall in love with every girl you see, *fratellino.*"

"No, I don't think—"

"That's your problem, Niccolò," Gabriel says. "You *think* entirely too much." He hands me a wineskin. "Drink up."

With mixed emotions, I drink a gulp of vino. My chest swells with joy at no longer being excluded from my brothers' escapades, yet I am scared silent by the idea of going to the bordello. I cannot deny that I too have secrets I don't confess to the priest—unmentionable dreams about Giovanna's handmaiden—but this is not the way I envisioned first touching a woman.

"You too," Gabriel says to León. "I'm not leaving you here with my sister."

They push both of us toward the exit. León links his arm into mine, taking the pouch of wine. When he twists slightly back to look at Giovanna, Emilio smacks his head forward. I am glad to have León's company, although I am quite certain he wants to go even less than I do.

Maybe this is best for León. Loving my sister will only lead him to despair.

León hands me back the pouch. "It's okay to fall in love, Niccolò, just not tonight."

"Not tonight," I say, taking a healthy swig. "So I should leave my poetry at home?"

"*Sì!*" all three of them yell in unison.

"Don't let them corrupt you, my beautiful baby brother!" Giovanna yells behind us. "Don't go, Niccolò!"

"Don't go, Niccolò, don't go!" I shouted, bolting awake at my desk.

Where the—? What the hell?

Everyone around me snickered, and I slunk into my seat, pulling my cardigan sleeves over my fingers, covering my face with my hand.

That was not the history lesson I was supposed to be having. Annabelle leaned on my shoulder from behind, looking out to the rest of the class.

"You'd all be tired too if you had exclusive access to the hottest club in town and had the night we just had."

Le Chat? Is that why Annabelle's being so nice to me?

It didn't add up, considering how miserable she'd made my last few weeks at Sacred Heart after I dissed her on Halloween.

Her words silenced the room, and one by one our classmates faced forward, whispering about how cool they'd heard the club was, and with that I was rocket launched into the social stratosphere.

Mr. Noah, however, seemed less impressed. "And what name do they call you at the clubs, Sleeping Beauty?"

"Adele Le Moyne. French Quarter. Formerly of NOSA."

"Well, Miss Le Moyne, I hate to have to make an example of you, considering it's the first day of a brand-new semester, but I'm really in need of a research assistant, which might be the only thing more boring than detention—"

"What? No. I can't. I have a mentorship. And a job."

And a descendant to find!

"And now you'll have another."

This is not happening—

"Mr. Noah," Annabelle piped in. "Can't you cut her some slack this *one* time? I'm sure Adele is truly sorry and embarrassed enough over the disruption. And really, students falling asleep on the first day? You might want to revisit your syllabus."

"Annabelle," I shot around. "You're *not* helping."

But when I turned back to the front, Mr. Noah was stroking his beard, as if considering her reasoning. "I guess we could make an exception this *one* time. Good suggestion, Miss Drake. I'll look into revising the syllabus. Okay, class, since we only have five textbooks for the room to share, we'll take turns reading the first chapter out loud. The War of 1812!"

I turned back to Annabelle and mouthed, *Thank you.*

Who's Nicco? she mouthed back.

I shrugged, trying to look innocent.

When the bell rang, I couldn't exactly run away from her like I wanted to, considering what she'd done for me, so we walked out together. It was too normal and too weird. I went through the motions, answering her questions, but I could hardly focus. All I could think about was the dream. *Why are you dreaming about the Medici?*

Everyone headed to the cafeteria, including Annabelle, and I was left in the hallway, scrutinizing the depths of my imagination. *Why are you dreaming of Nicco?*

I paused at the door—at the red velvet rope in front of the staircase—and for a change, I wasn't thinking about my mom being up there. I was thinking about him.

Neurotic behavior pumped into my veins as I walked off campus. The impulse to obsess about Nicco was the last thing I needed right now. I *needed* to obsess over finding the last coven members and saving my mother. I needed to obsess over the near-naked situation with Isaac last night. I *did not* need to obsess over the fact that Nicco was possessing my dreams.

I made a deal with myself: I could think about whatever I wanted on the walk, but once I crossed the threshold at home, it was done. He was done. I did not need to be operating metalsmithing tools while thinking about Nicco.

But by the time I got home, my memories of him had exploded from a locked box into my consciousness, and I was fuming. Emilio had been right about one thing: never trust a Medici.

I paused at the kitchen door.

Breathe.

"Dad?" I yelled, setting my bag on the counter. I headed straight for his studio. "Da—"

He met me in the doorway with a finger over his mouth. "Shhhhh."

"What?" I whispered.

He stepped aside and nodded to the couch near the back wall. Isaac was there, sleeping.

"What happened?" I asked, suddenly worried. I pulled out my phone to see if I'd missed any messages.

"Nothing's wrong. He was so tired, I thought he was going to fall asleep on the bench. I was almost afraid for him to be handling any tools. I told him to go lie down, and he's been out cold for the last couple hours. He wanted me to wake him up when you got here, but I don't think it's a good idea. The kid is exhausted."

"Okay," I said. "Should I just skip metalwork today and go to work-work early?" Eagerness hardly described how ready I was to get the descendant hunt started.

He looked to my mountain of wire rings on the workbench and then back to me. The crease in his brow told me the answer was no.

"Okay," I said, unsnapping the tie from around my neck. "Be right back."

I ran up to my room to change. I wouldn't be doing anything messy in the metal shop today, so the question was: *What does one wear on the first day of work at a psychic tearoom?*

I stripped off the cardigan and button-down, tossed them on my bed, and flipped through the homemade dresses hanging in my closet. They were organized by fabric type, lightest to heaviest. After I flipped past the last two dresses, both velvet, I reached for another group of hangers hidden in the back, upon which hung some of my mother's garments.

I'd found a box of her things last year when this room was still the attic, and, despite having been in full-on angst mode, I hijacked the box, ironed and hung her clothes, but then pushed them all the way to the end of the rack, where they'd remain out of sight. Now my hiding and ignoring the clothes seemed like a metaphor for her life.

Freeing one, I pulled out an airy black dress with full-bloom red roses printed onto the fabric. I slipped it on. It had a high scoop neckline and bell sleeves that cinched at the wrists. The silky fabric puffed out as I twirled in front of the mirror, and I decided it was perfect for both the metal shop and the metaphysical. Not something I'd usually wear in the studio, but all I was going to be doing—from now until eternity—was bending and cutting metal rings. *Frigging chainmaille.*

Boots. Necklace. Wing-tipped eyeliner. And a spritz of my mom's perfume.

I bounced back down the stairs, marveling at the difference between six months ago, when I'd been crying and just wanting to leave my mother's Parisian home, and now, twirling in an ensemble that was more hers than mine.

Downstairs, the wire cutters and pliers were already waiting for me at the bench, along with a metal rod that my father had already coiled steel wire around with a drill.

"Aw, you did the fun part," I said, making him smile. Even though I was anxious to get to the tearoom, I'd be lying if I said I didn't love working in my dad's studio with him.

I pushed the coil off the rod and began clipping the little circles loose. When I had six, I pinched each one of them closed, and my fingers were already starting to feel sore from squeezing the tools. I wondered why I ever thought taking on a project as big as making a chainmaille dress was a good idea. I stretched my fingers out, did another six, and then wondered how much magical assistance I could use with my father only three feet away.

At first I used a little magic only when he turned away, but gradually the challenge became to see how much I could mentally pinch the wire cutters and squeeze the pliers even when he was close by.

At the end of the hour, he'd finished polishing a dozen bracelets, and I had another minimountain of steel rings.

"Wow," he said. "You're a pro."

"It's pretty Zen," I said, realizing that I might have gone a little *too* fast.

"Repetition is the road to mastery with this kind of work."

He came around the bench and showed me how to weave the rings together in sets of five. I was paying attention, but the late night was catching up with me again and I yawned, blinking back glossy eyes.

My father looked over at Isaac, and then back at me.

"Why are you so tired?" he asked.

"I'm not tired," I blurted out. "I'm not tired at all. I just can't see straight anymore after making all these rings." Guilt slid out of my voice, but I stuck to my story and kept my eyes on the metal as I connected the rings together.

He walked back to his seat across from me, and although I didn't look up, I could still sense his gaze. Another urge to yawn came on, but this time I kept my mouth clamped shut. It felt like my eyeballs were going to pop out of their sockets as it passed.

"You're wearing your mother's dress," he said.

"Oh." I was surprised he could remember such a detail. On second thought, looking at the intricate bracelets he'd carved, I wasn't. "I found some of her stuff in the attic. Is that okay?"

"Of course, sweetheart. It looks just as beautiful on you as it did on her."

"Yeah, right," I said with a little laugh. I was glad it didn't bother him, though. I was already growing attached to the dress.

"I stand corrected. It looks *more* beautiful on you."

His cell phone rang, which was always kind of shocking to hear since the reception so rarely allowed calls to go through.

He answered and then after a pause asked, "Are you *serious?*" He stood up. "Wait, can you repeat that?" He held the phone up so he could see the screen—the bars, presumably. "Hold on a second." And so the usual dance with the cell towers started; he ducked outside to try to get a stronger signal.

I snuck over to the couch and sat carefully on the edge, next to Isaac.

His hair had fallen in front of his face; I tucked it behind his ear, just like he always did, almost daring him to wake up. He didn't stir. And then I couldn't help but touch my lips to his, which were so noticeably soft compared to his prickly face and rough hands. Profuse blushing followed as I thought about all the uncharted territory those lips had discovered last night. And then, as if he'd read my mind, his hand slid over my hip. "Isaac!" I whispered. "My dad is—" But his hand stopped at my waist, and I realized he hadn't even woken up.

My father's voice became louder. I gently placed Isaac's hand back on the couch and hurried to the workbench, but I didn't get far enough before my dad stepped inside.

He looked over at the couch, and Isaac stirred, turning around the other way.

He whispered, "I thought we agreed not to wake him up."

"I didn't wake him up!" I whispered back.

He frowned.

"Dad. I *promise* you he didn't mind," I said, reaching for my coat and bag.

He frowned harder.

I kissed his cheek. "I'm going to work. Love you!"

CHAPTER 22
Bottom of the Cup

The shop was on a block of wall-to-wall brick town houses, all three stories high, each decorated with dark-green shutters and the kind of wrought-iron balconies that tourists stopped to take photos of.

I paused across the street, still trying to process the idea that I was about to start work at a psychic tearoom. Even with the magic and the witches and the vampires, it was still hard for me to believe in the whole psychic thing. If people could really tell the future, why the hell did so many people just die in this Storm?

My rational side was back to wanting proof—but then Isaac's words about me needing to believe more rang in my head, and then so did Papa Olsin's, warning me not to open the attic. How could he know something like that? Was it that I didn't believe? Or that I just didn't *want* to believe?

I took a deep breath and crossed the street. *Either way, I'm here to find our fourth witch.*

So I can strengthen our coven and figure out a way to save Mom.

A bell jingled overhead as I walked inside—kind of ironic for a psychic tearoom; then again, not everyone who worked here was a psychic. I wasn't. Nor were the Daure kids, at least as far as I knew.

The jingle didn't prompt anyone to come out. Part of me thought it would be polite to yell hello and announce myself, but I didn't want to interrupt a tarot-card reading.

I set my bag on one of the three black-and-white zodiac wheel tables near the front window and stripped off my jacket and scarf. I don't know if it was the childhood familiarity or . . . something else, but the shop had a soothing effect.

Water trickled from a fountain near the bay window. I cupped my hand underneath the gentle stream, just like I'd done when I was a child. My hand felt so much bigger now, but the water felt the same, cool and tickling. *Water.* Water witch. *Mind on the mission, Adele. You're here to find Morning Star's descendant, whose brother was* killed *by Giovanna Medici, if you've forgotten.*

The thought brought me back to the dream.

Giovanna had appeared almost exactly as I'd pictured her when I read Adeline's diary, only . . . human. I didn't want to think about the Medici being human. I didn't want to have dreams about Nicco that seemed so real they made me feel closer to him. I wanted to forget him. If it weren't for my mom being imprisoned with him, maybe I would have by now. *Yeah, right.* The water splashed up into my face, and a girl giggled.

I whirled around to the empty shop. There was a fireplace to my left and wall-to-wall shelves to my right, but no sign of anyone else.

Jesus, Adele, you're losing it.

You could tell that the large storefront was once a parlor room of some kind. Now two long glass-case counters ran along the back, displaying jewelry and blocking off the corridor that ran the length of the bottom floor, where the psychic booths were hidden behind curtains.

The shop wasn't stuffed to the brim like Vodou Pourvoyeur, or at least it didn't feel that way. Each display, from the crystal balls to the bamboo lutes, looked purposely placed and freshly dusted.

I moved through the shop, sucked in by the mystical oddities on the shelves, all illuminated by track lighting. I could have spent an entire day looking through the different crystals and teacups. Everything in Vodou Pourvoyeur felt historical, but here things felt futuristic, like they might have a portal to another dimension behind one of the curtains in the back. The Voodoo shop felt warm, while this place felt cool—less apothecary and more celestial. I'd never be able to choose which one I liked better. Despite all of their differences, they both shared one energy in common: both were welcoming and warning at the same time.

All along the right wall, black granite cases sparkled as if diamond flecks had mixed in with the stone; they displayed a potpourri of precious and semiprecious new-agey treasures: huge chunks of natural geodes and crystalline formations that looked like they'd been pulled straight from caves, and wands made of quartz and fluorite and lapis. No two were the same. Little signs—in handwriting that looked like it belonged to a wizard—listed off the healing properties of each and noted that they'd all been charged by moonlight.

At the baseboards all around the shop sat baskets of rocks and stones. Some were polished, some were raw, and others were metallic or opalescent. One basket contained bright-orange coral.

I walked toward the fireplace on the opposite wall. So many details were exactly the same as I remembered them from my childhood: the bearskin rug, the taxidermied canary in the brass cage, which was now on the mantel next to the Russian nesting dolls, and the glass box with the crown.

Like in the Borges' shop, candles and incense burned on the mantel, although the scent here was as different as the vibe: instead of earthen and woody, the tearoom smelled soapy, a mix of lilacs and rose and honey. Potted plants of ivy sat on top of the shelves and on the fireplace mantel, spilling all the way to the ground. When I was a kid, Chatham Daure showed us how to clip the ivy and grow it in a glass of water. I thought it was magic. Back then I loved this place, even though some of it—like the frozen-in-time canary—had terrified me. It was the kind of place where it seemed like anything was possible.

I knelt down on the bearskin rug, where I used to sit so often as a child, and waited.

As I stared into the hearth, my fingers threaded the hem of my dress. Codi Daure had once told me fairies lived in this fireplace. It was just after my mom left; I thought I'd never stop crying, and likely everyone around me feared the same. Codi, who couldn't have been much older than six, had seen my tears one gloomy afternoon and told me about the fairies to try to cheer me up. I'd believed him, without question. Jeanne made fun of me for weeks for believing in fairies, but I came to this fireplace every day that summer, hoping with all of my being for it to be true. Mrs. Philomena even let me leave elephant ears with water on the counter for them. The leaves always turned up empty the next day, and I was sure the fairies had drunk the water, because there were always trails of sparkles left behind on the leaves.

Later I realized Mrs. Philly had probably showed Codi how to take the dust from the bottom of the raw gemstone displays and sprinkle the leaves.

Even now it felt like the kind of place where fairies would hide, the kind of place where magic could happen.

"Unnatural deeds do breed unnatural troubles," came a guy's voice.

I jumped up. The booklover was leaning over the glass counter, a damp black curl hanging over his forehead.

How long has he been watching me?

"I'm sorry if I startled you," he said. "You looked so peaceful staring into the fireplace."

The comment didn't exactly lower my creeper radar. It sounded like something Nicco would say—and I wouldn't make that same mistake twice. I hadn't exactly forgotten the weird vibe the guy had given me that day in the café.

I let out a small laugh and approached the counter. "'Unnatural deeds do breed unnatural troubles'? In that case, I think you might have taken the wrong job. Maybe two wrong jobs if your first day with Isaac really went as I heard it did."

"You won't find me using the words 'wrong' and 'job' in the same sentence," he said. "We could have found ten bodies and I'd still be grateful for the job. Isaac is ace. The odds of finding two jobs in such a short time after arriving in the city is a miracle."

Why the hell would anyone move to New Orleans right now? The memory of Palermo's when I first met Gabe and Nicco flashed through my head. "Let me guess . . . You're looking for someone?"

His eyes slanted. "And how did you know that? Wait, are you a psychic? I thought I was supposed to train you on the counter today. Are you going to work in a booth, rather?"

I crossed my arms. This guy was hiding something, and I didn't like it. Why was he turning up everywhere all of a sudden? "What did you say your name was again?"

"Callis."

"Callis *what?*" I don't know why I'd asked him like that; I just had this tick in the bottom of my stomach.

"Salazar. Callisto Salazar."

Onyx jumped up to the counter and slowly walked over, tail in the air.

"Are you okay?" Callis asked as my arms crossed tighter.

"I've been down this road before. Cute guy with a strange name shows up to this dystopian town with a sibling in tow . . .'"

"I'm guessing we're no longer talking about Isaac?"

He held my gaze in the silence. His eyes were a hue of blue that rivaled the larimar crystal ball on the counter, the kind of blue reserved for Gerber babies or Hollywood starlets. And if I wasn't mistaken, they'd been accentuated with a light coat of eyeliner to match his black nail polish.

"I don't want to make you uncomfortable, Adele. You can ask me anything you please."

I wondered if they'd worked outside today. He was still giving Snow White a run for her money, but yesterday I'd almost been able to see his veins through his skin. "I'm not uncomfortable," I said.

"The way you're squeezing your fists indicates otherwise."

I looked down at my hands. It was a nervous habit I'd picked up since I'd come into my powers, sometimes having to contain rogue sparks.

"You seem uneasy, that's all."

"Why would I be?" My pulse picked up as I realized how defensive I was being. I looked down at my hands again. It wasn't just a nervous habit. I *felt* something. It was faint, but it was there: something supernatural. My eyes instantly searched for the nearest metal object.

He smiled a pinched-lip smile. Not a sinister or creeper smile, just a regular happy one, which freaked me out even more.

"Have you really never met another witch before?"

"W-what?"

And then I just stood there, looking at the leather cuffs on his wrists and the rings he wore on most of his fingers. This was all incredibly strange—*too strange*. Ren's nonbelief in coincidences rang in my head, but then again, wasn't it Ritha Borges who'd said, "Sometimes when things need to be found, they find you"?

His smile spread wider. "My God. Have you really not? Am I your first? You *do* know your boyfriend is a witch, right?"

"Isaac told you?" The words came out a loud yelp.

"No! Oh, sorry, no. He hasn't betrayed your confidence. We didn't talk about you, or about anything, really. I just noticed his mark. I didn't say anything, though, because I didn't want to freak him out, like I'm doing to you right now. He's quite muscly."

"Yes. He is."

His expression told me the message was received.

"What do you mean you saw his mark?"

"His Maleficium. Like yours. Whiiich, now I'm guessing you can't see yet."

My blank stare must have answered for me.

"Oh boy. Adele, the witch's Maleficium is one of the most special parts of growing into witchhood." His voice lowered. "Witchhood is a tradition of secrets, and the Maleficium helps you identify those truly of the magical community, which is why you can't see the mark of others until you can see your own."

My eyes slowly wandered to my left arm—I pushed up my sleeve. Nothing. If Isaac hadn't been going on and on for the last month about a triangle, I'd think this guy was totally full of shit. *But if this is really a thing, why doesn't Désirée know about it? She grew up a witch.*

He leaned over the counter, took my wrist, and turned my arm over. Just as his finger touched my skin, the tin shelf behind him tilted, sending another case of moon mugs crashing to their deaths.

I looked at him suspiciously, and he looked at me with a similar expression, both of us pleading innocence.

"Juuuuullllllliiiiiiieeeeee!" a voice bellowed from down the hall.

Callis grabbed a broom from behind a tall cabinet. "I keep telling them the integrity of the bricks is compromised, but they keep drilling the shelf back in and blaming Julie."

"She gets the blame for everything around here," I said. "At least she has been for as long as I can remember."

Ren would tout Julie as the French Quarter's most famous ghost, but here among the Daures, she was treated like a daughter or a sister, depending on which family member you were talking to.

Chatham came running out from the back. "Everyone okay?"

"Everyone but the moon mugs," I said.

"Missy, aren't you on the wrong side of the counter?" He unlatched the wooden middle section and lifted it up for me to walk through, and then he let out a little yelp as he squeezed my shoulders. "I think this is more exciting for me than you, so you'll have to beg my pardon, but you're just so grown up. It's just like when each one of the boys had their first day."

I was glad Callis was sweeping mugs, so he couldn't see how red my face was turning.

And so for the next couple hours, the nostalgic psychic and the shiny new witch took turns showing me the ropes. Chatham showed me how to book appointments, and how to ring a sale on the antique cash register that made a satisfying zing when the cash drawer popped open. All the while, I wondered if I'd get another moment alone with Callis. I had a million questions about these witch-marks. I couldn't wait to see Isaac to tell him.

"This thing," Chatham said, pointing to a tall piece of furniture with lots of narrow drawers like a library card catalogue, "is the customer database." It took up a large portion of the back wall.

I pulled out one of the drawers and ran my fingers over the cards. They were all filed alphabetically by last name.

"Every customer who's ever had a reading—since readings were legalized, that is—has a handwritten card on file."

I pulled a few out, learning the system: color-coded dot stickers indicated preferences like tarot or palm, and notes were taken on the back, like whether they wanted a female psychic or someone who specialized in near-death experiences, their birthdates and star signs, and who their reading had been with. Most had one name listed, maybe two, and others, who were not picky about who saw their future, had a list of readers. Some had names scratched off.

"The more you get to know your psychic, the more enriching the reading becomes," Chatham told us.

Most of the cards were single, but some people had ten. I held up a stack bound together by a rubber band.

"Mary Jo's been coming here for decades. We're her first stop after Mass."

"Wow, I didn't know people did both of those things," I said.

"There's more than one way to talk to God, honey, and don't let anyone tell you otherwise."

I looked to the clock on the wall and back to Callis, who was at the other end of the counter cleaning crystal wands until they sparkled.

Chatham took me on a lap of the shop, pointing out which items were made locally. We paused at a bookcase near the front window where shelves of metaphysical books were displayed. I ran my fingers along the spines: *Beginner's Guide to Stargazing, Encyclopedia of Crystals, Hauntings and the Haunted.* Some were as vintage as Mr. Mauer's collection, and others were new and glossy. Three on the end caught my eye. *The Art of Dreaming, Deciphering Your Dreams,* and *Dreamology.*

My fingers lingered on the last one.

"Dreams," Chatham said, peeking over my shoulder, "one of our most underestimated tools."

"What do you mean?"

"Dreams are the time our mind doesn't dictate what we think and see and imagine, what we remember, what we fantasize about. They are arguably the most important key into your own soul." He tugged *Dreamology's* green spine and handed it to me.

"Merci," I said. I pictured my stack of research books back at the brothel. "But just to warn you, my to-be-read stack is huge."

"At your leisure, sweetheart. I just think you might find it interesting . . . Call it a hunch."

There was something about a Chatham Daure hunch that made me wonder if I should move the book to the top of the stack.

The door opened, and Theis walked in—his walk said he was on a mission. He saw me and waved, but the serious expression never left his face.

"Excuse me." Chatham hurried over and gently steered Theis's studded leather-jacket-clad elbow to his booth in the back.

I drifted back to the counter before realizing I didn't know what to say to Callis. How to just go back to witchtalk? So then I was just silently standing in front of him like a weirdo.

"Yes?" he asked, looking up.

"Question . . . About these mal-ef-a—*marks*."

"Maleficiums."

"*Oui.* You said you can see mine. Where is it? What does it look like? Is it just the alchemical symbol for Fire?"

"Whoa." He started laughing. "I don't want to spoil it for you—seeing your Maleficium for the first time is a special experience."

"Especially if you saw it for the first time in the middle of the night in a graveyard, right after a séance?"

He laughed again. "Well, that would certainly be one hell of a first time."

"When will I be able to see it?"

"No easy answer to that, love. Whenever the universe decides you're worthy of it."

My mind spun. *What the hell does that mean? Who is this guy? More importantly, who else in this town has seen my mark unbeknownst to me?*

"One more question," I asked, my fingers threading my chain. "What if . . . it never comes?"

"Is your mother a witch?"

"No. She's, er, not really in my life."

"Your father?"

I shook my head.

"What does he do?"

"He's a metalsmith."

"Well, maybe you'll be a metalsmith instead."

"Instead of what?"

"Instead of a witch."

"*Huh* . . ." I tried not to sound horrified by the idea of *not being a witch.* "It's probably just the alchemical symbol for Fire," I mumbled.

He let a smile slip, but that was all I got.

CHAPTER 23

His and Her Marks

The water kicks my feet from under me and sweeps me away. It feels like I'm flying. Weightless. Only there aren't any clouds or peaceful horizons, and there isn't any serenity as we're carried into the current along with everything else on the street. I knock away a detached car bumper, and its sharp metal edge slices my arm. A stop sign smacks the back of my head, and I want to blink out. I want my mom to save me, like Pop did that time a wave caught me while he was teaching me to surf at the Rockaways. I wasn't under for long before he pulled me out, but I remember hearing my mom screaming from the beach. Screaming my name over and over again as she ran into the water to meet my pop as he carried me out.

Like they're screaming my name now, over and over and over. The sound gurgles as water pushes into their mouths.

"Isaac!"

"Isaac!"

But the girls don't know my name.

They called me Mister.

My phone vibrated underneath me, jabbing into my side. I wasn't drowning. A chemical smell pierced the air. Not the ammonia used to clean the stainless steel rooms, but . . . silver polish. My eyes pelted open.

I sat up and swung my legs down to the floor, the disorientation melting away. I was in Mac's studio. He was at the workbench polishing jewelry.

I walked over to the table, feeling oddly exposed, as if he'd seen everything running through my subconscious while I was asleep. Mac was the last person I wanted to know about the nightmare—other than Adele. He needed to know that she was safe with me, not think I was incapable of keeping people out of danger.

Adele's pile of chainmaille rings was noticeably larger than it had been earlier.

"You just missed her," he said. "She's really excited about that new job."

Or more coven members.

"I'm glad she's getting out of the café," I said, having to force my voice to work. "That place haunts her."

He nodded, still focusing on polishing the bracelet. "Her mom loved that tearoom. It's unbelievable how alike she and Brigitte are. Sometimes I wonder if she got any of my genes at all."

Mac had never mentioned his wife—ex-wife?—around me. I liked that he did, but it also felt weird since Adele never talked about her mother, like I might be invading her privacy in a roundabout way. Adele so rarely mentioned her, it was almost like her mother was dead—and just one more thing we had in common. I looked around the room at all the tools, the sculptures, the sheets of brass and rods of silver and gold yet to be touched. So much metal. "I think she definitely got some of your genes."

He looked up at me. "So who's Jade?"

My breath halted. I knew I shouldn't have gone to sleep here. *What were you thinking?*

"Who?" I asked, trying to play it off like my pulse wasn't racing.

"You screamed her name a couple times."

My eyes dropped to the pile of metal rings.

"Adele wasn't here," he said, putting down the rag. "Don't worry."

For a second I felt like I could breathe again.

"How long have you been having the nightmares?"

"I—I don't know. A few months, I guess." I couldn't look at him, but it was the closest I'd ever come to talking about it.

"I have a friend who's a trauma couns—"

"I'm fine," I snapped. *Don't get defensive, Isaac.* "There are thousands of people out there who deserve help before me. Real victims."

"PTSD is a real thing, son."

"I don't have PTSD. Just lack of sleep. I start work really early—not that I'm complaining—and I stayed up too late last night, that's all." *Because I had to make up for saying some really stupid shit to your daughter, who has the most vivid blue eyes I've ever seen and who I still can't believe forgave me.*

"I know you're not complaining, son. But please, if you ever change your mind . . . or if you ever need to catch up on z's, the couch is there."

I nodded.

"The couch, just to be clear. *Not* Adele's bed."

I looked him in the eye and nodded again, using all of my mental strength not to imagine Adele last night, the moonlight pouring through that perfectly thin T-shirt, which was now officially my favorite piece of clothing in the world.

My pen glided around the page in swirling curves, forming delicate tendrils of hair. Tiny bubbles trailed from the blonde's plump lips up to the water's surface. Bubbles were supposed to be fun, light, and weightless, but here they carried her last breath back out to the world. If you listened closely, you could almost hear the gurgle as her pensive eyes watched the bubbles carry it away.

The streets outside the café were so silent, devoid of people and cars, you could hear Ren's voice from two blocks away as he went on about someone named Alessandro, which meant they'd be here shortly.

I finished filling her eyes with ink, then set the pen down and emptied the carafe of coffee into the sink. Ren and his tour group would likely be the only customers for the rest of the shift, so they might as well get a fresh pot.

I ground the beans, looked at the chicory, and then ignored it, because it was disgusting. I couldn't understand for the life of me why people would ruin perfectly good coffee by adding it. Adele said I wasn't able to get the full effect until we were able to get milk, but again, why would you make something so gross that it was only drinkable cut with equal parts milk. Baffling. I flipped the switch on the machine to brew.

Even though I'd covered shifts at the café a few times for Adele, it still felt odd being on this side of the counter. Most of the time I just sat in my usual spot in the window, which I think actually attracted customers—nothing to do with me personally, but just seeing a live human as proof that the café was open. But today, despite the nap, I was still exhausted, and I felt better tucked away behind the counter, hiding behind the empty pastry cases and espresso machines. I almost hoped no one would come in.

Plus, it was easier to think about dead girls and cold touches and the whispers in the wind when I was sitting away from the sharp line of afternoon sun cast through the window.

I closed the sketch pad.

Ren rounded the gallery on the corner with the same perfectly timed joke about blue dogs that he told every day, and the group came into view and crossed the street to the shop.

"This is the best cup of coffee and chicory you'll find in NOLA," he said coming through the door. *Oops.* "And I'm not just saying that because it's the only one you'll find around these parts. And this is Isaac, the second-best barista downtown." He winked at me, and everyone laughed.

The group was made up of two couples, one older and the other midtwenties, and another four women who looked like they were together and who all appeared to be taken by Ren, just like the women always seemed to be. It made me chuckle . . . *if they only knew.*

I pulled down nine cups and began filling them with coffee. There's wasn't really a point in taking orders, because we didn't have much else. The group sat at a table along the red wall. One of the women, who had a midwestern accent, seemed extra enamored.

"And how are you this fine day?" Ren asked, leaning on the counter. I got a giant whiff of something sweet.

"Good God, Ren. Overdo it much on the cologne?"

"What ever do you mean?"

"You smell like you took a shower in orange juice or something."

"Not orange juice," the midwesterner giggled, reaching around him for a cup. "Grapefruit."

"I think it's lemon," said another.

"Dolce al limone!" he said with maximum Ren-level drama.

"I love it when he speaks Italian," the third girl whispered.

Italian? Since when was Italian part of Ren's act?

He turned back to the table, grabbed one of the girls, and twirled her around straight into a dip. For a second I thought he was actually going to kiss her. I think everyone in the room did.

It reminded me of another time in the café, when Nicco's brother had been twirling Adele around, and I kinda wanted to retch.

As the girl swooned and fell to her seat, Ren stepped back to the counter for his coffee, seeming a little dazed. He pulled his flask from the inside of his velvet jacket, took a swig, and started to screw the lid back on but then stopped and glugged the rest of it into his coffee cup.

"You okay, there, buddy?" I asked.

He tucked away the flask and took a sip from the cup. "Never better!"

Then as if to prove it, he ran to the front of the room and leaped up to a chair, making me cringe as it rocked on two legs, but he actually managed to stabilize it and land the move. We both breathed a sigh of relief.

He went straight into the story about a girl who died on the roof of Bottom of the Cup, back before it was a psychic tearoom. I thought about Adele and her first day, surrounded by psychics and ghosts, fingers threading her chain and telling bad jokes as she got more nervous. I picked up my phone to see if there were any progress updates.

Just a message from Dee:

Dee	14:12	I'm dying. I want to go over there.

I tapped out a response.

Isaac	14:37	Chill.
Dee	14:37	What do u think the odds of her finding a witch are?
Isaac	14:38	She definitely wants it bad.
Dee	14:38	I'd just feel better if I was the one making contact with our next sister.

Isaac	14:38	Brother.

Isaac	14:38	And stop worrying. She's got this.

Ren finished his story to enthusiastic applause and questions about paranormal activity. I topped off their coffees as he answered their questions, and then he shooed them out the door, muttering something about ghost children as they headed to the hotel across the street.

I poured myself a cup of nonchicory and sat back on the stool. Just as I picked up my pen, the door opened again and a pretty girl walked in. A customer coming in was already strange enough, but a gorgeous girl felt almost mythical. When someone did come through the doors, it was almost always a cop, a construction worker, or Ren.

I think she's wearing the same uniform as Adele's.

She approached the counter, her gaze and smile in sync—actually, everything about her was in sync, from her hand placed at her hip to the rhythm of her walk. Her crisp clothes and glossy hair made her look prim and proper, but the way she casually leaned on the counter before saying a word, completely confident that I would be into her, made me think she was after something. A thick, silver, chain-link bracelet with a flat heart that looked like a dog tag rested on her left wrist. Dee wore an identical one.

"Hi," she said.

"I hope you like plain ole drip coffee, because it's pretty much all we have. That or espresso straight up."

"I was hoping for something a little sweeter . . . She has long dark hair, innocent blue eyes, and a scar down her right cheek."

The mention of Adele's scar made me immediately uncomfortable—as if she knew I was the one who caused it.

"Adele's not here today. I can tell her you came by?"

I could have told her that Adele was just around the corner at the tearoom, but I figured that if Adele wanted people to know where she was, she would have told them herself.

"Oh well. I could have sworn she told me she was working today." She slowly pulled off her cardigan, arching her back unnecessarily. "Silly me."

"You could try texting her," I said.

"I'll do just that." She swung the sweater over her shoulder, and walked away.

It took me a moment to register what I'd just seen. "Hey!"

She paused just before the doorway and looked back.

I ran around the counter. "You have . . ."

"I have?"

I hesitated, and she walked out the door.

A mark on your arm . . .

"Wait!" I yelled, grabbing my peacoat from behind the counter—the keys were in the pocket.

She had a mark on her arm. And she'd *wanted* me to see it.

By the time I got the door locked, she was turning the corner.

"Where are you off to?" I yelled.

She looked back. "That depends. Where are you off to?"

Oh Jesus. Everything about this girl screams trouble.

I caught up with her, telling myself I'd just be a few minutes and that no one else would be coming into the café anyway. "I'm Isaac."

"Isaac Thompson. Son of the infamous Norwood Thompson. The one who's going to fix the city, right?"

I barely nodded.

"I'm Annabelle." She held out her hand. Her skin was like silk, but she shook with authority. "Annabelle Lee Drake." Her fingers slowly slid against mine when she pulled away, beckoning me to follow her—and also telling me to tread with caution if I didn't want to be in the doghouse again.

"So, how do you know Adele?" I asked.

We passed an oyster house, a hat shop, and a grocer's, all closed. She still didn't answer.

I probed. "Just from school?"

"Adele's the best, isn't she?" Buried deep under all of her sweetness, there was something patronizing about her tone. "I'm sorry about NOSA, but I'm *so* glad Adele got transferred uptown, or we'd have never met and become such good friends—"

"No offense, Annabelle, but I know about all of my girlfriend's good friends. Who *are* you?"

"I think the question you're trying to ask is, *Are you a witch?*"

My feet planted.

She glanced back, smiling, her head cocked slightly to the right, as if it was the most normal thing to say to a guy she'd just met. She continued to walk, and her stride stretched a tiny bit longer, and so did her smile when I caught up. I'd never spoken to anyone besides Adele and Désirée about witch stuff, and I had the feeling that talking about magic to the only girl on the planet who could make a school uniform look good was a bad idea.

"Yeah," I said, "maybe that's what I meant."

"Then maybe *I* should be asking who *you* are."

"I'm someone whose name you knew before we met! And whose café *you* came into."

Her arms crossed.

"Fine." I shoved my jacket sleeve up my arm and unbuttoned my shirt cuff, revealing the mark.

One of her eyebrows lifted. "We *are* kindred spirits . . ."

It was a pretty docile reaction compared to what I was feeling. *She can see it. Someone can see it. I'm not going crazy.*

"Have Adele and Désirée gotten their Maleficiums yet?" she asked, walking from the slate sidewalk to the middle of the street and continuing down the road. It's not like there was any traffic to hold up.

I ignored her question and followed, starting to wonder if she was leading us somewhere in particular or if we were just wandering.

"I heard," she said, "that if your Maleficium doesn't surface by the birthday after your Elemental, you lose your magic forever—even your memories of it. You just slip back into the mundane as if it never happened."

"What? My *what*? How do you know all of this?"

"How do you *not* know? You're a witch with a Maleficium, so you've clearly come into your Spektral magic. It can't be your Astral if you're really as green as you're making yourself out to be."

"Spektral magic?"

"Oh, you really are like a little puppy." She paused, turned to me, and touched my face. "Can I keep you?"

I pushed her hand away and kept walking. *I already hate this girl.*

She fell into step next to me. "Spektral magic is your secondary power," she explained as we walked past antique shops and art galleries and jewelry shops—all closed until further notice. "The one that comes after you've mastered your Elemental."

"I—I don't have a secondary power." I tried to feel like I wasn't following her around like a lost child.

"Sure you do—otherwise you wouldn't be able to see your mark. And you sure as hell wouldn't be able to see mine."

My phone buzzed. I pulled it from my pocket without taking my eyes off her, like she might vanish before I was able to shake her down.

My eyes flicked to the message:

Adele   14:48   ISAAC! Did u seriously not notice anything weird about Callis?

She huffed as if in disbelief that something could possibly be more important than our conversation. I quickly banged out an answer, debating whether I should mention the perhaps-a-little-too-coinciden-tal Annabelle encounter.

Isaac	14:49	What's NOT weird about the guy? I actually thought he was a vamp at first.
Adele	14:49	Wow. Okay. No. By the way, found out about ur arm <3

When I looked back up, Annabelle was already walking off. I dropped my phone back in my coat pocket and ran to catch up.

"Hey, Annabelle, did you by any chance talk to Adele about the Maleficiums?"

"No. I wanted to, but she ran off before I had the chance."

Hmm. "So back to this Spektral power?"

"It's not like the universe would give a witch all their magic at once. You have to earn it, prove you're worthy before moving on to the next stage. Your Maleficium, your mark, is like Mother Nature's way of initiating you. If you never earn your mark, it all fades away and you just become an extraspecial mundane person. A tycoon, a street-corner psychic, a cancer curer, a prolific artist—you know, someone extraordinary but not magical."

"Is your whole family magical? Like Dee's?"

"Hardly. I've pretty much been on my own."

"Then how do you know all this?"

"Oh. I—I guess I've just picked things up here or there. At first it was freaky. For a while I just thought I was really . . . *persuasive.* I was already used to getting my way, but then after my sixteenth birthday, if I wanted something, all I had to do was . . . ask. It didn't matter if it was a teacher. My parents. Thurston. I borrowed a car from a cop once, just because."

"That's kinda rad."

"I know! It was extra hard for me to tell I was coming into my magic, because there are no physical signs of Elemental magic for Aether witches."

"You're an Aether witch?"

She held out her arm so I could see her mark, a black circle with line work that matched mine. "Aether."

I pushed my sleeve back up and held my wrist out to her. The marks were in the exact same spots on our forearms. "Air."

"I've never met an Air witch."

I pulled a breeze around her head until her long red hair stood straight up, causing her to *"Eep!"*

I twirled my finger into a spiral, and the breeze gently twisted her hair into a crown on top of her head, something I'd practiced on Adele a bunch of times. I figured Annabelle would take it down straight away, but instead she just slowly spun around with her arms out, letting the remaining magical breeze brush over her face.

"That's so cool. You can actually control the wind . . ."

When we hit the edge of the Quarter at Canal Street, we turned back around and kept walking the way we came.

"So, are you in a coven?" she asked. "Or anything like that?"

Avert.

"Wait, if you have your mark," I said, "then you must have your Spektral power."

The store behind her, which sold stripper clothes, suddenly came into view *through her chest.* I blinked, and she literally disappeared before my eyes.

"That is *effing*—you can evaporate?"

A hand swept slowly across my jaw. "Invisibility," she said, her voice soft.

"That is so crazy."

"It's not that crazy," she said as she reappeared. "For a *witch*." She smiled again, but this time like a normal girl, no smirk or hidden agenda.

"Yeah, I guess it's no crazier than being able to change into a bird."

"No way."

Without much thought, I grabbed her hand and pulled her into an alleyway next to a shop that sold antique swords and coins. Even though there wasn't a soul around, I looked both ways down the narrow passage and then up to all the windows overlooking the alley.

When it seemed clear, I walked backward into a darker, danker area. She crossed her arms, giving me a questioning look.

Then I sprinted back toward her and leaped into the air, wings spread, and swooped up over her head.

"That is so cool!" she yelled as I soared up into the sky.

I zoomed down the length of the alley, out to the street, and circled back. And then dove again, landing on the ground in front of her.

"You can *fly*!" she yelped as I retook human form.

"Yeah, I guess it's part of my Elemental magic."

She was jittering with excitement when we walked back out to the street, heading toward the café. "Have you ever met another witch of your kind?"

"Another Air witch? No. Just Adele, and Dee." I didn't feel like I was breaking code, because she'd mentioned them first. She already knew they were witches.

Is it possible that I just found a descendant? My fingers raged with prickly sensations as I tried not to freak out. I turned the corner, and she followed, and suddenly we weren't just wandering. She knew it, and I knew it, even if I didn't want to admit it to myself. *I was leading us.*

Observe.

Witch? *Check.* Aether? *Check.* Cosette Monvoisin was a beauty, and this girl definitely fits that bill . . . *Might not be an actual correlation, but, check.* I walked faster. She kept up.

I had an idea.

Adapt.

We turned another corner. There was a very easy way to test Annabelle's ancestry. Take her to the mother of all invisibility spells. It wasn't like I'd let her in the house or tell her our secrets; I just wanted to see what would happen if I slipped through to the other side of the spell.

My confidence grew as we walked two more blocks, but when the brothel was within view, fear knocked against my chest. *Bad. This is a bad idea, Isaac. What if your plan works? Then what?*

I ignored my own questions, too overwhelmed by the prospect of finding the next descendent. I could already envision myself telling Adele and how happy she'd be. She and Dee were so hell-bent on putting the rest of the coven together. *They want this.*

We closed in on the gate.

Abort. Abort. Abort. Walk past it, Isaac.

But my gut told me she was one of us.

Then, for once in my life, I did the smart thing: I disengaged and readapted the plan. I kept walking.

Internally, I breathed a sigh of relief, knowing I'd just averted disaster. And most likely a huge fight with Adele.

Annabelle stopped.

Shit.

She looked up at me. "Do you feel that?"

"Feel what?" I stuffed my hands into my coat pockets.

"I know you can feel it too."

She took two steps to the left, then two steps backward, as if playing some magical game of Hot and Cold. "What is that *feeling*?" she asked me again. "That *magic*."

"I—I don't know."

"You're lying. You brought me here because you wanted me to feel it, just like I wanted you to see my mark."

In a split-second decision, I walked up to the gate and grabbed the handle. "Wait right here," I said.

"Oooooookay."

I passed through the gate, closed it behind me, and while pacing back and forth behind it, blurted out, "I think spirits have been contacting me. Guiding me. Something? I heard them *say my name*." I peered through the vine-wrapped bars at her, heart pounding.

"See." She smiled. "The universe *is* giving you your next gift."

"You—you heard all that?"

She raised an eyebrow.

I gripped the two bars framing my face. "Does that mean you can see me too?"

"I'm the one with the Spektral invisibility, not you." She gripped the bars just above my hands and slowly stroked the iron, twisting her hands up and down. Fascination washed over her face, making my pulse accelerate.

She dragged her gaze from her left hand to her right and then met mine. "What is this place?" She was smiling, but her eyes shone with fear, her voice practically a whisper.

It was just how I felt around my own family's magic at the convent. I wanted to tell her she didn't have to be scared. *She deserves to know about her own magic.*

Dominate.

"It's a spell," I said quickly, before I lost my nerve. "An invisibility spell, with a few enhancements on our part. I'm guessing you feel it so strongly because . . . it belongs to you."

"I didn't cast this spell."

"No, it was originally cast by another Aether witch."

"What happened to her?"

"She died."

Her eyes pulsed.

"Sorry! In like the 1700s. And I think *you* inherited the spell."

The fear in her eyes turned to rapture. "Witches inherit spells?"

And then I was the one smiling. "I guess I'm not as green as you think."

"Well?" she said. "Are you going to let me in?"

CHAPTER 24

Fourth Time's a Charm

Customers came in and out of the tearoom, some locals, some having traveled from outlying cities to ask questions about their fate. Chatham hung in the background, stocking shelves and rearranging merchandise, but really I think he was listening in, watching as Callis taught me how to fill out the forms for astrological birth charts.

"The information provided has to be precise," Callis said. "An incorrect hour can throw an entire chart off."

Chatham's partner, Edgar, came out from the hallway, kimono trailing. "Darling!" he said with Ren-level enthusiasm. "How have I only now been able to greet you on your first day?"

He pulled me into his arms, and I got a big whiff of his rose-scented chest.

"Because you're more popular than Madonna around here, Mr. Ed," I said, squeezing him back.

"Adele, how many times do I have to tell you, Mr. Ed was a horse, of course. My nose isn't *that* big."

Callis chuckled in the background.

It was so nice being around people instead of being by myself at the café, I bobbed back and forth between not wanting them to go away and wanting to get Callis alone so I could interrogate him, especially about these marks. Excitement bubbled as I thought about telling Isaac.

The phone rang, and Callis answered. After a quick greeting, he processed a credit card transaction and looked at Chatham. "A Ms. Nora Murphy on the line for a tarot reading."

"Thank you, sir," Chatham said, and slipped into his booth for the phone reading.

"Would you like some tea?" I asked Edgar.

"Only if you'll drink it with me."

I made a pot of vanilla chai rooibos, and he sashayed to the front with the sugar and faux cream. We sipped tea at the table by the window while he explained the differences between palm readings, tea-leaf readings, and dream consultations.

I tried to listen attentively and not obsess over the other witch in the room, but I kept sneaking glances at Callis, who was polishing brass chalices, the faint chemical smell mixing with the floral incense burning on the fireplace mantel. *Is he a descendant?*

"Now let's talk about the psychics," Edgar said. I was acutely aware that he'd noticed me glancing back at Callis, and I hoped he didn't get the wrong idea.

I angled my chair so Callis was out of my sight line completely and I could give Edgar my full attention. "Should I take notes?"

He laughed. "Oh, honey, some of the things I'm going to tell you should never be committed to paper. Now, Marita is our most temperamental psychic; she loves peppermint patties. We keep a bag for her behind the counter. At least we did before the Storm."

We finished another pot of tea as he gave me a rundown of all the psychics' individual quirks, sensitivities, and ego boosters. When he was finished, he implored me to make myself at home. "Don't be afraid to ask questions or touch things. You need to feel comfortable here. Lots of different people means lots of energies to mine."

"I already feel comfortable here." In a weird way, I'd trained my entire childhood for Bottom of the Cup.

Chatham appeared behind the counter to collect Edgar for his next appointment. When he got up, he hugged me and said, "I can see his initials."

"Excuse me?"

"Your future husband. Do you want to know the letters?"

I couldn't tell if he was joking or not, but then his serious brow made me jump up. "No!"

Chatham and Callis both laughed.

"Edgar!" Chatham yelled. "Leave her alone." Onyx sprang to his shoulder.

"How awkward would that be," Callis piped in, "if it *isn't* Isaac?"

I turned to him. "How awkward would it be if he *is*?"

They all laughed, but then the look on Edgar's face dropped—just a tad, but I caught it.

Oh no, my future husband is some kind of monster. I'm going to marry a beast, and it's all unfolding in Mr. Ed's mind right now.

"What's wrong?" I asked.

"Oh, nothing, baby." He was clearly lying. "I just always had this little fantasy that you and Codi would end up together, take over the shop—"

"Mr. Ed!"

"Adele, call me Edgar, or I'm going to take back this job!"

"Fine!" I yelled, laughing and shaking my head. "But me and Codi? Can we *please* not say things like this in front of Isaac? Papa Olsin already completely freaked him out."

"Oh, is he bothered by the metaphysical?"

"No, nothing like that. I just don't need things to get any more complicated than they already are."

I waited for him to make a crack about me being sixteen and not knowing complicated, but instead he squeezed my shoulder. "I hear ya, sugar."

He and Chatham retreated to their individual booths behind the hallway curtains, and a gray-haired lady walked in from the street.

She had on a pencil skirt the color of Pepto Bismol and pearls the size of peppermints. She put a crumpled wad of cash on the counter in front of Callis, and I offered to walk her back.

"No need, sugarplum. I've had this appointment since before you were born. No Storm is gonna keep me from seeing my Eddie."

I opened the counter for her to pass and watched as she waddled down the hallway and disappeared into Edgar's booth. When the curtain stopped swaying, I turned back to Callis.

Now that I finally had him alone, there was no quick and easy way to transition back to our previous conversation. I'd come here to find a witch, but I hadn't expected it to be this easy. I hadn't come with a plan.

I hoped he'd bring it up again, but he opted for the mundane: "The most important thing to remember is that under no circumstance can a customer be permitted behind a curtain without an appointment."

"Got it."

"No matter what they say or what kind of trickery they use."

"Got it."

"And make sure your cell phone is always silenced. Chatham hates hearing ringtones. He says it disrupts the energy."

"Got it."

There were a million things I wanted to ask him about magic and about these marks—or Maleficiums or whatever he called them—but something prevented the words from coming out. I was too used to hiding everything magical, to wrapping it all in secrets and excuses. Every time the words got close to the tip of my tongue, my fingers and toes rippled with energy. I don't know if it was just excitement, or a warning, but it reminded me of being around Nicco and that made me extra cautious.

Maybe it was just me finding it hard to trust anyone after being so wrong about him.

Callis turned to the record player and sifted through some vinyl. I investigated a rack of incense with ethereal names like Midnight Garden, Nymph's Tears, and Graveyard Dust—special blends that Chatham's sister, Fiona, made in the back of the shop. I pulled out a stick of Jumping Jupiter and held it under my nose. It smelled like gin.

If the Daures hired Callis, he must be okay? Psychics should be extra-good judges of character, right?

I took the incense stick to the little wooden slat carved with stars on the mantel, and I glanced over at Callis, who was still flipping through records, before lighting it with my pointer finger.

As I watched the smoke drift, the music, something probably entitled "Sounds of the Forest," dripped through the speakers like a light rain on lily pads.

"Sorry," Callis said, giving me an apologetic look.

"I would expect nothing less."

I ran my fingers over the book spines on the shelves next to the fireplace. *He said he's in town looking for someone. What if he's looking for me? The coven? What if we've been looking for each other?*

"So, Callis, where are you from?"

"A simple question with a complicated answer."

"Everyone was born somewhere," I said, walking back to the counter. Nicco had attacked me in the bell tower when I brought up his past—it might not have been the smartest method of moving the conversation forward, but it had certainly been effective.

"In my case, a tiny town in a distant memory."

"So you don't have any ties to New Orleans?"

"I've always felt a special kinship to the city . . . in spirit. But not consanguineous ties, if that's what you meant."

Morning Star's descendants could have ended up anywhere, right? After all, Susannah's had ended up in New York. Isaac didn't know he had any ties to NOLA before he ended up here.

I leaned against the counter, fiddling with the medallion around my neck. I even flipped it over, just in case he'd recognize it like Nicco and Gabe both had. The necklace didn't draw Callis's attention, but I did catch him glancing at my arm again. It felt like an invitation to be more direct.

"So, what kind of witch are you?" I mentally crossed my fingers for Water.

His weight shifted, and his gaze dropped.

"Sorry, you don't have to tell—"

"It's fine."

He picked up a three-inch candle made of swirls of white and purple wax from an impulse-purchase basket on the counter. He stared at the wick, squinting. His brow creased as a little wisp of smoke emitted from the wick. He exhaled loudly. "Well, that was pathetic," he said, waving the smoke away. "But I should be well used to it by now."

A Fire witch?

There was a little charred spot on the wick, and an even bigger one on his ego. He appeared genuinely upset and embarrassed. What kind of Fire witch couldn't light a candle? *Shit, is he really a witch? Unless . . .*

"Callis, do you know about mixed magic versus preserved magic?"

"Yes, of course."

"Is that why . . . ? Your magic—?"

"No. My family's been of the Fire variety since the dawn of time."

"Then . . . what happened to your magic?"

"Well. That's the reason I'm here, in New Orleans." He hesitated, as if carefully monitoring my reaction. "I'm looking for someone. *Someones.* Brothers."

The one little word got my complete attention, though I knew better than to let it show.

"I've been told they've used many aliases over the years," he continued, "Cartier in France, and Carter here in the US, but their baptismal names are Emilio and Niccolò of the house *di Medici, di Firenze*."

Suddenly I felt like I was having an out-of-body experience. "Oh." My heart raced so fast it was hard to speak at a normal speed. "Were they here during the Storm? There's a website to report missing people."

"They aren't missing. Well, they are, but not because of the Storm. 'Hiding' might be a better word. I've been tracking them for . . . well, it seems like ages now. A locator spell led me to New Orleans, but just as we got to the Vieux Carré, they disappeared from the map. If I didn't know better, I'd say they'd used magic."

"Oh, they're witches too?"

He looked directly at me, his expression stern. "They're vampires, Adele, and they are *never* to be trusted."

"*Pfft*. Why would anyone ever trust a vampire?" My throat went dry, and my hands found the charms dangling at my waist. "I know I'm pretty new to all of this supernatural stuff, but why would anyone actually go looking for a vampire? That seems like the exact opposite of what a reasonable person would do."

"Who said I was reasonable?"

I couldn't tell if he was evading the question, so I just waited, unafraid to meet his gaze.

"I'm looking for Niccolò and Emilio Medici because I'm going to kill them."

My mouth pinched shut, but a noise expelled from the back of my throat.

A spoon rattled against one of the zodiac tables behind me; I flipped around, but before I could stop the metallic reaction, the spoon knocked the cup and saucer to the floor, shattering them both.

"Julie!" I scolded, grabbing a rag and spray bottle of cleanser, glad to have an excuse to walk away.

HOLY SHIT.

Breathe.

"I know what you're going to say," Callis said behind me. "That killing them won't bring my magic back."

Not what I was going to say.

"But maybe," he continued, "it will prevent another witch from suffering a similar fate—if I can save just one witch from losing their magic, it will be worth it."

I carefully picked up the chunks of porcelain and took them to the trash can behind the counter. "So . . . what do the Medici have to do with your magic?" I was sure I'd said the name too casually, but if Callis suspected I knew something, he didn't let on.

"I was a very powerful witch before the Medici attacked me. Before Niccolò and Emilio Medici tortured me—fed off me like the unhallowed, diabolical lusus naturae they are." His eyes fell to the counter. "For weeks they held me captive, taking turns draining my blood, and my magic, and almost my life."

Tears pricked my eyes.

"I'm just grateful for my baby sister," he said. "Otherwise I'm not sure there would be a reason to wake up each morning. For what is a magicless life for a witch?"

"That's . . . that's . . . *horrible.*" I had no reason to doubt Callis. In fact, everything he was saying added up. Nicco had admitted to me that he and Emilio had tortured people in the past—here in New Orleans, even—when they'd posed as the Carter brothers. I guess Nicco and Emilio had roared through more than just the 1920s together if they'd gotten Callis too.

Are you really surprised that they continued to hurt people through the century? He threw you out of a window two months *ago, Adele.*

But I was still surprised . . . for some reason, hearing that Nicco was a monster never got easier.

"I'm quite certain they're still here," Callis said. "I may not have my full level of magic, but a witch's intuition is always their strongest asset."

He smiled at me, and I quickly wiped my eyes.

"And if they're not still here, well, I think I've fallen a little in love with this city, even in its half-dead state. I've never had a problem with the dead—only the undead."

I didn't know what to say or how to react. I could feel the horror dripping from my face.

"You look frightened."

I shook my head, since I was apparently unable to produce words.

"I'm sorry, maybe I shouldn't have told you about the vampires, but then again, you should be warned."

"Callis, when did you arrive in New Orleans?"

"All Hallow's Eve."

I looked back to the candle, and so did he.

"Adele, don't think me weak because I've lost my Elemental magic. There are other ways. I'm going to get them. I'm going to get their entire clan."

That's exactly what I'm scared of.

I left the shop, entering the nighttime air, a frazzled sack of emotions. *A real-live victim of the Medici.* My chest shuddered at the thought of Callis killing the vampires. I couldn't think about it. I couldn't think about Callis killing my mother. Whatever happened between Nicco, Emilio, and Callis is between them. *I will* not *let Callis kill my mom.*

My hands sparkled like the Fourth of July.

"Shit!" I whispered, shaking them out.

I pulled my coat tighter across my chest and picked up the pace. We had to find the other coven members.

It was hard to imagine someone surviving the infamous John and Wayne Carter. I guess the brothers got more than they were bargaining for when they caught a witch. That seemed to be the Medici's fatal flaw: underestimating witches.

I felt the vibrations of my phone through the thick wool pockets: *7 missed calls: Désirée Borges. 10 missed calls: Isaac Thompson.*
What the hell?

Désirée	4:41 p.m.	u need to call me. Right now.
Isaac	4:45 p.m.	Please call me before u talk to Desiree. I can explain. I swear.
Désirée	5:39 p.m.	DO THEY NOT HAVE PHONES AT THAT PLACE?!?!?!?!?

I didn't even get a chance to read the rest of the messages before the phone rang.

"I'm a few blocks away," I said before Désirée could speak.

"Good. Because I'm about to either kill your boyfriend or kiss him."

Something felt different even as I walked through the gate. Not danger, per se. Intensity. Désirée and Isaac were on the porch, in the cold, clearly waiting for me.

"What's wrong . . . ?" My voice trailed off as I saw her. "What. Fresh. Hell?"

"I can explain—"

"You?" I yelled up to Isaac. "*You* brought Annabelle Lee Drake here? *Here?*"

"I hope you like being single," Désirée said to him, and ran down the stairs.

Isaac ran down the set on the opposite side, and they both got to me at the same time.

Then, by some sick twist of fate, Isaac, Désirée, and I were standing in the yard while Annabelle stood on the porch of our headquarters, arms crossed, smiling her sweet, bitchy smile at me. She even had the audacity to wave.

Isaac's voice was pleading, but my attention went to Désirée first.

"Don't look at me," she said. "Birdboy says she's a witch, but she's been unwilling to prove it to me since I got here."

My eyes grew wide, and my hands went behind my back, fists clenched. *Breathe.*

"She's an *Aether* witch," Isaac said.

"Oh, is that how she was able to win you over?" I snapped.

"Thanks a lot. Could you give me a little more credit than that?"

"I don't care what kind of witch she allegedly is. Why would you bring her here?"

"I didn't mean—I just wanted—I tried to stop her from coming through the gate, but she rushed past me!"

"You're an *Air witch*. You couldn't think of any way to keep her out?"

"I didn't let her in the house!"

This can't be happening.

I took deep breaths as it all became painfully obvious: Thurston's unwillingness to leave Annabelle despite his feelings for Georgie, Mr. Noah bending to her will so easily. I'd always known there was something unnatural about the way Annabelle got everything she wanted, how everyone around her worshipped her.

Isaac's voice softened. "She's an Aether witch, Adele. She saw through the invisibility spell."

Is he saying? "You . . . think she's our fourth? *Our* Aether witch?"

"I know it. Just as much as we know this place belonged to Cosette Monvoisin."

I looked at the way her hair was twisted into a crown on top of her head, and then to Isaac, and my teeth pressed together. Whether she was a witch or even a future coven member, I still didn't trust her as far as I could throw her, and I did *not* want Annabelle Lee Drake knowing our secrets—especially not about my mother's new family. "What did you tell her?"

"I didn't tell her anything!" Isaac whispered. "I saw her mark, and she saw mine, and she told me about Maleficiums."

"About what?" Désirée asked.

"Yeah, Dee?" Annabelle yelled down from the porch. "Why didn't you explain his Maleficium to him? Unless you don't know about—? *No.*"

It was a good thing Dee wasn't a Fire witch, because, based on her expression, the whole house would have blown. *What alternate universe did I step into where Annabelle Lee Drake knows something about magic that Dee doesn't?*

No one else said anything for a minute, and we had a good old-fashioned witches' stare-off, me rocking back and forth on my feet.

"Fine," Annabelle said. "I'll go."

"No," the three of us said at the same time.

"I don't want to stay where I'm not wanted, even if it's *my family's* invisibility spell."

"This *can't* be happening," I mumbled. "I need more proof."

Annabelle must have heard me, because she stepped to the edge of the porch and lifted her hands slowly to the sky. We all craned our necks to gaze upward. The barrier cloaking the property showed itself: an ethereal shield that twinkled under the nighttime sky like a borrowed net of stars.

"Whoa," Désirée said.

It was impossible not to be impressed by something so beautiful. *Dammit.*

The three of us looked to each other, Isaac's eyebrow raising, implying that it was enough evidence for him. Dee's stern brow released, and that left everyone looking at me.

Despite thinking everything about this was a bad idea, I tossed my hands in the air.

The three of us hopped up the steps to the porch, and Annabelle pounced on Désirée, as if she'd just been told she'd gotten through Rush Week.

Dee stiffened, shock still in her eyes. It must have been weird for her, having known Annabelle for so long. But then her uptown smile spread across her face, and they were hugging, Annabelle going on about how *of course* they were sisters in magic, because they were also sisters in life.

I was elated to have our fourth, but I kind of wanted to throw up, just a little. I took solace in the fact that Dee was using the tone she reserved for her dad's publicist when he was forcing her to do something on camera.

Annabelle Lee Drake is a key to saving my mother?

Isaac's hand slid around my waist. "She's legit," he said, leaning in. "And I've seen her Spektral power. She can—"

"You've done magic with her?"

"*Shit.* I thought this is what you wanted."

I turned to him, smiling, snaking my arms around his neck, and pulled him close. "I'm kidding." His heart was racing—I knew he didn't want to mess up the coven. I knew he didn't want to mess up *us*.

"Nice job," I said. "One encounter with her, and you figured it out. I've been going to school with her for a semester, and Dee's been best friends with her since pre-K."

"Well," he said, making an effort not to gloat, "we have matching marks. It helped."

I pulled myself closer and whispered, "Can you please never use the words 'we' and 'matching' together in reference to Annabelle again?"

"You know, you're kinda hot when you're jealous."

Just as his lips nearly touched mine, Désirée cleared her throat.

I turned around.

"So," Annabelle said, "when do we do the binding ceremony?"

I moved to the front door. "Can you give us a second, Annabelle? We'll be quick."

"Sure. Go do your witchy tribunal or whatever. I'll just . . . wait here."

The three of us walked inside and into the blue room.

"Just to be clear," I whispered, "we are *not* telling her anything. No Casquette Girls Coven, or curses, or vampires. We can't trust her yet."

"Then how will we re-bind the circle?" Isaac asked. "If we're lying to her about her past?"

"Binding her in will just have to wait until we know we can trust her!" It was difficult to keep my voice from rising.

"Adele's right. It's too major. A wrong move like that could bring the whole coven down."

A mouse-like sneeze came from the corner of the room.

"Dammit, Annabelle!" Isaac reached down, scooped his hand into Dee's jar of salt on the coffee table, and tossed it toward the doorway. A salt outline of a girl appeared.

"Busted," she said.

"Way to prove we can trust you, Annabelle," I said, trying not to reel from excitement by the fact that she was *invisible*.

"I don't want to be outside. I want to be in the witchhouse, with the witches. I'll prove myself, whatever you want! I'll make you want me in the coven."

"Spoken like a true Aether," said Désirée.

"I'll also make you regret the day you were without an Aether." She reappeared. "My persuasion power is *very* useful. Surely there's something you need—something I can get for you."

"Okay. Figure out why all of my aunts are at my house right now," Dee said with a smirk. "One's in from Dallas and the other from

Savannah having secret little cabals with my gran. All *we've* learned from
our spycasting is that something bad is happening in the spirit world.
Maybe if we figured out how to fix it, she'd see why I joined this coven."

"Secret cabals? Retrieving secrets is kind of my specialty."

"Annabelle, you can't magically coerce Ritha," Dee said. "Get over
yourself."

"Ouch. Who needs to coerce anyone when you have invisibility?"
A sly smile spread across her face.

A similar smile transferred to Désirée. "I like the way you think,
Annabelle Lee Drake."

"That's why we're besties."

I turned to her. "*Dee*, spying is what got you kicked out in the first
place."

"Exactly, so what do I have to lose?"

"Oy vey." Isaac looked to me.

I sighed, sharing his sentiment.

"Well then, it's settled," Annabelle said. "We leave after curfew. In
the meantime, what do we do? Make potions? Talk to the dead?"

Désirée huffed. "If it were that easy, we wouldn't have to spy."

"Well, it should be that easy," Annabelle said.

"Why?"

"Because we have Isaac, and he can talk to ghosts, duh?"

I looked up at Isaac, who slid his arm around my hip and pulled
me near. "I swear I just figured it out today."

My eyes slanted.

"And I was standing *inside* this property when I told her. I didn't
think she'd be able to hear me!"

CHAPTER 25

I Spy

"Isaac, why don't you give Annabelle a tour of the house?"

There was something about the way Adele asked that made me feel like she really meant, *Why don't you distract Annabelle for a while?*

So while she and Dee went back to the breakfast room to confer, I crossed our new recruit to the other side of the house, careful never to take my eyes off her as we meandered through each of the front parlors. I was glad everyone had calmed down, but there was still something slick about Annabelle. Three was supposed to be a crowd, but Adele, Dee, and I always got along just fine, even after Adele and I got together. Four meant teams could be formed. Teams within the coven were not good.

"I loooove New York," she said, from the corner, looking over to me as her fingers strummed an upright harp, filling the room with an ethereal wave of music. "My mom takes me and my sister there twice a year."

"Oh yeah, for what?"

She moved on from the harp to a tea cart that held booze that looked as old as the house. "Shopping. Broadway shows. Frozen hot chocolate from Serendipity."

I'd never been to Serendipity for a twenty-dollar cup of cocoa, but it was so easy to picture her there with all the other tourists. Then on to Fifth Avenue with an arm full of shopping bags, her chauffeur catching z's in the driver's seat in a parking garage, waiting to take them back to the Waldorf Astoria so they could lounge before dinner at Tavern on the Green.

"I'd love to go to college there, but Drakes go to Vanderbilt. Maybe I could go up north for grad school. Where are you going?"

"Um . . . I don't really know. I'm sure a GED is going to destroy my apps, so probably nowhere."

"Please, your dad knows *the president*."

"I'm not really thinking about the future too much right now, just trying to help people have a present. But, uh, SVA and Pratt and Parsons. That's where I applied. And technically Columbia, my pop's alma mater."

"I've never heard of them, sans Columbia."

"They're mostly art schools."

"*Aww.* I can totally see it now. You and Adele in art school together in New York, living in a loft, staying up all night at coffee shops, going to student film screenings and underground parties."

I turned away, pretending to examine a painting on the wall of a Parisian street scene, unable to keep myself from blushing as she pretty much described my dream freshman year. But I knew it was just a fantasy. I could see the Red Sox moving to New York before Adele would. Not that she had anything against New York. I just couldn't imagine her leaving New Orleans, no matter how bad it got here.

"I always thought I'd do pre-law, just like my parents, but ever since I've come into my magic, I've started to think about journalism. Can you imagine? As an Aether? People would tell me anything. I'd be able to scoop everyone."

I laughed. "I'm not sure if that's terrifying or badass."

She smiled.

There was nothing in any of the rooms that I thought a girl like Annabelle would find cool, but she seemed to be fascinated by everything and handled anything she touched with care. I explained how the house was when we arrived, and she showered us with praise over all the improvements we'd made. It was only by playing tour guide that I realized how much we'd made the bottom floor of the brothel our own. The front two parlors were still fit for lounging, but the dining room now looked more like an Old World apothecary. The kitchen looked like a chem lab, with bottles and vials and cauldrons covering most surfaces, and the library was covered with stacks of books and papers with all of our research, most of which I'd also covered with sketches. The back two rooms with all the windows, one dubbed the sunroom and the other the breakfast room, were now like two big greenhouses. With the help of some special Earth juju from Dee, the plants looked tropical-island worthy.

Annabelle seductively swept her hand across a fern. "This place is so spectacular."

Every move she made—every time her hips turned, or her weight shifted, or her eyes hung on you—it seemed precise, as if she was trying a little too hard to be sexy. It slipped away as soon as we crossed the hall and joined the other girls in the breakfast room.

"Ready to hit the Borges' shop?" Annabelle asked.

Adele looked up to her. "Why do we have to go? You're the one with the invisibility."

"Because we're a coven? I mean, you don't *have* to come. I don't want to make you do anything you're uncomfortable with."

I pulled Adele away, as I could see her mentally pouncing on Annabelle. "Come on." I swept her hair away from her eyes. "It will be fine. If shit hits the fan, I'll fly us out of there, and these two can deal with the wrath of Ritha."

I was joking, of course—I'd never leave Dee behind—but it was enough to get Adele to slip her hand into mine.

"Fine."

Outside, Annabelle paused at the gate. She turned back, excitement in her eyes. "I just got an idea." She took my free hand in her left and then Dee's in her right, and we were all linked. Then we just stood there for a second in front of the gate.

"Adele?" Dee asked.

Adele released my hand, stepped forward, and twisted the handle manually. Dee and I exchanged a glance—it was perfectly clear to both of us that Adele wasn't okay with Annabelle knowing anything about her magic.

When she came back, I squeezed her hand.

She reciprocated, but not without a worried glance my way, reminding me that she still thought this was a bad idea.

"Don't worry, Adele," Annabelle said, "the Borges can't catch us if they can't see us." She closed her eyes, inhaled deeply, and began to whisper words I couldn't make out. The invisibility shield once again revealed itself to us. A sparkling, iridescent bubble.

Annabelle didn't gloat. She stepped forward, pulling us behind her in a chain, and then looked back at me. "I need some breeze from behind. *Gently.*"

I nodded, and a swirl of wind brushed over our shoulders. As we walked through the gate and away from the property, the shield pushed out ahead of us and broke away from the mothership—a little satellite shield surrounding us.

At first there was a lot of awkward bumping into each other as we tried not to step outside of the bubble, but then Dee and I stepped behind Adele and Annabelle, making it easier to sync our strides.

A guy pedaled leisurely down the street on a bike, apparently not worried about the curfew, right past us without so much as a glance or head nod. Ignoring us would have been normal in New York, but here, it meant he definitely couldn't see us.

As we continued past closed shops and bars and boarded-up houses, Adele ignited the dormant gas lamps on the houses, lighting our way. "So cool," she said, unable to hide the excitement in her voice. "I feel like a twinkling fairy." Her excitement instantly lightened the mood.

Annabelle gave Adele the smile I'd seen earlier, when we'd been alone and she'd let her guard down.

"There's one way it could be cooler," I said.

Annabelle scowled.

I concentrated on the bubble, unsure I could even pull it off. I imagined one of my feathers floating through the air.

Light as a feather, breezy as a bubble. Light as a feather, breezy as a bubble.

Air swirled around us, and when I opened my eyes there was a slight change in gravity as we rose a foot off the ground. Squeaks came from the girls as we floated another foot higher. Then another and another until we were drifting along the rooftops of the two-story houses.

Adele turned around, smiling with pride and delight, and the only thing that kept me from grabbing her and kissing her was the floating magic needing so much concentration.

I could only hold us that high in the air for two more blocks; then we bobbed up and down lower to the ground, the girls gasping each time the bubble rose.

When we got to the block behind the Voodoo shop, I lifted the bubble high again and floated us over the Borges' tropical courtyard, giving them the same view I got every night. For a second I wished I was alone with Adele, floating among all the alluring plant life.

I blew us toward the alleyway that connected the courtyard to the main street, and we bobbed up and down along the side of the house. Voices became audible as I lobbed us over the gate.

"Is that Theis?" Adele asked.

I hovered the bubble about three feet off the street near the front of the shop. A guy was standing on the steps, and Ritha was in the doorway.

"What's he doing with my gran?"

"Who's Theis?" Annabelle asked.

"Ren's boyfriend," I said.

"Who's Ren?"

"How much time do you have?" Adele answered with a laugh.

Ritha handed Theis something in a pouch. "Do you remember the instructions? That's not kiddie stuff." He nodded. "If this doesn't work, you let me know immediately. We might have a much bigger problem on our hands."

"Thanks," Theis said. "It's going to be fine. He's just under a lot of stress with the house and the insurance agents, and he's been drinking too much."

"Then why are you here if you don't think there's a problem?"

"Well . . . he's never used 'to stop the voices' as an excuse to drink."

"Voice? Or voices?"

"I don't really pay attention to his gibberish when he's tanked."

"My advice would be to start. Pay attention when he's drinking. When he's sleeping. Or any other time he thinks no one else is listening."

Theis looked nervous as he kissed her cheek good-bye. It was weird. Like some kind of magical drug deal.

We watched as he continued down the street and turned the corner. The last time we saw Theis while we were hiding behind an invisibility spell, Nicco was sinking his fangs into his neck for dinner. I could almost guarantee that Dee and Adele were recalling the exact same memory.

I turned back to Ritha—her arms were crossed in front of her chest. "Désirée Borges, if you think I can't sense you from fifty feet away, my own grandchild, my would-be heir, then we are even more disconnected than I imagined."

She went inside and shut the door without looking back. The lock snapped. The whole cool tone and calmly locked door seemed much worse coming from a Borges than yelling and slamming things. Adele looked back at me with an expression that said, *Ouch.*

"This was a stupid idea," Désirée said.

"I'm sorry," Annabelle piped up.

"I knew better. I just want to know what's going on. I'm not used to having any secrets with my family. Whatever, let's just get out of here."

And with that I raised the bubble, and we soared above the city at rooftop height.

"Hey look, it's Onyx!" Adele said, trying to change the subject. She pointed down as we floated high over the Daures' courtyard.

I dipped down so she could see the cat before I realized there was a woman there, sitting next to him on the fountain.

"Isaac," Adele whispered. "We don't need to trespass!"

"I'm sorry, it's not exactly easy to navigate a four-person bubble!"

I knew I wouldn't be able to gain enough momentum to rise again without bouncing off the ground. We dropped even lower.

"Onyx, what if I never see Alessandro again?" the girl said, sniffling and holding her head in her hands. "What if we never find him?"

Shit. Now I felt like a real jerk, invading this girl's private moment. *Chill out, Isaac. She can't see us.*

Adele shot a look back at me.

"Sorry, just getting bounce!"

Our feet touched the ground, but just as I was about to push off again, the girl looked up from the cat—straight at me. Her hard gaze caught me off guard, and my magic fumbled, leaving us grounded.

"Protégez la," she said, directly to me.

"Come on, Isaac," Adele said nervously. "I don't want to get caught snooping here on my first day of work."

"Ye of little invisibilty-bubble faith," said Annabelle.

I didn't take my eyes off the girl.

"Protégez la!" she said louder.

The cat stood straight up, back arched, and hissed.

I bounced us back into the air, but the girl's gaze didn't break from mine. Her neck craned as we rose higher over the fence. *"Protégez la! Protégez la!"*

I slipped my arms around Adele and pulled her into my chest, focusing on the bubble and not the girl at the Daures'. Adele tried to twist around, but I just held her tighter.

We bobbed down the street and floated over the gate. When we were mere inches off the ground, the bubble dissipated back up into the dome and our feet touched down, back to regular gravity.

Annabelle and Dee led the way back up to the house, excitedly talking about testing the limits of the invisibility spell, but Adele hung back. As soon as they were out of earshot, she twisted around to me. "What's wrong? Your heart was racing up there."

When my words didn't come out immediately, she said, "I'm sorry for snapping at you. I just know the Daures are pretty private."

"Protégez la," I said, or tried to say.

The words drew a smile from her. "What? Was that French?"

"What the girl said back there."

"What girl?"

"Back at t-the . . ."

Her brow dipped in concern. *She didn't see her,* I realized. *Did any of them?*

"Are you okay?"

"I'm fine," I said, not wanting to alarm her with the message. "Let's go in. It's cold."

She nodded, though she definitely didn't look convinced.

We crossed the threshold, and the door closed behind us. The deadbolt clicked into place, but I turned back to test the knob anyway.

Adele crossed her arms and smiled. "Don't trust my magic enough to lock a door?"

"What? No, I just want to make sure you're safe."

"You're starting to sound like Mac."

"You didn't find a dead girl in a pool today."

She frowned, which wasn't my intention.

"Come on." I draped my arm over her shoulder and walked her toward the blue room.

Protégez la?

CHAPTER 26
Blue Room, Blue Book

I knew I'd brewed the pot of chamomile tea strong, but judging by the quickness with which everyone relaxed, I assumed Désirée had spiked it with her enchanted herbs. Isaac lay across the sofa, his head in my lap and my arm awkwardly pulled across his chest. Every time I tried to reclaim it, he pulled my hand back, which was the only way we knew that he was still awake.

Dee was sitting on the floor on the opposite side of the coffee table, legs stretched out, one ankle crossed over the other, and Annabelle was next to her, explaining the three levels of witch magic: Elemental, Spektral, and Astral.

Isaac's fingertips slowly stroked my arm, putting me in a meditative state. I could still hear their voices in the background, but my mind drifted thinking about Spektral powers and these marks and wondering when mine would appear. The only thing out of the ordinary in my life, currently, was Nicco appearing in my dreams. Dreams that were so vivid and detailed they felt more like memories. Nicco's memories. Nicco's dreams.

Nicco.

Callis wants to kill Nicco.

How am I going to explain to Isaac and Dee why we can't let that happen—without telling them about Brigitte?

"Jesus, Annabelle," Désirée said with disbelief and a spring of annoyance. "Who gave you the witch 101? Have you been having secret sessions with Ritha?"

"No, but if I'd realized studying under your grandmother was an option, I'd have started a long time ago."

I couldn't help but feel a twinge of jealously that Annabelle and Isaac were ahead of the magical class with their Maleficiums. Isaac was older, but with Annabelle it was just annoying.

"You're not going to tell me Arlo and Valentine are Aethers too?" Dee asked. "Actually that would make total sense. Everything your dad touches turns to gold."

"No. Neither. My mother is a master of many things, but they all involve old money, martini shakers, or black Amexes. Not magic."

"Wait," I said, "our Aether witch's mother is named *Valentine?*"

Isaac's chest shook with laughter under my palm.

Dee's eyebrow raised at Annabelle. "So?"

"So, what?"

"So how the hell do you know all of this stuff?"

It did seem like she was evading the question.

"Oh." Annabelle began tidying up our usual smattering of things on the table. "We had one of *those* Christmases when an estranged relative pops up looking for money. A great-aunt in Nashville I didn't know existed. She blew into town just before Christmas and was gone by New Year's, but she taught me a few things. I guess it was just meant to be, because I had my first bout of invisibility while she was visiting, and then this thing appeared on my arm. She told me magic can be triggered by being around other witches."

Isaac squeezed my hand.

A rattling noise drew everyone's attention underneath the coffee table—to the porcelain bowl sitting on top of Désirée's grimoire. It still held a bunch of random objects left over from when we did the location spells.

The bowl rattled as Dee pulled it out. She glanced at me.

I shrugged. *It's not me.* I shook Isaac, and we both sat straight, watching the contents of the bowl vibrate as Dee fished around for the culprit. She pulled out the heart-shaped locket that Isaac had found on our first night here.

She held it in the air, and the locket swung once, twice, and a third time like a pendulum . . . toward Annabelle.

Isaac and Dee both looked to me permissively, which felt strange. "Who are we to deny Cosette her heir?" I said, and Désirée handed the necklace to Annabelle.

"I think it's more Adele's style than mine. Who's Cosette?" she asked, almost giddy. Not an emotion I'd ever seen from her.

"And then we were four," I said, my fingertips tingling.

I wasn't ready to go all the way by binding her into the coven yet, but I lit a fire under Désirée's cauldron, brewed some more tea, and we told her how all of our ancestors had been in a coven together, and Dee made Annabelle a gris-gris in a little red sack that matched ours.

We told Annabelle everything we knew about Cosette, Lisette, and Minette—except, of course, the part about two of her great-something-aunts being killed by Gabriel Medici, and that Lisette had joined the ranks of the undead, and now eternally slumbered in our school's attic. And because the night went so well, I even pulled out the necklace she'd given me and slipped it back around my neck. My collection was starting to feel complete: the feather from Isaac, gris-gris from Dee, the heart from Annabelle, the medallion from Adeline, and the sun from my dad.

"Is that your grimoire?" she asked me, nodding to my bag. Adeline's diary was partially sticking out of the top.

"I wish. I don't have one."

"Me neither."

My gaze dropped to the locket around her neck, and something occurred to me. I was surprised I'd never asked him before: "Isaac, where did you first find your grimoire?"

"In my great-grandparents' basement."

"Just, like, randomly?"

"I was cleaning out their house for my grandpop after his mom passed. Sorting everything into piles: trash, Goodwill, and to-keep. These two blackbirds were perched outside the basement window. When I was finishing up, I opened it to get some air, and the birds zipped in and flew around the room, knocking over all of my stacks of clothes and books, and about a million VHS tapes—completely wreaking havoc. They finally landed on top of a large leather-bound book, and lo and behold, it was this one. My grandpop didn't know what it was and said I could keep it."

"That's kind of cute," Désirée said. "The two little blackbird familiars."

He turned to me. "Why?"

"I was just thinking . . . When I found Adeline's necklace and diary, they were so well hidden no one without my kind of magic would ever have found them. Birds helped you find your Air grimoire. What if Cosette's most precious items are also hidden using her kind of magic?"

Désirée sat up and crossed her feet beneath her legs. "Aethers' base element is Spirit. They can control things with souls, like people."

"So where would Cosette hide her things?" I asked.

"Some Aethers have other illusionary powers like glamouring," said Annabelle.

"Glamouring?" I asked.

"The ability to change one's appearance, like hair color or even cosmetic changes, like a new nose. Really strong Aethers can even completely alter their physical appearance."

"Come on," I said, standing. "There's got to be something in this house. A trapdoor. A secret chamber. A magical hidey-hole."

"Well, let's take a proper tour," said Désirée, slipping her grimoire into her bag. "But this time we stick together. Maybe our collective magic will produce something we've missed?"

She grabbed a few candles and a stick of sage. Then she paused and pulled a large jar from underneath the table and handed it to Isaac. "You take the salt. You never know . . ."

We explored the rooms on the second floor, knocking on walls and listening for hollow caverns, pulling books from shelves and pressing the statues carved into the fireplace mantels looking for secret levers or switches that would reveal hidden drawers or revolving walls. We searched hundreds of mundane hiding places, from pillowcases to cigar boxes to the bottoms of vases, but nothing tingled or lit up a sixth sense. Not even for Annabelle.

We moved up the stairs to the third floor, Isaac leading the way with his weapon-like flashlight, and me trailing the group with a swarm of tiny flames.

"Last floor," I said when we reached the top.

Frustration emitted from Annabelle in waves.

"There's always the attic," Désirée said. "We know you have a thing for attics, Adele."

She and Isaac both snickered.

"What?" Annabelle asked.

'Nothing," I said, shooting Dee a death glare.

Isaac took us straight down one of the halls to a closed door. "The forest entrance," he said, shining his light on the wooden door's carving.

"Wow," I said. "It's enchanting."

"Let's hope it's enchant*ed*," said Dee.

With a quick mental flick, I pushed the handle down, and the door opened.

Immediately upon entry, I noticed something different. There was an electrical charge in the air, like on the first day of autumn.

"Do you feel that?" Désirée asked, taking slow steps around the room.

"Yes," we replied simultaneously.

We all took slow steps around the enormous empty room. As we circled, Isaac opened all the windows, letting the moonlight in.

Our paths led us back to the center. To each other.

"I want to try something," Désirée said, pulling out her grimoire. She set it on the floor and took the jar of salt from Isaac. "Cup your hands," she said to Annabelle.

Désirée poured the salt into her hands until they were overflowing, and then set the jar down and smoothed her hair. "Isaac, when I tell you to, kick up the air."

He nodded, and Dee gestured for the three of us to join hands, surrounding Annabelle in the middle with the salt. She glanced down at the page and then started an incantation:

From the world, you've stayed hidden,

Four witches are we with good intention,

With the heir who can unblind,

Slip off the veil for us to find.

She repeated the lines, and we joined in.

Whatever that electrical feeling in the room was, it came tenfold. First my toes and then my fingers tingled as the magic pummeled through the room.

Annabelle's hands began to tremble so hard some of the salt spilled to the floor. A light glowed from her palms, giving the crystals a silver, neon-like effect. "Hurry, Dee!" Her voice bubbled with excitement.

Désirée yelled the last line of the chant. "Now, Isaac. Now!"

He jerked his hand, and a puff of air shot the salt up and exploded it outward over our heads. We shielded our faces as the tiny crystal grains rained down, showering the entire room.

Then there was silence, like some magical bubble had burst.

"Holy shit," I whispered.

The air glittered with suspended salt particles in sweeping lines and whorls. Then I realized: the salt wasn't floating. It was resting on invisible objects, now revealed.

A million crystalline specks outlined an extravagant four-poster bed with a canopy and a mound of pillows. Around the room were a pair of loungers, a standing mirror, a room divider strewn with dresses, an open wardrobe filled with hats, and another with shoes, and a vanity covered with antique tins, jars, and perfume bottles. A large fireplace had become visible against the far wall.

"And there it is, the madam's bedroom," Désirée said. "All it took was three bound descendants, an Aether, a jar of salt, and a revealing spell."

"Talk about secret service," I said.

Isaac smiled at my cheesy joke, and I teetered around, mesmerized by the sparkling outline of the hidden room.

Annabelle walked to the window, where moonlight bathed a salt-outlined piano. She pressed a key on the far-right end. It dinged. "This is so cool."

"Cosette Monvoisin must have been one powerful witch," said Dee.

Annabelle looked at us. "Hell yeah, she was."

"It's so beautiful," Isaac said.

And he was right. Every object revealed by the salt gleamed like a constellation in a moonlit galaxy. "And it's all been here the whole time. Hidden from plain sight by magic." Cold ripped up my spine in a violent shiver.

"Is it just me," Dee asked, "or did the temperature just drop?"

"Not. Just. You," I answered.

In the light of my fire orbs, I could see Isaac's breath plume.

His head whipped to the right.

"Isaac?"

He flung himself around again, brushing at his neck.

I tugged his arm. "Are you okay?"

He nodded, but the crease in his brow told me otherwise. The cold swept between us and around us and then he took off, as if following someone.

"Isaac?" He stalked straight to the salt-outlined fireplace. I followed a couple steps behind. "Are you okay?" I touched his back as he stared into the unlit hearth.

"Stand back," he said.

A breeze picked up around us, and ash began to drift from the cold hearth.

"Do you see something?" I asked.

He knelt down, pushing air into the hearth and then pulling it back out. Chunks of burnt wood and coal tumbled out onto the floor with it—it was as if he was digging deeper into the house with his Air.

I knelt beside him, not wanting to be near the flying debris, but too worried to leave his side.

The look on his face was stern, and his eyes kept slipping shut, as if he was concentrating.

Désirée and Annabelle ran up behind us, egging him on. Centuries of soot and decaying brick billowed out from the fireplace. I began to cough; Isaac pulled me under his arm. With his free hand, he yanked a gust of clean air from the back of the room and whipped it around the four of us, the vortex shielding us from the debris ripping out of the fireplace. I closed my eyes, trying not to cough. He pulled me tighter into his chest, and we all huddled together. It felt like the wall was crumbling before us.

Then the energy tapered, and Isaac's grip loosened. The vortex dissipated around us, and we all looked up. Our side of the room was covered in soot, save the clean circle surrounding us.

The hidden fireplace was completely cleaned out and seemed so much bigger now that it was empty.

"What the hell was that about?" Annabelle asked.

Isaac shone his flashlight into the hearth, and the rest of us drew close around him to peer in. Four of the bricks at the back were trembling, grinding out of their mortar.

Désirée extended her hand, and the mortar crumbled away like sand. Two bricks gently flew out and into her hands, the other two into Isaac's.

We all looked back to Annabelle.

"You don't think I'm going in there, do you?" she said.

Isaac rolled his eyes, set the flashlight down, and crawled into the fireplace.

I stayed close, shining the light over his shoulder. He looked back at me with trepidation before stretching his arm into the opening between the bricks. He patted around blindly.

"Nothing," he said, looking back to us. "It's empty."

"There has to be something!" Annabelle yelped.

"Let me see," I said, pulling him out of the way.

We switched places and I crawled into the fireplace. Warmth emitted from my body as the space got smaller around me. *Breathe, Adele, you're not trapped.* I inserted my hand into the hole and stretched my arm, feeling around, trying not to think about cockroaches and spiders crawling up my fingers in retaliation for disturbing their home. *It's just an empty compartment with smooth, cool walls. No. No it's not.* "It's metal! A metal box!"

"So?" Désirée said.

"Don't you think that's a little strange?"

I shut my eyes to focus on the metal. I imagined it parting ways, just like Adeline's box in our attic. My hand slipped down farther, and Isaac gripped my calf as if he were worried I might get sucked into another dimension.

I slapped around the metal cavern, gasping as my fingertips touched the edge of something.

"What?" asked Isaac, his voice sounding distant.

I inched a teeny bit farther in, scraping my shoulders on the brick. *Jesus, how tiny was Cosette?*

"I think I have something!" I grabbed the thick tome and launched myself out, straight into Isaac's chest, knocking him over.

Breathing heavily with excitement, I pulled myself up. "Sorry! I'm always so scared those metal compartments are going to chop off my hand." My right arm was covered in soot all the way to my neck.

All six of their eyes were glued to the book clutched tightly against my chest.

"Oh. My. Goddess," Désirée said. "Is that really . . . ?"

"Cosette Monvoisin's grimoire," I answered, blowing ash from the hair that hung in my face.

The fireball at my shoulder broke into two, and then into four, and kept dividing until tiny little lights were floating all around Annabelle's head like a halo.

"La femme d'or," I said, smearing away more dust from the cover. I handed it to her. *"The Golden Woman."*

CHAPTER 27

Murder by Proxy

Isaac and I practically had to give ourselves sink baths to wash off our soot-covered limbs and faces. We probably snuck in too many kisses in the process, because by the time we walked back into the blue room, Dee and Annabelle were visibly annoyed. Whatever. We were the ones who'd done all the dirty work.

We all sat on the floor around the coffee table, staring at the unopened book.

The leather cover was the same baby blue as the ceiling, and there was a gold insignia with a scroll of words under the title, also in French: *"Honi soit qui mal y pense."*

"Shame be to him who thinks evil of it," I translated.

The book was thick and the pages uneven. It seemed both like it had seen a lot of action in its day, and was also perfectly preserved. Just like Susannah's sketchbook, Adeline's diary, and Marassa's grimoire.

Annabelle held her breath—I think we all did—as she slowly opened the cover. Désirée leaned in and Isaac leaned back a tiny bit, as if it might be booby-trapped.

The inside cover was lavish compared to Susannah's and Marassa's simple leather-bound books; it had navy-blue endpapers with silver threads woven into the design. Three lines of French were centered on the first page—handwritten with sharp, straight precision and yet with trailing loops of casual femininity. The combo made Cosette seem dangerous—very femme fatale. I thought about the pirate she'd sent plummeting to his death after he'd fondled her sister.

A look of confusion tugged Annabelle's face. She turned the book to me, I assumed for translation.

"Non, ce n'est pas correct," I said, reading it to myself. I flipped the page, and then the next, and the next. "This can't be!" I flipped through the pages faster, but they were all the same: lists of names—Deveux, Lagenstein, Drake, Alsace, Thurnau—next to addresses and sums that looked like financial figures. Line after line after line of men. All men. "It's not her grimoire. It's just the stupid brothel ledger."

"No!" said Annabelle. "After all that?"

Isaac turned the book his way and slowly turned the pages.

"I'm so sorry, Annabelle," I said. "I really thought . . ." I felt heartbroken, betrayed by the magic, and it wasn't even my grimoire.

"Come here," he said, pulling my hand. "What if this *is* her grimoire, and she just liked to keep all of her secrets in one place?"

The joke wasn't enough to make me smile, but I crawled to his side of the table and draped myself over his back, chin on his shoulder while I read the pages. On each line there were also initials—sometimes one set, sometimes multiple sets, and margin notes, all in French. Some of the words I didn't understand at first, but there were patterns of them like a code. My back stiffened, and I sat back on my feet.

"What?" Isaac asked, turning around. "What is it?"

"Not spells!" I yelped. "It's just notes . . . on customers. Girls. Positions. Other sexual . . . preferences."

His lips pinched, trying not to laugh as my cheeks flushed, but then one look back at Désirée and all three of them burst.

"I hate you guys," I said, pushing his shoulder. I moved to the velvet chair, shaking my head and trying not to smile.

"You sure you don't want to translate it?" Désirée asked.

Isaac high-fived her.

"Quite sure," I answered, folding my legs, nose in the air.

"It might not be a grimoire, but it certainly contains all of the secrets of La Nouvelle-Orléans," Isaac said.

A snort expelled from Désirée's nose, and she buried her face behind her arms. Even I couldn't help giggling, and then the laughter went around the room in delirious waves.

"Well, this sucks," Annabelle finally said, wiping away tears. "But it makes me so happy to know how frazzled my mother would be if she knew our fortune was started by the original madam of the French Quarter."

Her phone buzzed, and she quickly pulled it to her chest.

"Oh," she said. "Gotta go."

"Annabelle? It's like midnight," Dee said. "Where could you possibly have to go?"

She stuttered with a response, but then Désirée continued: "Mommy and Daddy Van der Veer just go to sleep?"

"Precisely." Annabelle batted her lashes with exaggeration.

Isaac looked at me, and I mouthed, *Her boyfriend.*

Part of me still didn't want her here, but most of me didn't want her to leave, because then the three of us would be alone and I'd no longer be able to put off the inevitable. I'd decided I wasn't just going to tell Isaac and Dee about Callis. I was going to tell them *everything*.

Callis. The Nicco dreams. Brigitte.

"It's fate. Sisters in magic," Annabelle said as she gave me and Dee tight hugs. *If only Brooke could see me now.*

As Isaac walked Annabelle to her car, Désirée plopped next to me on the couch, an uncouth move for Dee. "Am I the only one in complete shock that Isaac and Annabelle are the first to get their Maleficiums?"

I put my arm around her, trying not to laugh. "*Non. Pas du tout.* It's soooo annoying."

"What's so funny?" Isaac asked, walking back into the room, stretching out his shoulders like he did fifty times a day.

"Oh, the usual," Désirée said. "Turns out my best friend of twelve years is the witch-sister we've been looking for night and day."

He sat on my other side and yawned. "You're welcome."

My fingers dropped to the charms on my chain, threading through each one. I had to say something before I lost my nerve and shoved everything back to a deep, dark corner of my mind. I stood up and paced away from the couch. "You're not the only ones who found a witch today."

Both of their heads turned directly to me.

"Callis. He's a witch too."

"*What?*" Isaac asked.

"Excuse me," Désirée said. "Who's Callis?"

"This weird guy who works with Adele at the tearoom. And he just started working with me too. This morning."

"He's a witch and he started working with *both* of you today? And no one got around to telling me this until now?"

"This is the first second we've been alone!" I said.

"Hey, I thought he was a vamp." Isaac held up his bandaged hand.

"So you . . . *stabbed yourself?*" asked Dee.

"I was testing him."

"He's not a vampire!" I said. "He's a vampire hunter."

Isaac stared up at me.

"Can you try not to look so turned on right now?" I plopped back down in between them.

Breathe.

I lay my head back against the couch. "He's here to kill Nicco and Emilio."

Isaac jumped up. "I knew I liked that guy."

"He tracked them here Halloween night using a locator spell, but *apparently* our spells are blocking his."

"What's his beef with them?" Isaac asked.

"Captivity. Torture. You know, the usual. The one who got away, now seeking revenge."

"Man, I knew Callis wasn't to be underestimated!"

Désirée turned to me. "So what you're saying is that the only thing standing in the way of this so-called hunter and Nicco and Emilio is *us*?"

"*Oui*. But not just Nicco and Emilio . . . Gabe, Lisette, the whole lot."

"So, if we gave them up," she asked, "we'd be, like, killing them all by proxy?"

"Yeah, we'd be proxy murderers. *If* we told him where they were. Which we are not going to do." I looked at Isaac as he sat back down. "You realize telling him would be breaking coven code times a million?"

"Chiiilllll. I'm not going to aid and abet." He pulled me close and kissed my hardening jaw.

"*Ugh,*" said Dee. "Get a room."

He ignored her, lightly holding my chin. "Those are our vamps. If anyone's going to kill them, it's going to be us."

My forehead pressed into his. "You do realize how effed up that sounds?"

"They're vampires, Adele. Killers. Unredeemable monsters. Why do you still not see that?"

"Do you think he's our fifth member?" Désirée asked. "Our Water witch?"

I turned back to her, his arms slipping around me. "All signs point to no. He says he doesn't have any ties to New Orleans, and anyway he's a Fire witch."

"Like you?" Isaac asked, his brow furling.

"Apparently, but he lost his Elemental magic in the vampire attack. At least that's what he told me."

"You don't believe him?" he asked.

"No, it's just—I've only had two conversations with the guy."

"How many conversations did you have with Nicco before you trusted him?"

I pulled away, heat ripping across my shoulders.

"I'm sor—"

"Don't bother." I got up, grabbing my coat and my bag. "I'm sick of your apologies."

"Great," Désirée said.

"Come on. I didn't mean it like that."

"That's the thing, Isaac. You did." I was done sharing for the night. I hurried out of the room.

"I swear, I'm going to design you a magical muzzle," Désirée said as Isaac scrambled up.

But he was too late—the front door banged behind me, and I mentally snapped the lock as I ran down the porch steps.

"Adele!" Isaac yelled from inside, shaking the handle. "Let me walk you home!"

I picked up the pace. It wouldn't take him long to go out the back, and I didn't want him following me.

Thank God I didn't tell him about Brigitte.

I walked onto campus in a huff. The metal fastener holding the red velvet rope across the bottom step unclicked, letting me pass, and then reattached itself, hiding the evidence that anyone had come through.

The steps creaked as I ran up the stairs.

I went faster, afraid I might chicken out. By the time I got to the third floor, I felt like vomiting, but I opened the padlock, went through the room with the statues of Mary and down the slatted hallway. Two little orbs of fire lit the dark path all the way to the attic door and its mélange of locks.

I wasn't here to open them. I wasn't here to break the seal.

I was here because the coven wasn't getting me any closer to saving my mother, or to the Count, or to figuring out why the Medici were after me in the first place. If I could just figure out what they wanted, they could go away and leave my mother alone. Callis could chase them across the universe for all I cared. *And then what happens when you get her out, Adele? She and Mac will get back together, and you'll just be one big bi-natural family? Human, witch, and vampire?*

Just because she was a vampire didn't mean she had to be a killer. I had to believe that.

Maybe I'd been wrong about the coven being the way to help Brigitte. If I couldn't tell them, how could they ever help? All of the people who could give me answers were on the other side of this door. Nicco—even with all of his secrets, even if he had tried to kill me—was still the one who brought out my Fire for the first time. *He's* the one who pushed me to find the coven. *He's* the one who warned me about his family. And now I needed him to tell me more.

Twice I'd fallen asleep in the building, and both times Nicco had invaded my unconsciousness. Maybe it was a coincidence, but maybe it was . . . something else.

I slid down to the floor, back against the door, feeling more like a guard dog than tempted by the locks in any way.

Despite already being sleep deprived and despite the late hour, I was the furthest thing from tired now that I was thinking about Callis's threat and my mother. I took off my coat and draped it across my chest like a blanket, trying to get more comfortable.

When I closed my eyes, all I saw was Nicco at the Waffle House, flashing me his not-so-innocent smile, and the night in the bell tower—when he told me not to trust him, which only got me more worked up. My heart raced, like it was pounding against the door, trying to wake him up for answers.

I lay down on my side and pulled my bag underneath my head, but hard edges poked my cheek. I slid it out—the book Chatham had given me earlier, a thin hardback, 1970s or '80s maybe, bound in black canvaslike fabric.

I swear it was green in the shop.

The title, *The Witch's Dreamscape*, shone in silver foil, the letters crafted by the sweeping strokes of an artist.

I sat up. The book Chatham had given me was called *Dreamology* or something weird like that.

Did I pick up the wrong book?

I opened the cover and turned the page:

THE WITCH'S DREAMSCAPE

by OLSIN DAURE

What the hell?

I flipped the page.

Then it was as if Papa Olsin was speaking directly to me:

A
note from
the author: Dear pupil,
if you are reading these pages, it's
likely you're about to embark on a new magical
journey, and for that I wish you the best. Please heed,
entering the dreamscape, whether yours or another's,
is not for the lighthearted. It's for those seeking a
deeper level of truth. Enter at your own risk,
for you might not like what you see,
and you might find the
very thing you
seek.

I want the truth.

I flipped the page again, not sure if I was more confused by Papa Olsin being the author of a book for witches or excited by how much my fingers were tingling.

This must be right.

Rule #1: The Breath

Rule number one in dreamwork is to *maximize your REM cycles.*

It's not just about getting enough sleep; it's about achieving deep sleep. Imagine you're standing on the threshold of a house. The door is locked. A box floats before you. In order to unlock the door, you have to empty all of your anxieties into the box and leave them outside. Pour in all of your worries, your doubts—anything that will keep you closed inward. In order to see the things you want to see, you will have to open yourself up completely to the depths of your soul.

Now, relax. Take deep breaths. And let's go.

"Grrreat," I said. *Breathing, relaxing, and letting go: all things I'm really good at . . .*

I unclasped Annabelle's heavy necklace from around my neck, let my hair down, and inhaled through my nose.

See the void. A blank canvas, either bright light or dark nothingness. If you're a beginner with dream magic, master your own dreamscape before trying to connect with someone else's.

"Too late."

I shut the book and pulled out my thermos of tea, along with a little vial I'd swiped from the coffee table when I scooped up my things. Désirée's sleepytime potion. I thought about the instructions again. *Dream Magic . . . Could that be my Spektral power?*

Instead of putting just a few drops into my tea, I knocked back half the bottle. *Ugh.* I swigged the tea, washing away the potion's bitter taste.

The release of anxiety was almost immediate. My eyes slipped shut, and I imagined I was in front of a house. It was on a cliff, overlooking the sea, waves roaring down below.

This is silly.

I went to the door and turned the knob. Locked. I stood there, staring, listening to the waves. And then, between the sounds of the water crashing over rocks, I heard a voice. His voice.

"Bella. Bella, la scatola. Guarda."

"Nicco, I don't understa . . ." My voice faded as I looked at the ground.

A simple but elegant black box rested on top of the limestone step. I picked it up and removed the lid. Empty.

I thought about the fight with Isaac, and suddenly a black feather floated into the box.

Whoa. I picked it up and examined it. Thinking about our fight at the brothel made me think about Annabelle joining the coven. Her silver necklace appeared next to the feather. I thought about Callis's mission and my mother and all the secrets I was keeping from my father, and the box got so heavy, I had to put it back on the ground. I closed the lid, and the door's lock clicked.

The knob turned, and the door slowly opened. I stepped over the threshold.

"Bella?" Nicco called from deeper inside the house. But instead of welcoming me, he asked, "What are you doing here?"

I followed his voice down a long hallway, until I got to a doorway with nothing but blackness beyond.

"Nicco?"

I took another step and plunged into the darkness.

Falling. Falling.

Falling.

For the first time since Halloween night, I allowed my mind to completely give itself over to Niccolò Giovanni Battista Medici.

CHAPTER 28

Another Night, Another Dream

THE SECRET MIRACLES *of NATURE*

AN EXPLORATION of ANATOMY
Bernardino Tuviani the Miracle Worker
Teatro dei Rinnovati, Siena
7 febbraio 1612

The energy is high in the piazza as I wait outside of the theatre for León. It's close to the peak of carnival season, so the markets are open late and people are rushing to finish their preparations. Music floats over from a nearby corner—a boy plays a lute for a girl twirling through the crowd with a ribbon, another sells flowers to the people as they wait for tonight's show.

I nervously read and reread the flyer, trying to hide my face from the people on the street. We are so close to the university, it will be impossible not to run into familiar faces. Tonight I'd be less embarrassed to be caught standing in front of the Siena bordellos, for the theatre is featuring a guest surgeon, a professor from Padua, whom I am very much looking forward to meeting, much to the dismay of the vast majority of the heads of academia. They call him a quack and a charlatan, just as they call any man who dedicates his life to surgery rather than to medicine.

I contemplate going in without León as more and more people rush in through the doors. There are physicians—both local and from neighboring communes—as well as barbers, pharmacists, students, and droves of curious spectators, all happily paying twenty soldi apiece for an evening's entertainment.

What could possibly be happening tonight that would be more entertaining than the dissection of a human body?

Just as I decide to go in on my own, Ruscelli, the dean of the school of medicine, walks past, the sleeves of his gown billowing as he animatedly speaks with two other scholars and a gaggle of their favorite students, the sons of Tuscany's elite. "Disciples" is a more appropriate term, for they follow Ruscelli around like he is Hippocrates himself.

"Why am I not surprised to find you here, Medici?" Ruscelli says, and his followers all stop. "Attending lectures from charlatans? Next thing we know you'll be telling us that you are leaving university to open a barbershop to perform your own surgeries." The old man shows not a shred of emotion, but his disciples snicker.

"Have you transformed lead into gold yet, Niccolò?" asks one of his more petulant pupils. "Found the philosopher's stone?"

"Shall we start calling you a mage?" asks another.

"If learning medicine from human experience makes me a magician, then so be it," I say, a bold statement that makes the other students quiver. I've already been thrown out of school once for presenting my ventricular theory, positioning the heart as the blood-producing organ rather than the liver as the great Galen has dictated. Not that getting expelled matters when your father is the university's sponsor. "Besides," I say, "not everything can be learned from the books of antiquity."

Ruscelli scoffs. I'm not sure which offends him more: my intrepidness for the occult, or my disdain for Aristotle.

"Spoken like a true Medici. You'd better watch out for that empirical influence of your household, Niccolò, or you will soon find yourself falling from star pupil at Siena to its greatest disgrace. Just like your tutor is falling with his heliocentrism."

"God forbid we not be the center of the universe," I say with a boldness birthed from my bloodline. It silences the students—noblemen they might be, but Medici they are not.

Of course, Ruscelli insists on having the final word. "Maybe you'd be better suited for the Platonic Academy if you are so indignant regarding our curriculum."

All eyes go to the books under my arm, and I regret not having hid my copy of *De humani corporis fabrica* in my sack.

"Niccolò!" someone yells through the piazza.

León, finally.

People part ways, letting him pass.

"Oh, they're multiplying," says the old man. He moves on, and his crowd follows, two of the boys in the back craning their necks to peek in through the doors.

"Did I scare them off?" León asks.

"Indeed."

"You'll be thanking me later for being tardy. After a bit of haggling at the apothecary and a lot of bribery, I managed to get everything on your list."

"*Eccellente*, and you can tell me all about it later!" I tug his sleeve, leading him through the crowds into the enormous theatre. We push through more people in the lobby eagerly waiting for the auditorium doors to open.

"Shall we go to the box?" León asks, referring to our family's private viewing area.

"No, that's not the vantage I'm hoping for tonight."

"*Bene,*" he says, grabbing my arm.

We slip through a door that leads backstage.

"Niccolò! What a treat to have you in my house tonight on your birthday!" Giacomo, the theatre manager, says. "Shall I escort you and Signor León to the Royal Box?"

"*Non, grazie, Giacomo.* I am more interested in the fine detail of tonight's demonstration."

"*Sì, sì!* Right this way!" he beckons.

We turn, and he escorts us through the dangling rigs and pulleys, directly onto the candlelit stage, which has been transformed from the set of *La favola d'Orfeo* to an intimate circle of seats surrounding a marble slab—the makeshift dissection table—sectioned off by a wooden barricade.

The circle of seats is boxed with four rows of benches for the theatre's top patrons. Giacomo leaves us, and for a moment it's just León and me on stage, and the cadaver resting on the table beneath a cloth. An astringent perfume permeates the air to mask the smell of the corpse. He was a criminal, a murderer fresh from a fatal day at the gallows—a foreigner—so his family doesn't have to suffer the embarrassment of his insides exposed for anyone who can pay the price.

A moment of tranquility encapsulates me as I take in the silent stage and the empty theatre, four mezzanines high, the roars of people muffled by the closed doors. I imagine the theatre full, not of the barbaric crowd about to enter, but respectful, curious people all interested in learning medicine for the advancement of human health. The fantasy is intoxicating.

A few other sons of noblemen who dare to watch the demonstration from an arm's reach join us on stage, and soon all the seats are taken.

The theatre doors burst open, and the crowds pour in, shouting and jostling for the best spots in the balconies, which, from my vantage on the stage, appear to rise all the way to the heavens. They push and shove, screaming lewd things, waving goat skulls and wearing horns, groping at each other's body parts, acting out the dissection to come.

Tuviani's assistants enter. One sharpens his razors at a table upstage, while another polishes his tools in a marble basin so they gleam for the audience. I feel a twinge of jealousy watching them and do a mental inventory of each tool, eager to learn about Tuviani's methods.

Despite not having the overwhelming support of the faculty, my first two years spent away from Firenze have been the best of my life. Joining the ranks of academia has helped me realize that I do not have to choose between art and science, for the questions of existence are questions of both.

León and I are Medici, whether by blood or name, so while we have an obsessive respect for the humanities, the quest for the truth usurps all else. We could never be content with merely the words of Galen and Aristotle from the pages in the library, for without testing radical ideas, how else would the world ever progress? The ancients look at anomalies as instances to be discarded because they break from the mold, but we see them as opportunities for new discovery. We go to the barbershops to inquire about farming our own leeches, and to the apothecary to investigate the origins of dragon's blood, and to gypsies in small villages to learn about remedies using olive oil, and to the alchemists to learn about the distillation of minerals—all of which drive the scholars mad.

We stay up all hours of the night, drinking wine and debating the roles of sensory experience and empirical evidence in natural philosophy, and then spend all day in the lecture halls and the libraries with equal fervor.

Pairing me with León, who loves the natural sciences just as much as I do, was the most brilliant thing my father has ever done. León is truly gifted—not that you would ever know from the way he speaks about himself: eternally humble, eternally grateful for my father's patronage.

We travel back to Firenze once a month, always with a group of students and professors who would give their firstborns for a tour of the

Medici archives, perhaps the most comprehensive collection of antiquities in the world. The collection has grown tenfold under my father's control, for he has the Medicean obsession with looking for truth in the world—in humanity.

And so in our quest against a priori, we do not spend our days arguing the academic status quo; we spend our nights proving them wrong, and so here we are at the theatre.

Just when my nerves settle down after the run-in with Ruscelli, the Albizzi brothers sit next to us. I *loathe* the Albizzi brothers, who wave the flag of the old guard at every given opportunity.

"So, Niccolò," says Francesco, the younger brother, "how is the transmutation going? Have you produced any gold yet?"

Madonna mia! You ask one simple question about transmutation during seminar and you are forever labeled the alchemist.

"Can I help it if metallics are my favorite of all earthen materials?" I say, sharing a glance with León.

"Never was a Medici who loved anything more than coin."

"He loves your sister more than coin," León says, drawing snickers from everyone within earshot, and his comment becomes reason one million and one why I am eternally grateful for his friendship—and also for Lucrezia Albizzi's interest in my "poetry" last winter.

Before the conversation can escalate further, the star of the show walks out onto the stage in a feathered velvet cap, a ruffled doublet, and gold cloak so gaudy he looks more like a commedia dell'arte character than a man whose work is destined to be added to future medical-school curriculums. He smiles at the audience before approaching the table. *I suppose one has to sell tickets, and it* is *carnival season.* His beard is trim, and his hair is polished and kept in a youthful fashion compared to the mummies who teach us throughout the year. His brow has a thick crease, and his eyes are beady, as if permanently stuck in a state of contemplation.

Giacomo comes out onto the stage and quiets the audience. "*È con grande piacere che vi presento.* From the University of Padua, Doctor Bernardino Tuviani at the anatomy table."

The audience roars as Tuviani lifts the barricade surrounding the marble slab. One of his assistants removes his cloak and doublet, and another rolls and pins his shirtsleeves. A third ties a protective robe over his clothes.

Giacomo addresses the crowd once again. "And at the lectern, Siena's own Doctor Matteo Ruscelli!"

My heart sinks, for I didn't realize tonight would be a debate rather than a simple demonstration of internal medicine. *So that's how they packed the house so tightly. With Ruscelli here, the argument is guaranteed to be the spectacle of the century.*

"One of the most distinguished and celebrated authorities on medicine," Giacomo continues.

On medicine of ancient times, perhaps.

But still the crowd roars, as most of the university is in the house, many of whom would take any opportunity to stay in his good graces. The very best way to do that, however, is to memorize his arguments, for that is the very essence of the school of medicine: to memorize first the infallible wisdom of the ancients, and then every rebuttal to modern arguments that challenge the old wisdoms.

"Without further ado," Giacomo yells with fervor, "let the show begin!"

Ruscelli dives straight into a lecture—a direct rebuttal to one of Tuviani's recent publications on the proper technique for bloodletting—and vigorously defends Galen's method in doing so.

Tuviani, seemingly unbothered by the words, removes the sheet as Ruscelli preaches in the background. Those of us seated in the circle gather closer around the table. I take the best vantage point, directly across from Tuviani.

As Ruscelli's tone becomes more sharp, Tuviani picks up a blade and carefully makes the first incision. He continues to open the chest cavity from neck to pelvis. As he saws bone and peels back each layer of tissue and muscle, his assistants quietly clean up the liquid that drains from the cadaver.

I watch in wonderment. León takes feverish notes on the man's techniques and his theories regarding blood and the venous system.

As the night progresses, Ruscelli's ardor grows grander, as does the length of his sentences, only pausing to suck in breaths. His lecture becomes more cutting as Tuviani calmly cuts, moving from organ to organ, explaining their function and connection before separating them from the cadaver and holding them up. Tuviani quickly becomes the favorite of the crowd, whose cheering grows proportionally with the amount of blood that oozes from the cadaver.

I can't tell what drives Ruscelli madder: Tuviani's candor or the calmness of his responses.

With the crowd roaring, Ruscelli's disdain crescendos, and he is practically frothing at the mouth as he wildly gesticulates his concluding remarks. Tuviani, up to his elbows in blood, finally yells, "And today, I prove Galen wrong about the phlebotomy!"

Gasps rise from the orchestra, where most of the students are sitting.

From the crowd, a voice says: "Because Galen didn't know the correct placement of the vein. He had never seen one. Now, who other than a fool believes something that the evidence contradicts!"

"Who? Who said that?" Tuviani asks, and it's not until all eyes swing to me that I realize it was I who had spoken.

For the first time that night, the audience truly hushes. León's expression is near terror.

Instead of refuting me, instead of humiliating me, Tuviani says, "Go on, then."

"There—therefore, the best point for revulsion would depend on the location of the festering wound, because the blood flows circularly through the body . . . to the heart."

He laughs deeply. "To the heart? But certainly you believe that the heart is the organ through which the life-giving spirits flow to heat the body. And the liver is where all four of the humors are produced, including blood?"

My answer is undoubtedly going to get me expelled from school again. "Well, according to my calculations—"

"Calculations!" shouts Tuviani. "Who brings mathematics, an empirical approach, to medicine?"

The medical students in the crowd erupt in laughter, and I make the mistake of turning to Ruscelli, whose head looks like a pustule about to rupture.

Sì, undoubtedly going to get me expelled.

"I should have you at all of my demonstrations," Tuviani continues, "speaking out such unfathomable ideas, so as to make my own theories more palatable!"

"The valves," I say, keeping my voice steady despite the lingering laughter from the crowd. "They are tiny, but they are there. Near-invisible flaps, keeping the blood flowing in a single direction to the heart."

"*Sì*, in a dreamer's world, *passerotto*, but there is no hand so delicate as to manage the handling of veins for the proof." He turns back to his assistant for his scalpel.

"Mine is."

"Yours is what?"

"My hand is so delicate."

"It has *never* been done before."

"As far as you know, but I've performed the procedure."

León's eyes grow wide, and I realize I've given away the fact that we practice on cadavers.

"On calves!" I quickly add. "I've done it on calves." If the authorities knew how much of my weekly allowance supports grave robbers, albeit in the name of science, I'd be imprisoned for the rest of my life, and if they knew how much I spend under the table at the apothecary, I might be tried for heresy, a crime difficult for even the Medici to appeal.

"Well then, my young friend, why don't you give us all a demonstration? Never mind that the fine people paid good money to see one of the most renowned anatomists in all of Europe do a complete dissection. Shall we instead watch you perform your own little experiment?"

The rhetorical question is meant to put me in my place, but what the foreigner doesn't understand is that there is no place in Toscana where a Medici would feel out of place—and at the surgery table is where I feel most in my element.

The theatre crowd gasps once again when I lift the barricade and step to the table.

"Leave it to a Medici to move from calf to human with such confidence," says Ruscelli.

Tuviani's eyebrow rises at the mention of my name, and then he dramatically hands me a scalpel, as if my assistant.

I wave my hand politely. "I have my own." I pull a small case from my purse and remove my knife. "I am very particular about my tools," I say, and pray that Tuviani is impassioned rather than humiliated by what I am about to show him, for humiliation is not my intention. I just love anatomy more than anything—because I love people more than anything.

Shuffles come from the auditorium as everyone tries to get a better view.

I lean over the body, paying particular attention to its stillness in contrast to my own movements. I slow my breath, and all the sounds in the room fade away. Everything fades, until it's just the corpse and me. My eyes slip shut. I envision all of the organs, just how León has drawn them a hundred times from our cadavers.

I use a little sleight of hand to misdirect my audience and ensure all eyes are focused exactly where I want them—on the blade and the incision, and not the way I grip the handle.

The scalpel makes contact, and I focus on the beating of my own heart, listening for the flow of blood missing from the cadaver. The scalpel moves slowly with the grain of the heart membrane, and I angle the blade carefully so as not to penetrate a single extra layer. Before I can ask, León removes a curve of wire from my tool purse and hands it to me.

"Light, please," I say.

Tuviani's gaggle of assistants hold candles nearer as I slip the wire into the vein, careful only to probe it so that the little flap protrudes without ripping.

"Lens!" Tuviani yells, and his assistant hands him a magnifier. He peers back at the vein and then to me, and then to my knife.

I pull the scarf out of his apron pocket to wipe the blade.

"Obsidian," I say. "I find the glass blade so much more precise."

"Well, young Medici," he says, "you have perhaps the most delicate touch with a scalpel I have witnessed on three continents."

"You could almost say I don't touch it at all."

León and I share another glance, and I know he is mentally scolding me for being so brazen.

Ruscelli gives me a different kind of look, one that very clearly says, *I hoped you enjoyed your stay in Siena.* But I do not care, for Tuviani has made this birthday one that I could never foresee being topped.

For the rest of the demonstration, I make sure not to interfere. I go back to taking notes, but I can sense the excitement in Tuviani's speech.

After the seminar, Tuviani invites us to his dressing room backstage. One of his assistants pours wine into chalices while another vigorously scrubs the caked blood from beneath his fingernails.

"Niccolò and León," he says, "I will be in residency at La Sorbonne starting this spring. Please know you have an open invitation to Paris." He shakes his fingers dry. "Don't be scared, Niccolò. Don't ever be scared of Ruscelli or any of them. And don't waste your breath trying to change their minds. It's like trying to stop the plague from spreading."

"And I thank you, *Professore*, for daring to take on Galen, and for the grandest birthday present I could have ever dreamt of."

"*Tanti auguri!*" he yells, slapping my shoulder.

"You should come with us to Firenze for the celebration," says León.

"What a grand idea!" I turn to Tuviani. "You must accompany us back to the palazzo as my guest. I know Father would love to meet you."

"And it would be an honor to meet the grand duke of Tuscany."

"It is done, then. We leave in the morning. And you will have to stay for my sister's wedding next week. It is sure to be the most elaborate celebration in Florentine history." I hook my arm around León's neck, just like my brothers always do to me. "And so tonight, to mourn Giovanna's future with the Neapolitan prince, we will get very, very drunk."

CHAPTER 29

Le Chat Noir

I swallowed the last sip of beer from the bottle and spun my phone on the bar.

There must have been a hundred people packed into the ballroom behind me, dancing to the brass band, half of them singing along and the other half shushing them so the club didn't get busted, but I felt completely alone.

I'd circled the whole Quarter after Adele ran out of the brothel, and I'd called her a bunch of times from her front door, but she wouldn't answer.

I spun my phone again.

I shouldn't have made the comment about Nicco—but I just didn't understand why Adele cared about what happened to him and his brother.

The later the night got, the more I was warming up to Callis's mission. As long as the vampires were in the attic, they'd never be out of our lives.

Now I couldn't stop thinking about what Adele had said about Callis's magic. *Is that why he's so sickly looking? From being drained by Nicco?* I knew one thing for certain: if Nicco had destroyed my magic, I'd hunt him down to the end of the earth or die trying.

I picked up my phone and scrolled through the contacts until I got to Callis's number. Both of us being witches made me feel like we had some kind of automatic bond.

Or maybe it's because we share a common enemy?

The music got louder as the band built up the last song of the set, and so did the crowd.

The bartender, Mia, uncapped another bottle of beer and swapped it with the empty one. I knew it was from Mac's secret stash, because the city hadn't seen a delivery truck since pre-Storm. All they really slung was moonshine, which was perfectly appropriate given the bar's illegal operating status, but not something he'd let me drink, being underage. Not that I wanted to. The stuff tasted like rocket fuel.

"Haven't seen you here in a while," she said as I took a swig.

I used to hang out here a lot, with AJ and Chase. Being with the other first responders was the only reason Mac ever let me in.

"Yeah, I guess I've been busy."

"Busy with Mac's daughter?"

I smiled affirmation, and luckily more customers came up to the bar before she could prod me for details. I took another swig and spun my phone again, worrying that I'd *really* wrecked things this time.

I wished I could enter some kind of parallel universe where I could team up with Callis, burn down the attic, and rid the world of Nicco and Emilio and their entire clan for good, while in this universe I could just be together with Adele without the lingering threat of the Medici. I pecked out a one-line message to him: *Want to get a beer?*

Instead of hitting send, I hit the back button until the message vanished. I was already in a world of shit with Adele—a couple beers, and a meeting with a vampire hunter would lead to God knows what, but I could almost guarantee it would be the opposite of fixing things.

I could only imagine the number of enemies the Medici siblings had made throughout their immortal lifetimes. You'd think with something like eternal life, they'd want to do something good for humanity, like cure cancer, or end world hunger, but I guess that's the thing. They weren't human. We were just a food source to them.

"Don't you have to be at work in a couple hours?" Mac asked, appearing behind the bar with a crate of moonshine.

"I'm off tomorrow. I mean, I have to work at the café for Adele, but that's not really work. It's just showing up."

He pulled out a bottle of beer, flicked the cap into the garbage, and took a sip. "It's very kind of you to take those shifts, Isaac. What happened to Bertrand and Sabine is horrific, but Adele is taking it worse than I expected."

Because she blames herself for their deaths.

"It's no big deal. It gives me time to work on my portfolio." I opted not to tell him that I didn't really care about my apps anymore because I'm sure that dropout wasn't a quality he wanted in his daughter's boyfriend. *If I'm still her boyfriend.*

"Let me know if you want me to look over it for you. Or if you need a recommendation letter. I know you're worried about your applications, but with all the work you've been doing down here, I can't see how a school would hold it against you."

I hated that he was being so nice. It made me feel even more guilty, like I'd slighted him too by fighting with Adele. I took another sip of the beer, finding it hard to look at him.

"Something wrong?" he asked.

Just that I can't get your daughter to understand that vampires are monsters.

"Something to do with Adele?"

"She told you?" *Shit.*

"No, Isaac. I grew up in this bar. I know when a man is sulking."

"Oh. I'm not sulking."

"*Yeah.* What's the problem?"

"It's . . . um, there's just something we don't see eye to eye on."

He crossed his arms. "What kind of something?"

When I looked up and saw the concern on his face, I realized what he thought my nervous blather might be referring to. "Not that! I completely respect your daughter."

He uncrossed his arms and took another swig of his beer.

"I swear." My heart raced. "It's something more . . . ideological, I suppose."

He chuckled. "Well, good luck."

Behind us the audience began clapping in time with the music.

"Whatever it is, don't push her. Trust me. I have sixteen and a half years of experience. Give her some space." His gaze moved over my shoulder. "Well, now I've seen it all."

I turned around. The crowd was circling a man and a woman, cheering them on as their dancing became more dramatic. He flung her around like she was a rag doll and snapped her back against his chest, their eye lock never breaking despite the twirling and dipping, like they were about to get it on in the middle of the dance floor.

"Is that?" I squinted. "Is that Ren?" I looked around the room for Theis and his usual gaggle of gothic groupies, but they were nowhere in sight.

The singer held the last note, and the crowd roared as Ren pulled the woman close and planted one on her lips. *Ugh.* "I didn't think there was enough moonshine in the world."

"Ren making out with a woman?" said Mac. "The apocalypse is nigh."

A couple songs later, Ren appeared at the bar next to me and ordered a drink.

"New friend?" I asked, nodding toward the crowd where the woman still danced with a group of friends.

"She's no Violette," Ren said, "but it's a fool who seeks to outdo perfection."

"Who's Violette?"

"*Pfft!* Only the love of my life!"

"*What?* What about Theis?"

"Don't bring up that vagrant around me!"

Mac crossed his arms again, this time with a different kind of worry on his face.

I looked back at the woman, but before I could ask another question, I was being lifted off the stool by Ren, who'd grabbed a fistful of my shirt at the collar.

"Don't even think about it, Yankee!"

"What the hell?" I yelled. "Don't even think about *what?*"

With as little force as possible, I pushed him off—I didn't want another black eye—but he came right back at me, even more aggressive.

Mac jumped over the bar and then shoved his way between us.

"Have you lost your goddamn mind?" he said, holding Ren at bay until he released my shirt.

I was glad—the last thing I needed right now was to be throwing punches in front of Adele's dad. But still, what the fuck?

Ren's gaze flipped back and forth between us. He pulled the flask out of his jacket pocket and downed the rest of it. "I'm sorry. She just gets me so worked up."

Mac looked at me in disbelief. All I could do was shrug.

He grabbed Ren's flask and then paused. "I don't know if I should confiscate this or refill it to the brim."

I stumbled into my room, stretching my arms and yawning profusely. Another downside of fighting with Adele was no perching. But it was after 0200 hours, so maybe sleep wouldn't be so difficult after all.

Yeah, right. At least I didn't have to work in the morning.

I slipped my phone out of my pocket, kicked off my shoes and jeans, and hoisted myself up onto the top bunk. Lying on my back, I sent up a silent prayer that when I unlocked the screen, there'd be some sign of reconciliation from Adele.

There were three unopened messages but none from her. All three were from my pop, who I'd been actively ignoring all day.

Pop	10:43	Hello, son. Just a reminder that the Pulitzer ceremony is next week, including the press dinner. You're expected to arrive an hour early to each for photos. I'll have a coat and tie for you.
Pop	13:08	Isaac, confirm receipt of message.
Pop	15:25	Isaac, just in case it wasn't clear, your attendance at these events is not optional.

Post-0200 hours seemed like the best chance to respond without starting a conversation.

Isaac	02:13	I think it's best for all involved if I don't go. I never want to see that guy's face again.

My phone vibrated. *Of course he responds.*

Pop   02:15   You will be there unless
you want to go back to
New York.

I dropped the phone down to the bottom bunk so I wouldn't risk throwing it across the room and then punched the pillow a couple times trying to fluff it up. *I'm not going.* I never wanted to see that photographer again and had no plans to ever go back to that bridge.

Medical choppers fly low overhead, kicking up winds and stirring up the stink of open sewage from somewhere nearby. Sirens blare in the distance.

Triage has been set up on the roof of a bank, which is only about two feet above the water—the closest spot out of the flood zone was too far away for medical emergencies—so we're in the middle of it.

I look down at my right hand gripping the edge of a steel table while one of my crewmates refills the gas tank in the small motorized rescue boat. My skin is ghost white and streaked with black oily mud, and my fingers are caked with layers of orange spray paint and wrinkled beyond recognition. *How long have I been out here?* It must have been fifty hours since I went out with the crew, since the first breach . . . maybe more.

"Son, are you listening?"

"What?"

The captain in charge of our ward is staring at me. "Go get some sleep. You're no use to anyone if you injure yourself."

"I'm fine, sir."

"That wasn't a request. Four hours and you can return. We'll be here." He points to a motorized pirogue. "Take the boat to the St. Claude Bridge. Someone from the next crew will bring it back."

I no longer have the strength to argue.

Even my reserve energy wanes as I scramble into the pirogue. I cruise a couple blocks at no-wake speed. The melodic hum of the engine over the rippling water makes my eyes droop shut more than once, but there's no faster way to get there unless I want to swim. God only knows what's in the floodwater. Snakes, rats the size of cats, and debris hidden beneath the murky surface waiting to impale you.

The tips of trees sticking out of the water show the edges of the streets below the surface. Red peaks and black peaks rise from the water intermittently. It's hard to reconcile that they're the roofs of houses.

My skin crawls as an eel slithers through the water alongside the boat. I watch the creature until the bridge up ahead draws my attention.

Finally.

I moor the boat and walk up the long ramp to the bridge, where two National Guard members are standing with some medics. My permanently waterlogged boots feel like they weigh two tons.

"Sorry, kid," the taller officer says to me when I reach them. "Ground transportation already left . . . They'll be back in an hour."

I can't wait another hour.

"It's fine. I'll walk."

"You're still looking at three feet of water minimum on this side of the canal, deeper, closer to the river."

I hold up my pale, water-wrinkled hands. "I've been in it for the last two days. I'll live."

"Do you have a weapon?" he asks.

"Uh, no."

"Living is debatable, then. There are looters rampant on this side. It's mayhem."

"I just want to get to base camp so I can sleep and come back out."

He nods approval. "It's not too far. Just don't veer off St. Claude until you get to Franklin. Then it's a straight shot to the dock. The sooner you veer off, the deeper the water."

I start down the ramp on the opposite side of the bridge, cherishing my last few dry steps. I hit water again before I get to street level.

It quickly passes my ankles and then my shins as I wade down the street. St. Claude looks like it was a main thoroughfare. Now overturned cars float down the street, and there was no signs of people, no voices or music . . . just the sloshing of the water as I walk. I pass a body shop, a dollar store, a post office, and house after house, all destroyed. Some buildings are missing roofs or walls, others just piles of brick and timber resting atop slabs of partially submerged concrete. And this was the unbreeched side of the levee.

Up ahead, a bright-purple house with pink decorative trim that looks suited for a gingerbread man sits in the murky water. Pieces of lethal-looking metal and wood from other buildings have collected against the front. I slog by.

As the water creeps up past my knees to my thighs, I try not to think about eels or snakes or anything else that slithers. *Maybe this wasn't the greatest idea.*

A shadow passes over the surface of the water nearby as something swoops overhead. I turn back, shielding my eyes from the sun, trying to catch sight of the bird. *Was that an eagle?* It seems implausible in the city. I freeze.

A man is on the bridge, up in the metal frame that lifts the drawbridge. I squint to get a better look—he's facing my way, shooting a long lens straight at me. *Fucking bastard.*

I turn again and walk faster, pulling my knees up through the water. It's incomprehensible that people have come to the city and aren't helping with rescue. There are seniors in retirement homes and hospitals without electricity and water, yet this asshole's hanging out on a bridge taking photos for some newspaper editor sitting comfortably in a corner office with a view of Central Park.

I splash my way down the street. When I glance back, I see his lens follow me. I shoot him the bird, yelling choice words I hope he can hear over the two copters coming our way.

A faint noise gives me pause. I stop, straining to listen. *Was that a cry or . . . ?*

I wait, but all I hear are the receding copters and sirens in the distance. With an uneasy feeling, I continue on through the floodwaters, which I could swear are rising—they're now nearly midthigh.

I stop again. *Barking.* A series of sharp, continuous yelps are coming from down the street, somewhere to the left, toward the river. I catch a blur of sandy-brown movement as a dog leaps from the roof of a car and lands in the water with a heavy splash.

Its floppy-eared head bursts up through the surface. I wade forward to meet her as she paddles toward me.

"I gotcha!" I say, scooping the dog out of the floodwater, which now reaches my hips.

She has a collar with tags and a white spot over her right eye and is a little too big to be held, but I can't just leave her to swim.

Over my shoulder, I see the photographer turn, following me with his lens. I can feel his energy, like he's about to get something good.

"It's just a dog, asshole!" I yell. I know it's impossible, but I swear I can hear the click, click, clicking of his stupid camera.

"Don't worry, girl. We're getting out of here."

She shakes uncontrollably and barks in my face.

"Calm down, I'm gonna get us out of the water, I swear."

She doesn't stop barking as I walk away. I hold her tighter, trying to make her feel safe, but she squirms and kicks. "Shit!" I yell as she launches herself into the water.

She paddles back over to the left side of the street, where the porches are submerged underwater and where I was told not to veer off into. "Do you have a death wish, dog?"

I wade out and try to scoop her up a second time, but she twists out of my hands again, this time growling. She paddles toward a residential side street, relentlessly yelping, and then I get it.

"Shit."

She doesn't want to be rescued. She wants to be followed.

I chase after her, splashing against the water. Her yelps become more excitable, and I know we're finally understanding each other: someone's in trouble. I scoop her up and propel us forward, holding her high as I wade through floating wreckage. An ominous feeling sweeps over me as the water rises to my waist and keeps rising. It reaches my chest, almost too deep to walk in, but the dog seems riveted on a group of houses a few doors down.

A chain-link gate floats by, and I glide it out of the way and push off into the deeper water with the overwhelming feeling that this is leading to nowhere good. The dog yelps louder.

Observe.

I swim across slowly, careful to feel my way and avoid snagging myself on any dangers unseen in the dark water. Waves begin to knock us as I paddle forward, and the dog continues to yelp in a sharp, uninterrupted string.

"Spot!" a tiny voice shrieks. "Spot!"

I jerk to the left. *A girl?*

More copters pass overhead, making it impossible to hear.

"Mister! Mister! Mister!"

"I'm coming!" I yell, more waves pushing over my head and into my mouth. Between the copters, the barking dog, and the splashing water, it's hard to hold on to her voice. "I'm coming! Just keep talking!"

Adapt.

The waves become stronger; I dive through the water, take two long strokes, and hoist myself into the drowned bed of a Ford F-150. I pull the dog in, wipe water from my eyes, and try to stand.

"Help!"

My head turns sharply, and I see her—a few houses down the street, a young black girl in a pink dress, clinging to a tree branch that has bowed into the water.

"I'm coming!"

A rumbling sounds from beneath the truck, and I feel the whole vehicle lift gently from the ground. I pull the dog onto the top of the cab, knowing it's probably too slick for her paws, but there's no more time. The water's coming.

"Help us!"

Dominate.

Without thinking, I kick off the side of the truck and dive toward the tree. *Fifty yards, Isaac. It's just fifty yards.*

My arms pound the water.

Dominate.

"I'm com—" I try to yell, but water rushes into my throat, and suddenly I'm being hurled underwater.

I flail, trying to break the surface, and when I finally do, I barely hear the girl's voice over my own gasping.

I kick and punch against the waves. I know if I lose her voice, I'll lose her for good. When I see the pink dress again, in the water, the waves try to take her, but I grasp her ankle.

I pull her close, swing her over my back with my right hand, and grab the closest anchored object with my left—a thin tree. "Hang on tight!" I yell.

Her skinny arms circle my neck in a near choke hold. I feel the tree shaking loose from the ground. "Tighter!" I yell.

"Jade!" she shrieks.

The debris sweeps past us faster and faster, and I know the breach isn't over. I knock away a mailbox that's coming straight at us and search for some kind of safety to get us to.

"Jade!" she shrieks again.

"Hang on!" I yell as the next wave of water comes tunneling toward us, crashing into my mouth and over our heads. Her tiny arms wrap tighter around my neck as it sweeps my feet. I kick and fight, trying not to let the current take us. Just as it pushes us under and her tiny arms wrap tighter around my neck, I see her. I see Jade.

CHAPTER 30

Forever the Alchemist

My eyes blinked open into the darkness, the void extending my false identity for a moment longer. Then I remembered I wasn't Niccolò Medici. I wasn't a nobleman born of the Florentine elite. I didn't have a sister or two brothers I loved deeply, nor did I have a burning desire to aid humanity. I was just a witch girl lying on the floor in the dark, stalking a vampire boy's dreams. Just a French Quarter Rat with dream magic who knew it was way past curfew but whose curiosity had not been satiated. The human Nicco was such a stark contrast to the monstrous Medici, it was impossible to turn away. I wanted to know more. I needed to see him.

I curled onto my side, pulling my coat over my shoulder. I wasn't ready to go back to my own life yet.

I wasn't ready to let go of him.

"Tanti auguri! Tanti auguri, figlio mio!" my father says. "How has it been twelve months since I've last kissed you, my son? Have you grown? You are nearly as tall as Gabriel!"

I match my father's hug as best as I can, but at eighteen I don't have close to his width.

"Nor can I believe it's been an entire year, Father. Yesterday it felt like we'd been gone for an eternity, but now that we are home, it feels like we only just left."

"The more of the world you see, Niccolò, the faster time will go," he says. "We will have the grandest celebration for your birthday, but first I have a surprise for you, to help you settle back in the palazzo."

The way he uses the word "settle" scares me. "Gabriel already told me of your surprise, Papa: you have brought Maddalena Morosini over from Venezia."

"*Sì*, it's true, but she is certainly not the surprise I intended for your birthday."

"*Bene.* I don't want any distractions."

"Niccolò!" he says with fatherly disappointment. "What is the problem with Maddalena? Gabriel tells me you were quite taken with her when you met in Venezia. So much so that she met up with you again in Paris! *So much so* that the two of you disappeared for three days, nearly causing her brother to challenge you to a duel!"

My cheeks grow hot, and I wonder if Gabriel has also reported back to Father each of my shits.

"Is your life something you risk for a girl you do not love?"

"I would have won."

"No doubt, my son, but killing your future bride's brother is not the path to a healthy courtship!"

"*Bride?*" I do not try to hide my horror.

"Do you deny your feelings for her?"

"I like her fine—she's exceptionally beautiful, and charming, and she could outwit even the surliest curmudgeons at the French salons. And has quite the capacity for philosophy, and—"

My father smiles.

"But—but I am not interested in love, *Padre*, and certainly not in marriage! I want to focus on my work. The trip abroad has given me such a renewed interest in my craft, I can think of nothing else! Besides, Gabriel is five years my senior, and he is still not married!"

"*Sì*, well, sometimes I think Gabriel Medici out in the world as an eligible bachelor does more good for our family than having him actually married to one poor woman."

We both laugh, but I am absolutely serious. Love is not something I desire. I just spent the last year observing how love crushed León. Love had, in fact, been the reason for our yearlong trip abroad.

Tuviani did return to Firenze with us and stayed as my father's personal guest to Giovanna's wedding. That night, and for many after, he had León's and my complete attention—not just for knowledge of medicine and anatomy, but also for his intriguing anecdotes of his younger years. He'd spent very little time at his first university before going out on his own, wandering from school to school, from Lisbon to Moscow, and from Uppsala to Crete. He stopped in every mountain and seaside town in between to gain the folk secrets of the gypsies and the back-kitchen recipes of *le vecchie streghe*. A true Renaissance man of experience.

"It's the things you learn in life, not in school, that you will remember when you are older, Niccolò," he said at dinner after the wedding.

Sometime after too many glasses of wine and too many dances, I realized León was missing. I spent the rest of the night looking for him, eventually enlisting my brothers to help.

It took hours, but we finally found him sitting on the bridge on the outskirts of town, in a near-catatonic state, partly induced by the barrel of wine we'd drunk, but mostly due to the nuptials.

In all the years since he first laid eyes on my sister, he'd never spoken to me of his relationship with Giovanna, but that night, sitting on that bridge, he cried over it. We three sat next to him, our legs dangling over the edge as the river filled with his tears. If there was a medicinal cure or a magical concoction that could have taken away his pain, I would have walked to the moon and back again to fetch it for my friend.

Love took a piece of León that night.

One year later I can still see the effects. He is just as brilliant, just as kind, and just as grateful for everything he has, but there is also an emptiness, like a tiny hole has pierced his soul, and a part of him leaks out each day—not enough for the average passerby to notice, but enough for me to see, making it my duty to follow him around with a bottle, collecting the lost parts of him so they will be there waiting when he is ready to be whole again.

So that is how I decided that we both needed an adventure.

If I was ever to have words fit for the paper on which my poems were written, I needed to see things, touch things, feel things that were outside of my everyday existence. Gabriel had never been able to get me on one of his diplomatic trips, nor could Emilio get me on one of his less-than-diplomatic romps, but the thought of learning all the secrets of the European greats thrilled me.

And I just knew that if we searched hard enough, we'd find the cure for León's heartache.

Gabriel volunteered to be our guide, and who has been in love more times than Gabriel Cosimo Medici? Who is better equipped for dealing with broken hearts?

One month in Venezia turned into two, and then we spent a third entirely in Sicily. My letters made Father so excited, he arranged for us to tour all of the *magnifiche capitali* of Europe, presenting me to all of the great families of the continent. We went through Vienna, Prague, and Budapest, the forests of Germany and hills of France, and across the sea to London. His generous trip had a twofold mission, and Gabriel saw that both were equally satisfied: we were to observe all of the European advances in botany, astronomy, and alchemy, note all of its medicinal discoveries, and unearth all of Europe's magical secrets. But also in meeting the great families, entertain as many queens' daughters as we could, which I grew quickly bored with. They were a mere distraction from a great cause. Except . . . when Maddalena turned up with her brother in Paris.

Paris captivated us for three months. We visited surgeons at La Sorbonne and smoked Egyptian hashish at salons with charlatans at night, and at some point the hole in León's soul shrank and shrank, and his smile began to gradually come back.

"Well," my father says, "that is just the thing I want to hear, Niccolò, that you are ready to dedicate yourself to your work." He beams with excitement. "Although, I am sure my brilliant son can do this *and* also find some time for Maddalena Morosini, who might be the most beautiful woman I have ever seen. And if you ever tell your sister I said that, I will cut off your fingers."

I smile and hug him again, finding myself not so frustrated that he invited Maddalena over from Venezia.

"I hope in your grand sojourn you have learned deeply from many institutions, have found great inspiration from our friends abroad, and are ready to hone your talents here in Firenze."

"That is exactly what I am trying to tell you, Father. I am eager to find focus on my work."

He removes a candelabra from the wall. "Then you must follow me now for the real surprise."

My father's cryptic tone is usually reserved for battle tactics with Emilio or banking strategies with Gabriel, so it is with great enthusiasm and curiosity that I walk by his side as we make our way through the palazzo, twisting and turning down staircases, moving deeper and deeper underground.

He dismisses the guards as we go, and soon the tunnels are completely dark, save his candelabra. There is no one but us, hurrying past empty dungeons from centuries past. I've only been this far underground once before, when I was about ten—playing a game with my brothers in which the basic premise was them leaving me alone in the dark and waiting for me to find my way back, crying and nearly pissing myself with fear.

Our footsteps grow louder the deeper we go as all other sounds fade away, and it feels like we have left the planet and entered the nighttime sky, for there could be no other place as dark. I marvel at how my father is able to navigate. His authoritative steps make it seem like he's traveled the route a hundred times before.

We come to a set of metal doors so large one would think they'd be only fit to guard a fortress. He holds the torch out to me. "Happy birthday, Niccolò. Your family and your destiny await."

I shine the fire closer to the metal—the doors are not embossed with the Medici coat of arms, but three interlaced diamond rings, which I know to be a favorite marker of Cosimo the Elder.

"I don't understand, Father. This palazzo wasn't yet built when the elders ruled Firenze."

"The palazzo above wasn't, but the palazzo below was."

He opens the doors, but on the other side, there is only another tunnel. A path is lit by torches mounted on the rock walls.

As we continue, more tunnels branch off, but we do not venture off the path, and I truly feel like the tunnels were lit by the gods of antiquity and we are journeying a secret path to Elysium.

And then my father stops. We are at a dead end, a wall of rock. Again he looks to me.

"Go on," he says. In the light of the flames, I can tell he is trying not to smile.

"Father, I know that you hold my talents in high esteem, but walking through stone was not a subject covered in our curriculum."

"Which is why, now, you will learn from me."

Just as I begin to laugh, he walks forward, and with a turn he disappears.

"Madonna mia!" I step forward with caution, hand extended. When I am close enough to touch the wall, I see the invisible path off to the right.

My hands swat back and forth as I pass. *"An optical illusion,"* I whisper. A simple trick of the eye, but one that takes a true master of paint and stone and sculpture.

The trick is immediately forgotten as I turn the corner and enter a space so cavernous I can hardly understand how it exists. The underground hall must be bigger than the grand hall aboveground in the palazzo. Bigger than San Lorenzo.

There is no natural light, but the arched ceiling is painted midnight blue and is covered in fragments of reflective glass. It takes me a moment to realize it's a twinkling depiction of all the major constellations and the planets glowing among them. A masterful nighttime sky.

"I see Galileo has left his mark here." I nod up to the four moons of Jupiter painted among the stars.

"Sì."

"This ceiling . . . The curvature would impress even Brunelleschi."

"They say he was quite impressed with himself when he built it." My father chuckles to himself.

"How—?"

Flames whip around the room, and sconces all throughout the hall are suddenly lit.

"What science is this?" I whisper.

"Just like all of the greats are forever immortalized in our great halls," my father echoes.

The mirrored glass on the ceiling reflects the flames, casting even more light onto the enormous statues. I step to one of the long walls, and my gaze pulls to the frescos that extend down from the ceiling. They're unfamiliar scenes of classical mythology, but with very recognizable strokes—the whimsical colors of Botticelli and the realism of da Vinci. Between the frescos are portraits of all the important Medici by Michelangelo and Raphael. And along both lengths of wall are the largest crypts I've ever seen, marble sarcophagi carved by Donatello and fit for kings.

"Father, keep me in suspense no longer, I beg you." I walk back to the center of the room where he is standing, watching me. "What is this place?"

"The bones of our ancestors, Niccolò. One day I will be here, and you will too, resting with the greats."

"Unless, of course," Emilio says, stepping out from a shadow cast by a gargantuan statue of Hermes, "he succeeds with his duty."

"He will," Gabriel says from the opposite corner.

They both move to stand at Father's sides.

"What—what is going on? What about the crypts at the basilica?"

"Those are the crypts for the people, Niccolò. *Here* is where we protect our souls, our bones, and our secrets. This is where you will take your place in greatness." He gestures to a set of doors at the end of the hall.

I walk toward the door, and they follow behind me. As I draw near, it opens, as if they commanded it.

I don't know what I expect to find, but the ghosts of my grand-fathers might have been a lesser shock. I freeze, paralyzed by the sight before me.

The room is not as long as the great hall, but the ceiling is just as cavernous. It's ablaze with light from fireplaces—shelves glitter with glass bottles and jars, and long benches on either side are scattered with more scientific instruments than I saw in all my travels, some whose purpose eludes me. It is perhaps the most sophisticated laboratory in Europe, if not the world.

Standing in the middle, waiting for us, is León.

"Welcome, my brother," he says, and then turns to my father. "I've set up everything to your specifications, sir. With a few *extras* that I knew you would like, Niccolò." He points to a set of obsidian knives.

Emilio spits on the ground at León's feet. "You dare to bring *him* down here, Father! Entry is by bone and by blood! And we all know *he* is neither." He draws his sword and points it at León.

My hand goes to the hilt of my dagger, as does Gabriel's, but León just looks at Emilio and takes a breath.

My father's voice booms throughout the chamber: "Don't you dare draw your sword, Emilio! I am the head of this household, and I have invited León into the circle. I trust him with Niccolò's life."

"Well, we all know you hold nothing in higher esteem than Niccolò's life," Emilio says through gritted teeth, but he sheathes his weapon.

"Watch your tongue, Emilio," Gabriel says, his hand still on his blade.

"Non capisco, Padre," I say, already moving on from Emilio's outburst. "What is this place?"

"This is your new home, Niccolò," my father says. "Yours and León's, if you choose to accept the duty that falls upon you by your bloodline."

"As if one's blood is one's choice," I say, slowly walking around, my hand grazing over brass scales, Galileo's *occhiolino*, and his telescopes. The room's contents seem equally split between astronomy, mathematics, and alchemy: an assortment of glassware and an apparatus for distillation is ready for minerals; maps of the world are stacked on workbenches, pinned down by metalworking tools; and spices from the Far East line four full shelves on the wall. Another shelf is tacked with botanist diagrams, and another has rows of jars sealed with wax, containing floating specimens—eyeballs of various sizes and a heart too big to be a goat's. Some shelves rise all the way to the domed ceiling, which has openings that allow airflow back out into the caves; half are filled with books and half with scrolls. Empty tables await cadavers, and empty cages with wall chains await . . . I look at my father.

"This is a very old laboratory," he says. "Different times called for different measures."

I gaze around again at all the ancient tools and modern inventions and feel a ripple of excitement. "If León and I can use this laboratory, Father, we will doubtless become the best surgeons in all of Europe."

"You will become much more than surgeons," my father says. "Niccolò, you will be the first to create the Elixir of Life. Your work here will elevate the Medici back to the greatest family in Europe."

I laugh. "The Elixir of Life is a thing of legends. All those who have tried have failed."

He smiles. "That's because all who have tried were alchemists, charlatans, and magicians. *You* are a Medici. Surely you don't think I let you continue on this medicinal path so you could pull teeth and treat syphilis? I have been priming you since birth, Niccolò. You will be the one who unites the microcosm with the macrocosm.

"You will be the one who draws together all the knowledge of medicine and mysticism to create the substance mankind has so desperately searched for since time began. The power of the heavens, of life and death itself, distilled into a potion that defies mortality."

If only my professors could hear the way my father speaks, they'd get the true effect of the grandeur of the Medici tongue.

"Your brilliant mind and your magical touch will take my work to places I could never imagine. Here you will no longer be stifled by the Aristotelian teachings of the university, nor will you be controlled by papal rule. Here you are bound only by your own dreams. And once the Elixir is complete, just think of the people you will be able to heal. You will not be one who treats the plague; you will be the one to *eradicate* the plague!"

"You have high hopes for me, Father, and I love you for that. I just hope that I won't disappoint you."

"It is not possible. I have waited with paternal excitement for this moment since you were born." He looks at each of my brothers. "Just like I waited for each one of my children to take their places in the family."

He beckons for me to follow and walks to a grand podium in the center of the room, upon which rests an aged tome.

The book is opened to a handwritten page. Scrolled across the top in Italian, rather than the Latin or Greek I expect based on how old the book looks, are the words:

MEDICI ELIXIR della VITA ·

Paragraphs turn into pages, and pages, and pages of notes, charts, diagrams on distillation and transmutation of the elements.

"You will take the helm, just as your grandfather did before you, and his grandfather, all the way back to Cosimo the Elder. They will all be here with you. Take guidance from their spirits, and finish the Elixir, Niccolò. I always knew it would be you who would take my place here."

I turn to my brothers, who have been unusually quiet throughout my father's speech, giving it even more gravity. Both of them smile at me crookedly, but with pride, and I wonder how long they've had to keep this secret. I hook one arm around each of their necks, as it's difficult for me to come up with words that express my feelings.

I have my calling, and it is neither sword, nor cross, nor coin.

In my old age, it won't just be poems I write, but history.

Creating the Elixir will be more important than the victory of war or acquiring wealth or land—for the Elixir will change our world. It will be *truly* magical, worthy of a place in antiquity, like the relics my father collects from ancient times.

"I bet you didn't think we could top the birthday when Bianca made you a man?" Gabriel says.

"No . . . No, I did not."

My father embraces me. "You are more than a man, Niccolò. You are a Medici."

The church bells boom high above us.

How can we hear the church bells from so far underground?

They grow louder, echoing in my chest, and when my father pulls away, I blink because I swear I can see the podium *through his chest.*

"Father?" I reach out for his shoulder, but my hand passes right through him. "Father!"

"Gabriel!" I yell, turning to my brothers, but they fade away too. The flames in the sconces go out one by one until the room is pitch black and I am alone. "León? *León!*" I scream until the sound of my voice fades into nothingness.

And from nothingness comes schoolyard chatter, and I am awake. The bells at St. Mary's church clang next to the attic.

It's seven a.m.

Shit.

CHAPTER 31

Twin-Flames

January 11th

My phone buzzed as I looped the little metal rings together, a pair of needle-nose pliers in each of my hands. The clusters had turned into rows, and the rows into patches, and now I had a two-by-three-foot section of chainmaille, and the mountain of little rings was shrinking.

I glanced down at my phone.

Désirée	**12:37 p.m.**	Is ur house arrest over yet?

I set down the tools and punched back a message.

Adele	**12:37 p.m.**	No. My dad even told Isaac that the terms of my grounding exclude him from the metal shop.

Being grounded for the last two days sucked, but it made not talking to Isaac easier. And I was definitely *not* talking to him. I looked over to his empty space at the worktable, to the sculpture of a coconut he was working on. He'd told me it reminded him of the island illustrations in Susannah's sketchbook. I told him it reminded me of the Krewe of Zulu. He'd carved each little coconut-shell hair with meticulous precision, just like the wisps of the feather.

I slipped on my coat, grabbed my bag from under the table, and continued the text conversation on my way to work.

Désirée	12:38 p.m.	Isaac should probably stay clear of Mac, anyway. And srsly, ur the only person on the planet who could get grounded for hooking up and still have their virginity intact.

My fingertips blushed as I texted the response.

Adele	12:38 p.m.	That's not why I got grounded. I got grounded for not coming home. My dad just assumes I was with Isaac.

The cool breeze felt good against my face after being cooped up. My father had even made me call into work. At least he had calmed down a little.

Désirée	12:41 p.m.	This is the part where u tell me where u really were, if u weren't actually hooking up with our other coven member.
Adele	12:42 p.m.	Um... Later. Not a convo for text.
Désirée	12:42 p.m.	u can't stay mad at him forever, u know?

And with that I put my phone away because I still felt like I could, in fact, stay mad at Isaac forever. I hadn't returned any of his messages— for whatever reason, "sorry" wasn't enough this time—which meant there was a zero percent chance of him not showing up during my shift.

Despite the inevitable confrontation, I was eager to get to the tearoom. I had a laundry list of magical things I wanted to investigate, most of which had to do with dreamcasting, as Papa Olsin called it in his book. If it was my Spektral power, I sucked at it, and no wonder I didn't have my mark. Despite my jailbird status, I'd snuck out the last two nights and gone to the attic to try to connect with Nicco, to no avail. It was like the dream magic had suddenly stopped working. But most importantly, I needed to know if Callis had made any progress with his *plan*.

And that frazzled my nerves as I opened the door at Bottom of the Cup.

He was behind the counter, sweeping up what sounded like large chunks of glass. "I'm beginning to come to terms with the fact that she hates me," he said, clearly frustrated.

I walked over. "Who hates you?"

"Julie." He dumped the dustpan into the bin. More broken moons.

"Why do they keep hanging that shelf?" It seemed illogical even for the Daures. I took the broom from him and finished sweeping as he held the dustpan steady. Onyx leaped onto the counter and supervised. "Thanks for covering my shift yesterday."

"No problemo. Isaac told me you've been grounded."

"Mmmhmm."

"Aaand that you're not speaking to him."

I did my best not to look annoyed—this was not something I wanted to discuss with Callis. "Did you tell Isaac? About your . . . mission?"

"Yeah, he didn't know anything about Niccolò and Emilio."

Every muscle in my back eased. It was such a moment of relief, I worried Callis might have noticed. Not that I really thought Isaac was going to rat, but then again, he hates vampires *so* much. Especially Emilio. *Especially* Nicco.

"I figured he didn't know anything."

"Unless it happened in the last two days?"

I smirked.

"None of my business." He held his hands up.

The phone rang.

"Bottom of the Cup Tearoom?" I answered.

"I need to speak with Olsin, please," quivered a woman on the other end.

"Okay." I glanced at his appointment book. "He has an opening in, like, ten minutes."

"I don't want an appointment. I just need to ask him a question."

"I'm sorry, ma'am. All psychics are by appointment only."

Click.

A little girl entered the shop from the hallway. She couldn't have been more than eight or nine, but her long black ringlets tied up into a floppy white bow made her look younger and doll-like. Her thin-lipped smile and deep-blue eyes looked just like Callis's.

I smiled at her, but before I could introduce myself, the phone rang again.

"Bottom of the Cup?"

"Hi, it's me again. Jessie. I just need to ask Olsin a question. It will be fast, I promise."

"I'm sorry, Jessie, but we can't transfer any calls unless you have an appointment."

She burst into tears.

I covered the receiver and mouthed *She's crying* to Callis.

He shook his head.

"I'm so sorry, are you sure you don't want to make an appointment?"

"No, thank you." *Click.*

"Always an appointment," Callis said.

I nodded and hung up the phone.

He turned to the little girl. "Celestina, this is Adele. I told you about her. She's a friend of Isaac's. Do you remember him?"

Her head bobbed.

"Nice to meet you, Celestina. I really like your bow."

The phone rang a third time. I answered, but someone reached from behind me and pulled it from my hand. Papa Olsin.

"Go look under the porch steps," he said into the phone before handing it back to me.

"Um?" I held the receiver back to my ear, but the lady had already hung up. And Papa Olsin was already shuffling back down the hallway, mumbling to himself.

Callis shrugged.

"You're pretty," said the little girl.

"Merci beaucoup, toi aussi."

Before I could translate, she replied, *"Pas aussi belle que toi."*

"Celestina!" Callis yelled.

A giggle slipped from my lips. *"Ton accent est parfait!"* And it was the truth—her accent *was* perfect.

"I'm so glad you've been watching the films I gave you," Callis said to his sister, and then looked at me. "She really is the cleverest little girl."

When I looked back to her, she was running toward me. She threw her arms around my waist.

"Celestina!" Callis stepped toward us. "I'm sorry. She doesn't get much interaction with children her own age. Or girls really, ever."

"It's okay," I said, trying to hide the startled look on my face. I patted her head. Vibrations came from above us. *Oh no.* I shoved her out of the way as the metal shelf above us tipped, and my arm flew straight up, shielding myself—the metal shelf froze in midair right above my head.

Callis dove onto the counter, arm outstretched, as a crystal ball tipped over its edge. "Got it."

All I could do was breathe loudly and bring my hand to the shelf so it looked like I was physically holding it up. Celestina's eyes grew big.

Callis swung over the counter and helped me lift the shelf down without tipping any of the other crystal balls.

Two long screws rolled around on the brick floor. "What the hell?" I whispered, picking them up, momentarily forgetting there was a child in the room.

Callis looked at me. "I told you she hates me."

The phone rang a fourth time. I hesitated before answering.

"Thank you. Thank you!" The woman was now crying hysterically. "I found her. I found Goldie under the porch just like Olsin said. We've had that puppy for twelve years. She was like our baby."

"*Whoa* . . . Glad we could help."

I hung up the phone a little stunned, both by the psychic experience and from nearly getting my head crushed by a crystal ball.

Callis ushered Celestina back upstairs while I lit a stick of incense called Ocean's Breeze, hoping it would have a calming effect.

"Are you okay?" he asked, reentering the room from the corridor.

"Yeah, fine." I leaned on the counter, trying to find a position that looked natural, but everything felt awkward because of the question I was trying to formulate in my head. How does one just bring up a vampire hunt a second time without sounding suspicious?

He looked at the two screws on the counter and then held the shelf up against the wall and stared at me, waiting. I hadn't told him about my metal powers, but I guess it was obvious after seeing me catch the shelf midair. My hand whipped to the screws, and they floated to the shelf; I twisted my finger in a circular motion, and the screws bolted themselves back into the brick.

"I have this sense," he said, testing the shelf's integrity with his palm, "though I'd hate for it to be true, that they're being protected by magic. Niccolò and Emilio. Like they've coerced a witch—or, worse, threatened one with violence—to protect them."

I laughed nervously, placing the grapefruit-size, smoky-quartz crystal ball back on the shelf. "That seems kind of silly. Why would vampires need protection?"

He smiled at me. "You underestimate me."

"No, that's not what I meant—I'm sure you're the best vampire-hunter witch person ever." My tone turned more somber. "You certainly have enough motive."

"I've been getting stronger—"

"*Oui*, you look better. I mean, not that there was anything wrong with the way you looked before." He smiled again as I stumbled through the words. "You just look healthier."

"I am healthier. The best I've felt in . . . a very long time. This city has done wonders for me."

"Does that mean you're getting your Elemental power back?"

He sighed. "Alas, it will take a lot more for me to get my Fire, if ever at all."

He looked at the basket of candles on the counter, and my heart broke a little. I pulled one out and set it on the counter between us. "Just try."

He faced me meekly, like he appreciated my enthusiasm but that it was a lost cause.

"Come on."

It felt strange, *me* coaching someone with their magic. It made me think of Nicco and the bell tower, when I was coming into my Fire. Then again, everything in the last couple days made me think of Nicco, and thinking about him nonstop frustrated me to no end. I didn't want to think about Nicco the human—*the humanitarian*. Especially after what he'd done to Callis.

He let out a sigh, and then focused on the fresh wick. I put up a wall in my mind so I didn't accidently light it, giving him false hope.

A line crinkled across his forehead, and a little puff of smoke wafted from the wick where a burn mark appeared. His face turned red as he continued to struggle with it.

"It's okay." I gently touched his arm.

His eyes popped open wide. My gaze dropped to the candle. The wick now had a flame of unnatural proportion. A flickering in my peripheral vision drew my attention. We both looked out to the shop.

Every wick in the room was lit: the candelabras across the fireplace mantel, the small candles nestled in chunks of crystal on the glass shelves, and the tea lights in brass boxes with star cutouts. It was almost romantic. For the first time in two days, I suddenly found myself wishing Isaac was near.

"Show off," he said.

"Sorry, I didn't mean to."

"Please don't be sorry." He walked around the counter, looking at the flames as if it was the first time he'd ever seen fire. "Did you say your magic came from your mother's side?"

"No."

"So it's Le Moyne magic, then?"

"*Oui*, but before La Nouvelle-Orléans, we were the Saint-Germains, of Paris."

"Saint-Germain? And I thought I knew all of the Fire-witch family lines. We're quite rare, you know?"

"I didn't. And I wish I knew more about the Saint-Germains. Sometimes I feel like a loser when Isaac and Dee are poring over their grimoires, learning their family secrets."

"You don't have your family book of magic?"

My head shook.

"I know the feeling . . ."

"In other news," I said, "I think I'm coming into my Spektral power." I immediately regretted saying it. I didn't want to sound braggadocious.

"That's magnificent!" His eyes dropped to my arm, even though I had a sweater on. "Have you received your Maleficium?"

"No . . . but soon, hopefully. Dreams. It's something to do with dream magic."

A slight look of disappointment appeared on his face.

"What? Is that bad?"

He looked to the shelf and then back to me. "No. Call it a hunch, but I have a feeling your Spektral power isn't something as basic as dream magic. For you . . . it's going to be something bigger."

I tried not to scoff. "Thanks for the vote of confidence."

"But there's no magic I'd ever discourage you from mastering, Adele."

"Well, thank you, old wise one."

He tossed a rag at me. I tossed it back.

"Fine," he said, "I'll dust. You make us tea."

"Deal."

Jars of loose teas lined the wall behind the counter. I thought we had a collection at the café, but this wall had more teas I'd never heard of than ones that I had. I pulled down a mason jar labeled *Dandelion*, unscrewed the lid, and sniffed the flowers.

"Good for the liver," Chatham said, walking in from the hallway.

"It should be a bestseller in this city."

He laughed and squeezed my shoulder. "Glad to have you back. Please don't scare your dad like that again."

"Glad to be back," I said, and meant it.

In my time in purgatory, I'd thought a lot about the Daures, and Bottom of the Cup and the locator spell pointing us here, and about the witch's book with Papa Olsin's name on it. How they were employing two witches at once. What if . . . Chatham was a witch too?

What if one of his kids is the descendant?

I suddenly found myself hoping it was Codi. I didn't know why; he'd just always been someone I trusted. One of the few.

I started to say something but then stopped and scooped dandelion tea into two star-shaped tea infusers.

What was I supposed to ask? *Are you related to a Native American princess-witch who was in a coven with my aristocratic great-something-grand-witch?*

Chatham waited patiently, which made me feel even more like I was right, like he was leading me to the water. *The water. Water witch.*

"Did someone read the book I gave them?" he finally asked when it was clear I was at a loss for words.

Even the totally appropriate question felt loaded with subtext, like he was looking for a way to facilitate an important discussion—start with some chit-chat about basic magic then work up to discussing the history of our intertwined witchhoods. Is that what growing up with a witch-dad would've been like?

"*Oui.* I read it six times, and I have a million questions." I pulled the book out of my bag. I was ready to talk to anyone who might be able to help me with my dream "problem." It was like I'd totally lost control of the magic the last couple nights. My brow scrunched as I looked at the cover. "What the heck? This isn't the—"

"Something wrong?"

My head spun. *What the hell?* The book was now green, and the title was *Dreamology*, just like I'd originally thought.

Chatham gave me a knowing smile. "Everything okay?" He looked at Callis, who was across the room dusting the Russian nesting dolls, and then back to me, as if another presence in the room might be the reason for my shyness.

I crossed my arms. *Why is this so much harder than talking to Ritha? Ritha was practically a stranger when I asked her about coven stuff. Chatham Daure has known me my* entire *life.* Maybe that's what made it so weird to reconcile.

A furry little head knocked against my arm. I stroked Onyx gently, which immediately calmed my anxiety.

Chatham watched me with keen interest.

"Adele, if you're curious about your dreams, go and talk to Papa. He's just back there in his booth. You'll find no better source on the subject matter."

I hesitated.

He smiled. "He had a stroke, Adele—he wasn't abducted by aliens. I know he seems a little different now, but he's just listening. He says he's closer to Ma more than ever since the stroke, and that's why he's so quiet, because he can hear better now. Don't be shy. He'd love a visit."

"O-okay." I don't know why the idea of walking down the hall to the old man's booth made me nervous.

Onyx leaped off the counter and padded down the corridor, as if he knew that following a cat would somehow make it easier. It did.

Jewel-toned velvet curtains lined both sides of the hallway: cobalt, chartreuse, and a burgundy that matched the shit-kickers on my feet. Papa Olsin's curtain, a gunmetal gray, was all the way at the end. It had always been his booth. Mrs. Philly's grape-juice-colored curtain was directly across from his and had been vacant since she passed a few years ago.

"Papa Olsin?"

"I've been waiting for you," he said, which seemed appropriately psychic. And appropriately esoteric.

He sat in the muted light of a Tiffany lamp with stained-glass lilies. The booth was dark without being creepy. Shelves behind him contained a jumble of yellowed papers and quartz pendulums, but the table before him, covered by a saddle blanket, was completely bare except for a deck of tarot cards and tape recorder used to produce souvenirs for tourists.

As I sat down and said hello, my gaze was drawn to the display above the bookshelf behind him: a magnificent collection of dream catchers in a variety of shapes, sizes, and colors, interlaced like a giant web, protecting Papa Olsin, the spider.

Our eyes met. "I read your book."

"And now you want to know about twinning?"

Twinning? "I was hoping to talk to you about . . . my dreams."

"Dreams . . ." His gaze was caring, like Chatham's, but distant. They had similar noses too, and now that I was so close, it felt like I was looking at a future version of Codi, which instantly made me feel more comfortable. "Dreams are the mind's way of processing the helter-skelter of the day, sorting all those thoughts, ideas, emotions, experiences—deciding what's worthy of your long-term memory, what's earned a key to your heart, and what goes out with the garbage. When you take a journey through your dreams, you might find things you never intended to face again, but you can also learn deeply of yourself."

"But what if . . . what if it's not my own dreams I'm trying to navigate?"

"In time, Addie. Dream-twinning is too advanced for you at this stage. You must start by mastering your own dreamscape before connecting with a partner's."

"Too late."

He sighed and pushed the tarot deck to me. I became more nervous as I shuffled the cards—twice—and I pushed them back. He flipped the top card. The Hanged Man, reversed. "Sometimes we find someone we complement so well, the puzzle pieces can't help but connect. Who is your other half?"

"He's just a friend."

"The truth, but not the whole truth." He flipped the next card. The Four of Pentacles.

"I don't know what he is."

"More of the truth, but not the whole truth."

I began to thumb through the charms hanging at my waist.

He flipped a third card. The Page of Swords. "You want to help this person."

"No!"

His dark eyes rose to meet mine.

"I don't want to help him. I want to help my mom."

"And therein lies the problem, Addie. When you lie to yourself, you are closing off your heart chakra. If it's answers you seek, you must first be willing to see the truth."

My heart chakra felt like it was knocking against my chest. *What more truth could there possibly be for a guy who threw me out an attic window?*

Definitely. No. More. Truth.

"Dream-twinning only occurs in very special relationships," Papa Olsin continued. "Love asks simple questions, which deserve simple answers, but people tend to overcomplicate matters of love."

My stomach jolted. *What? Love?* "Surely there could be other reasons?"

"Surely. And usually there is magic involved."

Of course there is.

"Entering another's mind is a precious right, Addie. You must be gentle with his dreams. Dreams are a person's everything. Their memories, their hopes, their desires, their fantasies. Dream-twinning is not for the fainthearted. It requires a level of maturity few can handle, which is why you should only dream-twin with someone who you are willing to share your entire self with. Entering the mind of another is the closest you'll ever get to touching their soul—well, almost." He smiled.

I was sure my face went as red as my heart chakra.

"Complete trust is required on both parts, for you might see things about each other that you never intended to share. When entering the dreamscape, everything you see is through the eyes of the dreamer. What they think, what they feel. It is their interpretation of the truth, which might not be objective."

"Is there a way for me to have better control when we're connecting?"

"Dream magic is not about control. It's about letting go—letting go of the part of your mind that is analytical, the part that is critical and judgmental. If you want someone to expose their soul, you must desire it, and they must desire to share it. Few, if any, could take it from another at will."

"How do I let go, then? How do I just open my mind?" Even as I said the words, I felt myself clamming up. Suddenly I was worried about exactly how much of myself Olsin Daure could see.

"It's not about opening your mind, Adele. It's about opening your heart."

"How do I do that?"

He laughed gently. "It cannot be taught, my dear. Nor is it something that can be achieved by magic." He smiled again. "You know, you were always Philomena's favorite."

"I miss her."

"I miss her during the day." He winked and then got up. He reached to the wall behind him and took down one of the dream catchers. It was small, about the size of my palm.

"Hang it above your crown chakra when you sleep, but be ready for whatever comes."

"What does it do?"

"It catches your dreams, of course. It will protect you from them if you need protecting, or it will amplify them . . . if that's what you seek."

"Merci beaucoup."

"You are very welcome. And, Adele, proceed with caution. If you enter someone's mind, you can't cherry-pick what's presented to you. Memories are easier to navigate, but if you get caught in another's fantasyscape . . . just remember, you entered at your own risk." He fanned out the stack of tarot cards, pulled one from the middle, and flipped it over. Justice. "You are playing with a dangerous mind, Adele, and that is the one thing he can't protect you from."

"I—I know . . . I'll be careful."

He stood and hugged me good-bye, and I exited the curtain, feeling perhaps more confused than when I'd entered but with an overwhelming sense of calm.

Did I just tell him my mom needs help? Did we just have a conversation about Nicco? And how am I going to get Nicco to trust me if he won't let me back in his dreamscape?

And how am I supposed to open my heart?

Isaac's voice floated down the corridor and jolted me out of the daze—he was out front, talking to Callis. I ignored it, mentally going over everything Papa Olsin told me. I looked down at the dream catcher in my hand as the information shuffled around in my head. *Did we just talk about magic?*

The only thing that became more clear was that I needed to talk to Codi.

I pulled out my phone.

Adele   **4:53 p.m.**   CODI! How's life? Coming home from school anytime soon?

I hung back for a second, waiting to see if he'd respond and also to avoid my pending confrontation with Isaac as long as possible. Another cell phone, not mine, dinged in one of the booths nearby.

I lingered in the hallway, gazing at Mrs. Philly's booth, and then typed another message:

Adele   **4:55 p.m.**   I need to ask u a few things of the family-matter variety. Sorry for vague-texting. <3

Another ding.

I yanked back the grape-juice-colored curtain. It was dark inside the booth, and even darker when I dropped the curtain behind me. My pulse raced as I pecked out another message:

Adele   **4:55 p.m.**   Codi?

A screen illuminated the pocket of a hoodie on the table.

I pulled out the phone and saw my own text message staring back at me. *What the . . . ?*

CHAPTER 32

Julie

My plan had been to wait outside the tearoom for Adele, but it felt stalkerish; plus it was cold. Not that it was much warmer in the shop. I buried my hands in my pockets, looking into a cabinet that contained a hundred different decks of tarot cards: fairies, sea creatures, skeletons. I didn't know anything about tarot, but I liked the art, and it helped me focus less on the tearoom's energy that made you feel like anyone here would know more about you than *you* knew about you. It was unsettling, to say the least.

Callis was behind the counter on the phone with a customer, who, from the sounds of it, was giving him a hard time. A dark-haired girl, a few years older than me, was on the other side of the room, crouching next to the shop's black cat, petting it. She looked up and caught me staring. I glanced away, back to the skeleton cards.

The waiting was driving me nuts. I'd hoped Adele would be working alone, so I could beg her to talk to me. She'd never stayed mad at me this long. Even with Nicco locked away, we're in a fight because of him, *and* it was my fault, which was twice as annoying. Why couldn't I just keep my mouth shut about it? It made me hate him even more.

I exhaled loudly and approached the counter as Callis hung up the phone.

"Hey, Adele's in the back with Papa Olsin," he said. "You look tired."

I shrugged. *What's new?* "So, on a scale of one to ten, how mad at me is she?"

"Hmm . . . she didn't want to talk about it, but she in no way let on that all was lost—and she didn't blow anything up when I mentioned you, so definitely not a ten."

"A grand gesture," said the girl from across the shop.

I looked over to her. She was still petting the cat, who was now stretched out on the floor, in total heaven.

"What?" I asked her.

Callis started to repeat himself, but I waved for him to stop.

"Actions speak louder than words." She gazed up at me. "You need a grand gesture."

"Like what?"

"Isaac," Callis said. "Who—?"

"Like what kind of grand gesture?" I asked. She looked familiar.

"Something that lets her know you won't do it again. That you've moved on from whatever upset you enough to upset her."

"Ohhhhh," Callis said. "*Her.* Of course she's talking to you."

I turned to him. "Huh?"

"Nothing," he whispered. "She never talks to me. Girls like you."

"You do remember that my own girlfriend isn't talking to me?"

I turned back to her, wondering if Callis was into this girl or something. "You know Adele?"

She watched me as I walked over but didn't stop petting the cat, who looked like he might scratch my eyes out if I interrupted his massage. His ears flattened to the sides, raising the hairs on my arms. Ever since I'd come into my Air powers, I'd developed an irrational fear of cats.

"They'll never love us in the way we want them to," she said, scratching his head.

"Who?"

"She was a sad little girl, but now she's strong. Now she's *la belle fille du Vieux Carré.*"

"The cat?"

"Adele. They think they love us . . ."

"Who are you?"

"Sometimes love isn't enough. She dreams of another. She told Papa Olsin."

Jesus, this girl is weird. Of course Callis would be into her.

"You know, my friend over there—"

She stood, an intense look spreading across her face. "He'll never get me."

"Ha. Okay." I looked back at Callis and shrugged apologetically.

"Never," she said. "I'm strong."

"Okay, I got it."

"I won't end up like Alessandro."

"Who's Alessandro?"

"He was my friend, but now he's gone. It's up to you to protect Jade, or she's going to end up like him."

"How do you know about—"

"Protégez la."

"What?"

"Protégez Jade."

"Jade's dea—"

"Protect Jade!" Her hands hit my chest, shoving me back a few steps and making me stumble. I tried to catch her hand, but she dashed through the opening in the counter and disappeared down the hallway as I regained my balance.

What the fuck?

"What was that all about?" Callis asked. "Who's Jade?"

"No one," I snapped.

His eyebrow rose, but I didn't say anything else as I walked back over. He leaned on the counter. "Well, thanks for trying."

I appreciated him not prying further.

"I'll have Celestina work on her. Who can resist a nine-year-old, right?"

"You'd be surprised exactly how much she can resist," Chatham said, appearing in the hall doorway, arms crossed.

Callis stood up straight. "Chatham, can you help me choose between these two different crystals I've been contemplating?" He grabbed the closest two out of the glass counter case.

The way he immediately changed the subject gave me the vibe that the girl was off-limits, like she was Chatham's daughter or niece or something. But from the slight excitement still emitting from Callis, I also got the feeling he wasn't going to give up so easily.

Godspeed.

The cat jumped onto the counter with the kind of grace I'd grown to appreciate over recent months, trying to perfect my own swoops, and took two steps toward me.

"Meet Onyx," Chatham said.

I sucked back my irrational fear and held out my hand. Onyx gently buried his head into it. Sometimes I wondered if other animals could sense it in me—the crow part. I liked to think they could.

"He likes you better than me," Callis said, showing me the scratch marks across his arms.

"At least someone likes me today," I said to the cat.

"Chatham?" The voice made my pulse pound like a freight train. Everyone turned to Adele, who was now standing in the hallway.

"Yes, my dear."

"Codi's at school, right?"

Who's Codi?

"Yeah, baby, you know that." Onyx jumped onto Chatham's shoulder.

"In Tuscaloosa?" she asked.

"Yes. What's wrong?"

She held up a phone in her right hand. In her left, a University of Alabama sweatshirt hung limply to the floor. "Then why did I just find his phone?"

"You angel! And I didn't think he could love you any more than he already does. He's been looking for that ever since he returned to school after Christmas break."

She handed them both over.

"I swear. That kid. Typical, right? The son of psychics, and he can never find his things." There was a slight stutter in his voice.

"It was in Mrs. Philly's booth."

"I hope that means he was practicing. He's got the gift for the cards—maybe even more than you."

"*Ha.* For the millionth time, I have no idea how to read tarot cards."

"You just have to open yourself up, Adele. Open yourself up."

She looked a little puzzled.

"I hope you got everything you needed from Papa?"

She nodded. "I think so . . . We'll see." Then she looked at me without saying anything. Callis shot me a look of sympathy.

"Hi," I said, trying not to sound meek.

She repeated the greeting without enthusiasm, a mere formality in front of friends. I knew it. They knew it.

She told them good-bye and came around the counter to me, in silence. I touched her shoulder as she walked past, but she didn't pause, leaving me no choice but to follow her to the door.

Just as I stepped outside, I felt it.

"Isaac." The word crawled over my neck like an icy whisper. *"She'll never love you like you want."*

I whipped around just in time to see a wave of green rocks pelt through the air from a basket on the right wall. "What the—?" I yelled as they smacked my chest.

Chatham leaned over the counter as the stones rolled down, clanking against the brick floor. He looked at the empty basket on the shelf and then to me.

Callis hurried over and scooped up some of the rocks, pausing to examine one in between his fingers. He looked directly at me. "Jade."

I didn't say anything. It took all of my energy just to stand there and not freak out.

He went back behind the counter, and like clockwork the shelf behind him came tumbling down, and the mugs smashed to the floor.

He groaned.

Chatham crossed his arms. "I'm beginning to think you're right, Callis. Maybe Julie really does hate you."

"Who's Julie?" I asked.

"Oh, you know, the family ghost," Callis answered.

I laughed uncomfortably and went after Adele.

We walked a few steps down the street—me still trying not to freak out about what just happened. I didn't know if we were walking together or if I was just following her. It wasn't a good feeling, but at least she hadn't sent me away.

"Adele, I'm sor—"

A group of people turned the corner, spilling into us.

"I can guarantee," said Ren, "if you drink enough purple *drank* you *will* see the red beady eyes of Jean Lafitte on Bourbon Street."

He stopped in front of a three-story, mint-green, paint-peeling town house, twilight creeping in behind it as if Mother Nature was Ren's personal set designer. The place was grimy at best, but the ironwork curled so fluidly, like *The Starry Night*, between the second and third floor balconies, you couldn't help pause and look.

Is that the place where . . . ?

Out of habit, I gently grabbed Adele's elbow. "That's the house where I first met Callis," I whispered. Now I wanted to hear the story.

She looked at me, puzzled.

"He was squatting there, with Celestina."

"Jesus."

"Yeah. I'm glad they have some place to stay now." It felt good to be actually conversing.

"If I can direct your attention to this pole holding up the second-story gallery?" said Ren. "Does everyone see that cluster of spikes sticking out high up?"

Heads tipped upward, and everyone nodded.

"And what do you think they were for?"

"To keep out burglars?" said a man from the crowd.

"Correct, a colonial alarm system! The spikes were meant to discourage robbers from shimmying up the poles and getting in through the windows. It's also said that French fathers welded them to scare the Romeos away from their Juliets."

He smiled, hung on to the pole with one arm, and swung around, letting us all know that the real story was about to come.

I kept one eye on Adele, in case she was ready to bolt. It had taken two days to get her to acknowledge me. I didn't want to blow my chance to talk to her. She was only a few inches away, but the distance felt so huge she might as well have been in New York.

"The year was 1840," said Ren. "It was a cool January night, not unlike this one. Monsieur Gardère, the patriarch of a well-to-do Creole family in the Vieux Carré, took his wife and four of his daughters out to dine on turtle soup and frog legs in the Faubourg Marigny. His eldest daughter, fifteen-year-old Violette, had stayed home sick. Halfway through the étouffée, Papa got *that feeling* that papas get. With a throaty grumble, he stood from the table, claiming he'd forgotten his billfold back home. 'I'll be back before the bread pudding arrives!'

"As his carriage crossed Esplanade Avenue, he regretted having allowed his children to be born so far from France. 'Violette is never coming into town for carnival season again,' he grumbled. 'She can stay back at Chatsworth until she's married, safely separated by the bayous from these *garçons de la ville.*' He coaxed his horse to trot faster.

"You see, the real crème de la crème of New Orleans society lived most of the year upriver on their family plantations, but spent New Year's to Easter in the city.

"By the time Monsieur Gardère reached his Royal Street home, he was in such a state of panic that he barely had the reigns looped before he jumped from the carriage.

"He made sure his step was light as he entered the house, but it was too late, for he'd shut the front door too hard, warning his daughter of his presence. The sounds of scurrying feet from above enraged him, and he paused on the stairs, wondering whether he should go back to his study to load his gun.

"*'Non!'* he decided. *'If it's that scruffy fruit peddler's son, then the sight of the barrel alone will put the fear of God in him!'* A precious hunter's moment was lost with the thought.

"He took the stairs three at a time, thinking about that pretty-faced boy's hands touching his firstborn, but when he burst through Violette's bedroom door, he found her in bed underneath the duvet, fast asleep, just as he had left her two hours before. Alone.

"The faint scent of citrus tickled Monsieur's nose. His back stiffened. 'Where is he?'

"'Where is who, Papa?' Suddenly awake, Violette did her best to hide the fear brought on by the sight of the gun; after all, her father was a banker, not a barbarian.

"*'Dis moi la vérité!'* Your cheeks are bright pink. Tell me the truth!'

"'I have a fever, Papa, of course my cheeks are rouge.' She smiled as innocently as she knew how, covered her mouth, and pushed two gentle coughs past her lips.

"Monsieur sat on the edge of her bed and tenderly touched her brow. Her smile reminded him of what it was like being fifteen, back in Bordeaux, where people were more civilized, back when social order meant something. *Why did the Lord give me five girls?* he wondered right before the sound of bending metal scraped through the air.

"Monsieur's head slowly turned to the window. Violette trembled as the metal creaked again. Monsieur leaped from the bed to the window, nearly ripping the curtain down. Violette sprung to life like a windup ballerina as Monsieur pushed the heavy window open all the way to the ceiling.

"'Voilà!' he yelled.

"The sight of the fruit peddler's son hanging over the wrought-iron balcony both enraged and delighted Monsieur. Now able to revel in the fact that he'd been right all along, he let out a hearty laugh as he aimed his gun, the barrel of which he thought was empty.

"'*Non, Papa!*' Violette screamed for all of the neighbors to hear. '*Je l'aime! Je l'aime!* And he loves me too!'

"The flush drained from Violette's cheeks as she watched Alessandro's knuckles turn from pink to white as he struggled to hang on to the slick metal. The terrified boy was strong from pushing his wooden fruit cart, which was always loaded down with heaps of lemons, oranges, and Violette's favorite, *pamplemousse*, but the winter air was damp, and little beads of condensation covered the balcony railing.

"Tears dripped from Violette's eyes. 'Stop this, Papa! I will never disobey you again!' She begged him to put down the weapon, but Monsieur was fixated on Alessandro's ragged clothing, overwhelmed with the notion of this unkempt boy ruining his daughter's life.

"Underneath his tattered jacket, Alessandro's forearms quivered, and his biceps spasmed. Soon his entire body shook. His legs danced in the air as he hung over the three-story drop. He cried out for mercy in Italian, his native tongue, as each vertebra in his back felt like it was sliding down with weight. *'Dio mi salvi!'*

"Praying a father's threat was stronger than the young boy's love, Monsieur Gardère sighed in concession, prepared to put down the gun and offer his hand to the boy. But Violette, who had grown hysterical, grabbed her father's shoulder, sending the weapon aimed toward the sky. A gunshot exploded, startling all three of them, but most of all poor Alessandro. His grip slipped.

"The gun clanked to the ground, and through the cloud of gunpowder smoke, Monsieur grabbed Violette's waist as she leaped over the balcony, screaming, desperately reaching out for Alessandro.

"The poor boy might have escaped the botched rendezvous with nothing more than a few broken bones, but, to his misfortune, a spike caught him on the way down, and, as the locals say, 'Ripped his skin open like an unraveling sweater.' The spike had hooked his hip and tore his abdomen straight through to his thigh. From chest to toe, the fruit peddler's son was filleted like a catfish.

"Violette hung over the rail, her gaze locked on the terror-filled eyes of the fruit peddler's son. Unfortunately, Death had not taken its toll before Alessandro hit the ground, and for a brief moment, he lay splayed out on the street, staring up at his own flesh, his manhood, and his intestines, hanging down, taunting him like a rope he could use to climb back up to his love's arms."

Jesus Christ. My hands folded below my belt.

"Blood gurgling from young Alessandro's mouth, he made it known to his beloved Violette that he would be waiting for her in the next life. *'Io sono tuo, mia bella!'*" Ren dragged out an Italian accent for maximum possible effect.

"And so, folks, on that cold January night, it wasn't just Violette Gardère who saw her lover's Romeo bits. They dangled from the spike, on display for the entire neighborhood to see. I'm sure it's safe to say that every teenage boy in La Nouvelle-Orléans thought twice before sneaking into the bedroom of *la belle* he was sweet on."

Ren took a dramatic pause, and for the first time in my experience, no one clapped after one of his stories. We all just stared up with sheer horror at the spikes sticking out of the pole that supported the gallery. The iron spikes jutted out every which way for maximum damage.

"Is that *true?*" someone whispered.

For Alessandro's sake, I hoped it wasn't.

"Now, folks, I told you to have your cameras ready on the tour because there's always a chance you'll capture paranormal activity here in La Nouvelle-Orléans." He pulled out his phone and tapped the screen a few times. "Here's a picture from my personal collection from back in November." He held it out for everyone to see.

Everyone closed in, oohing and ahhing.

When the phone passed to Adele, I peered over her shoulder, along with a guy with a crooked toupee. "That's nuts," she said.

The image looked like just a street shot at first, but as my eyes focused on the negative space, the form easily came into view. I shivered. Coming straight at the camera, straight at Ren, was the figure of a man, dark and translucent like a smokestack. *Flying? Floating?*

"That's bullshit," said the man with the bad hairpiece. "Basic Photoshop."

"Excuse me, sir!" Ren yelled, stepping right into the guy's face. "I can assure you that no such enhancements were made, and if you take issue with the concrete evidence in front of your face, this might not be the tour for you!" He was so worked up, spit uncontrollably flung from his mouth onto the guy's face.

A couple girls giggled, and the guy fell back into line, but something about Ren's dramatic style felt off. It wasn't that the guy didn't deserve it, but it did seem a bit out of character for Ren, who usually enjoyed the odd heckler or skeptic. I turned to Adele, who also looked a little taken aback.

As the tour group began to move toward the tearoom, Adele caught Ren's eye and waved good-bye, then began walking away without even a glance at me.

"Hey," I said, hurrying after her. "Can I walk you home?"

"Do I have a choice?"

"Yeah. You always have a choice, Adele." I suddenly felt like I'd punched myself in the gut, like I'd given her permission to break up with me.

She sighed and resumed walking. I took it as a sign that it was okay to follow.

She didn't say anything at all for the remaining blocks, and I managed to keep my mouth shut. The silence seemed better than anything I could come up with.

When we got to her house, the awkwardness came tenfold. It had been a long time since I'd dropped her off without kissing her good night, but I got the feeling I was about to remember what it was like. The iron gate unlocked as soon as she touched the handle, and each moment became more dreadful than the one before as we walked up the steps.

"Can I come in?"

She shook her head without looking at me.

"Okay. I can give you some space."

"I don't need space, Isaac, and I don't need any more apologies. I need you to stop blaming me for what happened. Don't you think I feel guilty enough about everything? About the Michels? About the Wolfman? About everyone else who got killed?"

"*What?* Jesus, Adele, I don't blame you for any of that."

"How do you think I feel every time you rub Nicco in my face?"

The door clicked as she mentally unlocked it.

She got halfway through the threshold before I grabbed a hold of her arm. I knew she was running away because she was about to cry and didn't want me to see, but I pulled her back anyway.

"I'm sorry, I swear, that's the absolute last thing I wanted you to feel."

Her eyes stayed glued to the ground.

Without thinking, I touched her face so she'd look at me. "I know my words don't mean anything right now . . ."

She nodded, her eyes glistening.

"But I'm going to find a way to prove to you how sorry I am."

I leaned in and kissed her quickly on the lips, knowing the affection wouldn't be returned, but it seemed like it would hurt less than not kissing her at all.

As I walked away, it felt like I'd been kicked by a Clydesdale.

"Isaac?" My heart stopped. "You should take this."

When I turned around, she was holding something out.

This is it. She was giving me back the necklace, the feather. She was breaking up with me.

I walked back, my chest tight, trying not to show the fear on my face.

"I think you need it more than me," she said. "You look like you haven't slept in days." She passed over the object and then slipped through the doorway and closed it behind her.

I stood there for a second, on her stoop, catching my breath, staring at the dream catcher in my hand.

CHAPTER 33

Elixir of Life and Death

Breathe, Adele.

Sucking in a big swig of air seemed to make my heart ache more, watching through the peephole as Isaac walked away.

When he was out of sight, I ran upstairs and changed into light-blue jeans, thicker socks, and the woolliest black sweater I could find—it had been freezing at the convent last night. I shoved an extra sweater in my bag, rebuttoned my coat, and was out the door before I could think any more about the laundry list of bad decisions I was making: disobeying my dad, lying to Isaac, and soon to be breaking curfew. Not to mention the dream-twinning.

I hustled down the street, focusing on the visible breath slipping from my lips into the night air and watching carefully for any sign of Isaac. If I ran into him on the way to the attic, that would be the sure way to end things. And I didn't want to end things. Not at all.

I thought about how much he probably would have liked Nicco and León back in the day, the do-gooders of their time. By the time I reached the convent, I was almost in a trance, the need for answers possessing me. I wove through the maze of hedges in the convent courtyard, climbed the old staircase, and unlocked the giant padlock on the first attic door.

Three little orbs of light floated over my head as I stood in front of the final door, grounding myself. My fingers swept the locks, careful to not open them as I wondered what my mom looked like on the other side. A vampiric Sleeping Beauty, or an emaciated, decaying monster? *Are they in pain?*

I turned around, trying to put her out of my mind, and slid down to the ground against the door.

And there he was, standing on the other side of the room, staring at me in disbelief.

"Isaac!" I yelled, jumping up. "It's not what it looks like! I swear!" Before he could say anything, my defensiveness switched to offense. "I can't believe you followed me here!"

"I did *not*," he snapped. "I was sitting on the roof when you walked through the door. How did you not see me? You've clearly lost it."

Panic flooded my veins. I knew we wouldn't make it through this fight again. *How did we even make it through the first one?* The words blurted out: "I think I'm getting my Spektral magic." It was the only Hail Mary I had.

His eyebrow raised.

"I've been having these dreams—and I got this book on dream magic. I was going to tell you the other night, but I knew you'd get mad."

"Why would I get mad? And what does your *magic* have to do with being at the attic?"

"It's called dreamcasting, and it's kind of like . . . dream telepathy. Connecting with people through their dreams."

He looked to the door and then back to me. It didn't take a genius to figure it out.

"Have you ever broken the seal?"

"No! I swear!" I thought about making something up about connecting with Lisette, trying to get information, but I was sick of lying, and hiding, and fighting. "But the only person I've been able to connect with is Nicco."

He sighed. The kind of sigh that scared me. My chest tightened.

And then he turned around and walked away.

"Isaac?" Tears rose to my eyes. "Isaac! I just want answers to why they're after my family! I didn't do anything wrong!" I shouted his name again, but it didn't matter.

He was gone.

I stood there, halfway between the two doors, tears pouring down my cheeks. "I just wanted answers . . ."

Then he reappeared, a huge heap of fabric folded under his arms: a stack of blankets. They must have been in the room with all the statues.

He walked straight past me and stopped near the locked door. He looked back. "Is this close enough?"

I nodded, trying to stop the tears.

He dropped the blankets to the floor. "So did you find anything out?"

I shook my head, still in shock. I looked down to the blankets and back to him. "You're not mad?"

He stepped in front of me and wiped the tears from my cheeks with his thumbs. His voice was soft. "Don't you think I want to know why a clan of vampires is after you? Even if it means . . . whatever this is."

"But you hate Nicco."

He nodded and let me go. Then he pulled the dream catcher out of his pocket, walked to the attic door, and hung it from one of the locks. He turned back to me.

"But I love you."

I froze, trying not to let the shock sprawl across my face.

"Don't worry, you don't have to say it back." He took my hand, pulling me down to the blankets with him. "But what's the point of me not saying it? We both know it's true."

I smiled, and he smiled, and he fluffed up the pile of blankets for maximum cushion.

"You're staying?"

"Unless you want me to go."

I shook my head. "I don't want you to go."

"Well, let's get your Maleficium," he said, lying back.

"So you're just going to watch me sleep?" I tried my best to sound playful.

"I have no intention of watching you do anything. I've slept a grand total of six hours in the last couple nights." He pulled out his phone. "I'm setting the alarm for midnight. Do you think that will be enough time?"

"Yeah, and that should be plenty of time before my dad gets home."

"Good, I don't want him hating me."

"Abouuut that . . . I got grounded because I forgot to set my alarm the first night I came here to test the dreams, and Mac was waiting in my room when I got home the next morning—he thinks I slept at your place."

"Wait, what?" He sat up. "So he thinks we—but we haven't even—shit!"

"I'm sorry," I said through clenched teeth.

"Why didn't you tell him you were at Désirée's?"

"I did, but he'd already called Ana Marie, freaking out, and she told him I wasn't there."

"So, you snuck out on a dream-date with Nicco, and now your dad hates *me*?"

"But you love me," I squeaked.

Before I could stop him, his fingers attacked, poking my ribs. "This is not funny!"

"No tickling!" I cackled, trying to crawl away, but he pulled me back.

I twisted around and lay next to him, my cheek cradled into the crook of my arm. He did the same. "He'll calm down eventually," I said.

"Like, before he kills me, or after?"

"Hopefully before." My fingers laced together with his, and I pulled his hand to my lips and kissed it. It was the first time I relaxed in days. Isaac had that way about him—an aura of calm that made you feel like everything was going to be okay—even when lying on an attic floor, even knowing I was about to go into Nicco's head. A swell of tingles rushed through my chest to the tips of my fingers, still woven with his. The sensation of supernatural energy. *Magic. Our magic.*

"And it wasn't a date," I said.

He squeezed my hand. "Yeah, I know."

"Do you realize how weird this is?"

"What, the curse? The dream magic? Camping out in a convent?"

"All of it."

"Adele, I can turn into a bird."

"And I love that about you."

He swept the strands of hair out of my face, and I don't know who was smiling more. Or, with our legs intertwined, whose eyes fluttered shut first.

Next to me on the workbench, León scoops a heap of brimstone onto a brass scale, and the powder puffs out around us in an ethereal haze.

The door opens, and Emilio's voice wafts over. "You're one year older, *fratellino.*" His voice sounds strange in the laboratory, for there are so rarely words spoken down here by anyone other than León and myself. "I've brought you a present."

"I'm in no mood for celebrating," I say without looking up, for the mercurial mixture I'm bringing to boil is a delicate, time-consuming process, and I don't want to ruin the batch.

"But I've heard you've made great strides with the Elixir! Or is that just Father's usual hyperbole when it comes to your accomplishments?"

I still don't look back, only fantasize about how quickly Emilio could duck if I sent a copper dish spinning at his head. "I know not what remarks Father has been making. We've made progress, but it's difficult to work on a medicine whose effectiveness can only be tested by killing the inflicted!" I knock the book, my notes, and the scales from the table in one swoop—everything but the mercury. "This is not a job for me, Emilio. It's a job for you!"

"I couldn't agree with you more, but alas, it is you who Father has chosen. It is you who he says possesses the *real gift* of all his children. *Tanti auguri, Niccolò.*" He tosses a vial onto the workbench.

The vial, sealed with wax, is the kind used by military physicians to distribute opiates to the wounded on the battlefield, but the substance it contains now is crimson.

I break the seal, pull out the glass stopper, and smell the substance. *Blood.*

"Not that I need a laboratory to make history, my brother," he continues.

I put the vial down and return my focus on the flame beneath the glass pot, making sure it doesn't grow too strong.

"Rest assured that after this trip, I will become a legend. There will be songs sung and poems written of the night Emilio Lorenzo Medici became the greatest hunter in all of Europe—the greatest hunter in the history of mankind."

León and I glance at each other, and I am sure we are wondering the same thing: *How drunk is he?*

"The one who first caught a vampire."

I finally turn my attention to Emilio just as he dumps a body onto the table with a loud thunk, knocking over the mixture. I jump out of the way before the glass smashes onto the bench, but León yelps as the mercurial backsplash catches his hand.

"Dannazione, Emilio!" I yell, grabbing the nearest cloth and drowning it in a bucket of water kept beside the table. I bring it to León's hand, which is already bright red.

León gapes, but his gaze is fixed on the corpse behind me. "Could such a creature exist?" he asks.

"She is in front of your eyes, is she not?" Emilio says.

I look down at the bedraggled girl, whose head rests on her piles of loose pale braids. The hem of her silver gown and the layers of skirts underneath are dirty and torn. She appears quite dead, but other than the ashy color of her skin, there are little to no signs of decomposition. Then her fingers move—not the twitchy jerk of rigor mortis, an intentional curling of the fist.

Rage overcomes my curiosity. "She's alive? How dare you bring someone down here! This place is known to no one—not even our mother!"

"No one but us, and now her," he replies with a smirk.

"I knew Father was mad to give you access to this laboratory; you are nothing but an imbecile!"

"Oh, how you will regret saying those words, baby brother, once you see the magic that flows through this diabolical creature."

"Diabolical creatures do not possess magic," says León, squeezing his injured hand tightly. Sweat pours from his brow, and only then do I realize he's shaking.

"Let me rephrase. You will regret saying those words once you see the anatomical makeup of this creature. Does that pique your interest, Niccolò? Is that academic enough for you?"

I fetch a bottle containing an iodine tincture. The liquid swishes as I cross the room for a clean rag, looking back at the girl, who doesn't seem to have moved again. I break my gaze from her for only a second as I reach also for a bottle of olive oil, which we keep by the barrel around here for such instances. Ours is far more . . . special than the bottle on the dining table.

I dab the olive oil onto León's wound, and he curses. The burn is blistering and clearly far worse than he has let on. My frustration and curiosity battle each other as I douse a second rag with the tincture and apply the cloth to his skin, wondering if I should make a stronger salve. My gaze darts from the girl to the tome on the podium, to the girl, and then back to León.

"But, Emilio," he says, "if she is really a vampire, how did you manage to capture such a dangerous foe?"

"A magician never reveals his secrets," my brother says, a clear jab at our refusal to talk about our own research.

In Emilio's case, I'm guessing his secret is a combination of inventive weaponry, an irrational lack of fear, and unadulterated stupidity. "So this is the secret mission Father has had you on?" I ask him. "To hunt a vampire?"

"Not just any vampire. This is the one they call *il cacciatore di streghe.*"

"The witch slayer?"

"Yes. I caught her in France after she attacked Étienne Deshayes's sister—an unfortunate loss of a powerful woman. No doubt Étienne will be looking for revenge."

"Then why did you not deliver her to Étienne?"

He takes the vial of blood from the workbench, removes the stopper with his teeth, grabs León's hand, and rips off the rag. León howls with pain, but before he can pull away, Emilio pins his hand to the table and pours the liquid directly over the wound.

I reach for a bowl to start the salve.

Emilio yells, "Keep your eyes here, Niccolò!"

And then I no longer need to be told to watch.

"What's happening?" León asks, writhing in pain as Emilio holds his arm in place. "What's happening to me?"

Despite hearing the concern in his voice, I cannot answer, for I am speechless.

"Madonna mia," I finally say, grabbing the magnifying lens from my apron pocket for a closer examination.

I quickly move the glass away again, double-checking that it isn't playing tricks on me. "Emilio, what sorcery is this?"

He comes closer, peering at the wound, and for the first time in a long time I want to kiss my brother.

"M-m-my skin. It's healing."

"It's regenerating," I say, mesmerized.

León's face is as pale as a ghost's, sweat dripping from his brow.

"How does it feel?" I ask.

"Nothing more than a slight tickling sensation."

We watch as the blistering wound shrinks until the skin is soft and pink as if newly formed, not white and hard like the scar tissue expected after such a burn. I trace my fingers over the spot where the wound was.

"Un miracolo," I say, kissing the new skin, which is just as soft on my lips.

"This is why I didn't bring her to Étienne," Emilio says. He kisses the top of my head. "Happy birthday, Niccolò. Don't ever forget who brought you this miracle, baby brother."

León holds his unmarked hand up before his eyes. "Niccolò, do you understand what this could mean for medicine?"

"I can think of nothing else." My mind reels, too fast for me to keep up.

"Niccolò," my brother says, "as exciting as this is, you might want to prepare yourself for the celebration starting soon upstairs."

"To celebrate you catching the vampire?"

"No, stupido, for your birthday! There is an exceptionally beautiful girl upstairs expecting your company."

"*Clearly* I don't have time for such frivolities now."

"I'll be sure to let Gabriel know. He'll be delighted to take her off your hands."

His comment doesn't rouse me. I stalk to the other side of the room, to the podium. Gabriel knows my affection for Maddalena is unwavering no matter how little time I spend upstairs during her visits. I'd planned on dining with her tonight, but now . . . now it is not a possibility.

A loud clank comes from the corner. I turn to see Emilio locking the large cage. The girl, who was not much more than a corpse just a moment ago, is standing inside, clutching the bars.

He tosses the long iron key to León, although I'm not sure why. "Her name is Séraphine Cartier, and she killed more than twelve of my men before I was able to kill her."

"Except that clearly you didn't *kill* her," León says.

"Dear León, if there is one thing I am certain of in this world, it is when I have killed. But this particular woman has a little habit of coming back to life." The way he looks back at the creature in the cage makes me wonder what else happened between them.

"Niccolò," he says, "do you still have the dagger I gave you? Sometimes one must do whatever is necessary. After all, you are a Medici. If the need arises, drive it directly through her heart. There are always ways to make death *finale*."

And with that he departs.

"I guess if you want to hear the hunter's story," says León with a smile, "you'll have to go to dinner upstairs. I'm sure he'll be telling it from atop the table."

A mixed set of emotions stir in my belly as I step toward the cage. It is nearly impossible to believe that this fragile-looking girl is the monster Emilio claims her to be. She looks more like one of the cadavers the grave robbers bring us than a girl who's killed a dozen men. Her whiteish braids fall nearly to the floor, disheveled in a way that isn't too different from the girls who scurry from Gabriel's bedchamber in the middle of the night. Only her cheeks aren't flushed; they are gaunt and sunken. In contrast, her eyes are crystal clear, pale like the glistening peaks of the Alps under the winter sun. Both sleeves have been torn from her dress, revealing skin silvery like a sardine. She struggles to hold herself upright. Her fingers, long and spindly, grasp the bars tightly.

I step closer to the cage, mesmerized. My heart races, thump-thumping even harder when I reach out to her face. My fingers gently graze her cheek.

Thump-thump.

Thump-thump.

"He's a stupid boy who puts his finger next to the dragon's mouth," she says, her voice threatening and inviting at the same time. Her words are Italian, despite her French name and her French accent.

"You don't look like a dragon."

She smirks. "A very stupid boy indeed."

Thump-thump.

Light floods the laboratory.

What?

The lock drops with a loud clank, and the iron bars are cool to the touch as I open the door and enter the cage.

No, this is not what happened. Séraphine would have slaughtered me had I gone into her cage. She was on the brink of starvation.

"I need your blood," I say, gently at first. Then I repeat it, over and over, each time with more rage as the monster cowers in the corner. "I *need* your blood!"

"Get out!" she yells. "Get out!"

The light becomes brighter, until I can't see anything at all. I can only hear her yelling, over and over. "Get out!"

"Get out!"

Thump-thump.

Thump-thump.

"Get out!" I scream into the total darkness.

I can't move—I'm trapped.

In the attic.

Adele is here. She's so close. *I knew she'd come for me.*

The weight comes back. The heaviness. The slumber. *No. No. Per piacere, no.* I struggle violently in the cassette, but it doesn't move.

Because I didn't move.

Magic.

I fight the darkness, fight the break in the dream, but Nicco's fighting too—fighting back. Fighting me. *Hold on to him, Adele. Hold on.* I wrap my arms around the dream and drift back to Florence before my consciousness is poked fully awake. Before I lose the sound of his heartbeat.

Thump-thump.

Knock-knock.

For hours León and I sit drinking wine, marveling at the possibilities Séraphine brings us. We are going to heal all of the ailing in Firenze—in all of Toscana!

Knock-knock.

We both look to the door in confusion. Neither Gabriel nor Emilio nor my father are the kind of men to knock before entering. And no one else knows the door exists.

The sound comes again.

"Is someone *kicking* the door?" I ask.

León stands, hand on the hilt of his sword, as I go to the door and unhitch the handle. The door swings open, and Emilio stumbles inside with another girl strewn across his shoulders—this one in a much fancier golden dress. Cascades of honey-colored curls obscure her face.

"*Madonna mia, Emilio,*" León says. "Have you got another? Maybe they *will* sing songs about you."

"No, not another." There is alcohol on his breath. "But I've had the most brilliant idea!" He speaks with such enthusiasm, the girl bobs up and down against his back.

I'm fixated on her gown; there is something familiar about it.

Emilio pulls her body over his shoulder and sets her down on the table far more gently than he tossed Séraphine. "You are going to need a steady food supply for the vampire."

The girl stirs—and I pause to process what my brother is actually saying. I know he is drunk, but this is lunacy. The girl stirs again, her hair sliding from her face.

In a fit of fury, I grab Emilio by the chest and slam him against the stone wall. "Are you *mad?*"

"Oh, don't be such a dandy, Niccolò. It's the perfect solution. *She's* the perfect solution."

I slam him a second time, bringing rage to his eyes. "Are you actually suggesting that I *feed* Maddalena to a vampire?"

Séraphine hisses in the cage behind us, shaking the iron bars with the strength of a Titan. Luckily, León's reinforced them.

"That's exactly what I am suggesting, brother. This will provide you with an endless supply of blood to feed the vampire, take the pressure off you to marry, *and* spare us from having to listen to the girl pine for you upstairs all day long! Everyone wins."

"You disgust me, *brother*—and now it is clear to me why Father never picked you for this duty. This work is about the betterment of human life, which you have no regard for whatsoever! You are no longer welcome here!"

Emilio tries to push me away, but I smash him back into the wall. "Do you understand me?"

"*Sì, fratellino.* But do not disillusion yourself, Nicco. Your duty is about the advancement of the Medici among the great families, not the advancement of mankind."

We stare at each other for another moment before I release him.

"Calm down, Nicco. I will put her back where I found her."

"Do not touch her. Just get out."

Cursing under his breath, Emilio leaves the chamber, slamming the door like a child. For a moment, I'm too overwhelmed by my own shaking to tend to her.

"Niccolò?" comes a meek voice from the table. "What is this place?"

I take a deep breath before falling to her side. "Do not fret, *bella*. You are safe. You are with me. I will get you back to where you belong." I scoop her into my arms and lift her up.

"If I am with you, then I am where I belong."

"*Sì*, but not here . . ."

"Shall I help you bring her upstairs?" León asks.

"No. This is my mess, and I will clean it up. You stay here with her." I nod to the cage. "Do not do anything until I get back."

"Of course."

Before I make it out of the great hall, Maddalena is asleep on my shoulder again. It's clear that Emilio has given her some kind of sedative. The thought of my brother administering tonics is frightening, but at least I don't have to worry about her seeing the secret Medicean tunnels. I can only imagine what my father would do to her if he found out she was here.

I move quickly through the dark underground, and then through the palazzo, and up all of the stairs to her guest chamber, getting a firm reminder that I need to spend more time fencing under the sun and less time working.

I set her gently on the bed, wondering what exactly Emilio gave her. Smiling, she whispers my name, causing me a swell of relief.

"*Sì, bella?*"

"You're here?"

"*Sì.*" I say nothing else lest I stir her memories, which now hopefully seem like a distant dream.

"I am so glad." Her Venetian accent seems stronger. It instantly brings me to the Adriatic, to the memories of when we first met. It was less than two years ago, though it seems like I've known her forever.

I stroke her cheek with tenderness. "But now I must go back to my work."

"You could stay here." Her hand slides over my wrist, and I can feel when she tries to pull herself up to me, but she lacks the strength, making me again wonder whether I should stay to monitor her throughout the night. I lower myself beside her and rest my head next to hers on the satin pillow; it is impossible not to get lost in her budding smile.

My fingers reclaim the place on her cheek, and for a moment I wish we had never left Paris and come back to Italy. "*Tesoro mio*, you are more beautiful than the sun's rays."

Her lashes bat, like I knew they would. "Tell me about your work, Niccolò . . . It takes up all of you."

It hurts me deeply to hear her say it and draws me nearer. "Not all of me," I say.

Her lips are now so close to mine it is impossible not to meet them with a kiss, for just one gentle moment. I start to envision myself on top of her, and I pull away. I know if there is just one more kiss, one more moment, I will have to have her.

Focus, Niccolò. There is a vampire *in your laboratory right now. A vampire.*

The quest for knowledge overtakes me—the only thing that could usurp my desire for her.

"You think I am too silly to understand it?" she says. "Is that why you won't tell me?"

"No. No, not at all. I never think you are silly."

"Then you don't trust me to keep your secrets? What was the place with the twinkling lights?"

The question surprises me so much so that I don't move away when her mouth comes back to mine. Her kiss draws out a desire to tell her everything—the science, the Elixir, and everything about my family.

I cup her cheek as my lips pull from hers. It is too dangerous to tell her my secrets. "Do you trust me, *bella*?"

"More than the sun trusts the moon to watch over the Earth while she rests each night."

Her words make me smile, and my hand settles on her waist. "You are my sun. You are the center of my universe." Her hand slides over my jaw, and I can feel how much she desperately wants me to stay. "Be assured that the reason my work consumes me is humanitarian. My mission is to prolong the most delicate thing in the world: the human heart."

"It brings me joy, Niccolò, that you consider the heart to be a delicate thing." She drags my hand over her breast to the top her chest. "Because you hold mine."

I nod.

Thump-thump.

Thump-thump.

"You don't have to go," she tells me again, and I want to stay. I want to kiss her.

And I do kiss her, the kind of kiss that shows us our future together.

Thump-thump.

No. No. No. I didn't kiss her again. I left. I went back to the laboratory. Back to León and Séraphine.

Thump-thump.

As I taste her, I can envision her swollen belly and our joy together during the summers in Venezia and the autumns in Toscana.

Thump-thump.

You should have stayed, Niccolò.

She suddenly jerks away, breaking the kiss. "Get out!" she yells. "Get out!"

Light floods the room. I can't see anything at all. I just hear her yelling over and over, "Get out!"

It's not her yelling; it's me yelling.

"*Get out!*"

Thump-thump.

Thump-thump.

"*Get out!*"

Everything goes dark. I can't move. I can't yell. *I'm trapped.*

There are no sounds of the Adriatic in the dank air around me. It's not Maddalena's heartbeat that thumps against mine. *It's Adele's.* I can feel her. I can hear her heart. I can smell her heart.

I'm starving.

She's so close. I want her. I want her here, next to me. But not in Florence, not in the seventeenth century. Not in my head. *No. No.*

No!

Get out!

"*Esci!*"

"Nicco!"

I woke up gasping. I could feel him. Not Nicco the human, but *my* Nicco. I heard him speak. I felt him—his pulse, the fear.

His heavy hand on my waist.

I turned over and was almost startled when I saw Isaac there. A tiny fireball danced over us—his eyelashes cast dark shadows against his cheeks, and his expression was peaceful. Just as I thought about getting up, he stirred, pulling me closer, and breathing in his scent changed my mind. I wanted to kiss him, just one gentle touch, but I knew it would wake him, and where it would lead. Instead, with as little movement as possible, I reached into my bag for the vial of sleepytime potion.

The feeling of Nicco kicking me out of his dreamscape filled me with uneasiness. I knew he didn't want me to unlock his secrets, but I also knew there wasn't much time left tonight.

I chugged the potion back before my conscience could drape me with guilt. A part of me knew this was wrong, that this went way past a violation of privacy. But I wanted answers. I needed answers.

Nicco, I get that you think hiding things is the best way to protect me, but letting me in is the best way to protect you.

Otherwise . . . you're going to be in there forever.

For a while everything was just darkness, but I knew I was getting close to something. Otherwise he wouldn't be fighting back so hard.

León looks to me as he stokes the fire in the hearth. "You should take the night off, Niccolò. I'm sure Maddalena grows weary of dining with your *madre e padre*. She's been here for a whole month, and you've hardly gone upstairs. Are you no longer fond of her?"

"Of course I am still fond of her! I am more than fond of her! But I'm sure Giovanna and her daughters are keeping her well entertained while I'm busy."

León's bright eyes dim ever so slightly, and I immediately regret mentioning Giovanna's children.

"Niccolò, just because I have loved and lost does not mean you should deprive yourself."

"I have the rest of my life to be with Maddalena, but there will be only one to first create the Elixir of Life." I look at him. "Well, two in this case."

"You might be surprised how little you'll care about the Elixir if it costs you your love."

"We are on the brink of finding the right combination. I can feel it," I say, pouring a tonic of carefully distilled minerals into the pot of Elixir, noting it in the margin of the Medici tome, next to the date.

León sighs loudly, but I ignore that too, turning the page to catch up on my notes.

I dip the quill into the pot of ink and pause to reflect on the last few weeks, wanting to commit only certainties to the pages of the book. Needless to say, our interest in phlebotomies has turned into an obsession ever since Séraphine came into our lives.

When my thoughts feel precise, I move the feather across the top of the page:

SUI VAMPIRI

> *As she is confined to her cage, we have not been truly able to test her strength, but based on the way she threw a bloodletting fleam at León—nearly killing him—it is apparent that even in her weakened state, she is inhumanly strong.*

I underline the last two words.

> *She is violently insistent about being freed, to the point where she thinks nothing of self-harm, slamming her body against her cage, intentionally cracking her own bones so she might slip through the bars. I have told her countless times there is no possibility she is getting through the metal, but she does not hear my words.*
>
> *She either does not believe me or does not care for her bones—why should she when every part of her appears to heal so rapidly? I can only conclude that her own blood affects her in the same way it healed León.*
>
> *Her eyes appear to lose coloration the closer she gets to starvation, although with her eyes naturally being such a pale shade of blue and the laboratory so dark, I cannot*

confirm this at the time. Her enlarged canines protrude when she is angry. Or when she is lustful. Or when she is reaching the point of starvation.

Anatomically, other than her blood, eye color, and canines, she appears to be exactly like a human. The key difference in her physiology seems to be her sustentative nutrition, which at the present moment is comprised entirely of human blood.

I set the quill down and run my hands through my hair, trying not to get too frustrated by the words. We tried giving her the blood of pigs, which she spat back at León, and the blood of lambs, which she spat back at me. This was followed by calves' blood and then goats', but nothing seems to bring her back to health other than freshly extracted human blood.

Not that we wish for her to be at peak health, but we cannot stand to lose her. This marvelous creature is surely the answer to modern sickness. If her blood, when applied to the human body, can have such a great effect as healing León's burn, it could be the basis for a revolution in internal medicine. It would tumble the entire old guard of physicians!

If finding those answers means León and I bleeding ourselves to feed Séraphine—then so be it! I return to the page.

We have yet to determine the exact amount of fresh human blood required by the vampire to survive, but Séraphine gets one vial per week from each of us, in exchange for one of her own.

As I dip the quill into the ink, I think about how having Séraphine in our laboratory has changed our routine completely. We spend our days working on the potion for my father, and our nights rigorously attempting to distill Séraphine's blood to the very essence of its healing properties.

> *We add drops of vampire blood to salves, oils, and tonics. We add it to soap. And we have seen great success in healing minor afflictions such as rashes and infected wounds. But the longer the blood has been extracted from its source, the lesser its potency, until it has no more healing qualities than the blood of a frog.*

I push away the book and move to the hearth to stoke the embers. *Focus on the Elixir, Niccolò . . . not Séraphine.* I pull out the pot, the quicksilver and brimstone, the salts and the measuring tools. And the rest of the night goes as nights always do. A careful eye on the measurements, and a careful eye on the pot, while careful words are read from the book.

When it's finished distilling, I pour the potion into a round-bottom flask and wait for it to cool so I can parse it out in measured doses to our fresh batch of rats, which is my least favorite part of this duty. I live to heal living creatures, not poison them.

León comes to the workbench and begins tidying up. When he returns from the basin he says, "Nicco, I'm doing this for your own good. You need to take a break."

"What?" I ask, looking up. "No!"

I jump up, but it's too late; he's already brought the flask to his lips and swallowed back its contents.

"León!" I yell, shocked at the risk he has taken, but also enthralled to the point of jealousy by his gumption.

"Now," he says, wiping his lip, "we'll make another batch tomorrow. It's too late to start one now. Follow your heart, and take the night off. I will stay here and watch Séraphine if it means you having a night of pleasure with your love."

"Brother, if you think for a second that your little act of foolery hasn't solidified me staying in the lab for the rest of the night to watch over you, then you really do not know me at all."

"Madonna mia!" He throws his arms up in the air. "I'm sorry, Maddalena," he cries, looking up at the ceiling. "I tried."

I laugh, and so does he, and when we turn back to the fire, Séraphine is watching us from behind bars; the warm glow from the fire cast over her face makes her look almost human.

I pour wine into chalices, and for the rest of the night, record León's vitals, eagerly awaiting some kind of change.

As the dawn approaches, my eyes droop, and León encourages me to once again give up and go upstairs, to Maddalena's bed.

"You know, Niccolò, even your twinkling Medicean eyes won't hold her attention forever. She's desired by more than one Roman duke."

"Let them come and try to get her attention. I will slay each one of them. But tonight there is nothing that will take me from you, brother. Not even Maddalena. I will stay with her tomorrow, *te lo prometto.*"

But as we doze off at the table, I dream of nothing but her—the scents of the Adriatic, the taste of her skin, and the way her fingers feel in my hair. Her arms circle my chest, and she whispers in my ear, "You want to be immortal, Niccolò Medici?" *Why does she sound French,* I wonder, but before I realize that the arms are not Maddalena's, Séraphine's fangs sink into my neck.

My dagger releases from its sheath and plunges into her leg as she drinks from me, which only seems to make her more excitable—each of her pulls renders me further and further into helplessness, until the pain stops. It's as if I've been dosed with some kind of sedative. I know she's still behind me, her fingers moving through my hair, but there is no more pain. There is no feeling at all, just weightlessness. Her fangs slide into me a second time, bringing me to a euphoric state.

But how did she escape? My pulse slows to near nothingness.

She withdraws from my flesh and whispers in my ear once more. "I will give you endless life, my precious little boy."

I awaken on the laboratory floor, my cheek cold from the stone. The clockwork timer is rattling. I swat at it and miss. The noise rings through my head like a stampede of horses, and my hand scrapes through a pile of glass looking for it. My eyes squint open to find several broken boiling flasks surrounding me, but I can focus on nothing but the noise.

I grab the timer and hurl it across the room. It smashes against the stone wall, the sound jabbing my head like a million daggers.

Something is wrong. *Why am I on the floor?*

I reach for my waist. My blade is gone. Still squinting, I turn and see it lying a few feet away on the floor, dark and sticky with blood. Behind it the cage is open . . .

I spring up, hardly able to comprehend what my eyes have revealed. My hand goes to my neck as the memories pour back. There's a slight sensation, but I feel no wound. Nothing at all.

"León?" I call out, suddenly frantic. "León?"

The room is empty, but there's a pool of blood on the floor.

I follow a bloody trail out into the great hall—dark splashes and footprints at first, and then mere droplets, as if the person bleeding was moving with speed. *Or healing?* A memory flashes: my dagger slicing through Séraphine's leg, and her laughter as I plunged it deeper. Her words: "Don't worry, Niccolò. You have pierced me, but it is also you who will heal me."

"León!" I yell, following the droplets of blood up the stairs.

They become farther and farther apart, until they lead me to my own bedchamber.

I open the door to a familiar voice. "Nicco?" Maddalena asks.

She is standing in the center of my room. I have to shield my eyes from the sunlight pouring in through the window in order to see her face. "Maddalena? What are you doing in here?"

"Waiting for you."

I stumble toward her, blinking in the light. "But why are you standing here?"

"She told me not to move." Her voice shakes. "That you would come."

I push aside her flowing hair, exposing her collarbone and everything else beneath the thin chemise.

"She told me that you'll finally want me. For good."

I suppress every urge, but then her head turns up, her lips dangerously close to mine.

"Do you?" she asks. "Want me?"

My mouth moves against hers as I speak. "More than Icarus wanted to touch the sun." *It is only her I want.* My lips press into hers as she pushes my doublet off my shoulders and then pulls my tunic over my head.

It has always been her.

I tug the ribbons of her gown and let it fall to the floor, regretting every moment I haven't spent with her. Our kisses become feverish, and I lift her up to the bed. I have touched her skin so many times before, but now it feels softer than the finest talc.

Softer on my hands, softer on my lips. Softer against my chest as my body brushes hers.

The wanton way she pushes away my breeches makes me kiss her harder, and the need to make up for lost time consumes me.

She flinches.

I taste the blood in my mouth and stiffen harder. *"Scusami,"* I whisper, but the taste sends violent shudders through my shoulders, down my spine.

Move away from her, Niccolò. Now.

"Don't stop," she whispers, the look in her eyes changing from shock to desperation. The same emotions pummel through me as she pulls me close. "Touch my heart, Niccolò."

My kisses move across her jaw, to the soft skin under her ear, and then farther down, until my lips reach the place on her neck where I can feel her pulse. *I can hear her pulse.* I want to taste her. *I need to.* Her body tenses, but her leg wraps around my hip and snakes into mine. Every noise that escapes her throat encourages me to take her. *Taste her.* My desire to touch her heart consumes me so completely, I don't notice when my kisses end and my teeth sink into her—all I can feel is her heartbeat thudding faster. She arches closer, her body begging for me, but it's her whispers that make me shudder.

"Prendimi, Niccolò. Prendimi, amore mio."

I suck harder. The world is only her. And red. Her body relaxes, and pulling the blood becomes easier. Her thumping heartbeat fills my consciousness, so strong and yet so delicate. It beats in time to her whispers of my name: "Niccolò-Niccolò." Her arms circle my head. "Take me, my love."

And I do, until her muscles go limp and I collapse on top of her.

I awaken to the sound of my name, but it's not my *bella*—it's a desperate cry from outside the door. "Niccolò!"

Giovanna.

My eyes pop open, and I jump up, stumbling off the bed—off Maddalena—away from the windows and the piercing light.

"Niccolò!" my sister cries again, closer now in the hallway mezzanine.

I grab my dagger even before pulling on my breeches—unable to comprehend the sight before me: Maddalena, covered in blood, my chest stained red. *"Vita mia!"*

"Niccolò!"

I run to the door and barely have it open before Giovanna—a flash of red chemise—jumps into my arms. "Niccolò!"

"Are you injured, *angelo mio*?"

She stiffens and inhales a deep breath. Her head snaps toward my door, which I hadn't closed completely. "Who do you have in there, Niccolò?" she asks, the words a near snarl.

I have to hold her tight as she tries to leap past me. I can't let her into the room. She must not see what I have done.

A door on the right side of the mezzanine slams open, and Emilio runs out in a vicious rage. "Where is she?" he yells, his hands sticky with blood. "I am going to shred her into pieces. Where is Séraphine!"

The door to the left opens, and Gabriel, unclothed, walks out, stretching his arms. He is covered in blood from mouth to chest. Behind him in the room, a tangle of naked bodies are strewn over his bed—not an entirely uncommon sight, except that today they too are all bathed in red.

"I need more," he says.

"*I* need more," Giovanna echoes. "I always hated him, Niccolò." A desperate mix of confession and exhilaration in her voice. "*You* hated him . . ." I assume her husband is drained in her bed. "I need more, Nicco. I need more."

I imagine Séraphine running through the palazzo, taking our lives and then breathing life back into us, one by one.

"*Madre e Padre*," I whisper, and together we run to the master bedchamber.

Our father lies on the bed, lifeless and bloodless, next to our mother, who looks just as beautiful in death as she was in life.

"No, no, no," Gabriel says.

My chest heaves, and Giovanna sobs loudly.

The only one still quiet is Emilio. He simply stares at our parents, rage building in his eyes.

"León!" Giovanna suddenly gasps. *"Dove è León?"*

"He—he was working alongside me in the laboratory last night," I say, "but when I woke on the floor, he was gone. There was just a pool of . . . blood."

"No!" Her expression is that of a grief-torn lover. "No!"

The four of us split up, each of us visiting one of his favorite rooms first and then exploring the rest of the palazzo, but there is no sign of him, just more slain cousins and servants and guests. And more of Giovanna's screams echoing down the hallways.

By the time we reconvene on the loggia, my own panic is setting in. Everyone is dead, all except for Giovanna's children, who are missing.

I wonder aloud whether I really checked the laboratory thoroughly— we turn and race down the stairs together and through the tunnels and the great Medici hall.

Everything is just as I recall: the cage door swung open, broken glass and instruments strewn about, and two pools of blood on the floor. One is mine.

Emilio stalks from Séraphine's cage back to the door. "There are two sets of footprints," he says, examining the ground. "One a man, the other a woman."

I turn to him. "What are you implying, Emilio?"

"He's trying to ask," Gabriel growls, "how did the vampire manage to escape?"

Emilio huffs. "Isn't it obvious, brother? León set her free. And in return, she set *him* free."

In a flash, my blade is touching Emilio's throat. He bats it away, slicing his hand without notice. "This is all *your* fault," he says, pinning me against the wall. "You have always trusted him too deeply. You and Father have always been blind when it comes to León."

"It's not possible," I say, but then my attention moves to something even more troublesome. "No. It's not . . . possible."

I shove Emilio, and he slams into the fireplace—hard. My new-found strength is surprising, but I spend no time considering it further. I tear around the room, inspecting the tables and knocking things over as I search frantically for the Medici tome. "It's gone. It's gone! Everything. All of our research. All of our family secrets!"

"This was his plan *all along!*" Emilio yells, pounding the table so hard the wood cracks.

Something more horrific dawns on me. "Last night. León drank the Elixir last night."

"You see!" Emilio says. "All this time, he was only here for the Elixir. He was waiting for this moment for the last six years!"

It feels like the entire laboratory is crashing down around us. I could not have been this wrong about León. I trusted him more than anyone. More than my brothers, my sister, my lovers. More than science.

"I trusted León," I say, "but I promise you, if he has betrayed me— if he has stolen from us—I will hunt him to the end of the earth until our pages are back in our possession. I vow it."

"No, Niccolò!" Giovanna says. "León would never steal from us. He is one of us!"

"Where would he go first?" Emilio asks her.

"San Germano," Gabriel says when she doesn't answer. "The palazzo."

"It's been shut for years," I say. "Why would he go there?"

Gabriel looks at Giovanna, and she bursts into tears. "Did you really think I didn't know of your rendezvous spot?"

"We leave immediately," I say.

"No, Niccolò, no!" Giovanna bangs her fists upon my chest. "He would never betray us! He loves me! *Ti ama!* He loves *you*, Niccolò."

CHAPTER 34
Dead Dogs, Dead Girls

"No, Niccolò, no!"

At first the words sounded distant. I reached for Adele as I woke. She wasn't next to me anymore. She yelled again, and I sat up in a panic. *She opened the door. He's here.*

"No, Niccolò!" she cried out again in the dark room. *"No. No. No!"*

She was huddled against the door, knees to chest, rocking not so gently back and forth, a little flame whizzing above her head like a halo.

I fell next to her. "Hey!" I whispered. "Hey."

"No. Nicco. No."

"Adele. Wake up. It's just a dream." I gently shook her shoulder, trying not to scare her more than she already was, but she just kept moaning the same words.

"Baby, it's just a dream. He's not here!"

Her eyes snapped open.

She looked to the piles of blankets and back to me. I could tell that she was wondering how she'd gotten next to the door.

I softly rubbed her shoulder. "What happened?"

"I—I don't know." Her eyes became wide and glossy.

When she didn't say anything else, I pulled her onto my lap, not knowing what she needed. Her arms immediately circled my neck.

"It's okay. You're safe. It's just me." I held her tight, trying not to think about whatever was happening between her and Nicco. "Breathe."

And for a few minutes she did just that, and I whispered soothing words into her ear until her pulse slowed.

Tears dripped from her eyes onto my shoulder. "He killed her," she finally said. "He killed Maddalena."

"Who's Maddalena?"

"Just a girl who loved him."

"Baby, he's a monster."

"I know." She wiped her eyes. "But he wasn't always."

"It doesn't matter what he used to be. It matters what he is now."

I desperately wanted to know what had happened—what she'd seen, why he was showing her, and most of all why she cared. But she didn't say anything else.

And I didn't ask.

He was on the other side of the door, and I was here with her, and I wasn't going to wreck it, despite every part of my being wanting to go straight to Callis and take care of this ourselves. I wanted this bloodsucker out of her life.

But I'd promised her I wouldn't do anything stupid, so instead I hoisted her up. "I want you to meet someone."

"It's almost midnight."

"She doesn't mind being woken if you have a tennis ball."

We walked through the dark streets quickly, heading out of the Quarter and through the Marigny. The walk and the fresh air did us both good, and by the time we got to the little park, she wasn't squeezing my hand as tightly.

Alys Arden

I was convinced there was nothing Stormy's tail wagging couldn't fix—even the ethereal version of Nicco Medici.

I whistled twice, and she ripped through the park gate.

"Why are you so smiley?" Adele asked.

"Her, of course."

"Who?"

"Here, girl." I dropped to my knees as Stormy jumped up, licking my face.

"Isaac . . . you're freaking me out."

"Stormy, I hate to break it to you, but you're no longer the number-one lady in my life. I've met someone." I held her up, and she sniffed Adele's palm with curiosity.

Adele pulled back, hugging her arms. "Cold."

"You don't like dogs?" I asked, setting Stormy down, unprepared to hide my horror if she didn't.

"I—I like dogs."

"I know she looks ragged, but don't be scared of her." I bounced the tennis ball on the ground a couple times and threw it high across the park. Stormy tore off after it. "She's the hero, not me."

Adele watched as Stormy brought the ball back, dropped it at my feet, and leaped back, waiting for me to throw it again.

"We've been together since the day the levees broke." I threw it long across the park, but when I turned to smile at Adele, I realized she looked even more worried now than when we'd left the attic. "What's wrong?"

"Um . . ."

I'd thought bringing her here would cheer her up. Instead she looked frightened. *Did I make a wrong move?*

Stormy ran back with the ball.

"You're doing that," Adele said.

"Doing what?"

"Bringing that ball back. With the wind. You're messing with me."

412

"Messing with you? I thought the dog would make you smile. I always find her therapeutic. Maybe it's just my anthromorphic magic side."

I bent down to get the ball back, looking up at her.

She sucked in a deep breath. "Isaac . . . there is *no dog*."

Stormy jumped up my leg, scratching at my hip. She didn't want to give up the ball this time.

I let her keep it. "What do you mean?"

Adele gaped at me, and if it weren't for the complete concern on her face, I'd have thought she was losing it.

"Adele? Are you okay?"

I turned back to Stormy, but she was gone. The tennis ball bounced lifelessly on the ground.

"What the eff?" I spun around. "Where'd she—?"

Then Stormy blinked back—rematerialized from nothingness there on the street, as if she'd never left. She bit down on the ball as it started to roll away.

"Stormy!" I shook the ball out of her mouth, but this time I could see my fingers through her muzzle. *No. There's no way. She made it. We made it. All of us except Jade.*

I hurled the ball across the park.

"Isaac?" Adele's hand touched the small of my back.

My eyes started to sting. I don't know why. Just the tender way she touched me, like something was wrong.

"What are you seeing?" she asked.

Stormy raced across the dark park as the ball soared above her. My hands tore through my hair and settled on the top of my head.

"No, don't go there," Adele said, stepping in front of me, her hands circling around my torso. "Don't lock yourself in that dark part of your mind."

"She has to be here . . . She has to be . . . because if she's not that means . . ."

She's dead.

A lump formed in my throat. I could hear her running back to us, panting, her paws crunching against the dead grass. I felt the ball drop against my shoe.

"Look at me, please?" Adele said, touching my jaw.

But I couldn't. I broke away and picked up the ball. Stormy was the hero, not me. If it weren't for her, they'd both be dead. I chucked the ball across the park again, sucking back the tears.

How did that girl at the tearoom know about Jade?

I turned to Adele. "At the shop, was there a girl with long brown hair and a white vintagey dress?"

She shook her head. "No. Just me, Callis, and Chatham, and Papa Olsin in the back."

"And Onyx?"

"And Onyx," she echoed.

"The girl?" Adele asked. "Did she speak French?"

Protégez la.

I nodded, still unable to look at her, still trying not to think about that morning the levees broke—when we nearly drowned. When some of us *did*.

Adele's arms slid up around my neck, and she pressed against me until my own arms circled her, hugging her tight.

"There's a reason that you can see them, Isaac. It has to be your Spektral power."

"I don't want this power," I said, taking her hand and beginning to walk. I left the tennis ball on the ground.

Adele sped her steps to keep pace with mine as we headed back toward the Quarter. Stormy followed us but stopped at the train tracks like she always did.

She barked relentlessly as we walked away, but I refused to look back.

We didn't say much on the walk to her house, but when we crossed under the oak-tree branches on Esplanade, I realized it was me who was crushing her hand now.

I was grateful when she finally said something, and it wasn't about dead dogs or dead girls.

"*San Germano,*" she whispered. "They followed León to *San Germano*. It's Italian for Saint-Germain." She looked up at me. "I—I think my family might have been the one to start this whole thing—the feud with the Medici." Her eyes dropped to the ground as she mumbled about someone named León. "I think *le Comte de Saint-Germain* might be the reason Nicco's whole family was murdered and he and his siblings were all turned into vampires. And now they're hunting us to the end of the earth. That's why Adeline locked them in the attic, so they couldn't hurt her or her father."

I stopped in the middle of the street and turned to her. "*No one* is going to hunt you down," I said with assurance. "I don't care if your ancestor boiled them in hot oil, you are not going to pay for something he did hundreds of years ago. Do you understand?"

She nodded.

"It doesn't matter whose family started it. We ended it."

She nodded again, looking up at me. I moved closer until our lips touched, and I kissed her in the middle of the curfew-silent street. Even if every resident on the block had stepped outside, I wouldn't have broken the kiss. I was done fighting. I was done with the insecurity. I was done with Nicco Medici.

When she broke away, she whispered, "We ended it."

She slipped her hand back into mine, and we rounded the corner onto her block.

"*Shit.*" She yanked me back a few steps before she peeked her head around the corner of a vine-covered brick building.

I looked out over her shoulder. "Shit."

Mac was entering their front door.

"He's going to kill me," she whispered. "He always checks on me when he gets home from work—like since the day I was born."

"Can you open your window from down here?"

"Of course." She raised her hand a few inches, and the window slid up with it.

We walked down the block, and when we were nearly in front of her house I quickly looked both ways down the street, smiling. "Are you ready?"

"For wh—?"

Before she could protest, I ripped my hand back, pulling a tight gust down the street. It rushed up from the ground, grabbed her around the waist, and spun her up through the air. A gleeful yelp slipped from her lips.

"Shhh!"

I directed the air forward so that it gently pushed her through the window. Well, almost gently—she landed on the floor with a thud. A moment later she leaned back out the window, reeling with excitement. "I love you!" Her mouth snapped shut, as if the words had escaped by accident. "I mean—I don't mean—I don't know what I mean . . ."

"No take-backs!" I yelled, too loudly, but I couldn't help it.

I turned away so she couldn't see my big goofy smile, and I was gone, soaring the rest of the way home.

CHAPTER 35

Witch Killer

January 18th

Isaac's voice wafted out through the glassless windows of the Marigny Opera House foyer, making me smile a dippy smile. Clipboard in hand to check in straggler volunteers, I bounced down a few steps, closer to the street curb and into a patch of sunlight. I still didn't understand how saying those three little words could have such a physical impact.

It felt like I'd had a stomach full of butterfly chrysalises, and those words had made them start magically hatching over the last week. Some had hatched one by one, others by the dozen, depending on how much I was thinking about Isaac. It made me feel silly, and it made me perpetually blush, and it made me want to hide under a blanket. *Is this what love is? How are you supposed to know?* I don't even know why I'd said it, but now, with the butterfly invasion, I must have meant it. *Right?*

Over the past week I'd buried myself into things because I was sure that everyone around me could tell I was acting weird, that everyone could hear the delicate wings in my stomach, brushing against my organs, jittering my nerves.

I dove into homework. I called Brooke and e-mailed Codi a million times, never getting a hold of either of them. I made a dress from the last of the Paris-purchased fabric I'd been hoarding, a plum-colored silk. Today it was Johnnie and Veronica's mentorship fund-raiser: a neighborhood effort to restore the music venue and convert the outer-lying buildings into temporary housing for displaced musicians. Alphonse and Klara Jones were funding the project with a benefit record they'd just released. Isaac had organized his entire crew to volunteer for the weekend, and there must have been a hundred other people here scattered throughout the grounds. My dad even ungrounded me for the occasion.

A young couple with two children approached.

"A lot of the kids are helping out in the backyard," I told them as I wrote their names down.

A hodgepodge of brass musicians were set up in the street, playing all the local hits, their trills echoing throughout the neighborhood, encouraging all to come out and help.

Again Isaac's voice echoed out over the shrill of a saw—he was showing a group of my classmates how to rip away the walls without destroying the marble floor. Another butterfly hatched.

Most everyone I knew back in town was on site helping out. My father was erecting a statue he'd made of Allen Toussaint, Callis had a team in the back doing landscaping, and Annabelle had found the least dirty job she could: handing out water and Kool-Aid with the senior squad and Celestina.

Car doors slammed shut, and I looked up to see two blacked-out SUVs parked at the curb. An enormous suited man opened the back door of the first SUV, and Désirée stepped out in designer jeans, sneakers, and a souvenir **I ♥ NOLA** T-shirt. Next came Ritha and Ana Marie. Morgan Borges and various other mayoral staff members got out of the second car.

Désirée hopped up the steps toward me.

"Is that a ribbon in your hair?" I asked.

"Give me a sledgehammer and something to hit, or I'm going to murder someone."

"Team Isaac it is. Foyer."

She walked straight past me, ignoring the shrimpy guy with a fedora, tortoise-rimmed glasses, and a camera who was calling her name from the curb.

More people approached, but my attention fixed on Jeanne and Sébastien, who were hurrying down the street.

"Put us to work," she said as I greeted them both with tight hugs.

"Actually, I have the perfect job for you, Jeanne." I handed her the clipboard. "I'm ready to get my hands dirty again. Why don't you take over here?"

"I do like a good system," she said, scanning the list.

"*C'est parfait,*" Sébastien said as I took his arm and we walked up the stairs and through the foyer, where Isaac's team was creating an acoustical collision of power tool screeches, and then into the cavernous space where Chase's team was removing all the drowned pews. The venue wasn't an opera house at all but a converted nineteenth-century church. It still retained most of its original form. Stone archways led from the foyer all the way to the stage, where the altar had been, and arched windows lined the long walls. Every pane of glass had been blown out by the Storm, giving the old structure a medieval feel. Sunbeams poured in, spotlighting the multicolored patterns in the terrazzo floors.

"So what did Isaac think of the paper this morning?" Sébastien asked.

"You really have a warped sense of an average teenage morning."

"What do you mean?"

"Nothing," I said, trying not to laugh. "Isaac's been here since five. I really don't think he read the paper."

"Wait. Have *you* read today's paper?"

"Er . . . no."

"Which do you want? The *Times* or the *Pic*?"

Oh shit.

He pulled them both out of his messenger bag and handed me the thicker one. The front page had the photo of Isaac.

UNNAMED HERO IDENTIFIED

Isaac Thompson, Son of Acting FEMA Director

The young man in the now globally famous photo, appropriately titled *The Day the Levees Broke*, has been confirmed as eighteen-year-old Isaac Norwood Thompson of New York City, son of now-acting FEMA director Norwood Bowen Thompson. The photo was taken by Julian Roddick the morning after the hurricane, which is now officially the biggest economic natural disaster in US history, with over ten thousand deaths. The photo captures Thompson holding a little girl up above the water as waves crashed over them from the Industrial Canal levee breach. She's now been identified as Rosalyn Jackson, age six.

The article went on criticizing the atrocity that was FEMA, debating whether Isaac's dad was cut out for the job. *Pfft. Is anyone cut out for that job?*

Jory leaned over my shoulder and took the paper from my hands. "The Corpse Whisperer's in the *New York Times*?"

"That's not funny," I said, trying to take it back, but Chase reached over and grabbed it. A small crowd gathered around us as the paper was passed around, eliciting hoots and exclamations. I gave up trying to get it back.

The pages of the *Times-Picayune* in Sébastien's hand fluttered in the breeze. My hair blew in front of my face, not wildly, but enough for goose bumps to prick the back of my neck. I turned, looking for him—Isaac was just standing in the front entrance, watching blankly from a distance.

A woman with a flannel jacket and a matching fur-trimmed trapper's hat set the *Times* on the floor and clapped, slowly and purposefully, with admiration.

All heads looked to him, and everyone clapped with her.

More people came in from outside: students, first responders, lots of neighborhood folks, even the mayor. The newspaper fluttered away—Celestina chased after it and then ran back to Callis.

The chandelier began to sway, and the breeze poured in through the blown-out windows like flooding water, but no one blinked an eye, because in south Louisiana, no one ever questioned a cool breeze; you prayed for them.

Callis glanced at me from across the room, and Désirée motioned for me to do something.

I hustled over to Isaac, who was gazing out at the crowd, a million miles away. The breeze picked up.

"Hey," I whispered, sweeping my hand over his lower back. "Just smile."

"Aw, guys," AJ called out, "did you know we've been working with a hero this whole time?"

A bunch of people in the crowd laughed playfully.

"Of course we knew," said Betsy, whose southern accent rivaled Dixie Hunter's.

"It will be over in a sec," I whispered. "Just smile."

"I don't want to smile."

"Well, you're going to have to channel your inner southerner and suck it up."

The corner of his mouth cracked. "What a very New Yorky thing to say."

"Learned from the best."

Désirée folded her hands into boxes around her face.

"What is she doing?" Isaac asked, now really trying not to smile.

"Voguing. I think?" It was quite possibly the only time I'd ever seen Désirée do anything silly—it was confusing. Funny but confusing.

"The award ceremony is tomorrow." Isaac's voice mellowed along with the wind. "I've tried everything I can to get out of it." He turned to me. "Do you think . . . you could come? Maybe Mac would even want to come to this stupid thing?"

For something so "stupid," he sounded completely stressed out about it. I hooked my fingers in his. "Sounds like the kind of thing he'd wake up for."

He kissed my cheek, which brought on insta-blush.

"All right, break time's over," he said to the crowd, and just like that he switched back into work mode and sent everyone scattering. When he thought no one was looking, he grabbed the copy of the *Times-Pic* from the floor and dumped it in the trash.

He scooped Celestina up, throwing her up to his shoulders. "We have a new recruit," he said, moving his team to the back of the church, where the altar would have been. "I hear she has years of experience with electrical work, which is just what we need."

She erupted with giggles.

My heart swelled a little. The image was a stark contrast to the one of Nicco killing Maddalena, which still roosted in the back of my head a week later.

A hand touched my shoulder. "It frustrates me how impossible it is to hate that kid," my father said.

"Dad, you don't need to hate him." I sighed. "I wasn't even with him the night I broke curfew."

"You mean the night you didn't *come home*, leaving me to think you were dead?"

I nodded.

"Then where the hell were you?"

"I . . . broke into the school library and fell asleep reading from one of the textbooks since we don't have our own copies; the next thing I knew it was morning." It was getting increasingly difficult to lie to my father. *I hated it.*

His brow crinkled. I prayed the story was ridiculous enough to believe. "Why didn't you just tell me that?"

"Uh, the whole breaking-into-school part seemed a bigger offense than sleeping with—*at*—sleeping *at* Isaac's."

"Jesus, Adele, you nearly scared me to death. You have to be more responsible. *Curfew. Crime.*"

"I know. I'm sorry. But don't be mad at Isaac."

"I'm not mad at him . . . I'm just not as ready for the next phase of your life as you seem to be. The phase with boys and college, and without *me*."

From the way he tensely squeezed my shoulder, I knew there was more coming. "And also—You know, you can tell me if you're thinking about having . . . Just. You can tell me anything."

"Dad."

"I'm serious, Adele. I just want you to be safe. I know I'm not your mother, but if you need anything I want you to come to me. And I promise no harm will come to Isaac."

"Got it. You can tell me anything too." I smiled up at him. "And thanks."

His arm slid around my shoulders, and mine slid around his waist, and we both just stood there for a minute, watching Isaac work—me really hoping he wasn't imagining the things I was imagining.

"I worry about him," he said, kind of out of nowhere, but kind of a long time coming. "You know there are trauma counselors on base specifically for first responders? I looked into it."

"He won't even talk to *me* about it."

"Of course he doesn't want to talk to you about it. He's in love with you."

"*Dad.*"

"Be careful with him, sweetheart."

I don't know how we went from my father telling me he wouldn't hurt Isaac to him telling me not to, but we both just stood there for a minute, watching him, and the butterfly wings inside were back to brushing against my heart.

The band moved to the backyard, and more and more people showed up: the Daures and Blanche. Ren and Theis with a live-in friend whose green hair had faded to a bile hue. Most people in the city had gained a couch dweller or two or ten: friends and family waiting for FEMA trailers, or for insurance claims, or for their jobs to come back.

There must have been three dozen people working in the backyard, draining fountains of sludge, picking up trash, raking leaves, hacking back bushes, and pulling up dead trees. A group of children gathered up the scattered bricks that used to be the footpaths.

Callis dropped a shovel to the ground and tugged a tree root. Seeing him made me think about Nicco, which curdled my Isaac warm and fuzzies like spoiled milk.

I should have hated Nicco even more after the front-row view into his monstrous behavior, but somehow it had the opposite effect: it made me empathetic, which made me disgusted with myself.

Day and night the argument went full circle in my head. *Nicco hadn't always been that way—he doesn't deserve to be eternally trapped.* Always landing back on the fact that he was a monster *now*. A monster who was after me and my family. A monster who'd terrorized Callis. A monster who needed to be stopped.

But, then, whatever logic I applied to Nicco I had to apply to my mother, which was infinitely harder. And the more I humanized my mom, the more I humanized Nicco, and it was just one eternal Möbius strip. Clearly, I'd be the first to go in a zombie apocalypse.

Callis's face dripped dirt and sweat while he wrestled with the slippery root. He looked so much healthier, cheeks even showing a little color. I hoped he was on the road to getting his Elemental back.

"Do you need some help with that?"

"Please," he said, holding the root out to me. "On the count of three."

He counted off, and we both heaved, but the root didn't budge. God only knows how many decades—or centuries, even—it had been buried in the ground.

We tried again, but I slipped and landed on my ass.

I laughed. "This is really a job for Dee."

"I beg to differ," he said, wiping sweat from his brow with his forearm. "You could do it. You're just not trying hard enough."

I lowered my voice as I stood. "Oh, I meant *magically*."

"So did I."

"Yeah, maybe if the tree was made of iron. Or silver. Or steel."

He softly laughed. "Is that what you think? That your telekinesis is limited to metal?"

"Given that I've never been able to move anything but metal. *Oui*."

"Get up. Grab the root." He came behind me, gripping it as well. "Close your eyes, and picture the root."

"Uh, okay."

"Don't think of it as a root; think about it as positive space. When you're ready, think about the ground. Now don't think of it as dirt and grass and earth. Just think of it as all of the negative space surrounding the positive space—the root."

I let out a little laugh.

"What?"

"Nothing. You just sound like my dad."

"Clearly, a brilliant man. Okay." He lowered his voice. "Telekinesis is about *moving* objects, but you, my dear, are better than that. Don't think about moving this object. Think about *re*moving it. *Evulsing* it from one point of negative space—the ground—to another, the surface. Mentally excavate the positive space from the universe, and place it in another point."

"Scratch that. You sound more like Copernicus."

"Focus."

My eyes slipped shut, and I mentally pulled.

Mentally pulling turned into mentally straining. It was like trying to hear something so faint you're certain the sound isn't there.

His hands slipped over mine, and a jolt of energy shot up my arms, knocking us back to the ground, Callis involuntarily breaking my fall.

"Yeah . . . exactly. Like that," he said, pushing me off as heads turned our way.

A round of applause came from the nearest volunteers—the root had ripped out of the ground all the way across the yard. It must have been thirty feet long. Nervous laughter slipped from my lips after having used magic so openly in front of so many people. Not that we'd done anything superfishy, other than rip out a pretty large root with the combined muscle mass of a large turkey.

"See," Callis said, standing up. "You need to stop underestimating your power, or you're never going to get your mark, and then you risk losing it all."

"Thanks for the vote of confidence."

He offered me his hand and pulled me to my feet. "I'm just saying . . . you're stronger than you think."

"Thanks." And this time I meant it.

He picked up a shovel, and I wondered why it had taken me so long to warm up to him. Without thinking, curiosity poured out of my mouth: "Why did they hurt you?"

He pressed his foot onto the shovel, breaking up the next root. He didn't say anything, but his jaw tightened, and I could tell he was remembering it.

I don't know why; I just suddenly needed to know. I needed to know why Nicco would do something so heinous. He dug into the dirt more, and I dug into him. "You never told me, but captivity? Torture? It doesn't seem like a random act of violence."

He slammed the shovel back into the root.

"You're right, Adele. There was nothing random about their violence. They did it because I'm a *witch*."

"Why would that matter?"

"Because they're witch killers."

A laugh slipped from my mouth before I caught my tongue. "No, they're not."

He looked at me sharply. My response had far too much authority. Too much familiarity. "I mean, I've never heard of that before. Vampires hunting witches?"

This time when he slammed the shovel into the ground, he left it standing and turned to me.

Shit.

"And what exactly *do* you know about vampires, Adele?" His arms crossed and he stepped closer.

"Nothing." My heart pounded against my chest. "Nothing."

"Do you want to know how I *know* they're witch killers?" He slowly circled, vulture-like.

My head bobbed.

"I know this because Niccolò and Emilio Medici didn't just capture and torture me and drain my magic and life. They captured *my coven*."

"What?"

"They captured, tortured, and drained my entire coven. And I can assure you, there were others not as lucky as me and Celestina."

"*Celestina?*" I gasped. "She's just a little girl."

"A little girl who will have eternal nightmares, thanks to the Medici."

"But why would they—?"

"Don't seek logic or reasoning with monsters, Adele! If you think for one second they aren't trying to eradicate your coven, you are *gravely* mistaken." He grabbed my arm. "Niccolò and Emilio are manipulative, conniving predators without a shred of humanity left. Do not be a fool."

"Hey," Isaac interrupted. He was standing next to us with Celestina, both of them holding up cans of water for us. "Everything okay here?" His eyes dropped to Callis's hand on my arm, which he immediately released.

"All good," Callis said, but his tone implied things were far from good. "Just discussing Adele's proclivity for the dead."

I turned to Isaac. "I don't have a pro—"

"Like this beast." Callis reached down for the root. "She helped me uncover it."

Isaac handed me the can of water with one eyebrow raised, as if he thought Callis was nuts.

Callis leaned casually on the shovel handle. "And I have a feeling she's going to be the key to uncovering more of the dead. Oh, wait, that's you with the dead. I guess with her I should say *undead*?"

Isaac crossed his arms. "What's that supposed to mean?"

"It means that you don't have to stand with your fellow witches, but don't try to stand in front of us, or we will take you down too."

"*We?*"

Callis turned back to me. "The rest of my coven will be here by tomorrow night, and we will sniff out Niccolò and Emilio, with or without your help." He took a deep inhale. "This city, it's so perfect for our kind. So much strength around every corner." He stepped closer to Isaac. "You surprise me, though. I really thought we'd be on the same page about this little situation."

Isaac's jaw clenched, but he didn't say anything.

Callis looked to me. "Despite not being magical, one of them certainly seems to have a spell on you. I hope you're strong enough to break it before your coven ends up in their trap."

"*Hmph.*" Isaac smiled curtly. "Maybe it's the Medici who should worry about traps."

"Tell me." Callis's eyes narrowed. "Where they are."

"No," I said.

"Are you protecting them?"

"We're not getting involved."

"Oh, but Adele, by standing in the middle, you are involved. You're tied to this by magic, and, I suspect, by *blood.*" He smiled cordially. "In the future, just remember there was a point when you had a choice over which side to fight for. In the meantime, Adele, I hope you stop closing yourself off to your magic. It would be a pity to lose one of ours."

"Adele?" said a tiny voice. Celestina's eyes were wide. "Why do you like the monsters more than us?"

My heart jerked. "I don't—"

"Come on, love." Callis held out his hand to her. "I'm going to take care of you, I promise. We don't need them."

As we watched them walk out, Désirée and Annabelle stepped next to us.

"Soooo," Annabelle said, breaking the silence. "Anyone want to tell me who the emo siblings are?"

Luckily, Désirée cut her off: "We have to go," she said to Isaac.

He sighed, turning to me. "Sorry, it's this stupid dinner for that photographer. Are you okay?"

"I'm fine. Go."

Désirée pinched his cheek. "Welcome to the government needing your face to soften their brand image."

Isaac swatted her fingers away, rolling his eyes. "Let's get this over with."

Annabelle put her arm around me as they walked off. "I guess that leaves you and me for the after-party."

Commotion came from the other side of the yard—Ren stalked across the grass, waving a small pouch in his hand.

"Did you think I wouldn't find this?" he yelled to Theis, who was weeding a flowerless flower bed with his bile-green-haired friend and Sébastien.

"It's for your own good!" Theis yelled, standing up.

Ren's giant hands slammed into his chest, sending him flying.

"Theis!" I screamed as he landed dangerously close to a concrete angel's broken wing.

We ran over, along with everyone else in the yard.

"You need help, Ren!" yelled the green-haired guy, jumping into the usually gentle giant's face. He was heavier than Theis but significantly shorter than Ren. "You're becoming a psychopath!"

Ren shoved him too, mumbling something incoherent. It sounded like drunken babble, which wasn't exactly strange for Ren. He grabbed Theis up from the ground and cocked his arm.

A man jumped in between them. "Dad!" He took Ren's punch in the shoulder, sparing Theis's face.

But then Ren tried to swing again.

My dad grabbed his arm and twisted it behind his back, muttering, "Now I know you've lost your goddamn mind." I knew it wasn't the first drunk guy's arm he'd twisted, but still, it made my pulse hammer.

Two other guys rushed over to help, and I couldn't help but stare, unable to believe what was happening. Ren might have been big and more often drunk than not, but he was one of the friendliest people I'd ever met. Everyone in the Quarter knew that. And he'd never taken a swing at my dad.

Detective Matthews ran out of the church with some others. He was in jeans and a Saints jersey but seconds later was cuffing Ren.

"Désolé. Désolé!" Ren apologized. "Now, you don't have to do that. *Je suis désolé.*"

"Come on, Terry," my dad pleaded with the detective.

"Mac, you've bailed him out enough. Let's see if a night in a post-Storm OPP does him any good."

My dad shook his head.

"Mi dispiace, mi dispiace," Ren pleaded over and over. *"Mi aiuti per favore!"*

Was he speaking Italian? Ritha and Ana Marie approached Detective Matthews, and they all went into the church together.

Everything about the scene was *so weird.*

"Pick you up in a couple hours?" Annabelle asked, going straight back to high school norm.

"For what?"

"The after-party!"

"I'm not really in a partying mood, Annabelle." Callis's threat was ringing in my head now that the commotion was dying down. *What exactly did he mean by his coven sniffing them out?*

Her head tilted to the side as she looked straight at me. "Come on, Adele, you deserve to let loose after being grounded all week."

"You know you can't, like, mind-meld me, right?"

"Sorry." She smiled. "Force of habit."

CHAPTER 36

Bloodsucker

I was thinking about Nicco when I got into the shower, I was thinking about Nicco when the water ran cold, and I was still thinking about Nicco when I flopped on my bed in a T-shirt and leggings, wet hair soaking through the pillow.

The Medici were a lot of things, but I just didn't believe they were witch killers.

Maybe it was me being naïve or an idiot, but it just didn't add up. Then again, things hadn't added up since the night in the attic when Nicco gripped my hand too tight and spun me around the room.

I'd suppressed the dream for most of the week, not wanting to see Nicco covered in Maddalena's blood, not really wanting to see him with her at all, but now I was analyzing every second of it. I thought about León—lover of science and of Giovanna Medici. And how their rendezvous spot had been in San Germano.

The León from Nicco's dreams being an accomplice in the Medici's murder-vampire-turnings was almost unfathomable after seeing their friendship. My pulse skipped. It couldn't be true! León really loved

Nicco—and Giovanna. But the question weighing heavier on my mind was: Could *Germano-Germain* really be a coincidence?

Was León really Adeline's father, *le Comte de Saint-Germain*?

The lamp near my vanity blinked on and off with a soft sizzling noise.

Even though I sought the truth, a part of me wished I'd never seen that particular dream. I didn't want any of my family members to have betrayed Nicco.

News flash, Adele. Nicco betrayed you.

Like León betrayed him?

Would León really conspire with a vampire? Why *did* he drink the Elixir that night? Is that why he was trying to get Nicco out of the laboratory that night? Theoretically, if León did free Séraphine, and now he's still out there somewhere—why would the Medici think I could lead them to him? Clearly they know far more about the Count than I do!

Pop.

The lightbulb in the lamp on my vanity exploded, and tinkles of glass rained onto the floor. *Dammit!* We should have stock in lightbulbs the way I went through them.

There were two ways to account for León-slash–the Count still being alive: Séraphine had turned him into a vampire, or the Elixir of Life was real.

Based on Adeline's diary comments about her hereditary powers in 1728, the Count was a witch . . . so unless he'd somehow been a vampire before he became a witch, the only reasonable explanation for him still being alive was—the Elixir had worked.

Was León Medici-slash-Saint-Germain an immortal witch?

The hairs on my arms pricked. I sat up, looking around the room as if someone else might be there. Of course, there wasn't, though I swear I sometimes felt Adeline like she was still here.

A small flame rose from my hand. I lay back down, bouncing it in my palm. The question still lingered, tugging at my heart: *Did León really betray Nicco, stealing the Medici tome with all of his research—the Elixir?*

They were like brothers.

Then again, I could imagine Emilio doing such a thing.

As humans the Medici had lusted after immortality, but why would *vampires* care about the Elixir? They were already immortal—but, four hundred years later, could they really just be after revenge?

I guess if you thought someone had a hand in turning you into a monster, the resentment would go as deep as Atlantis. Especially for Nicco, who'd dedicated his life to aiding humanity. It broke my heart knowing he was turned into the very thing he despised the most: a monster who preys upon people. The flame whizzed around my head.

I hated thinking about Nicco as deadly. I hated thinking about him feeding on Callis. My pulse picked up. With all of this family feud echoing in my head, it made me wonder: *Is Callis really just after revenge?* Something told me no, despite him being so forthcoming with information, unlike Nicco. And he seemed genuinely interested in helping me with my magic.

Then again, Nicco had always seemed to have a vested interest in my magic, though Nicco had never threatened me—only his brothers had.

My fists balled, containing the sparks, as I thought about Emilio's fangs ripping into my mother.

Why did Nicco care so much about that Elixir?

He's immortal—a *vampire*.

Unless he thought . . . that it could change him?

Was that why he wanted it so badly? To save himself . . . to grant himself a way to live without being a monster? Surely if there was a way to reverse his condition, he'd have figured it out after all these centuries. Why would he care so much about a missing book?

If Nicco believed the Elixir could save him . . . does that mean *Adeline's father could help me save my mother?*

Was that my bargaining chip—the recipe for the Elixir? If the Count still had the Medici tome, how the hell would I ever get it back?

I got up from the bed and slipped into my boots. I hadn't wanted to go back in Nicco's head, because I wanted to hold on to the human version of him—the Nicco who wanted to be a great surgeon, the Nicco who wanted to help me, protect me. But now, more than that, I needed to know about the Nicco who threw me out the window and who killed Maddalena. I needed to know, for sure, whether León was the Count, and whether he really had anything to do with Séraphine's escape. The answers could be the key to saving my mom—and to saving Nicco, though I wasn't ready to admit I might want to do that.

I put on my coat, and my mind flipped back to Callis and the mention of his coven. *What if they're watching me?*

"Ugh!" I screamed, and the lamp on my nightstand burst, shattering glass all over the floor, darkness enveloping me. Maybe Callis was right: I needed to trust myself more. Three little orbs of fire rose from my palm and hummed around my chest.

What if I don't need to be so close to Nicco to connect? It's magic, not engineering.

The fireballs buzzed faster, zipping around me in circles.

Then the closet door creaked open as if beckoning me. And I felt her. It was like Adeline was there, telling me to press on.

I traded my coat and boots for my witch box and a pillow.

Sitting in front of the Saint-Germain safe, I placed candles in a wide circle and uncorked a bottle of rose water. The floral notes wafted out as the water flowed into a metal bowl my dad had made when he was first learning to metalsmith. The scent immediately made me want to breathe deeper. Relaxing was not one of my key strengths, but it was exactly what I'd have to do to make this work—even though thinking about Nicco, the attic, and the centuries-long family feud made me the opposite of relaxed.

I plucked sprigs of dried rosemary and eucalyptus out of the wooden box and added them to the bowl. Then I cast the rest of the witchy goodies aside and positioned two picture frames on top of Adeline's diary next to me. The first was a photograph of my mother on a bridge over the River Seine. She had on a bright-red skirt, and the wind was puffing it out, and she must have been close to my age because we looked nearly identical.

Next to it was a photo of all of us—Brigitte, Mac, and three-year-old me in cut-off overalls, sitting on the slate steps in front of the cathedral, feeding bread crusts to the pigeons. *French Quarter Rat since birth.*

I crossed my feet under my legs and extended my hands, palms-up, ready to receive energy from the universe. Open to the magic.

My eyes slipped shut.

With a deep inhale, I felt all of the candles light around me, the flames shining through my eyelids. Hints of rose and herbs transferred from the water to the air around me, and into my lungs. The medallion became heavier against my chest; it vibrated, and the hum of the metal made me feel Adeline guiding me. Keeping me safe. I could relax because she was with me.

One by one, the nails and boards popped out, revealing the metal box underneath. This time when I parted the metal, I wasn't scared. This was our family's magic. *My* magic.

Out came the diary, and other things I'd stashed partly because I didn't want Isaac to find them, but also because I never wanted to see them again.

I shook the folds out of Nicco's green-and-black-checkered flannel shirt and slipped my arms through it, then I pulled out his jacket and put it on too. I instantly shuddered.

Leather and soap.

His scent was something I'd nearly forgotten. Now it felt like he was right there in the room with me too.

I can do this. I can open myself up to Nicco and come back in one piece.

I hope.

I went over everything Papa Olsin had taught me. This time there were no teas, no potions. Just me and my magic, and him.

A Saint-Germain and a Medici.

A witch and a vampire.

Me and Nicco.

The air is different in New Orleans.

It holds the scents of fry and the peppery blends the locals drown their seafood in, and the buzzing of cicadas, and the stomps of jazz pianists. It smothers your senses with a slight hint of intoxication, making you want more. Maybe that's why vampires have always loved it here. Or maybe the feeling is just due to the blood settling under my tongue.

My shoulders relax as the hunger is satiated.

I look back, like I always do. The guy is wandering down the street, disoriented but very much alive. I didn't take too much. He'll never know the difference, and I'll be held over for a while.

Now to find Lisette Monvoisin, the girl Gabriel claims to have made a part of this family but has no recollection of doing so. As if Martine isn't enough.

If it weren't for his hysteria over not finding her, I'd chalk it up to an eighteenth-century, absinthe-induced fantasy. If it weren't for the fact that blood-drained bodies have been dropping all over the Vieux Carré since the day the attic opened. Since the day *she* released them. Adeline's descendent . . . *His descendent.*

I must find Lisette tonight. I can only sweep her victims under the chaos of the Storm for so long. The last time I overheard that nitwit detective, he said the body count for the recent French Quarter crime wave is up to a dozen—if he only knew how many bodies I've carried out to the swamps.

Until Lisette learns how to control her feedings, she's a liability to all of us. The only thing that might be a bigger threat is Gabriel becoming unhinged over losing her.

The morning light creeps into the sky, and I sense footsteps nearby—a vampire who was never taught how to go unheard. No one has told her to silence her breathing. No one has taught her how to hunt. I quicken my pace.

Two sets of footsteps? The sharp click of new shoes. Human footsteps. They grow faster, and Lisette's follow suit.

She's hunting. This would be a good opportunity to show her how to take just enough, and how to make her prey forget her; but really, teaching her is Gabriel's job. He made her.

The scent of freshly ground coffee wafts from around the corner. They serve the same kind at the café where Adele works.

No.

I inhale deeply and smell her shampoo, her freshly washed hair. She's just around the corner—Adele is the prey.

The clicks of her footsteps accelerate. She knows she's being followed. *Smart girl.*

The cool morning air sweetens with the scent of her fear. I pull my hoodie tighter and pick up my pace down the broken sidewalk. *Three. Two. One.*

Slam.

Adele bounces off my chest, but my arm darts around her, yanking her back up; her arms fling around my neck. As soon as she regains her balance, she tries to break away, but I hold her tighter. "Shhhhh."

She doesn't listen; I shake her hard as the second set of footsteps approaches us.

On the other side of the street, she appears, walking past us, bright-blond hair hidden beneath the hood of her cloak.

Lisette Monvoisin.

She smiles daringly at me, but the heartbeat pressing against my chest holds my attention.

Fury builds at the thought of what might have happened if I hadn't been here to intervene. *What I'd have done to Gabriel's child if she'd gotten to Adele before me.*

For a split second my rational side considers dropping Adele and going after Lisette, who is a threat to all of us.

It's what I *should* do, but it's not what I'm going to do, not now that Adele is in my arms.

For weeks I've wanted to touch her.

This wasn't the oak-tree branch in the park I envisioned us sitting on, or the top of a Ferris wheel away from the rest of the world, or even my bed. Now it doesn't matter. I have her close—I don't want to let her go.

I file the sound of her heartbeat into my vault of memories and press her tighter as Lisette turns the corner, and just like that, I don't care where Gabriel's child is off to, or who she feeds on. Who she kills. As long as it isn't the girl in my arms.

If Lisette tries to touch her again, she'll regret it forever. *Niccolò, you're acting like a fool.* But I suddenly find myself not caring about that either.

Lisette's footsteps fade into the early-morning haze, and we're left alone. Only then do I realize Adele is shaking in my arms. She clutches me in fear, not desire.

She's scared of me.

She should be.

I come to my senses. "*Scusa*, are you okay?"

Tension releases from her shoulders as she recognizes my voice. She looks up at me with misguided relief. I don't want to let go.

The taste of blood still lingers in my mouth, but I am suddenly starved. I can't remember a time when I have felt *so* starved. When I have so truly desired something.

Her voice shakes. "Have you had any luck finding your family?"

I lean closer, trying not to inhale her scent too deeply, but I do, and then my lips are moving along the side of her jaw, tasting her skin. My fingers climb through her hair, to a place that can hold her head securely. Every vertebra in her back tenses, and her words continue, though whether they are of protest or pleasure I have no idea. I only hear her heartbeat accelerating.

It startles me how concerned I am with her heart.

A tear slides down her cheek and over her jaw, dampening her skin before it reaches my lips. When I taste it, I know that I'm too far gone.

"Nicco?"

My teeth sink into her flesh, pushing a soft moan from her mouth.

With each pull, her pulse slows. "Nicco," she whispers as she bleeds into my mouth.

Her arms fold over the back of my head, and I forget about it all. I forget about the chase. I forget about revenge. I forget about the curse. I forget about avenging our father. And I forget about León.

I lift her by the waist and step into the nearest alleyway. In the darkness, I continue to drink, and I have never felt truer to monster form. I suck harder. This is all I ever wanted. She is all I ever wanted. To hear her pulse. To taste her. To have her heart.

Thump-thump.

Her voice screams inside my head: *Nicco, you didn't bite me! This didn't happen!*

Thump-thump.

Thump-thump.

"Get out! Get out! *Get out!*"

It's not her voice. It's my voice.

Screaming inside my head.

I need more. I want more. *I want her completely. Forever.* And I take her until she goes limp in my arms. Everything goes red—and then black. I'm in the darkness, pleading.

"Please get out, Adele. I beg you. *Please* get out . . . There are things . . . you can never unsee."

She disappears from my arms. I reach out, but there's only blackness.

Thump-thump.

Thump-thump.

She refuses to get out of my head—out of my fantasies. *She fights back. All I can do is push her into a different day.*

The clouds pass swiftly through the black sky, and the stars twinkle down. My feet hit the pavement with purpose and frustration. Letting Adele out of my sight is not a risk I'm willing to take, not now that Emilio is in New Orleans.

I pull the flask of whiskey from my pocket, take the last sip, and hurl it against a Bourbon Street dumpster. It slams with an explosion of glass.

But then my adrenaline spikes—*she's near*—I feel her.

My eyesight pulses in the darkness, eager to catch a glimpse, and my hearing sharpens, ready to pull the sounds of her footsteps to my ears. *Why is she out on the street at this hour? After the curfew?* She should be at home, behind the Saint-Germain protection spells.

Her footsteps hasten, as do her breaths. She's on the next block. I quickly step around the corner so we collide, and again I catch her before she hits the ground.

"We really should stop meeting like this, *bella*," I say, feeling the alcohol warming my insides, "not that I mind it." Humor has never been my strong suit, but I am overwhelmed by a need to see her smile.

She doesn't.

She's panting but trying to hide her breaths. My hearing sharpens once more—her lungs struggle for air, an asthmatic condition, per-haps. He braids are disheveled, and her clothes . . . *are some of them are missing?* My thoughts flash to Emilio. "Are you hurt? Why were you running?"

Still she doesn't speak. She begins to shake. Then *he*—that incessant Air witch—calls her name, and she flinches.

I grab her hand and take off. *What are you doing, Niccolò?*

We run through the curfew-silent streets, away from his cries to her.

The only reason I haven't ripped him limb from limb is because he's protecting her too; I know he will at all costs, because he loves her. So for that he is useful, but still, she needs to learn to protect herself—as if such a thing is possible against my family.

She squeezes my hand as we run. Her power emanates in waves of warmth. The lights flick off as we hurry past them. She's getting stronger. I know she's the one who broke the seal. She'll be the one who leads us to him.

But for now I am leading her, through the garden, through the cathedral, up the stairs, and into the bell tower. Away from my family, away from everyone. It's just me and her and the moonlight beaming down through the window. Under the cast of silver, she looks even more like León, and her fingers go to the necklace, just like Adeline's always did.

She gasps for air as she leans over the stone ledge. She's angry. *Bene.* She's going to need that passion to channel the magic, to reach the Fire I know is there.

It's not fair for such a sweet, innocent girl to be dragged into this war, but we don't choose our families. And when our families have roots as dark and twisted as the briar patch we are tangled in, we don't choose our destinies either.

The cross breeze gives her voice a slight shake. "What are we doing here?"

"You're upset about something," I say, drawing her to the center of the tower and circling behind her. "I have an idea to make you feel better." My hands slide up her arms, raising chill bumps.

Her delicate shoulders knock against my chest, and for a moment I have to calm myself.

I sweep both of her braids to the left side. Her nervousness both saddens and intoxicates me.

"On the count of three. I want you to scream as loud as you can."

"What?"

"One," I whisper against her ear.

"Two."

Chills sweep down her neck.

"Three!"

I jump up and ring the bell and then protect her ears as she screams, buckling, pulling me down to the stone floor with her. I want to make everything better for her. I want to hurt whoever has caused her pain. I want to get her as far away from the Medici as I can.

I want *her*.

Stop it, Niccolò. Bring her home.

I lift her up. "Do you feel better?" I ask, her back still pressed against my chest.

"Yeah, actually," she whispers, turning around.

"Bene." I brush a tear from her cheek.

She peers up at me, her cobalt eyes just like his, burning with that age-old energy I know so well, and I vow to end anyone who tries to harm her, my family or not.

Bring her home.

I don't. The way she looks at me . . . Is it fascination? Infatuation? Or just morbid curiosity? Or is it possibly . . . something else? The longer she gazes at me, the more I wish it to be.

You're a fool, Nicco. Even if she does know about you, she'll never love you, not after she learns of the things you've done. She'll run from you, and that's what she should do now.

She doesn't. Instead she moves to the wall and slides down to the stone floor.

What do you know, Adele? Who I am? What I am?

Her smile makes me think she knows, and yet . . . she came here with me anyway. With a vampire.

Her teeth chatter, and I tell myself it's because she's cold, not because she's scared. I give her my jacket, and I want her to wear it forever.

We sit in the bell tower, and she asks questions, and I give her the answers. None of her questions are the right ones, but at times the undercurrent in her tone makes me rise in my seat.

She looks directly at me. "Did Adeline ever tell her father you called?"

With one little name drop, the undercurrent rips my feet out from beneath me, and I'm swept down the dark river. My jaw snaps shut, hiding the evidence of my desire. That was the *right* question. Definitely the right question.

My fingers cover my mouth. "*What* did you say?"

She stands up with misguided confidence. "Paris: 1728. Did Adeline ever tell her father that you called . . . *Monsieur Cartier?*"

I pounce, pinning her to the floor beneath me. Hearing her call me by Séraphine's name makes me seethe with need.

I want her to know everything—the urge to tell her all of my secrets almost overtakes me—but she cannot know. *Not yet.* It's too dangerous for her . . . and it's too risky for me. After all, she *is* a Saint-Germain.

And deceptive innocence is their key trait.

She radiates warmth, and it pulls me closer—a warmth I haven't felt since I was alive, since those days in the laboratory with León. Fire magic.

"Do you trust me, Adele?"

"*Sì,*" she whispers, sitting up to meet my gaze.

I want to press my lips into hers, but instead I slam her back to the ground.

"Never trust a vampire, Adele!" My fangs are exposed to her, but her eyes don't flicker. Her gaze pours into mine.

Nicco, this is wrong.

She lifts her chin, bringing herself closer, and I don't know if I lower to her or she pushes up to me, but my lips touch hers, and her mouth opens up to mine, and I can't resist tasting her. I slide my hand beneath her, and she pulls me even closer.

Kissing her isn't part of the plan, Nicco. I'd wanted to learn about her magic, and whether she could defend herself against my family—and against me.

But I want this more.

In her naïveté, she kisses me too hard, and my fang scrapes her lip, drawing blood.

I shudder violently against her. My lips move to her neck in a wave of feverish kisses. My arms crush her tighter.

"Stop, Nicco," she whimpers. "Stop fighting it."

Her fingers slip through my hair, and she presses me tighter.

This is the way, Nicco. To get what you want. Her.

Just next to her ear, I whisper, "It will be quick, *bella*."

My teeth plunge into her neck, and I shudder and shudder as I take her completely.

When she goes limp against the floor, I kiss her lifeless lips. *"Ti amo, bella."*

But then her hands push against my chest.

It's not possible. She's dead. I killed her.

"Get off!" she cries. *"Get off me!"*

Her hands shove me so hard I fly backward and crash against the stone wall, through the tower wall—and I'm back in the cassette.

In the attic, on my back.

In the darkness.

A wave of rage so great passes through me that my eyes flutter open, just for a few seconds, and my lips move.

"Get out," my dry voice croaks. *"Get out.* That never happened, Adele! I would never—I am not a monster! *Get out!* Get out of my head!"

I tore off his jacket and huddled in the corner of the closet, tears pouring down my face.

You were there, Adele. He didn't *kill you that night in the bell tower. He didn't bite you. He didn't even try.*

But it felt so real. It wasn't a memory—at least not completely—but it was in his mind, what he was thinking about as he lay there in magic-induced slumber, what he'd been thinking about during all of our times together—*killing me.*

I didn't need Olsin Daure to tell me I'd slipped from Nicco's dreamscape into his fantasies. Part of me had always wished I was in his thoughts, but reality came crashing down upon discovering the reason I was—because Nicco's strongest desire was to drain me . . . *to kill me.*

Does it make him any less of a monster that he didn't?

No. Because he had another reason for not killing me: he needed me to find the Count. And *that's* all Nicco ever wanted from me. That's what kept Adeline alive in 1728, and it's what kept me alive last fall. León.

Devastation swelled in my chest, making it hard to breathe. It was like I'd been thrown out of the window all over again.

I curled against the wall. Isaac had been right about Nicco all along, and so had Callis. The image of his fangs plunging into my neck made me wonder something I'd never considered: *Maybe Callis is right to rid the world of Nicco.*

I sat up, shoved the candles, herbs, and diary down into the hole, and closed it with one quick whip. I grabbed Nicco's jacket and locked the closet door behind me.

Nicco can go to hell. I'm done.

I traded the leggings for a pair of jeans, laced up my boots, applied some wing-tipped eyeliner, and sent a message to Annabelle.

Adele	**9:02 p.m.**	Still want an extra date to the party? <3

CHAPTER 37
Let Him Go

The last time I'd climbed into Annabelle's Porsche SUV involved hot pants and a blindfold, so I couldn't help being nervous as I clicked the seat belt in place.

"Nice jacket," she said. "Looks Italian."

"You have no idea . . ." *There was no point in letting good leather go to waste.*

"Did you manage anything?" she asked, turning off my street.

I patted the backpack in my lap, and it clanked. "Four bottles. Trust me, it's enough to send the whole party into an alcoholic coma."

"Cool. I swiped a case from the pantry. Mrs. Nicholson will never notice."

"Who's Mrs. Nicholson?"

"The housekeeper," she said, as if everyone in town knew Mrs. Nicholson. *Maybe they do, for all I know.*

When she continued down Esplanade and turned left at the river, I became really curious. "Where are we going?" I asked, the déjà vu coming back tenfold.

This time she wasn't evasive. "A requiem for Holy Cross. The boys are already there, hopefully with the bonfire blazing. It's freezing." She cranked the heater and flipped on her brights.

As we drove down the riverfront through the abandoned neighborhood into the Lower Ninth Ward, one horror after another popped into the flood of her headlights: houses that had been pushed off their slabs, crushed by telephone poles, even burned down to charred piles of tinder. People's entire lives spilled out into piles on the streets . . . generations of once-treasured things. And the spray-painted *Xs* contained numbers that weren't zeros.

As the images whipped past us, I thought about Isaac, and how he came here every day, helping strangers, trying to fix people's lives. I wondered what had really happened that day with the little girl in the photo for it to still be affecting him this badly.

Annabelle slowed to a stop. "Shit."

Half a block ahead was the now-infamous cruise ship that had ended up on the wrong side of the levee thanks to the storm surge and was now blocking the road. The cruise line, the insurance agency, and the government were all fighting over who was responsible for removing it. My money was on it staying there forever.

"Just take a left here," I said, and then directed her the rest of the way through the Storm-devastated neighborhood. Holy Cross was about as deep in the Lower Ninth Ward and as near the riverfront as you could get. By the time we parked, the mood was so somber, it was hard to remember we were going to a party.

I blotted my eyes dry on my sleeve and then waited as she reapplied her makeup.

The campus was pitch black, and even with her brights it was hard to see much more than the wrought-iron fence surrounding the once-magnificent property that now looked like something from a gothic novel. A few giant oaks still stood strong, their branches creating sprawling canopies over the walkway through campus, but most lay lifeless on their sides, uprooted by the high winds and soggy grounds.

I opened the car door—faint music came from somewhere farther into campus. The wrought-iron gate swung open in the riverfront breeze, someone already having cut the chain that had held it closed. *I wonder how many laws we're breaking tonight?*

The engine cut, and Annabelle stepped out with her case of booze. Cell-phone flashlights activated, we walked through the gate and down the path of dead trees, bottles clanking, our offering to *le fais do-do*.

Leaves crunched underneath our feet as we approached the mammoth three-story redbrick building, which even in its destroyed state still managed to be beautiful. It was at least a hundred years old. White scrolling ironwork, now covered in rust, framed the second and third story balconies in a fairy-tale-like way, winding and scrolling over the building like wisteria. Its rows of windows were blown out and boarded up, and now covered in graffiti, making me wonder if that had been part of tonight's requiem.

Feet scurried across the second-floor balcony, and a guy yelled, "Who's there?"

"The girls with the good stuff!" Annabelle yelled back, and smiled at me.

We held up our phones as he swung over the rail and half shimmied, half jumped down the pole to the ground. I recognized him from the fund-raiser.

"Need some help with that, Miss Drake?" he asked, taking the box from Annabelle.

A freckle-faced guy was right behind him. "Madame?" he asked me with an exaggerated bow.

I handed off the bottles. "*Merci beaucoup.* I'm Adele."

"Oh, we know who you are." They both smiled and ran ahead with the booze, yelling a chant that I assumed was the Holy Cross fight song.

"Did *you* make them do that?" I asked Annabelle, trying not to giggle.

"Nope. The credit is Bobby and Sampson Bradford's. Southern boys being southern boys."

We hurried to catch up with them.

Close to the building, a chain-link fence had been erected and topped with barbed wire to keep trespassers out post-Storm, but the boys had cut out a passageway.

The freckly one, who I think was Sampson, held it open as we ducked through. "You're going to want to run through to the other side of the building." Then they took off through the doorless entranceway.

As soon as we stepped inside, we both immediately started to gag—and then we ran—the stench of mold wrapping around us like an inescapable plague.

When we burst through the other side of the building to the back of the campus, I was gripping my side, trying not to throw up. I felt like we'd just made it through some rite of passage.

Dozens of kids were spread out on the dark, expansive lawn, chatting and laughing. I spotted most of the upperclassmen from Holy Cross, Sacred Heart, and Ursuline, their faces lit by the glow of phones, flashlights, and camping lanterns. One group had surrounded themselves with candles. Puffs of marijuana smoke hung in the damp air around them.

We walked through the crowd. Music played from shitty phone speakers, and nervous laughter and giddy shrieks came from girls who weren't quite drunk enough to flirt with the guys trying to inch closer to them.

Three students sprinted out of the building behind us, all with chairs held over their heads; then two more came out with crates of moldy textbooks.

"I found some dry ones, Preston!" one of the guys yelled as they ran past us.

Out in the darker part of the lawn, a curly haired blond guy *whooped* before carefully adding more broken furniture to a rickety tower made of smashed-up desks and broken chairs, floorboards, and shelves—anything that could be excavated by the football team and a crowbar.

The city was never going to rebuild Holy Cross, so it was destined to become nothing more than a time capsule of teenage memories, which made it both sad and cathartic watching students rip the school apart. We stopped at the furniture tower. A slight tinge of smoke lingered in the air.

"Is that supposed to be a bonfire?" Annabelle asked Preston. He was a friend of Thurston's who drove a car that cost more than my entire future college tuition. "You realize you're missing one key ingredient, right?"

"Everything's too damp to catch fire," he said. "But we will persevere, worry not!"

She winked at me, slipped her hand into his pocket, and tossed me a cigarette lighter. "Maybe Adele has the magic touch." She hooked her arm in Preston's and walked him away while I circled around the stack to the other side, out of their sight line. *If I can make this work, how am I supposed to explain it?*

I held my hands in front of two smashed chairs, keeping the lighter in my palm, until I could feel heat coming from the bottom of the stack. Tendrils of smoke curled out from the jutting floorboards. I bounced my hands, and flames crackled in the center.

"Not too much," I whispered as the flames grew.

Smoke billowed as the books caught fire and the tinder crackled. Heads turned, and then the cheers started. Flames ripped up the middle of the stack, bringing the crowd running to the bonfire, shouting.

"Finally!"

"It's a miracle!"

"Something like that," Annabelle said, bopping back to my side with a bottle of champagne.

Preston's arms circled around my neck. "You are a lifesaver." His breath was hot and alcoholic against my ear.

I tried not to visibly cringe.

"Let's get this party started!" Thurston yelled, running up behind Annabelle, swinging his arm around her shoulders.

She nearly dropped the champagne she'd been trying to uncork. She extended the bottle out to me, turning around into an instant lip-lock with Thurston. I grabbed it, happy for an excuse to scoot away from Preston.

Veuve Clicquot? Why am I still surprised?

I'd brought four unmarked bottles of moonshine—that pretty much summed up our two existences. The foil at the top of the champagne bottle was mutilated—clearly she'd never even had to open a bottle before. I ripped it off in one quick tear, twisted off the metal cage, and gave the cork one little push in just the right spot.

Pop.

It sailed into the fire, followed by an arc of bubbly.

"Oops!" I yelled, wondering how many dollars of champagne it was as the people around cheered. Preston's arm circled my shoulders again, this time squeezing me. He cheersed me with another bottle, and I took a sip straight from mine, the bubbles backing up in my throat and fizzing out of my mouth.

He leaned in, dangerously close to licking the champagne from my face, but I squirmed away before I was tempted to set him on fire.

He began loudly singing the Holy Cross alma mater. Thurston and Georgie joined, matching his volume, and the singing became more and more dramatic until the rest of the Holy Cross boys collected together around the fire, arms slung around shoulders.

Private school is so weird.

But no matter what school colors we wore, the sense of loss was something we all shared. Annabelle and I huddled together on two wooden crates in the ring of people around the fire, me with a careful eye on the flames.

People fanned out on the lawn, sitting on blankets and makeshift benches and flattened cardboard boxes, swigging every kind of booze they could swipe from their parents' liquor cabinets. Or, in the case of a lot of kids here, from their parents' wine collections. I'd never even drunk wine before I went to Paris.

The Holy Cross boys took turns running up to the schoolhouse and returning with the contents of their lockers to dump into the bonfire. They told stories about football games and senior pranks and homecoming dances. They sang their alma mater so many times I soon knew all the words. People laughed and people cried, and mostly people drank. A lot.

"You look intense!" a girl called out.

I turned to see Veronica and Johnnie approaching, both carrying plastic shopping bags full of stuff.

I stood, giving them both hugs.

"We made a pit stop on the way," Veronica said, lifting one of the plastic bags to me. "Johnnie said you were locker number 306?"

"You didn't!"

"We did."

Merci mille fois!" I didn't tell her the reason Johnnie knew my locker number was because he used to wait in front of it during our freshman year, causing me to constantly be late for class because I was so shy I avoided my locker until after the first bell.

I opened the bag and sucked in a deep breath. Tears stung my eyes when I saw the French-English dictionary Mémé had given me when I was little. I filed through the waterlogged notebooks; a photo of me and Brooke from the last Krewe du Vieux, now covered in black specks;

a sketch pad; and a huge roll of pattern pieces I'd drawn during my mentorship last semester.

"A fire!" Veronica yelled as she threw a black dress high up into the air toward the fire. "A fire is burning!" It ballooned open, and I recognized it from last year's production of *The Crucible*.

"Hey! I made that!"

Veronica had played Abigail. She spun around, tossing the rest of her notebooks into the fire and yelling more of the lines from the play: "God damns our kind especially, and we will burn, we will burn together!"

I sat back down next to Annabelle. "No one will ever burn *us*," she said, resting her head on my shoulder.

"No, they won't."

I giggled, and she giggled, and we passed another bottle of warm champagne back and forth, watching more students ceremoniously dump their possessions into the fire. All while Tyrelle slid sad notes up and down his trombone.

"None of it matters!" Thurston yelled, coming up behind us. "Only each other!"

He leaned over Annabelle's back, and her arms circled around his neck.

"Kiss me," she said. And he did, until he was crashing over us and I was pushing them away. They toppled onto the ground, getting laughs from the girls and hoots from the guys.

More kids went up to the fire, and more stuff was burned. Trig books, chemistry tests, sports jerseys, yearbooks—it all went into the fire between tears and sniffles. Most of the kids here were seniors. Six months ago they'd all had a pretty firm idea of what they'd be doing after graduation. For some of them it would all still work out; for others, their college funds were now paying for their family homes.

Everyone got their turn, and we moved on to a fresh bottle of bubbly. I needed to pee like never before, but Thurston was gone and I didn't want to leave Annabelle by herself—she'd been taking sips from the bottle at twice the rate I had.

I pulled Veronica away from her lip-lock with Johnnie and sat her in my place.

"Bathroom," I said, and wandered off.

We were miles from an actual functioning bathroom, so that left two options: popping a squat behind a tree or going inside the dilapidated building and testing my gag reflex.

I crammed Nicco's jacket sleeve over my mouth and dashed inside, phone in hand, lighting the way through the dank decay.

"Adele, wait up! I need to pee too!"

For some reason, hearing Annabelle say the word "pee" made me giggle, which was bad when your bladder was about to erupt. I neared the end of the hall and saw a door with a dress.

"Thank God," I said, half bent over as I barged through.

In the dark, a figure sprang away from the sink, where another guy was sitting.

"Shit!" I yelled as pants were jerked up and zippers zipped.

"Adele!"

I was out the door even quicker than I'd come in, running smack into Annabelle.

"I need to peeeeee," she said.

"Let's go upstairs. It's bad in there—dead-animal smell."

But then Thurston opened the door, yelling my name. His eyes opened wide, her flashlight in his face. "Annabelle!" He stepped out, pulling the door shut behind him.

"I have to pee," she said.

"There's another bathroom on the second floor."

She tried to push past him. "Come on, Annabelle," he begged. "Don't go in there."

Her eyes slanted, hearing the desperation in his voice. "Move, Thurston."

"No."

She looked straight at him, her eyes glistening. "Let go of the door, and move."

"Annabelle, I never wanted to hurt you."

"Move!"

He stepped away begrudgingly, a valiant but futile attempt to fight through her magic. I followed behind.

Georgie was standing there by himself. His voice trembled. "I'm— I'm sorry, Annabelle."

"Get out," she said to him.

Thurston reached for her arm. "Annabelle."

Georgie ran past us. A part of me wanted to chase after him to see if he was okay, but then Annabelle pushed past us and headed for the staircase, so I went after her instead.

"Annabelle!" I yelled as I reached the second floor, which was just as dark as the first.

When I opened the door to the bathroom, I could hear her crying in the stall.

I debated what to say as I squatted in the stall next to her, but then she spoke first.

"Here," she said, handing me tissues under the divider. *Thank God.* The toilet paper looked like it contained five hundred kinds of diseases. *Not an option.*

"Shouldn't I be the one handing you tissues?" I asked, finishing up.

"Ha." She sucked in a giant sniffle.

We both came out of the stalls and stared at the sink. The toilets hadn't flushed, because the water was cut. "We need Désirée's magical hand sanitizer," she said.

"Come with me." I led her down the hall and out onto the long balcony that overlooked the back of the property. "Hold your hands over the rail." I pulled the last bottle of moonshine out of my bag, unscrewed the cap, and poured it over her hands. "Multifunctional. Gets you rip-roaring drunk and kills germs better than soap!"

She didn't laugh.

After I'd poured some over mine, I handed the bottle to her. "And I promise it will also kill whatever's going on in your brain."

Her smile still didn't crack, but she took a swig from the bottle—and choked it back up over the railing.

"Told you."

She sank to the floor, and I sat next to her, legs sliding under the railing, feet hanging over the edge. A government-issued blue tarp, now shredded and ragged, hung from the roof above us, blowing in the breeze. Out on the lawn below, the bonfire blazed.

She handed the bottle back to me and burst into tears. "Why did he stop loving me?"

Oh God.

"I don't think he stopped loving you." My hand went to her back. "I think . . . he's just . . . *in* love with Georgie."

She cried even harder. I didn't know if I was putting words into Thurston's mouth, but I'd seen the way he looked at her and the way he looked at Georgie, and I knew if it were the other way around, Georgie would be the one crying on my shoulder.

"He's been my best friend since we were five. We've been to every dance together. We were supposed to go to Vanderbilt together. We were supposed to get married at the cathedral, after he proposed at the Eiffel Tower senior year." She cried even harder. "He's the only person who gets me . . . who doesn't think I'm a total bitch."

My arm slipped around her shoulders, and I felt like I was in an alternate universe.

"We don't think you're a bitch—the coven. And, seriously, you can do better than the Eiffel Tower. That's way too cliché for Annabelle Lee Drake."

She smirked. *"Merci beaucoup."* She took the bottle back and swigged, face contorting. This time she managed to hold it down. "I did kind of hate having to hide the magic thing from him."

"I know you don't want to hear it, but you'll find someone better for you."

"You're right: I don't want to hear it."

"You're the most beautiful girl in the whole school—in *all* the schools—and you have badass magic. Maybe you'll meet a witch, and you won't have to keep any secrets from him."

"Like you and Isaac?"

"Like me and Isaac . . ." I turned away as I said it and then drowned my accelerating heart with a swig of the moonshine. I'd been obsessing over Nicco ever since we left the fund-raiser.

"Who, in case you've forgotten, is insanely hot," she said, sensing something was up. "And he's from New York. And he can fly. He can *fly*, Adele."

"And he's a really amazing artist," I said, "and he wants to help everyone he comes into contact with. And he doesn't want to kill me, like Nicco does."

"Whoa."

When I didn't offer up anything else, she asked, "Is that whose jacket you're wearing, then? It doesn't seem like Isaac's style."

I almost told her it was my dad's. And if I hadn't been drinking, I probably would have, but instead I said *"Oui"* and took another sip.

She took the bottle and swigged again. "So my guy is gay, and yours wants to kill you?"

"Pretty much. Vampire boy problems."

Saying the words out loud helped me hear just how ridiculous it all was. I'd never spoken about Nicco to anyone. *I couldn't.*

"When we first met, I thought he was . . . my friend. Or something. Then I found out his family has been after mine for the last few centuries, and even then I stupidly thought we were on the same side.

When push came to shove, he chose them and threw me out a window. Literally." My teeth pressed into my bottom lip, holding back the tears. "I'd be dead if not for Isaac, and Dee."

"Sounds like this Nicco guy needs an ass-kicking. I'm available, by the way." Her words were starting to slur, possibly explaining her nonreaction to the fact that I'd told her he was a vampire. "Where is he now?"

"Taken care of," I said. "But thanks."

I took two more swigs of moonshine and looked over to her. My next words felt like they were ripping my heart out. "We just need to let go."

And then there was silence, all but the ambient noise of the drunken teenagers below squealing around the fire and puking behind trees.

"Yeah," she said, standing, then pulling me up.

She wiggled a ring off her finger. "Thurston gave me this for Christmas, in between the I-love-yous and the sex." She started crying again and then hurled the ring out into the darkness.

"Oh my God, Annabelle, that was awesome!" I pulled off Nicco's jacket and held it out in front of me. "There were no I-love-yous and no sex—just something that felt . . . magical."

She cheered as I threw the jacket as far as I could. It felt blasphemous ruining such a finely crafted garment, but I was too drunk to care.

"All I want is someone who loves me like Isaac loves you," she said, wrapping her arm around my shoulder as we both gazed out toward the bonfire.

"I know," I said, taking a deep breath. "I don't know what's wrong with me. I just can't get over Nicco's betrayal for some reason."

"Oh, the old 'I can't believe a vampire seduced me and tried to kill me'?"

I laughed. "Not all vampires. Just this one."

She kissed my cheek.

"Annabelle, there's something you should know about Nicco . . . and his family. Because it affects you too."

We sat back down, and after several more swigs of moonshine for both of us, I told her everything—everything except my mom's secret. I told her about Nicco and the curse, and Cosette and Minette and Lisette. She cried when I told her about Gabe and what he'd done to them.

"I want to meet Lisette," she said, eyes glistening.

I didn't tell her that she already had—on Halloween night—and that she'd called Lisette a freak.

"One day," I vowed, both of us seconds from passing out on each other's shoulders. "One day we're going to open the attic. I know it."

"Oui, Adele, oui."

PART 3

The Maleficiums

*If you don't hunt it down and kill it, it will hunt you down
and kill you.*

Flannery O'Connor

CHAPTER 38

Knockout

January 21st

If someone had slipped a one-way ticket to New York into my hand, I'd have walked off the bridge and gone directly to the airport. Anything to get out of this ceremony.

But there was no ticket. No red pill. No escape hatch or eject button. There wasn't even an airport. Just jerkoffs everywhere. Jerkoffs from my pop's office, and from the mayor's office.

I checked my phone compulsively in between shaking people's hands. No messages from Adele.

Where is she?

The powers that be had decided that the bridge—the same fucking bridge the jerkoff was standing on when he took the photo of me—was the perfect spot for the ceremony. It was the kind of bridge that opened for barges to get through, but the metal was so rusty and old looking I couldn't imagine it groaning open. The water in the Industrial Canal was thick and brown, though the sun's reflection gave it an almost-green tint. No matter which direction you looked out past the water, it was the same: destruction. Nothing but piles of dirty scrap wood, metal, and glass. Like the gods had played a giant game of Jenga with the houses.

A podium was set up in the center of the bridge, with three rows of seats behind it and what appeared like a hundred on the other side for the audience. Désirée paraded with her mother on the opposite end of the bridge, which was jerkoff heavy.

I adjusted my tie and shook more hands. My face hurt from smiling.

Half the people in town seemed to be here, and they all fit into two camps: In the first were the wealthy, cultured, artistic types, the museum directors along with their biggest benefactors, deans from the art departments of the local universities—who, if I was a different person, I'd be schmoozing with—and other generally rich people who'd come to ooh and aah. In the second camp were the first responders, rebuilders, volunteers from various NGOs, and the neighborhood locals.

What the fuck side is my father on? When we'd arrived in New Orleans, it was definitely the latter. These days, who knew? Reporters sifted through the crowds looking for "real people" to interview. Survivors.

I wandered down the side of the bridge that led into the Lower Ninth, as far away from the crowd as I could get, and pecked out a message to Désirée.

Isaac	**13:02**	If one more person tells me how brave I am, I'm gonna blow up this bridge.
Dee	**13:03**	ur def not allowed to say the words bridge and blow up in the same sentence around so many feds.

Isaac	13:03	Where the hell is Adele?

Dee	13:04	Probably suffering from a level orange hangover. Tyrelle said she and Annabelle were so wasted last night he had to give them a lift back to the Quarter.

I guess that would explain why she didn't return any of my messages last night.

Isaac	13:05	Do you think she's coming?

Dee	13:06	Calm down. You're going to be fine.

I looked up as helicopters flew overheard, getting aerial shots of the setting from the now-famous photo. All the media was here. And not just local, the big ones. CNN, MSNBC, the *New York Times*—no wonder my pop was stressed. He hated the media more than anyone. At least he used to. My phone buzzed again. *Finally.*

Adele	13:07	I'M SO SORRY! We're parking!! PLEASE DON'T HATE ME. xo

Thank God. I slipped the phone back into my pocket, trying to ignore everyone pointing at me from afar.

But then a little seven-year-old voice called my name from down the bridge and instantly made everything easier and harder at the same time. *Rosalyn.*

When I looked up, she ran away from her parents. "Isaac!"

I dropped to the ground, and she jumped straight into my arms, squeezing my neck just as tightly as she had that day the levees broke. I pressed my eyes shut as I lifted her up so they wouldn't tear.

"You're here!" she yelled.

"Of course I'm here!" I said as her grandparents approached. Neither Charmaine nor Marcus looked like they were holding it together very well. "I wouldn't miss a chance to see my favorite munchkin."

Her smile turned into a pout as I set her down. "You haven't been over to play with me."

"I'm sorry," I said to her grandparents before even telling them hello. "I've been taking on extra work with my crew." The truth was, I couldn't handle the visits after we'd finished the repairs on Marcus's brother's house where they were all staying.

"Baby, it's okay," Charmaine said, pushing my hair out of my face. "You don't have anything to explain to us."

I nodded. "How's the roof holding up?"

"Good enough," Marcus said, "thanks to you and Chase."

Rosalyn's small voice said, "I found a cat. We rescued her like you rescued me." She gripped two of my fingers and swung my arm back and forth. "Do you think Jade's in heaven?" She looked up at me, waiting for a response, and I felt the water on my chest crushing the words inside me.

I crouched down. "Yeah, munchkin. Jade's in heaven. Probably playing hopscotch with my mom."

Charmaine turned away. A lump formed in my throat.

"Who's that girl?" Rosalyn pointed behind me.

Adele was standing away from the crowd with Mac, staring at us. She waved, looking like she didn't want to interrupt.

I stood up, the lump in my throat still so big I couldn't form words without the risk of my voice cracking.

"See you up there," Marcus said, his hand on my shoulder.

I nodded my good-byes and rubbed Rosalyn's head without looking down.

When I reached Adele, I pulled her into my arms, lifting her off the ground—not something I would have *ever* done in front of Mac before, but I felt like I was losing it.

"Hey," she said softly, hugging me back. "I didn't mean to pull you away."

I held on to her tighter.

"I'm sorry we're late."

"Can we get out of here?" I whispered. "Anywhere but here."

A male throat cleared loudly, and in an instant, my shit was pulled together.

"Dad," I said, setting her down, "this is Adele."

She tried to hide her surprise as she told him hello.

"And her father, Macalister Le Moyne."

My father shook Mac's hand and greeted him with his usual style—the least amount of words possible—and then he gripped my shoulder as if I wasn't going to come otherwise. "We're needed on stage."

"I'll just sit with the Le Moynes until they call my name or whatever."

"Isaac. Stage, with the other people being honored. Now."

I nodded.

And with nothing but a stiff smile to Mac and Adele, my father turned and walked back up the slope.

Mac turned to me. "We'll sit in the front row, okay? We'll practically all be together. Everything's going to be okay."

"I'm fine. Really."

Adele reached for my hand as I walked away, her fingertips scraping mine.

I mentally cursed my pop for treating me like a kid in front of her—and in front of Mac. Norwood Thompson had never been a warm person, but he'd become completely callous over the last couple months.

He stopped to join Lieutenant General DuPont and the mayor, who were being interviewed by a newscaster. Her cameraman hovered over her shoulder with a boom.

I took a seat on the front row "on stage," choosing the one farthest from the podium, keeping my focus squarely on the ground. I didn't want to see the crowd. Or the helicopters circling above. I didn't want to see the front row, where Charmaine and Marcus were sitting with Rosalyn, who looked so much like Jade.

My father took the seat next to me, and I gazed straight out. No "Nice to meet your girlfriend" or "Sorry to make you do this, son." Just silence. Dee and her mom filed in behind us, and more people filled the rest of the seats. The award recipient took his place on the opposite end of our row. Not being able to see him brought a slight respite.

Mac and Adele sat in the front row as promised. Behind them, people filled all the chairs, and behind them, more people stood, another ten rows deep. My fingers tapped my knee. I thought it'd be easier if I focused on Adele.

It wasn't.

Click. Click. Click.

It was all I heard from the cameras of the photographers now crouching between us. In the distance, out of everything that had been destroyed, there was still a red-and-yellow ADULT VIDEO sign standing strong; that's what I focused on.

My phone buzzed, but I didn't move.

Everyone quieted as Morgan Borges took the spotlight at the podium. He had to yell his speech over the chopper blades pounding above—I fantasized about a ladder dropping down and lifting me away.

The mayor spoke about the courage of first responders and how many lives we'd saved, and it wasn't long before people in the audience were crying. When he finished, a representative from the Pulitzer Prize committee, a woman who looked like she left New York only for moments like this, stood up and talked about the need for disaster photography and its important role in investigatory journalism. When she introduced the photographer, everyone clapped like sheep—everyone but me. And Adele, who was staring at me with her hands frozen midclap, stuck between me and decorum.

The photographer spoke about his journey down to the South and his time spent waiting out the Storm.

Oh, the horror it must have been from his Canal Street hotel.

My foot tapped in time with my fingers against my knee.

He spoke about paying someone $500 to get a ride in their boat out to the Ninth Ward, and how the guy had abandoned him once the water started to rise, despite payment.

The speech, which seemed like it had been generically written for a national speaking tour, went on and on about how bad the sights were, describing houses and landmarks in great detail. *As if these people don't fucking know?*

"I held my camera over my head and waded through the water to this bridge, which would become my sanctuary."

He talked about how his entire career was about being fearless and brave.

Wind swirled over the crowd, blowing ladies' hair and making guys hold on to their fedoras. Désirée discreetly kicked the back of my chair, but I didn't care to temper my powers. The wind made the masturbatory speech harder to hear.

"I can't believe you're making me do this," I said to my father under my breath.

"Life isn't always about the things we want to do."

"Uh, no shit. Look around. Do you even spend time in neighborhoods like this anymore? The Norwood Thompson I know would never be at a celebration for a man who stood by and took photos while people were dying."

"Sometimes you have to pick and choose your battles, son. Showing face is an easy win."

"At my expense."

"You need to check your attitude."

"You need to check your priorities."

"I know you've been through a lot, Isaac. Please don't make me regret letting you stay in New Orleans."

"Letting me? Oh, now you're a parent? When's the last time you've seen me?"

"Isaac, this will be over in ten minutes, tops. Please just do this for me."

Mayor Borges called my name, welcoming me up to the podium.

I looked at my pop. "You're right. This is me . . . picking and choosing. Jade, not you."

The crowd clapped politely as I moved up to the podium, where the photographer stood smiling, so proud of himself. *Smug piece of shit.* The woman from the Pulitzer Prize committee beamed at me, holding his framed prize.

My hand curled into a fist. "Isaac!" my pop called. But it was too late. My two front knuckles cracked the photographer's jaw, causing instant pandemonium.

"Isaac!" Désirée screamed.

Yelling and cheering rose from parts of the crowd. I didn't have to look up to know which parts.

A cop came after me, but I pushed him out of the way and hustled down the bridge until I was close enough to the street below to jump off and run underneath.

As soon as I was out of sight, I dove into the air and took crow form. It was stupidly risky, but in that moment I didn't give a shit. All I wanted to do was fly away. And I did.

CHAPTER 39

The SS Hope

"*Holy* shit," I said, holding my skirt down as the wind kicked up. People around us were all aflutter. A few appalled, most cheering and hooting. The photographer was bent back, his assistant simultaneously trying to tend to his bloody nose and get a cell phone call to go through.

"I love that kid," my dad said, staring at the stage where Isaac had been.

"So do I . . ." My heart kicked up with the wind, realizing how much I really did. Sometimes his hotheadedness was brash and stupid, but other times it was just hot.

Not that I advocated punching people, but knocking out that jerk here and now took guts.

"I think he just earned himself a lifetime seat at any bar in the city. I mean, when he's of age."

Please. Like my dad didn't already let Isaac have a beer after work with the rest of his crew.

He looked at me. "You want me to go distract his father while you get a head start?"

"I love you, Dad," I said, wrapping my arms around his neck.

"I love you too, almost enough to give you my car keys, despite you not having your license yet. But I think you should run off that hangover."

Shit.

"We'll talk about it later . . . Just go."

The hangover-induced nausea passed by the time I hit Elysian Fields. At least I thought it did—it came in waves, so it was hard to tell. As I ran, I kept imagining the trouble Isaac would be in after the stunt. *Would his dad send him back to New York?*

The thought made my stomach turn again.

I hit the call button on my phone for the tenth time. *Pick up.*

When I got to Esplanade, I stopped on the neutral ground to catch my breath, wishing for teleportation powers. I leaned one-handed on an oak tree, sucking in air, trying to guess where he'd go. I called him again. It immediately clicked to voice mail.

Thank God I'd worn flats.

As I turned onto the brothel's block, I recognized Annabelle's Porsche parked on the curb.

Why would she be here?

Even though we'd made huge strides last night, I'd never thought about her just coming and going from the brothel as she pleased. Even though I'd told her *so* many things.

"Isaac!" I yelled, opening the front door.

I was sure he'd be there, but the house was totally silent.

"Annabelle?" I couldn't imagine her even being awake right now, let alone a functioning person, after how much she drank at the party.

I went through the parlors, and just as I stepped into the blue room, one of the pocket doors on the opposite side wavered, like someone had knocked into it. I froze.

"Isaac? Annabelle?"

Perfect silence, but I had a weird feeling.

I crept to the coffee table, lowered my hand into a jar of salt, and threw it at the gap between the doors. The salt sprinkled to the floor.

Nothing.

Chill out, Adele.

I ran through the hallway, through the kitchen to the sunrooms. The back door was open a few inches. I don't care what state of mind he was in: Isaac would never have left the house unsecure. We'd have to have a talk with Annabelle.

I locked it and headed back out the front, wondering if he'd just gone straight home—if you could call the navy ship home. He'd only go there if he *really* didn't want to be found; the only person who'd be able to find him there was his father.

As I walked down the street, ignoring the cramp in my side, another one of my calls went directly to his voice mail. *Ugh. Answer your phone.* I picked up my pace, heading toward the river, getting more worried with each passing block.

By the time I got to the dock, dark rain clouds were collecting overhead, making it seem later than it was. For some reason, the gloom made me feel like Isaac was definitely here.

As I drew near, the huge white letters painted on the side of the ship seemed to glow in the dull light: **SS HOPE**.

Kind of ironic.

The makeshift first-responder living quarters might have been a retired navy vessel, but the dock had been commercial pre-Storm, used for loading and unloading container ships, which meant there was security, but not military-base-level security.

I casually sat on a bench overlooking the river and listened to the waves splashing against the ship as I scoped out the entrance. A chain-link fence topped with looping barbed wire surrounded most of the dock. All metal. Might not be a total impossibility to sneak through with a little magic assist.

At the end of the fence, where the entry road ended at a barricade, an overhead halogen lamp illuminated an old security booth. *Great.*

I craned my neck to see if anyone was inside. *Dammit.* A security guard was wildly waving his arms in a way that could only mean he was listening to a football game on a radio. I'd never get past him without military ID or an escort.

There was a metal trash can about thirty yards to my right—an idea crept into my head—a totally Isaac kind of thing to do. I focused on it.

I can't believe I'm doing this.

The scent of burning garbage wafted over, and then burning rubber. Twists of black smoke billowed out, spilling onto the dock. I threw a little more energy its way, and flames danced out of the top.

Out of the corner of my eye, I watched as the security guard jumped up and grabbed his walkie-talkie. He ran out and past my bench, calling for backup.

Moving lightly, I slipped past his booth.

I descended a narrow stairway, following a sign that said **BERTHS.** I wasn't even sure what that meant, but the other options seemed more wrong. Belowdeck, a maze of dark corridors unfolded—dozens and dozens of gray metal doors lit only by the tiny emergency lights every few feet on the floor.

I'm never going to find him before I get caught.

I checked my phone. No signal.

Two guys in camo pants and white T-shirts turned into the corridor, blocking my path.

"Excuse me," I said. "Do you by any chance know Isaac Thompson? Where his room is? I went above deck to try to connect a call, and now I'm totally turned around."

"Way to go, Thompson," said the taller guy on the left, looking me up and down from beneath his cap. He smugly elbowed his blond-haired friend.

Gross.

I turned to the blond, who I hoped wasn't such an overt douche.

"It's 2-86-5-L, give or take a couple doors," he said. "Starboard edge."

When I still looked confused, he gave me directions.

"Merci beaucoup!" I hustled past them as they nudged each other, continuing to bro out.

"Thompson's got that hero thing down," the tall guy snickered.

"Shut up, dude. He deserves it."

Cringing, I moved faster.

A few more turns, another set of stairs, another turn, and I was standing in front of number 5.

I knocked lightly.

No answer.

I turned the handle slowly, fearing it might be the wrong room, and opened the door. The room was cold, dark, and smelled a little of cedar. It was sparsely furnished with only bunk beds and two metal lockers. A slip of light from the hallway shone on the figure lying in the bottom bunk, his back to me, but I recognized Isaac's shoulders.

His skateboard poked out from under the bed, and his sketch pad was on the floor, underneath his wallet and chain. I slipped in and gently let go of the door, and everything went dark. It hit me that Isaac had been living in this little metal cell for *five months* so he could stay in New Orleans and help people.

"Are you sleeping?" I asked in a soft voice.

"No." His response was neither inviting nor uninviting.

I didn't know what to say, how to get him to tell me what was going on inside his head.

I curled my fingers into a fist and then popped my hand open, gingerly throwing up a handful of dim fireballs into the air. They floated closer to him, shedding just enough light for me to see.

I slipped off my shoes and climbed into the bed next to him. He didn't turn around to face me, so I curled myself around his back, slipping my arm underneath his, and over his chest, wishing I could protect him from whatever this was.

I didn't push him to talk, and he didn't push me away.

Then he pulled my hand tighter against his chest. I buried my face into his shoulder blades and let the silence take over. We lay there, completely still, listening to each other's breath.

I could feel when his pulse slowed, and I worried that he'd calm down completely and fall asleep without saying anything—that he was never going to tell me what was wrong, and then just explode one day.

I climbed over him and settled into the space between him and the wall. The fireballs followed as I settled back in next to him. He looked at me, finally, and his golden-brown eyes were glossy but not teary, his gaze deep and dark with his secret pains.

My hand found his palm, and my fingers threaded through his. I wanted to ask him what was wrong, but saying that something was wrong just seemed like it would make things worse. "What are you thinking about?"

He just continued to stare until two words finally came out of his mouth: "It's stupid."

"I doubt it."

He fell silent, but I didn't urge him to speak—just listened to the rain outside pitter-pattering down on the ship and waited.

"Sometimes . . ." His eyes went from glossy to teary. "Sometimes I just wish my mom was here."

That was the last thing I expected him to say. All of a sudden, I felt like I was holding his heart in my hands. "If she was here . . . what would you say to her?"

Another long pause went by. His lips pinched together, fighting the tears.

"I'd tell her that I tried. I tried *so* hard, but—" His voice cracked. I didn't so much as blink.

"I'd tell her how I thought I was going to drown. How I can still feel that little girl's hand slipping away. Her hand. It was so tiny. I thought I had a grip, but then the water came and just . . . ripped her away."

I held his gaze through the tears forming in my eyes.

"If I could have just held on, I'd have rescued—" He became so choked up he had to stop.

"Isaac, you did rescue her. You *saved* her."

He stayed perfectly still as the tears poured out of his eyes in long streams. "No, I didn't," he said softly. "I didn't save Jade."

"Rosalyn, you mean?"

"There were two little girls. Sisters."

The tears blinked out of my eyes.

"Jesus, Isaac," I whispered, quickly wiping the tears away and propping myself up. I slipped my hand under the sleeve of his T-shirt and squeezed his shoulder. "It's not your fault."

"Yes, it is. I had her. I had them both. But then the water came . . . so much fucking water. Something—a sheet of tin roofing or something— hit us and sliced into my arm, and I let go. *I let go.* Rosalyn screamed as a wave swept Jade away. I tried to reach her, but the current jerked me under. All I could do was hold on to Rosalyn and fight the water."

I didn't know what to say, and I couldn't stop my tears anymore, so I just ignored them.

"I let go. I let go of Jade."

"Isaac, it's not your fault." Those were the only words that came to me.

He wouldn't meet my eyes.

"It's not. It's not your fault."

He'd clamped his arms together across his chest, but I wedged them open and squeezed myself against him, hugging him as tightly as I could. I wished I knew what his mom would say. I don't know how many times I repeated those four little words, but it felt like hundreds. "It's not your fault."

When his arms finally circled around me, I felt like I could breathe again. "It's going to be okay, I promise."

He began to cry. Not silent streams of dripping tears, but choking tears, and the sound made my heart crack into a million glass pieces.

I hugged him harder, and he crushed me against his chest, and we lay there until eventually he stopped shaking.

No more talking.

Just blackness and breathing and heartbeats, and my head on his shoulder and his arms around me, and silence for a while.

"Isaac?"

"Yeah?"

"Your mom would be so proud of you."

He sucked in a deep breath, his chest rising underneath me.

He gently stroked my arm. I imagined the photo of him and Rosalyn from the paper, and now I saw what he saw when he looked at it, and it was so much more horrifying. I also saw what he refused to see—that he was a hero.

He was *the* Hero. My Hero. He'd saved me too, on Halloween night.

"Isaac?"

"Hmph?"

"I love you."

His fingers paused on my arm. He kind of laughed, and he pulled me up from his chest. "I don't want your pity-*I-love-you!*"

"It's not a pity-*I-love-you!*" Suddenly I was trying not to laugh.

"It's totally a pity-*I-love-you.*"

My voice softened. "It's an I-think-you're-the-most-amazing-person-in-the-world-*I-love-you.*"

He didn't argue or say anything at all. He just looked at me and pulled me closer until my lips reached his.

His arms encircled me, and when we kissed, everything felt different. Everything felt *more*. Like we'd taken the heightening elixir. He wasn't like any other boy I'd ever kissed. As his hands slid up my back and into my hair, it felt like tiny bolts of static were emitting from his fingertips. *Magic.* I knew he felt it too when I touched him, because my mouth could hardly keep up with his.

Without breaking the kiss, he rolled over on top of me.

I fumbled at his shirt and pulled it over his head, his lips coming back to my neck. And for the first time in a long time, I felt like things might actually get better one day.

His hands swept underneath the silky fabric of my dress and over my stomach, and then so did his mouth, soft kisses, trailing up, pushing my dress all the way over my head. I arched so he could unhook my bra, and as more clothing slipped off and his lips met mine, I promised myself I'd tell him everything tomorrow.

Everything.

His warmth and kindness seeped out with every touch as his hands and lips found all their favorite places. My legs twisted into his, pulling him closer, and when my fingers traced up his back, he shivered. With our kisses, and limbs, and magic lacing together, I *knew* we were right together. I knew it more than anything. I slid my hand back down the curve of his spine, just so I could feel his body react to my touch, this time my fingers dipping into the waistband of his jeans.

His back stiffened. "Wait," he said, despite continuing to kiss me harder.

I didn't.

Then his hand cupped my face, and he pulled away. "Stop."

I yanked my hands away, face flushing with embarrassment. "I'm sorry! I thought you wanted to. I'm sorry."

"No. *No!* I want to. I just . . ." He kissed me again. "I have to give you something first."

My cheeks still burned as he leaned over to the floor. He grabbed the chain and swung his wallet up into his hand; then he lay back by my side, propped on his elbow.

I mirrored him, nearly naked and feeling kind of silly.

"This might be the stupidest thing I've ever done," he said.

Oh God.

"But I can't keep this anymore. I can't kiss you anymore not knowing . . ."

"W-what are you talking about?"

He fished through his wallet, and a condom dropped out.

"Oh."

"Not that," he said quickly.

"Then *what?*"

He placed a piece of metal between us on the bed. "This." It wasn't quite a square but a more complicated shape, like origami.

"What is tha . . . ?" My words drowned out as the memories trickled back.

"What is it?" he asked.

"I—I don't know."

But I did know, kind of. He knew too. It was a note, folded in a way that required vampire strength, or powers of the metal-witch variety.

I closed my fingers around it—Nicco had pressed it into my hand right after he asked me if I trusted him . . . right before he spun me around and threw me out the window. The next thing I remembered was being on the roof, Isaac removing it from my hand in my state of hysteria.

As I blinked away the memory, I saw the fear in Isaac's eyes, and I hated it.

"You've had it this whole time?"

His head bobbed up and down. "I'm sorry, Adele."

I leaned over to reach my coat on the floor.

His arms slipped around my waist. "I'm sorry. I didn't mean—"

I dropped the metal note into my coat pocket and turned back to him. I knew why he'd kept it. To protect me from Nicco, because I was too blind to see him for what he was.

A monster.

"Aren't you going to open it?" he asked.

"Not now."

"Why not?"

"Because . . . it's not going to change how I feel about you."

"Are you sure?"

"Oui."

It hurt my heart that he would even ask me that. "It's not going to change *us*. It's not going to change that I think you're the most amazing person in the world. But if I open that note, it will change this moment. If I open it, Nicco is going to be in the room with us, and I don't want him to be. I want to be with you."

His eyes held mine for a second before he pulled me close, and his lips smiled against mine as he kissed me. "I love you, Adele."

CHAPTER 40

Time

I huddled into my coat as raindrops shook from the oak-tree canopy. It was dark but not after curfew when I slipped off the ship, careful not to wake Isaac, because I knew he needed sleep.

Thank God I hadn't slept through the night—one day after being ungrounded.

Even now I wanted to go back. Thinking about turning around made a butterfly hatch. Suddenly I felt like I was floating down the street, smiling too much as I dodged the puddles down Esplanade Avenue.

In an effort to ground myself, I opened the string of messages that had accumulated over the last few hours. Most of them were from my father, first asking me where I was and whether I'd found Isaac; then, assuming I had, asking if Isaac was all right and letting me know that he was going to work. His emotional range was sometimes difficult to gauge over text, so I headed to the bar to settle his nerves in person. My phone buzzed again before I could put it away.

Désirée	7:06 p.m.	So, has Isaac totally lost it or what?
Adele	7:06 p.m.	He'll be fine. I think he has some kind of Storm-related PTSD.
Désirée	7:06 p.m.	Ya think?

I sucked in a huge breath and switched to the group chat, hoping it wouldn't wake him up. Surely his lack of sleep was exacerbating his anxiety.

Adele	7:07 p.m.	We should all huddle tonight. We need to talk about the new coven in town.
Désirée	7:07 p.m.	I can get to HQ after nine. I have to keep the shop open until curfew.
Isaac	7:07 p.m.	Should we invite Annabelle?

So much for not waking him up.

Adele	7:07 p.m.	If Callis really is serious about destroying all the Medici, one of her relatives IS at risk.

Isaac	**7:07 p.m.**	He seemed pretty serious to me. Plus, her invisibility could come in handy.
Désirée	**7:07 p.m.**	I've always been abt maximizing the coven's strength.
Désirée	**7:07 p.m.**	BTW, something tells me we're about to be swept into a supernatural shitstorm.
Isaac	**7:08 p.m.**	Why? What happened?
Désirée	**7:08 p.m.**	Tell you later. So it's settled. We'll re-bind the circle tonight.
Adele	**7:09 p.m.**	I'm glaaaaaaaad u guys feel that way abt Annabelle. Because I kinda might have already told her. That is, if she remembers anything from last night.
Désirée	**7:09 p.m.**	Little Miss Adele Le Moyne. Breaking her own rules. What exactly did u tell her?

Adele	**7:09 p.m.**	Everything? I think? It's kind of a blur. I suffered for it greatly, if it makes u feel better. Never. Drinking. Again.
Désirée	**7:09 p.m.**	Whatever. I'll prep some spells so we can test the extent of our collective powers.

I breathed a sigh of relief that Dee didn't seem to care about my slipup.

Isaac	**7:10 p.m.**	Callis's coven is probably way bigger than ours. Do u think they're all weak like him, magically? And all Fire witches?
Adele	**7:10 p.m.**	No clue. I'm not super eager to find out. We'll have to figure out a way to avoid the clash of the covens. Adding Annabelle.
Adele	**7:11 p.m.**	A, are you ready to be bound into the circle? Maison Monvoisin 9pm :)

Annabelle	**7:11 p.m.**	Sooooooo ready for to-night <3 <3

As soon as the meeting was set, I felt like alligators were wrestling in my stomach, and it had nothing to do with Callis or Annabelle or supernatural shitstorms.

I'm going to tell them about Brigitte—and that we have to figure out a way to help her.

Breathe, Adele.

I sucked in another big breath and sent Isaac one more message:

Adele	**7:41 p.m.**	You should go back to sleep... you could use the extra zzzzs.

Isaac	**7:41 p.m.**	You should come back to the ship and break more rules.

I bit my bottom lip, trying not to grin, and a butterfly hatched in my stomach in retaliation.

Adele	**7:41 p.m.**	Ha. I think three times is enough rule breaking. See you at nine.

When I walked into the ballroom, my dad was behind the makeshift bar, slicing cucumbers into thin discs. He didn't look up.

"Do you understand how a phone works?"

I could tell by the tone of his voice that he wasn't really mad. I crossed the room to the bar and sat on one of the stools.

"I could swear you do," he said, "because your fingers are always pecking on that expensive screen of yours."

"I'm sorry. I fell asleep."

"At *school?*"

"No, at Isaac's."

He put the knife down and looked up.

"Because you were so tired after sneaking out to a party after curfew and drinking underage?"

"Yeah."

"Is this some kind of rebellious phase?"

"No." I pulled away the knife, slid the wooden board to my side, and began cutting the limp produce while he consolidated bottles of moonshine and gave me a mini-lecture on responsibility.

I sliced a second cucumber. And then two lemons. But when he asked how Isaac was, I pushed it all aside and folded my arms on the bar, cradling my head just like I'd done when I was a kid. "There were *two* little girls, Dad."

"Jesus." He wiped his hands and came around to the stool next to me, anticipating what was coming next.

I told him the whole story. How Isaac had almost drowned. How that photographer took photos while he tried to save the little girls, instead of helping. How he'd searched for Jade until his dad dragged him away to be triaged.

Even though the story was hard to speak out loud, it felt good to tell him about it, to just be open about something. How we used to be about everything.

When I finished, I wiped my tears and pulled my hair out of the messy bun. As I tied it back up, he stood, but then paused, watching me.

"I know you hate it when I say it, but sometimes you remind me so much of your mother—it's incredible."

"I don't hate it, Dad."

And I didn't. Not anymore.

I arrived at the brothel an hour early as I needed some time to collect my thoughts. There was so much to tell: the León-slash-Count conspiracy, and how he might have helped Séraphine, and about Adeline killing Giovanna so she wasn't the one in the attic, and, most of all, my reasons for keeping Brigitte's secret for so long.

As I psyched myself up, turning the story over in my head, I became so anxious I couldn't sit still any longer.

I swept remnants of dried herbs from the floor, folded the blankets, and fluffed the couch pillows. I stacked Isaac's loose sketches and gathered up all of the paper scraps with handwritten shopping lists of things whose uses required imagination, like Hound's Tongue and bat leather—clearly Désirée's. I anchored them under stones and crystals. As I scraped wax off the coffee table with my fingernail, I suddenly had the overwhelming feeling that something was out of place . . . or missing?

I scanned the room, but everything looked as it should, just neater than before. I chalked up the strange feeling to my separation anxiety from Adeline's diary. I wasn't sure I'd ever been here without it. My medallion wasn't around my neck either. I'd been in such a hurry to get to the ceremony, I'd skipped a few steps getting ready. I suddenly had a strong desire to retrieve them.

I checked my phone: 8:40 p.m. *You'll only be a few minutes late if you hustle.*

I buttoned my coat all the way up and was out the door before I could give it a second thought.

A single fireball rose from my hand, floating ahead as I hustled down the porch steps. The stars twinkled above, some hidden by the haze of the full moon. As I crossed the yard, breath billowed from my lips into the cool night air. I shoved my hands into my pockets. Metal poked my fingers.

My feet stopped. My breath paused. And I was pretty sure my heart froze too.

How did I forget about this?

Well, I knew *how.*

For a second I just stood there spinning it in my pocket. I'd been *so* certain that Nicco and I were on the same side. That we'd get through the horror together, despite the odds.

Then he threw me out a window and changed everything—but not without slipping me this piece of metal first. Something he clearly hadn't wanted his brothers to see, and that he must have planned in advance. Something that Isaac had kept this whole time.

Instinct told me to take it straight to my father's studio and melt it into a stake, but my intuition—and my need for answers—would never allow that.

"Niccolò Giovanni Battista Medici, you're lucky I have my intuition, because it's the only thing that might save you from getting killed by Callis."

The bushes rustled around me in the breeze, and the little orb of fire whizzed around the note in my palm. One side had the folds of metal, and the flat side had an insignia scraped into it. I recognized it from Nicco's dreams. It was on the doors that led to the great Medici hall: three interlocking diamond rings.

Feeling the shape of the metal in my palm brought back the night in the attic so vividly—my hand on the cool metal doorknob, and Nicco pressed against my back. "Do you trust me, *bella?*" he'd said. The shock those words had sent through my body. And then he pulled me away, preparing to throw me away like I was nothing.

His last words echoed through my mind: "I'm so sorry, *bella . . .* but there is no other way."

Flames flickered in the dormant gas lamps lining the bricked foot-path to the gate—in and out, with the hammering of my pulse.

As I stared at the note, I felt the mechanisms in the front door unlock, and a wave ripple across the wrought-iron fence hidden beneath the ivy. The metal folds slipped away from each other, like a blossoming lotus, and every bit of metal on the grounds creaked, curling toward me, as if the entire property was leaning in to see the message.

When the pewter note finally lay flat in my palm, I recognized the otherworldly handwriting carved into the metal, but the words were near impossible to comprehend. I could almost feel Nicco with me, hear his barely there accent whispering the message into my ear:

I trust you.
Break the curse.
Niccolò

My hand shook as I reread the message over and over. I couldn't move. All I could do was stare at the note as the monster in my head slowly started to dissolve. Throwing me out of the window. *It was all a ruse to trick his brothers.* To give me the thing I needed even more than magic—the thing I'd asked him for.

Time.

Time to break the curse. Time to figure everything out.

Nicco had given me time.

Which I haven't done anything with.

That's why none of it had ever added up, why none of it had made sense—why his actions had made the whole world seem off-kilter.

I knew in my heart it was the truth, but I needed confirmation.

I tapped out a message.

Adele	**8:43 p.m.**	Nicco wasn't trying to kill me when he threw me out that window, was he?
Isaac	**8:45 p.m.**	Shit
Isaac	**8:45 p.m.**	I meant to tell you when I gave you the metal thing, I was just distracted!
Adele	**8:45 p.m.**	Tell me what?
Isaac	**8:45 p.m.**	That he knew I would catch you. How we planned it.

They'd planned it. All this time I thought Nicco had betrayed me—that he really was a liar and a monster—but it had all been based on that one moment. A moment he'd planned with Isaac. Now the pin was pulled and the monster was unhinging in my head, leaving only the boy I knew from my dreams. The boy who wanted to help people.

Who wanted to help *me*.

Isaac	**8:47 p.m.**	You opened it?
Adele	**8:47 p.m.**	Yes
Isaac	**8:48 p.m.**	Is everything different now?

Adele	**8:48 p.m.**	Yes
Isaac	**8:48 p.m.**	So you hate me now?
Adele	**8:49 p.m.**	No. It doesn't change the way I feel about you. It doesn't.
Isaac	**8:49 p.m.**	You have no idea how relieved I am to hear that.
Adele	**8:50 p.m.**	But it changes the way I feel about him.
Isaac	**8:50 p.m.**	What does that mean?
Adele	**8:50 p.m.**	It means he doesn't deserve to be in that attic, Isaac!!! He didn't do anything!!
Isaac	**8:50 p.m.**	HE TORTURED CALLIS AND HIS ENTIRE COVEN!

"But he saved me!" I hurled the metal note back at the house, screaming.

As soon as my voice faded away, I felt something in my hand again. When I opened my eyes, the note was back in my palm, and every single metal object outside the property was at my feet: Victorian courtyard furniture, gardening tools, and fixtures that held potted plants all surrounded me in a circle of tin, iron, and brass. Bright flames shone out of every gas lamp on the property, illuminating the crack in the wood where the note had hit the door.

My phone buzzed again:

Isaac	**8:52 p.m.**	Just hang tight. Are u at HQ? I'll be there in a few minutes.

With a little mental focus, I refolded the note and slipped it back into my pocket.

Breathe, Adele.

My fingers moved quickly across the screen.

Adele	**8:53 p.m.**	OK, but I have to run to my house to get ASG's things. I'll be back though. Promise.
Isaac	**8:53 p.m.**	Babe, we're going to figure this out.
Adele	**8:53 p.m.**	I know.

I'm going to figure this out.

I stormed into my bedroom, unable to pinpoint the actual reason I was fuming. There were too many emotions brewing in my belly to sort. I wasn't mad at Isaac, not really—though I was pissed that he was right about one thing: Nicco not trying to kill me didn't equate with the world being safer with him in it.

I was mad about plenty of other things, though. I was mad that Emilio had turned my mom into a vampire, and now she was trapped in an attic. I was mad that she'd killed those students twelve years ago, and somehow I justified that it wasn't her fault. I was mad that the Medici had hurt Callis. And I was mad that Callis was now threatening my mother's immortal life.

And Nicco's.

And even with all of that, I could only think about the fact that Nicco hadn't thrown me out of the window trying to kill me; it had been his backup plan all along because . . . he trusted me.

Unfathomably, he trusted me. And that meant I had zero reason not to trust him.

Never trust a vampire.

Nicco might have had his secrets, but he'd never threatened me, never lied to me. All he'd ever done was protect me—and now, after this note, it was hard not to believe the reason he'd kept his secrets bottled up was because he thought doing so was protecting me too. Even if his motives were questionable or self-serving.

I sucked in a sharp breath.

Above all, I was furious at myself—for losing trust in him, and for not doing anything to help him get out. I hadn't done anything to break the curse.

You found another coven member.

"It's not enough," I said as my backpack unzipped itself. I slipped the diary in. Now Callis was in town, *with backup*, and Nicco was still helpless. Was I supposed to just stand by?

I dumped some candles and other things from my witch box in too, eyeing Nicco's shirt, which lay in a pile of clothes on the floor. I stripped off the dressy clothes from the ceremony and slipped on the flannel, breathing in his leather-and-soap scent.

Maybe it will still help strengthen the connection. Like last time.

Dark jeans. Shit-kickers. Saint-Germain necklace. I ripped a brush through my hair and tied it into a braid.

I felt like I was getting into cat-burglar mode. I wasn't going back to the brothel—not just yet. Not until I knew for sure. I needed to see for myself why I shouldn't help break Nicco out of the attic. I needed to see what he really was—someone with a heart, or a manipulative, conniving predator without a shred of humanity left, like Callis had said.

And I couldn't take any risks of slipping into his fantasies—I needed to be where our connection would be the strongest. I needed to know the truth about what happened with Callis.

I needed to be near him.

CHAPTER 41

The Binding

I took a few running steps, my board dragging on the street before I let it drop and jumped on. It would've been faster to fly, but my legs wanted to move.

There'd been something doomsdayish about today since the moment I woke up. At first I thought it was because of the ceremony or yesterday's weird confrontation with Callis, but now I knew what it was . . .

I shouldn't have given Adele that note.

Just two hours ago everything was more perfect than it ever had been, my darkest secrets out, falling asleep with her in my arms, and the rain drowning out the rest of the world.

Giving her the note had been the right thing to do—if she'd found out after, she'd never have forgiven me—but still, now that we were arguing mere hours after leaving my bed, it was hard not to regret it.

I circled my arm, redirecting the breeze to create a tailwind, and steadied myself on the board as the wheels rolled faster.

I should have just thrown it into the river and played dumb if it ever came up.

And so Nicco's note continued to torment me, despite it being no longer in my possession.

As I neared the brothel, I felt the pulse of the protection spells. Two more pushes down the bumpy street, and I jumped off the board, kicking it up into my palm.

How did I forget to tell her about the plan?

I was just so shocked and relieved when she cast the note aside, I totally blanked on the part about Nicco and I planning her great escape. I just . . . got distracted.

I stopped short in the front garden. A giant pile of metal objects was in a circle in the middle of the yard—evidence that Adele had been here. I walked around it, wondering how long ago. After she'd opened the note? Or after she'd messaged me?

"Adele!" I yelled, going through the front door. "Désirée?"

No one responded, but I did a quick loop through the bottom level anyway. I thought about the pile of metal outside on the lawn and wondered how angry she'd been.

Calm down. She'll be back any minute.

It's not like she ran away to save Nicco.

I went back outside and sat on the porch steps, leaning back, stretching. In a weird way, I used to feel bad for him, for being trapped in the attic with his psychotic family, but learning what they'd done to Callis's coven—draining them of their blood, of their magic—had changed everything. Not that I expected anything different from a vampire, but Nicco was a master at making you think he was different. He was good like that. A manipulative monster. The biggest monster of all of them.

A witch killer.

I didn't know if helping Callis was the right thing to do, but there was no way I was letting Adele open that attic—not because I was jealous of Nicco and didn't want him around, but because the vampires were a threat to everyone in town, to the coven, and especially to Adele, even if she didn't realize it.

No more innocent people in this town were going to die.

I pushed the bracelets away from my watch: 21:27. She should have been back by now.

Dee was late too, and that girl was never late for anything; she was born with an agenda in hand. And where the hell was Annabelle?

I tapped my fingers on my knee, wondering if they were all together. What if Adele was trying to convince them to help her release Nicco from the attic?

Don't be a tool, Isaac. They're probably at the Borges'.

I thought about Nicco draining Callis and wondered what it would be like to have my powers taken away. Then I thought about how much I knew Nicco was in love with Adele.

And I thought about how much I was.

As the thoughts crisscrossed through my head, I was already out the front gate.

The shutters were closed at the Voodoo shop, but an interior light glowed faintly through the front-door transom. I tried the handle. Locked. I knocked. Nothing. I checked my phone again. No messages. I called Dee. No answer.

All three of my coven members were MIA. It couldn't be a coincidence. Something was off.

My ears perked hearing a shout from deep inside—muffled voices speaking back and forth. I stepped down the sidewalk to the alleyway gate and peered through the ironwork.

Gas lamps flickered on the walls, casting shadows down the brick corridor. I lifted my hand through the bars and wafted the air my way, letting the wind carry the voices. *Dee's voice.* I couldn't make out the words, but I was sure it was her. I took a few steps back and then, with a running jump, grabbed the top of the gate. With a little strain, and with one eye on the twelve-inch metal spikes sticking out the top, I pulled myself up and carefully leaped over.

In the cover of the alley, I morphed into bird form, because as a crow I didn't feel like I was trespassing on Ritha's property. I was just . . . flying.

I took the bend into the courtyard and flew straight up to the third-story balcony at the back of the camelback shop, overlooking the fantastical gardens. A great hearth, which I'd originally assumed was a fountain, danced with fire, lighting up the enlarged fauna and casting creepy shadows on the brick walls.

Désirée, Ana Marie, and Ritha were standing around the fire, arguing. Désirée's arms were flailing—very un-Désirée-like. Despite not being that far away, I couldn't make out what she was saying to her gran, though whatever they were discussing did not look fun. Ritha Borges no longer looked like the kooky grandmother I'd met right before the Storm, but a force to be reckoned with.

I dropped down to the second-story balcony to hear better, but everything was still a marble-mouth muffle. I lifted off again and swooped in a wide circle around the yard. Normally I wouldn't be down to spy on my best friend's family tiff, but the tense faces and animated arms made me wonder if the topic of discussion was vampires. Or maybe Ritha had found out about the new coven in town. Was that the supernatural shitstorm Dee had referred to?

I swooped lower, rustling the leaves of a tall banana plant. The voices became louder, but the words were no more clear. Just a louder warble. Ritha crossed her arms, just like Désirée always did, making her instantly look more threatening than any of the military guys I was used to being around. She said something to Ana Marie, but her words were still garbled, and I wondered if my magic really was failing.

I dropped inconspicuously into a patch of tall sunflowers, feeling a jolt on the way down. *What the hell was that?* I flapped up a few feet, and there it was again, a tiny zap, kind of like the jolt when I crossed Esplanade Avenue through the trapping spell.

"This is wrong on *so* many levels, Gran," Dee said, following the others to the back door.

Her words were perfectly clear now.

Magic. The jolt must have been some kind of silencing shield.

I sailed through the air after them, but just before I reached the shop, the door slammed shut. *Dammit.*

I swooped around the building. No open doors. No open windows. If I wanted in, I'd have to fly down the chimney; that is, if there wasn't some kind of magical barrier. Three long flaps, and I was high above the house.

Here goes. I held my breath as I swooped down.

Everything went dark, my wings scraping the bricks on the descent, but I focused on the light, and at just the right moment I swooped out and up, avoiding a crash landing.

Tiny caws coughed through my beak as I flapped around the candlelit room, shaking century-old soot from my feathers and blinking it off my eyelids. From the shadows, an enormous black cat appeared, glassy eyes glinting—I fluttered up to a curtain rod, my tiny bird heart exploding.

But the cat didn't move . . . It didn't seem interested in me at all.

Usually I could sense other animals near, or smell them at the very least, but instead the room had a distinct scent that reminded me of freshmen bio lab, mixed with orangewood incense.

My claws wrapped tighter around the rod as I realized there were animals all around. Birds. Foxes. Rabbits. An alligator on the floor. Loads of antlers were racked on the walls, all frozen in time. *What is this place?*

Scattered over the surface of a big butcher table in the middle of the room were lamps, magnifying glasses, and coffee tins filled with brushes and tools I'd never seen before. *The Borges do their own taxidermy?* Terror pumped through my veins, but then again, the thought of being immortalized in crow form after I died did seem kinda badass.

I took off and flew out into the hallway and down the stairs to the second floor. Just like the ground level, the second floor was a railroad, or a shotgun as they called it in the South. The rooms flowed into one another with no hallways. The first room had a lush carpet of brightly woven oranges and pinks, and the walls were covered with pieces of art similar to the ones hanging in the shop—at a glance they could be mistaken for paintings, but they were really made up of thousands of tiny beads sewn onto silk. I flew past a beaded mermaid, wondering if this was the room where Ritha's coven met. Throw pillows lay around the edges of the room, alongside drums, bells, baskets of candles, herbs, and other ceremonial things.

I slipped through the folds of thick black curtains into an even darker room and immediately braked, landing on the head of another time-stopped beast—the kind I hoped to never meet in real life based on the size of its now permanently growling teeth. A panther maybe? Its eyes glowed yellow. I'd stopped asking why a long time ago with the Borges.

All the windows and entrances in the room had been draped with heavy black fabric, and the only light came from low flames crackling in the fireplace and racks of candles dripping wax onto the mantel among statues of skeleton people. Mirrors of all sizes rested along the walls, reflecting the flames. Some were enormous, in tall wooden frames, some were wide and beveled, while others were smaller and had intricately designed frames of silver vines and rosettes, as if straight from a fairy tale. Across the entire room, shards of suspended glass hung from the ceiling at varying heights, like a room-size wind chime. *What the hell is this?*

I recognized the scent of burning sage.

A tiny caw of surprise slipped from my throat when I realized two men were on the sofa, both slumped forward, as if passed out, their faces obscured by the shadows and flopping dark hair—one had curls, the other dreadlocks.

Someone else, a small white-haired woman, was curled into the paisley armchair next to them, also slumped over and still as death.

What the . . . ?

Pulse pounding, I took off and flew low around the room, avoiding the strands of tiny glass beads hanging from the ceiling—the broken mirror pieces reflected everything below them, creating a beautiful juxtaposition of soft color and sharp edges.

Footsteps pressed into the ceiling above, shaking the strands of floating mirror shards, followed by rattling metal, like chains. Before I could inspect any further, voices rose from behind the curtain at the opposite end of the room. I landed back on the panther.

"You can't do this, Gran," Désirée said, walking into view with her gran and mother. "You have no right." She walked to each of the sitting people and placed two fingers on each of their necks, as if checking their pulses.

What the fuck?

"Désirée, they're not dead," said Ritha. "The spell is not going to kill them. Now I'm sure you have more important things to do with your coven?"

"Mom! What the heck? Gran has lost it!"

"There is a perfectly valid reason for all of this," Ana Marie answered, "which I'm sure your grandmother is about to tell you—"

"There is, and I won't. When you dismiss your family coven, you dismiss your privileges. Access is something you should have considered before removing a family grimoire from this protected house and using it to awaken your most powerful ancestor without closing the portal to the spirit world."

"I didn't know about closing—?"

"You'd *know*, Désirée, if you were here, where you're supposed to be, learning the powers of centuries of magic in our family! Leaving a tear to the other side makes the spirits of our ancestors vulnerable to the malevolent! And if the ghosts of our ancestors suffer, we suffer. Our magic will suffer. The whole magical ecosystem suffers when the spirit world is disrupted."

A moment of déjà vu washed over me. I'd heard these words before: the night I'd seen Ritha muttering in the garden. She'd said something about supernatural crimes, and destroying the . . . *binding*. Or everything will unravel . . .

"The spirits hold everything together," she continued. "You know this, child. All magical connection is bound to those who came before us. We must protect them. Protect the binding, protect the magic."

Spirits are the binding? I struggled to understand what they were talking about. Did spirits bind the natural world to the magical world? Did they bind us to our magic?

Are we the magical ecosystem—witches and spirits and magic?

But that didn't explain why a spirit would need protection. What could harm a spirit?

Protection . . .

Protégez la.

Protect her.

My fingers tingled, and the mark on my arm pulsed.

"Just because I joined another coven doesn't mean I betrayed the family," Désirée snapped, a slight shake in her voice. "I don't deserve to be shut out completely!"

"That girl is going to be trouble. Mark my word."

Girl? What girl? Adele?

"Just because it's not your coven doesn't make it trouble!"

Murmurs came from the couch. "Ghohhhhh . . ." It was the curly haired guy. "Ghooowich."

Ritha straightened, looking deeply unsettled.

"*What* did he say?" Ana Marie asked with a hint of panic.

"Witch," the man moaned. "Ghost. Witch." He gestured to me with a wavering hand.

The heads of all three Borges women shot my way, along with Ritha's hand.

Oh no.

The air around me exploded into smoke, and I fell to the floor in human form.

"Ghost witch!" the white-haired lady in the chair shrieked. "Ghost witch!"

Désirée's hand went to her temple.

I jumped up. "I'm sorry! I was worried about you! And *clearly* I should have been."

"Yankee!" The man's head of long black curls bobbed up with a burst of energy.

"Ren? What the hell is going on here?"

"You have to help me, kid. I've dried out, I swear! I don't even have the shakes anymore."

I stepped closer to the couch.

"Don't even think about touching him," Ritha said sharply, stopping me in my tracks. "The entity could transfer."

"What does that mean?"

The man next to Ren began to stir. Only when he jerked his arms did I realize they were all bound by ropes. "This is insane!"

Désirée's expression changed, like she'd put the pieces together. "This is an intervention!"

Ana Marie and Ritha turned to her. "Exactly, sweetheart," her mother said.

I glared at them. "Since when do interventions involve involuntary imprisonment?"

"When the problem is of the malevolent variety," said Ritha.

"*What?*"

When Ritha said nothing more, Ana Marie explained. "It's very dangerous. We don't know for sure that they've been taken by demons, but the hosts' strange behavior leads us to believe the entities are malevolent. Possibly parasitic."

Dee stepped closer to the tied-up trio, seemingly back to her usual self, like all of this was totally normal.

"What are you talking about? What . . . strange behavior?"

"Polarizing mood swings," said Ana Marie. "Aggression, other abnormal activities. That's how it all starts. We've tried mojo-bags and baths, and other means of extraction, but nothing has helped, and the longer the entities remain, the more violent the hosts' behavior becomes."

An image of Ren swinging at Theis flashed into my mind, but then a scream came from the floor above us, and another slam of metal, again, like chains rattling.

Dee and I stared up at the ceiling.

"She was the first one we found," Ana Marie said. "About two months ago. She's had a total seize of the mind. We're afraid the next phase may be final."

"Final?" I asked. "Like death?"

Another scream came from above. None of the Borges women wavered.

Ana Marie looked to each of us. "We're trying to help them before they harm anyone else or endanger themselves. Unrestrained, these people are a threat to anyone around them."

"You!" Ren yelled, trying to stand so suddenly, the whole couch jerked with the constraint before pulling him back down. He was looking straight at me. "I should have known that *you* were behind this all along!" His voice sounded different—deeper, and with a slight accent, kind of like when he was performing, but more foreign. European.

All six Borges eyes turned to me once again.

"This is all part of your diabolical plan to get rid of me!" he shouted. "First you move in on Julie—"

"What? Julie?"

"Now you think you can move in on my girl? Bring her back from the other side? Over my dead soul! I'm on to you, Yankee!"

Désirée looked at me with *what the eff* eyes, but in my mind things were starting to add up. Ren's recent erratic behavior—from the night he appeared to be having a heart attack on the street, to his orange-juice cologne, to him nearly going to blows over a girl at the bar. It all began to make sense, in a fucked-up, supernatural kind of way.

But it was something Julie had said the night in the courtyard with Onyx that bubbled to the top of in my mind: *What if I never see Alessandro again? What if we never find him?*

I stiffened. "He's not possessed by just any random malevolent entity."

Both Ritha and Ana Marie crossed their arms. Désirée had been in arms-folded stance pretty much since I'd dropped in.

I moved nearer to the couch. "Ren?"

No response.

"Ren."

He turned his head to the opposite wall like a kid.

"Ignore me all you want, Ren, I have plans tonight. A hot date. It's gonna be bangin'. I should probably leave now so I'm not late picking up Violette."

"Ti ucciderò!" he yelled, trying to Hulk out of the restraints.

The Borges didn't flinch, totally confident that the ropes would hold him. Magic, I guessed.

"Ti ucciderò!" he yelled maniacally. *"Vi ucciderò tutti!"*

"He's not possessed by some random supernatural parasite," I yelled over his hisses and snarls. "It's Alessandro, the Italian fruit peddler's son. Julie's friend! She's devastated over him being missing."

"Sì, sì, aiutami!"

"Who's Alessandro?" Ana Marie asked.

"Alessandro, one of the Royal Street ghosts."

They looked at me blankly.

"You know, the one who . . . got his *junk ripped off.*"

"Romeo going up, Juliet coming down!" Ren yelled enthusiastically in his normal tour-guide voice.

"The Romeo Catcher," said Dee.

"Exactly!"

She turned to her gran. "If the entity is just a common house-ghost, why haven't you been able to exorcise him? It should be a cinch for you. It's like your specialty."

"The entity might have been a friendly house-ghost at one time, but the way he's attached to his human host, draining him, it's an abnormal possession. It's parasitic, making it nearly impossible to detach or exorcise."

As Ritha spoke, my gaze stayed on Ren. His eyes drooped, weighed down by potato-shaped bags beneath them. His glistening curls, which usually sent middle-aged women into tizzies, hung limp over his shoulders, and his cheeks were sunken, like those of the skeleton-men on the mantel.

Désirée turned to Ritha. "What would make a house-ghost parasitic?"

"After death, the soul is still protected by a body. Instead of a physical one, it's an ethereal body—a 'spirit' or a 'ghost' as we call them in the natural world. But if something were to harm the spirit badly enough, it may release its soul, just in the way we release our spirits after death. In order to survive in the natural world, the soul would need to seek out a new spiritual body to connect to. Another ghost—"

"Even if the ghost is still inside another human!" Désirée finished.

My hands folded on top of my head. "So Alessandro's soul is, like, seeking asylum inside Ren, and . . . *draining away* his future ghost-spirit-body-thing?"

Ritha nodded. "If Ren's spirit is holding two souls, the imbalance is unnatural. Unsustainable. But perhaps more importantly begs the question, who—or *what*—is attacking the ghosts so gravely they are releasing their souls?"

"Anininiinanimimarrrrrummm," Ren mumbled incoherently. *"Anininiinanimimarrrrrummm Praaaaedator."*

I looked at Désirée. "That's what Marassa said the night of the séance."

Ritha's head flipped my way. "Marassa Makandal *spoke* to you? What exactly did she say?"

Dee answered for me. "'All souls will suffer.'"

"And that phrase," I added. "Animarum Praedator. She kept saying it over and over again. *Animarum Praedator. La protéger.*"

Ana Marie's voice became sharp. "Protect who? Désirée?"

"I—I don't know. I thought she was talking about Adele."

Which reminded me. I pulled out my phone: *22:07 hours. No new messages.* Something about that made me nervous. I needed to get out of here. I could come back to help Ren once I knew Adele was safe.

Ritha's gaze settled on me. "Animarum Praedator is Latin. It means *Spirit Predator.* What did Ren mean when he called you a ghost witch?"

"It's my Spektral magic . . . I think."

"You must be very gifted to have made contact at such a young age. It can take a lifetime for even the greatest witches to master contact with the dead." Her tone became pointed. "Ghosts are the hardest things in the magical ecosystem to hunt because of their ethereal nature—"

"Hunt?"

"But I imagine it would be much easier to hunt them if you can sense them. See them."

"Wait, what are you trying to say? You think I'm the one the ghosts need protection from? That I'm hunting ghosts? That I'm one of these . . . Spirit Predators?"

"Do you deny your connection to the spirit world?"

"What? No, but—"

"Mom, enough!" said Ana Marie.

"All of this started happening around the same time my grand-daughter started hanging around you. Halloween night. When you bound your coven."

"That's *ENOUGH*," Désirée said. "Leave him alone!"

"If it's not you, it's Miss Le Moyne," Ritha continued. "She's got a connection too. I'm certain of it."

"Adele cannot see ghosts."

"You have no idea about that girl."

"We're witches!" I yelled. "Not Animarum Praedators, or Spirit Predators, or whatever the hell. You know that!"

Ren's lips were pursed, and his brow crinkled. His face was so red it looked purple. He roared, "THE ANIMARUM PRAEDATORS ARE WITCHES!"

Ritha's eyes lit up.

I looked to Désirée, wondering if she was thinking the same thing I was—about the new witch who had arrived to town Halloween night, which was also about the same time I had started hanging around Dee.

The white-haired woman in the chair looked at me—her irises were as pale as her hair, like the color had been drained out of them. "I tried to warn you," she cried out, "but you didn't help me!"

Everyone's gaze hardened on me.

"What are you talking about?"

A draft blew through the curtain, gently rocking the mirror shards. The dangling glass chimed above us, and I saw her reflection in them as they swayed. My heart nearly stopped as I realized what all the mirrors were for. The pieces of glass didn't reflect the old woman, but the entity inside her: the blonde I'd found floating in the pool.

What the . . . ?

"I shouted to you, Isaac," she said, weeping, "but you couldn't hear me, so I left you a message in the dust! You read it, but you still didn't help me!"

"I'm—I'm sorry. I didn't know. I'm sorry."
The mirror. The message in the mirror.

ANIMARUM
PRAEDATOR

Her corpse didn't need protecting; her *ghost* did.

Ritha shot the Borges death glare at me. "If you have caused any harm to the spirits of this coven, you will be cast so far out of the witching world—"

"Don't talk to him like that!" Désirée yelled, and her arm shot to the window behind me, flinging it open. The girl was born to tell people what to do with her eyes, and I didn't need to be told twice.

In a poof I was gone, through the window, flying over the rooftops, adrenaline shooting through my veins.

I wondered if I should go to Adele's first, but the drowned girl's reflection pounded in my head. *The Animarum Praedator are witches.*

I turned on Royal Street, ready to rip Callis out of his bed. The house with the drowned blonde had been on his first day on the job.

Had she needed me to protect her from Callis?

Instead of helping her, I'd practically delivered her to him, hooking him up with the job and even leading him to her body.

Fuck.

But why would a witch be attacking ghosts?

CHAPTER 42

The Carter Brothers

As I pushed aside the pile of blankets on the attic floor, the little fireballs whizzed around my head. *You need to calm down.*

I slid down to the floor against the sealed door.

This is never going to work if you don't relax.

My eyes slipped shut.

I want to see it, Nicco. No childhood memories. No dark, twisted fantasies about killing me. *I want to see that night. I want to see the night you tortured Callis.*

And with that, the little balls of fire hovering around me fizzled out, and everything went dark through my eyelids.

The dream started in the same way all of the others did, with the beating of a heart—of *his* heart. The thump-thumping.

Come on, Nicco. You trusted me enough to ban yourself to an attic for eternity.

Thump-thump.

Thump-thump.

You have to trust me with this.

But all I saw was darkness. Nothing.

I imagined Callis bursting past me through the door and killing my mother. I could see the vehemence in his eyes as he plunged a stake straight through Nicco's heart.

I'm coming in, Nicco.

It's for your own good. You have to trust me.

I'm coming in.

I heard the crashing waves in the background. The front door was locked, but this time I flung my hand, and it swung open.

The thumping grew louder and louder, and suddenly I wasn't in the attic or the house on the cliff. I was in the doorway of an elegant room with a long dining room table full of people. Windows with plush green drapery lined the right wall. A china cabinet stood tall on the left, next to a buffet table with a silver coffee set and a stack of newspapers. A man was standing at the head of the table, bent over, fingers resting on the table. He looked up, and I gasped.

Emilio. I hardly recognized him, so dashing in the suit.

Thump-thump.

Thump-thump.

My gaze followed the thumping. Nicco was standing at the window, equally dapper, looking out, lost in thought.

Nicco? I held up my hands—they were my own, not Nicco's. I turned to my left, to a mirror over the buffet. The reflection was *me.* "Of course you're not him, Adele, he's standing over there," I mumbled.

He turned and looked straight at me.

"Nicco!" I fought the urge not to run over and throw my arms around him.

Dazed, he turned back to the window.

"Nicco!"

This time he didn't react. Nor did anyone else.

They can't hear you, Adele. Or see you. It's Nicco's dream. You're inside the dream.

I walked closer to the table, wondering what occasion called for everyone to dress so handsomely. All the ladies wore beaded dresses, finger curls or flapper bobs, and fur stoles around their shoulders. Some of the men's bowler hats looked pristinely vintage. Maybe it was one of those themed parties where everyone dressed from a different decade? This one would definitely be the Roaring '20s. Maybe '30s . . .

I moved closer to a man whose mustache could have really used a trim, which seemed strange compared to his formal attire. His skin was *so* pale. *Are they all vampires?* That would explain the lack of food on the table.

I waved my hand in front of his face just to be sure. Nothing.

His head fell forward, chin to chest.

"Sir?" I asked, momentarily forgetting they couldn't hear me. I leaned closer, and that's when I saw that his wrists were not only bound together but also bound to the table underneath.

I straightened up quickly and stared at the others. They were all *prisoners.*

"Nicco?" I quickly stepped around the table. "Nicco, what are you doing? What are you doing to these people?"

He turned and looked straight at me, as if he heard me but couldn't find me, and then he slowly turned back to the window.

"Why are you doing this?" I shouted.

Callis's words rang in my head: *Don't seek logic or reasoning in monsters, Adele.*

"Help me," a tiny voice called, the first words spoken since I'd been in the room, and they weren't much more than a wisp.

I know that voice. I moved down the table, past men and women, some older, some not—just like one huge family at Thanksgiving.

"Help," she cried again, small and helpless sounding—a little girl down by Emilio.

She was wearing a pale-blue dress with a big navy bow at her chest. Her long black hair was braided into two pigtails, curled on the ends. She was so gaunt and pale she better resembled a corpse than a vampire.

"Celestina!" I yelled, realizing I was exactly where I wanted to be. I rushed over and grabbed for her arm, but my hand went right through, as if she were made of air.

Her lips were cracked and bleeding, and she continuously licked them as she murmured, "Help." She looked up, I swear, directly at me. "Help." Her head bobbed to the side. "Help me, please."

She wasn't pleading to me; she was just delirious with . . . starvation? Dehydration? Blood loss?

I wanted to lift her up and run her out of there. "Nicco! Do something! This isn't you!"

But he didn't even look my way.

"It's going to be okay, Stina," said a voice across the table—another voice I knew, and another face I hardly recognized. Callis struggled to hold up his head. His skin was an ashy gray, and his dark curls fell over his glossy blue eyes.

"Callis!" I hurried around the table to him. "Callis, I'm going to help you." I fumbled for the rope around his wrist, but again my hand went straight through like I was made of vapors. "How can I help you?" I screamed.

This is a memory, Adele. They don't need your help. You know they survive. But how?

Callis's head fell back to the side. The shoulder of his jacket and the collar of his shirt were soaked with ten shades of dried blood, and there were two giant holes in his neck. Not dainty fang marks like I'd seen on Maddalena or Theis, but enormous bloody gashes, as if from multiple feedings.

No. The realization crashed around me. *This is Callis's coven.*

I dashed to the next closest person and the next, peering at their clothing just below their ascots and fur stoles and suit jackets. Though none of their wounds appeared as bad as Callis's, they all had fang marks and stains of crimson—all of them except Celestina.

"Oh, what, you're too humane to feed off a nine-year-old?" I screamed at Nicco before turning to Emilio. "I didn't think *you* were above anything, Emilio. Maybe there is hope for you yet?"

"Don't worry, Stina," Callis said weakly. "I'm going to get us out of here. And I'm going to get you something to eat."

In a quick whip, Nicco crossed the room. "No, you're not!" He slammed his fist on the table in front of Callis. "The only way you'll be leaving this room is as a pile of ash and bone hidden in my pockets, so I can dispose of you in the river."

"No, Nicco." My head shook vigorously. "No. This isn't you. I know this isn't you."

Emilio laughed in the background. "Did you really think you'd be able to spill Medici blood, Callisto? Aren't you supposed to be the leader of your coven? Have you really not learned anything in your years?"

He looked up to Emilio with a smile. "I've learned that people will always underestimate a little girl."

"*Cosa?*" Nicco asked as our heads all turned.

Celestina was gone.

"*What* did you do?" Nicco yelled at Callis. "Where is she?"

Callis laughed with what little energy he had left. I think if he'd been physically able to, he'd have spat in Nicco's face.

Emilio tore through the room, searching for her.

I dropped to the floor, looking under the table, scared for her life, despite knowing she lived to see New Orleans. But she wasn't there. Just the ropes that her bony little wrists must have slipped out of, and a pair of doll-like patent-leather booties. Glancing at all of the other shoes under the table, I suddenly felt like I was at a Roaring Twenties museum rather than at a costume party. The thick nude stockings, the beaded fringe hanging down from the ladies' dresses—exquisite detail, far too authentic for just *costumes*.

I quickly emerged.

Emilio whipped out the door, still searching, while Nicco whispered threatening things into Callis's ear, every word of which was about killing Celestina—*a child*. But rather than his words, my attention was drawn to his suit, which looked like it came straight from Jay Gatsby's closet.

I stumbled back a few steps, into the buffet. Out of the corner of my eye, I caught a glimpse of the top newspaper in the stack. It was crisply folded, like it hadn't been read yet.

Emilio came back into the room, exchanging loud words with Nicco in Italian, but I didn't turn around. My eyes were glued to the headline on the front page:

PROHIBITION ENDS AT LAST!

But Did It Ever Really Begin in New Orleans?

"What the hell?" I ran to the window, the curtain rippling as I rushed past. With my nose near the glass, I got the confirmation I needed. We were on Royal Street, on the corner of St. Ann. *This is the house of the Carter brothers.* These people weren't just victims of Nicco and Emilio; they were *the* Carter brothers' victims from Ren's story.

"*Adele?*"

When I turned around, Nicco was calling my name.

"*Adele?*"

Thump-thump.

Thump-thump.

"Adele, you have to trust me."

My eyes fluttered awake, my heart pounding. Thump-thumping. I held on to the scene in my head. Every detail. The rope shackles. The bite wounds. The threats. Everything was exactly how Callis had described it.

Callis and Celestina and the rest of his coven were the victims of the Carter brothers, but he'd left out one key detail.

The fact that it happened nearly *a hundred years ago.*

"What. The. Hell? Who are they? *What* are they?" How could witches stay alive for a century *and* still appear to be nine and twenty-five?

It didn't change the fact that they'd been tortured by the Medici, but it certainly gave me pause. Callis's half-truth was enough for my suspicion to run deeper. And, as always, one answer led to a thousand more questions.

I blasted out a message to Isaac, Dee, and Annabelle:

Adele	10:51 p.m.	Sorry I'm late. On my way back to HQ, now! Need to talk STAT. Callis is up to something.

CHAPTER 43

La sauvez

I circled the building twice. No signs of life. No lights. No noises. I wasn't even sure if the Daures lived in the Quarter. Maybe it was just Callis and Celestina who lived upstairs?

Without skipping a beat, I landed in an alley across the street so I could change form without causing alarm, and ran back to the shop. I pressed my face to the smoky bay window, trying to see if there was any activity deeper in the house. Maybe another chimney entrance would let me catch him off guard.

I pulled out my phone to call Callis. *And say what? Attacked any ghosts today?*

Then, as if in response, the front door slowly opened, bell jingling overhead as if to invite me in.

I dropped my phone back into my pocket and glanced over my shoulder, hoping to find Adele rushing down the street, having opened the door. But there was no one.

I peered into the dark shop and stepped across the threshold. Cold air moved around me like silky pythons, slithering around my neck.

Behind me, the door creaked closed.

"*Sauvez la,*" Julie whispered, her voice no longer strong and defiant but distant and ethereal.

"Julie?"

"*Sauvez la,*" she whispered again, and I saw her near the window, just for a blink before she faded away along with her words. "*Sauvez la . . .*"

"Julie!"

Something about the tone of her voice was off.

She was hurt. I knew it.

The last time I was here, she'd been so strong, so opaque, I'd thought she was human. She'd even knocked me back. Now she could barely speak.

A dim light in the hallway flickered on, drawing my gaze.

"Callis?"

The squeaks of twisting metal responded, then the rush of running water.

"Hello?"

"*He'll never get me,*" Julie said again, slowly brushing my ear, and this time I heard the real message.

He already had.

"Julie, are you okay?" A chill whipped around me, and I followed it, lifting the partition in the counter to pass through, glass crunching underneath my feet. "Are you hurt?"

She blinked in and out down the hallway, her long white dress fluttering, and disappeared into the lit room.

I followed her into the corridor, definitely with the feeling that I was trespassing. Definitely not caring.

I pushed a door open into rolling clouds of steam.

"Julie?"

Waving my hand through the wet air, I turned off the bathroom faucet. "Julie, did Callis touch you? Where is he? I'm going to help you!"

I moved slowly, not wanting to scare her; then I froze when I caught a glimpse of the mirror.

Julie, still blinking in and out, was leaning over the sink, smearing letters on the mirror:

MÉFIEZ-

My pulse accelerated, hammering in my ears. Was this her last-ditch effort to communicate?

VOUS

The French words compounded my anxiety, now thinking about Adele.

DE

English, Julie. English. But as more letters came into view a translation was no longer necessary.

CELELS

"Celestina!" I yelled. "Celestina did this to you?"

MÉFIEZ–VOUS DE CELESTINA

"Oui," she whispered against my ear, shivers jutting down my spine.

What had Callis said before Chatham had walked in? "I'll have Celestina work on her . . . who can resist a nine-year-old, right?"

My fist balled.

How many ghosts has this guy hurt because of me?

"Isaac, sauvez la."

I whipped around as the cold brushed my neck. "Julie, what does that mean?"

The door opened, and she floated into the hallway, blinking in and out, repeating the words.

"Julie?" I yelled, hurrying after her into the shop. "Julie?"

She wasn't there.

What's happening to her?

I flashed my phone on the ground. There was broken glass everywhere. Not just moon mugs—all of the jars of tea were shattered into a smattering of glass and dried herbs and flowers, crystal balls, and Tarot cards. Signs of struggle.

"Sauvez la."

When I looked up, she was standing in the middle of the room, her entire being fluttering just like her dress. "Julie!"

And then she blinked out completely.

"What does it mean, *sauvez la?*"

But when I said the words out loud, I got it, because the French word sounded just like the English: *save.*

She was no longer saying "Protect her." She was saying "Save her."

I thought about the girl's reflection in the broken mirror, and I kicked the leg of a wooden chair.

I'd failed to protect someone else—and now they needed saving.

I pulled out my phone. A message was flashing on the screen:

Adele	**22:51**	Sorry I'm late. On my way back to HQ, now! Need to talk STAT. Callis is up to something.

Thank God, she's at the brothel, but then I read the time stamp, and my pulse raced. *Thirty minutes ago.* If she'd arrived at the brothel and we hadn't been there, wouldn't she have sent more messages trying to find us?

The phone rang. Désirée.

"Did you get Adele's message?" I asked.

"Yeah. I tried calling her, but she didn't pick up. Not that it's totally unusual for her. Did you find Callis?"

"No, just another preyed-upon Royal Street ghost. We need to get the coven together, *now*."

"That's why I'm calling . . . I was starting to get worried, so I did the location spell on Adele, which of course didn't work because of my badass gris-gris. But then I did it on Annabelle, and it showed her at . . . school."

"School, like the Ursuline convent?"

"Yeah . . ."

"Why would she be there this late?"

"I don't know; that's why I'm calling you."

"You go meet Adele at the brothel and see what's up. I'll swing over to the convent and find Annabelle. She better not have any funny ideas."

"Don't worry, she won't be able to undo our spells. The only thing that would happen if she broke the Monvoisin part of the curse is the vamps would get their memories back from that night."

"Still. See you in a few." I went to hang up but then had one last thought. "Dee?"

"Yeah?"

"I thought you made Annabelle a gris-gris too?"

"I did. But I may have left out the one extra ingredient that blocks the locator spell. After ten years of being besties with Annabelle Lee Drake, you know better than to ever trust her one hundred percent."

I hung up and stalked to the door, glass crunching under my feet.

What the hell is going on in this town?

The only thing certain was that a supernatural shitstorm was brewing.

CHAPTER 44

Animarum Praedator

I ran down the dark stairs, trying not to make a sound, as if my footsteps might wake the slumbering vampires in the attic above. I hit the ground floor, wondering whether I should make a detour at Bottom of the Cup on the way to HQ, when a shadowy figure moved across the hall up ahead.

I knew that perfect ponytail.

"Wait!" I called out.

She hesitated, and I could tell she was wondering whether turning to me or running away was the best move.

I flashed my phone toward her. "Annabelle?"

"Adele?" she said, turning around, extra surprise in her voice, a hand on her chest. "You *scared* me." She hurried over and gave me a hug. "Everyone's so worried. What are you doing here?"

"What are *you* doing here?"

"Looking for you, silly. Dee and Isaac are freaking out." She flashed a stream of text messages up on her phone. "I told them I'd run over here and look since I had my car."

"Something's going on," I said. "We need to get back to HQ and make you official; then I'll fill everyone in."

"Definitely! Everyone's waiting for you to re-bind the coven."

I grabbed the front door handle, still not used to using my magic in front of someone other than Dee or Isaac.

"Not that way." She pointed to the back door. "My car's in the student lot."

"Fine. Let's hurry."

I paused as we stepped into the pitch-black courtyard; her hand lightly touched my back to urge me on.

It might have just been the chill in the air, but something felt off. A shadow moved out on the grass. I grabbed her arm. "Annabelle," I whispered, "I don't think we're alone."

"Of course you're not alone, love." *Callis.* Sounding disturbingly creepy in the dark. "We've been waiting for you."

We? "Funnily enough, Callis, you're just the person I wanted to see."

"He is?" Annabelle asked.

"Well then, it's fate who has brought us together."

Fate or Nicco . . .

I lifted my hands out to the sides and quickly folded my fingers flat against my palms. Flames erupted in the two dormant fountains, one on each side of the courtyard.

Callis was standing in the center of the arc of statues, on the grassy patch where our crew had hung out on the first day of school. A circle of unlit candles surrounded the whole patch. He turned to the fountain on the right. "And *that* is precisely why we've been waiting for you."

I don't like this. Not one little bit.

"I'll get you a box of matches for your birthday."

"Oh, it's not just any fire we're interested in. It's your fire."

Again with the "we."

"I just don't understand why *she's* so special," Annabelle said, looking at me.

"That makes two of us." Out of the laundry list of people who had come into my life since the Storm, Callis was officially of the variety I didn't want to be special to. Especially now—the way he was tenderly looking at me creeped me out.

"I don't want to fight, Adele. I have a proposition for you—"

"In a circle of candles behind a convent at night? How *romantic*, but I think you might be a little too old for me."

His arms folded, and a smile crossed his lips, like he was glad I'd figured something out. *But what had I figured out?*

"Age is relative," he said. "You of all people should know that, consorting with vampires."

"When *were* you born, Callis?"

"July twenty-ninth. Leo. It was a dark and stormy night . . ."

"What *year?*"

"Fifteen seventy? Fifteen seventy-five? Give or take a year or two. It starts to blur after the first two centuries."

I gave him a long, hard look. I didn't want to go against a fellow witch, but now that I was physically standing in between him and the attic—between him and my mother—I didn't want to play games either. This was as far as Nicco could get me, and now I was on my own.

Well, almost on my own. I looked at Annabelle, then back to Callis.

"You're older than Nicco, then," I said evenly, laying my first card on the table.

His face seemed to tighten, but he returned my gaze. "So Niccolò is the one you've been protecting? Figures. I wasn't sure, though. Emilio does have that bad-boy thing that all the girls love these days, right?"

"I don't know, Nicco didn't seem like much of an angel when he was whispering threats in your ear at that twisted dinner party."

"And how did Niccolò Medici tell you about that if he's trapped in an attic, slumbering—ah, of course. The dreamscape. *That's* why you think your Spektral power is something as vapid as dream magic. You really should spend less time with the Daures before your magic becomes as soft as theirs."

"A mighty big statement coming from a Fire witch with no Fire—"

"How adorable that you've been dream-twinning with Niccolò. Does Isaac know you're in love with him?"

I didn't so much as blink. "There's nothing to know."

"There's *always* something to know when it comes to the Medici. Especially Niccolò. That vampire has more secrets than the Mafia and the Illuminati combined."

"Sounds to me like you were up to something back then. Emilio said you were after their blood."

"It started with revenge back then, just like it's going to end with revenge now."

"I don't care what it started with; it's not ending with this convent." The medallion shook against Nicco's flannel shirt, and a Tigress I hadn't known lived inside me emerged with a deep-throated growl, scaring away any last hints of the doe-eyed Ingénue.

"Well, Adele, that depends on you. But first it's my turn to ask a question: I know why the Medici are after me . . . Why are they after *you?*"

"Why do you care?"

"Isn't that obvious? Anything, or *anyone*, the Medici would go to such great lengths chasing must be very valuable to them. And anything of value to them—"

"Oh, *so* valuable. A witch with no Spektral powers, as you were so kind to point out, and no magical family, and no grimoire."

He strolled over, only stopping when he was practically toe to toe with me. "But a witch who has budding telekinesis, and who has managed to get into Niccolò Medici's head . . . or his heart. I'm not sure which would take more talent." He paused. "Or which would be scarier."

His hand went to my jaw; I pushed it away.

"You underestimate yourself." He placed a hand on Annabelle's shoulder. "You both do."

When Annabelle didn't shrug him off, I pulled her closer. The way she was smiling at him made me think she didn't understand the level of creepiness we were dealing with here.

"Who are you, Callis? Why are you really after the Medici?"

"I've already told you, Adele. Those self-righteous, lordly pricks burned our grimoire and destroyed my coven—*my family*. They got us excommunicated from the entire witching world! But now, finally, they'll pay for what they did all those centuries ago."

"How are you *so* old?" I asked, thinking about the Count and his possible immortal-witch status.

"Our Spektral power was the only thing that even the Medici couldn't take from us, although I'm sure they thought it drained along with our Elemental magic when they *buried us alive* and left us for dead. It allowed us certain means to maintain longevity—it was the only thing that saved us in the sixteenth century, and it's the only thing that will bring us back to power now."

"Nicco was a toddler in the sixteenth century, and I know Emilio is tough, but a child? Come on."

"Their father wasn't a child. This family feud predates even your precious Niccolò—but enough history; let's move on to the future." The cold glint in his eye vanished, but his smile remained unsettling. "I know you didn't grow up in a magical family, Adele, so maybe you don't understand how the magical universe protects itself. Once a witch is stripped of his or her magical elements, it's permanent. They say it's impossible to get your magic back . . . and yet, we are about to prove them wrong."

I shrank back a little. Something about the way he said "we" made me understand that I was a part of whatever he had planned. *Don't let him intimidate you.*

From the corner of my eye, I glanced at the gate to the parking lot, judging whether we could make a dash for it—not that I'd leave Nicco and my mother unprotected, but Annabelle could get away and go get Isaac and Dee. I looked at her, wondering if she could use some Monvoisin coercion on Callis, or was he still enough of a witch to remain unsusceptible?

She must have had the same idea, because she had that look: the one I always imagined on Cosette right before she went all witchy-badass.

Sexy eyes and a slight smile, and she was looking straight at Callis. So this is what it was coming down to—the Tigress and the Femme Fatale. Me and Annabelle.

My fingers tingled with anticipation, ready to ignite if things went south.

"A witch's power is strongest within its coven," he said, "but in order to bind a coven, you must possess a grimoire, and in order to invoke the magic of the grimoire, you must have your Elemental powers. Do you see the conundrum? The Medici have taken all of those things from me, but tonight I'm getting them back." He looked at Annabelle and then to me. "And if the Medici are after you for the reason I suspect, then I may be getting back even more."

"Care to enlighten me as to what the hell you are talking about?"

"Care to join my coven?"

All I could do was laugh, because the notion was so ridiculous.

He smiled wider and walked back to his spot in the center of the circle. "If you stand with us, I'll tell you everything you want to know— more than you could even imagine about magic, about witches, and how we're going to become the most powerful coven in the world. You'll learn everything. Coven members don't have secrets."

"I've gotten pretty far excavating secrets on my own."

"I'll *bet* you have, darling. It's one of the reasons I know we're meant to be together—magically speaking, that is. But let's not get ahead of ourselves. First the grimoire."

"I don't have a grimoire, Callis, I'm no use to you!"

"I wasn't talking to you."

Annabelle turned to me, beaming. "*Me.* He was talking to me." She opened her enormous Hermès bag and pulled out a heavy book.

The brothel ledger?

"What the . . . ?" My fingers balled as the sparks flicked from my palms. She'd taken it from the house. I knew she was there this afternoon. I *knew* something was missing.

Callis extended his hands. "You did have a grimoire, Adele. You were just too shortsighted to realize how an Aether's grimoire hides itself."

Annabelle walked over to him with the book.

"*Annabelle!* What are you doing?" I hurried after her, but she set the book down in his palms and placed her hands over it. "Don't let him touch that if it's really your grimoire! He's not who he says he is."

"Focus," he told her. "Just like we practiced."

Practiced?

She closed her eyes, and her lips began to flutter, whispering words I couldn't hear.

"Annabelle! What are you doing? Stop!"

The brothel-ledger illusion slipped away, revealing a book of an entirely different sort. The cover was still the same baby-blue leather, but it looked older and more worn, and hardly able to lie flat, because the pages were stuffed with so many extra things: papers, dried flowers, feathers.

Annabelle opened her eyes and looked down, and the smile that appeared on her face was the most genuine thing ever worn by Annabelle Lee Drake—the ecstatic bliss of a cult member who's found her new home.

She flung her arms around Callis's neck, and he hugged her back, still holding her grimoire with one hand and gently petting the back of her head with the other.

I just stood there like a broken toy, mute and in shock.

When she finally released him, he reached up to stroke her cheek, and I swore for a second he was going to kiss her. "See," he said. "I told you, you underestimate yourself."

And then he did kiss her, on the forehead, with a look that might have meant there was more to come.

"Annabelle," I said in a low voice, "get away from him!"

She looked back at me, and the corner of her mouth crooked, letting me know that she wasn't some brainwashed child to pity. She'd known exactly what she was doing the entire time.

She played me.

She played all of us.

"We just needed my family's grimoire to bind our coven, but I told Callis I could get the Medici's location out of you too. You didn't even make me work for it, Adele. You just let me right in. Or maybe it was your boyfriend who was so keen to have me?" She battered her eyelashes my way.

More sparks shot from my fingers; this time I didn't bother balling my hands.

His arms slid around her waist, and he lowered his head next to hers, neither of their eyes leaving me. "You did very good, darling," he said to her.

I couldn't tell if he wanted to kiss her neck or slice her throat.

A stocky man approached from one of the side buildings. He had dark hair tied back in a long ponytail. "Callis, this is a bad idea. We don't need Aether magic in the coven. We'll find another way."

Annabelle's sly smile turned stern. She broke away from Callis and took a couple steps toward him. "If it weren't for this Aether witch, you wouldn't be about to get your *magic back*, because you wouldn't have a grimoire to bind your coven. And you still wouldn't know where your enemy is!"

"Annabelle, are you *insane*?" I shouted. "You can't join his coven."

"I can join yours; I can join his. Nothing's changed, Adele. I'm just the same popular girl I've always been."

"You have something he needs—that's it. You can't trust him! Let's get out of here, now. We can forget this ever happened." *As if.*

"Let me see. I could go with you to join a mixed-magic high school coven with two girls who don't even have their Maleficiums, or I could join the ranks of one of the most powerful covens in the history of witchcraft. *Hmm.* Tough choice."

"Most powerful? Callis doesn't have enough Elemental magic to light a candle; how is he going to bind a coven?"

She walked right up to me and got in my face. "You're right." She grabbed my arm and jerked me to her side, gripping me so fiercely it sent chills up my spine. "We do need more Fire magic."

Fear washed over me as the severity of whatever I'd gotten myself into came crashing down. This time I didn't have Nicco at my side, and I didn't have potion-powered witches at my back, weakening my enemies with magic and casting protection spells. I ripped my arm away, Annabelle's fingernails scraping into my skin.

"Come, now, Annabelle, don't hurt her," Callis said, walking closer.

My palms lit up. "You can't force me to join your coven; that's not how it works." I looked left and right in search of some magical assistance.

He smiled. "You won't find any metal back here, Adele. I've made sure of it."

"I hope you removed it all from a three-block radius," I spat, vowing to learn how to fight sans magic, starting tomorrow.

He stopped right in front of me. "What have they done to you, love? Even at such a young age, you are clearly an extraordinary witch. No doubt descended from one of the greats. I can see that—I can see all of your potential, and I can help you realize it. Yet you choose the side of those who think of you as nothing but a meal? The side of the monsters. The side you know has been chasing your family through the centuries, just like they've been chasing me. Niccolò Medici is nothing more than a predator that needs to be taken down. He's twisted your head. I promise, when he gets what he's after, you will be his reward. Every last drop of your blood will be his reward."

He brushed the loose hair from my face; I swatted his hand away again and looked him straight in the eye. "I'm not joining your coven, and I'm not betraying Nicco."

"Really? Even though he probably already has your death planned?"

In that moment, it suddenly became harder to ignore the fantasies I'd seen inside Nicco's head. *How he kissed me.*

"I bet he knows exactly how he's going to take you," Callis continued.

How he bit me.

"I bet he's counting the seconds down in his sleep as we speak."

How he drained me until my pulse slowed to nothingness.

"They are monsters, Adele. But we are Fire witches. We belong together, and if you'll let me, I can protect you from him."

"I don't need protection from him," I snapped.

I need to protect him.

And I need my coven.

Three on one was no good. On complete impulse, I pushed Callis away and made a run for it.

But he was faster, and as the fireballs rose out of my palms, his arm was already around my middle, his ring-clad fingers digging into my ribs as he lifted me into the air. I swung all of my weight against him, and we both fell back, hitting the ground. I let go of the magic and elbowed him in the ribs, *hard*. He grunted, releasing me. I scrambled to my feet, but he did too, right behind me.

A black blur up ahead ran directly at me, sprang over my shoulder, and collided with him. I whipped around as he fell backward, roaring, the hissing cat clawing at him.

"Onyx, no!" I screamed, but there was no cat.

Callis was wrestling with a guy in a U of A baseball cap.

The guy slammed Callis down on the ground. "Do you know how long I've been waiting for this?" His baseball cap fell off his close-shaved head.

"Codi!"

"Just get out of here, Adele!"

"You're a—? I *knew* it!"

As I stepped toward them, people descended all around us.

Callis's coven members?

"I'm not joining you . . ." My voice deepened, practically a snarl as I stumbled back.

Two of them grabbed my arms and hoisted me up. I jerked and twisted, keeping one eye on Codi. Another four of them pinned him to the ground. Instead of just restraining him, the guy with the long ponytail kicked him hard with a steel-toed boot.

A bone cracked so loudly, even Annabelle turned away from the sound.

"Nooooo!" I screamed, trying to yank myself out of their grip, my legs kicking up in the air, but they only held me tighter.

Flames erupted from my palms, but then something heavy smashed the back of my head. I fell to the ground, everything going dark.

"Adele . . ."

Cold. Stiff. Marble.

"Adele . . ."

My eyes peeked open. Little fireballs buzzed around my head with panicked energy.

"Adele!"

The sound of my name echoed through my brain, but cradled my attention. My head fell to the right, toward the familiar voice. Through the slits of my eyelids, I saw Codi—and suddenly I was fully conscious. I tried to move to him but couldn't. My arms were bound from behind. I was tied to one of the white marble statues. The convent courtyard.

Callis.

"You're alive," Codi said, his head leaned back against the marble nun in relief. He was tied to the statue next to me. "Are you okay?"

"How did you know I was here?" I jerked my wrists, but the more I struggled, the more the statue dug into my back.

"I didn't. I've been tracking Callis ever since he started at the shop, but he threw me off tonight. My guess is it had something to do with *that.*" He nodded toward the sky.

A glimmering dome twinkled over the entire property, just like the one at the brothel.

"Annabelle," I said through gritted teeth.

It could only mean that whatever they were up to, they wanted to be completely unseen and unheard. I jerked harder against my restraints, the plastic cord digging into my wrists, ripping my skin with every move.

"I've been watching him whenever he was around you, Adele, I swear. I never left you alone with him. We were always there—me or Julie. I'm sorry, Adele!"

Onyx. "How long have you known about—?"

"Whatever they're about to do, Adele, you have to resist, okay?"

"Codi, can't you just turn? Go get help! Go get Isaac and Dee. Or Chatham. Anyone! Just get out of here!"

"I'm not leaving you!"

"Go!"

"I-I-I can't." His eyes dropped down.

Mine followed. "Codi! Your leg!"

His pant leg was soaked through with dark liquid, and where the denim was ripped, white bone, pink with blood, protruded from his skin. I gagged.

"Adele! Don't look at it! Look at me."

Only then did I notice how pale he was. Sweat dripped from his chin.

"Calliiiiiiiiiiiiiiiis!" I screamed, and in a whoosh all of the candles ignited all around us.

His circle.

And then all of his people were stepping out of the darkness in long, dark, hooded robes.

His coven.

Callis emerged into the candlelight.

"Callis!" I half screamed, half pleaded. "Codi needs to go to the hospital!"

"Well then, let's get to it." He took his spot at the head of the circle. "The sooner we're finished, the sooner he can receive medical attention."

They're binding their circle. They have the grimoire, and now they have . . . me.

"That is," Callis added, "if he survives."

As his witches took formation around us—the brute on his left and Annabelle on his right—the supernatural energy ripped through my bloodstream.

"Annabelle! Codi needs an emergency room, now!"

She didn't so much as turn my way. *I know she can hear me.* "Annabelle!" I tried to bring a flame into my hand to burn off the restraints, but my palms were bound against each other.

Callis's voice was steady but aggressive. "Adele, this is your last invitation to rescind your coven and join mine."

"No. Chance. In. Hell!" I screamed, pulling against the ropes until I felt the bones in my wrists sliding apart. I fell back hard against the stone.

Concentrate, Adele. Concentrate.

I felt around for metal, but nothing called me. Nothing tingled. Well, not *nothing*.

"Then you leave us no choice but to take what we need."

His voice lowered, and his coven moved closer. Their hands clasped one by one. Annabelle released her grimoire into the air—it floated open in front of them—and she took his hand.

Together the two of them began to chant. The pages of the book fluttered in a swirl of wind; I desperately looked around for Isaac, my hopes rising, but it was just Mother Nature. The rest of the coven joined on the third verse.

"Adele, you have to resist!" Codi said, turning to me.

"Resist wh—?"

My own scream interrupted my question as I slammed back against the statue, banging my head. I could feel the blood trickling down the back of my neck.

Monstrous flames erupted all around the yard.

"He's siphoning your Elemental power!" Codi yelled over the chanting. "He's taking your Fire!" His head whipped to Callis, and I felt something cool pelt my cheeks. Water.

Water witch.

Codi had activated the sprinkler system.

Callis's eyes popped open, and his arm flung toward me.

I screamed again. It felt like my insides were being slowly drawn out, like Callis's coven was extracting my magic out with a giant magnet in the same way I drew metal objects toward me.

I tried to pull the magic back inside me, to hug it tightly and put up a mental wall, but it slipped through my fingertips, and out of my pores, and through every strand of my hair, my screams never ceasing.

There were too many in his coven; the tugging came from all sides.

The chanting became louder, and Codi continued to yell to me. My eyes smashed closed as the tugging sensations turned to slicing.

"Stop it!" I screamed. "Stop!"

Chanting and smoke. The sounds of kindling crackling and branches snapping became louder.

I forced my eyes open. All of the citrus trees around the convent, all of the bushes and hedges, were on fire. The shadows of firelight flickered against Callis's face—his smile of satisfaction.

Sweat dripped from my chin, and tears poured down my cheeks.

They're going to burn it all down. They're going to torch the convent—and everyone in it—using my Elemental magic. I'm burning them down.

I'm going to kill my mother. I'm going to kill Nicco.

And they'll have their coven bound. All in one fell swoop.

More sweat poured from my brow as I felt for the fire and pushed against it, but it was like trying to push a sand dune—the more I pushed, the more it caved in around us. Smothering us.

My chest tightened as the smoke filled my lungs.

"Adele, we'll get through this. I've got you!"

High above, the metal in the attic shutters called to me. Adeline's necklace bounced against my chest.

"I can't break the spell on my own," I muttered to her, my voice so raspy I was unable to hear my own words. *What did your father do, Adeline, to get us into this mess?*

"Adele, do not let him win! Fight back!"

Smoke billowed around us; I could hardly breathe.

What if I'm too late? What if I have no more magic left?

I forced myself to concentrate. I pictured them all: Lisette and Martine gently swaying from the ceiling. Martine humming a French lullaby in her sleep. Gabe, shackled and dreaming about undressing some Portuguese princess who had broken his heart. My mother, curled into Emilio's arms.

I'm not going to burn you alive, Mom!

And Nicco.

I pictured Nicco most clearly. Alone. Cold. Trapped. Slumbering inside *la cassette* and tormenting himself even in his sleep.

"Wake up, Nicco." Tears dripped as I said the words out loud. *"Wake up."*

A glow came from within his chest. Icy blue. I reached out for it, repeating the words of the slumbering spell as I mentally pulled. The spell wouldn't completely break without Dee and Isaac, but if the Medici wanted to live, they were going to have to fight through what was left of it and wake up.

Just as with the root, I mentally pulled on the spell. *It's just positive space that needs to be moved to a different point of negative space in the universe.*

Smoke continued to fill my lungs, but I focused and kept pulling.

I trust you, Nicco. I trust you.

"I trust you!"

Through the chanting and the screaming, a rooster's crow echoed out of the convent. Hopefully it was enough to wake them.

I twisted my hands and pulled at the ropes with my mind, trying to move them too. I tugged, desperately, but without any effect. With all of the tugging and pulling, I felt something else. Something metal.

Not just one thing—a thousand things pulsing toward me.

Suddenly I could sense every single nail in the attic shutters. I felt the stake turn slightly, wanting to come to me, and the locks on the attic door rippled—the locks my hands had brushed against so many times. All those times I'd wanted to open them.

Now I finally would.

I would not let Callis kill my mother.

Or Nicco.

You were wrong, Callis, you overconfident piece of shit. You didn't remove every piece of metal.

I mentally raised my consciousness to envelop the entire convent grounds and then ripped it back to me, bringing everything metal back with it.

The enchanted stakes shot down from the shutters like missiles, and a giant explosion boomed. Glass rained down on us.

And then everything went dark. No more fire. No more light.

I felt nothing.

Around me screams rose through the smoke and through the haze. The church bells rang, just like the first time I'd opened the attic, but now in the chaos, they reminded me of the night in the bell tower. Nicco had rung them for me that night, and now I rang them for him.

My magic was gone.

It was all I felt. Heaviness. Lifelessness.

In my delirium I smelled leather and soap as one tiny moment of relief came: one slice at my restraints and my wrists were free. I dropped to the ground. My cheek hit the wet, charred grass; I couldn't command myself to move farther away.

Through the smoke and screams, a blur of vampires tore through the yard—a blur of witches' throats being ripped open, but even that made me feel nothing.

His witches took my magic.

Then, through a momentary parting in the smoke, I saw Codi still tied to the statue next to me, his head hanging down limply.

No.

"Codi!" I shrieked.

In one final surge of adrenaline, I threw myself up and staggered over to him. I didn't know if they were my screams or the screams of others as I popped off what remained of the plastic ropes around his wrists, trying not to look where the plastic had melted into skin. "Codi! Hang on! I'm going to get you out of here!"

One last pop and he dropped to the ground, howling. "My leg!"

Thank God he's alive.

I fell next to him and wriggled myself under his arm. "All right, you're going to have to work with me here."

He nodded, squeezing my shoulder, and I heaved him up, both of us yelling.

Weren't we just eight years old? When did he turn into this heavy man?

Step by step, I dragged him off through the hazy ash as the screaming and fighting echoed behind us like a distant dream. Coughing, I directed us toward the convent door, praying that we weren't leaving a trail of blood behind. I knew I'd be the one who'd have to fend off anyone or anything that came our way.

I could feel Codi fading, more of his weight pressing down on me—with each step my knees shook harder, wanting to give in. "Come on, Codi, just a little farther."

Using my shoulder, he pulled himself up. I grunted, absorbing the shift in weight, and fought through each step forward, not letting myself buckle underneath him as we went down the dark hallway. Spots appeared around us as I dragged him past my history classroom. Greens. Pinks. Blues.

In the silence, I heard the ringing in my ears.

There was nothing left to do but hide. I threw us against the nearest door, pushing it open with my shoulder and letting it swing wide.

The dim, stone-floored room felt cave-like. It was mostly empty, other than a crucifix on the wall and a kneeling bench underneath it. The shattered window lay in pieces over the stone floor. With one last heave, I dragged Codi across the room to the corner, crumbling underneath his body weight, both of us sinking to the floor. I propped him against the wall.

"I'm going for help," I said, despite knowing I'd never make it anywhere, but I couldn't do nothing. *Just one foot in front of the other, Adele.*

And that worked for three steps.

My right knee hit the ground, and then my wrists, and my face hit the floor, and I was lying flat, cheek against the cool stone, using all remaining energy just to stay conscious.

I should have shut the door, I thought as everything began to blur. I stared out into the hallway. The alcove in the corridor wall encased a statue of Mary holding a baby with a crown and scepter, all blinged out in gold. I loved that gold. The metal.

I don't know why, but I loved that they were looking down on me now.

I wondered if my mother was here, somewhere, or if she'd run off into the night.

Had Nicco?

I hoped not.

I hope he's killing Callis.

If he wasn't, and if I ever got off this floor, I would kill him myself.

I now understood how you could chase someone through the centuries.

CHAPTER 45

Save Jade

I'd never flown so fast.

I zoomed down the street, not caring that I was pushing my tiny bones too hard. I had the perfect vantage for things I'd *never* wanted to see: smoke rising from the back of the convent, and supernatural energy radiating from the building like an A-bomb. The scent of fire wafted through the wind.

I flapped harder, tearing through the overwhelming feeling that I was too late . . . though for what I had no idea, other than that I was absolutely certain Adele was not at the brothel. Suddenly it was Halloween night all over again—Adele breaking away from the plan. Breaking away from the coven.

I should have gone to her house before Dee's. Before the tearoom. I should have found her first.

Up ahead, shimmering magic arced over the Ursuline property. It couldn't be the protection spell, or I'd have seen it before. This was something else. It glimmered more like . . . an invisibility shield.

Annabelle. Caws tore from my throat as I soared higher.

I swooped over the concrete wall, hearing little *tinks*, like metal raindrops hitting the bricked ground. They grew louder as I flew over the maze of hedges, preparing for a roof landing.

Then everything exploded in a deafening *boom*.

The shutters slammed open against the stone walls, and glass blasted from the window frames.

I'd imagined this scenario so many times over the last few months. Imagined how mad I'd be when it happened—an all-consuming, blinding anger. But it wasn't at all how I felt now. Instead I was filled with an all-consuming, blinding fear.

Not of the vampires. A fear that Adele was dead.

I fought the current, but then a magnificent wave of energy shot out, throwing me backward.

The church bells clanged as I tumbled through the air. I crashed into a magnolia tree, struck two heavy branches, then thumped onto the ground.

I hopped up onto my claws with the intention to take off, but instead I staggered, wooziness gripping me as I looked up at the open attic. There were only two ways Adeline's spell could have broken. The first was that Adele had broken it on purpose . . .

The second was that she'd been killed.

As everything went black, for the first time ever I hoped Adele opened the attic.

I peeked my eyes open and instantly fluttered up to my talons, outstretching my wings as I tried to find my balance. The church bells were no longer ringing. *How long was I out?*

Wind rustled through the leaves, and the lingering silence was far too definitive for my liking. Blood dripped from a nearby hedge, not far from a crumpled body of a guy my age.

Adele.

I soared up to the attic and shot straight through a window, high into the rafters, anticipating starving vamps. No one lurked below in the dark room, but the floor was covered in scattered objects: chains, broken statues, and stacks of long wooden boxes, several of them smashed. *The casquette girls.*

Something about the stillness of the air told me the signs of struggle weren't fresh. This was what remained of Adele's fight Halloween night.

No vampires, no blood. No Adele.

The attic's clear.

I swooped down and out the door, clearing the room where we'd slept on the blankets, the storage room, and the hallway, slowing only when I got to the door at the stairs.

The padlock was blown to bits on the floor, but that's not what concerned me. A girl's whimpering floated up from down below.

I hesitated, wondering if I should take human form, to be more prepared to fight, but then I pumped my wings, tipped to the side, and soared around the curve of the staircase toward the whimpers. The source was on the second landing. I stopped heavily on the stairway bannister above, scrabbling to hold my perch.

His blond hair was so disheveled, and so stained red, he was almost unrecognizable from his usual movie-star-looking self.

Gabe paused without detaching his mouth from the woman's throat and peered up to me like a wild animal deciding whether the next hunt was worth giving up the current catch. The woman's hair was too light to be Adele's. My chest nearly exploded with relief.

Even with his jaw clamped, he still managed to smile, and I fought the instinct to dive into him and peck out his eyes. He started drinking again all while holding the stare, daring me to turn, daring me to try to take him.

She whimpered again, and I knew I should drop down and help her. There was another body behind him. A guy—dead. He'd kill this woman too if I didn't do something. I thought about the stake strapped to my ankle.

Then I imagined Adele lying on another staircase with one of his brothers attached to her neck.

I took off again, beating my wings to pick up speed.

And that woman would die because of it.

I took the next curve sharply to gain momentum. At the bottom of the stairs, I'd have to decide—a right turn down the hallway toward the classrooms, or stay straight and go out the back door into the gardens. But when I got to the bottom, a clicking sound, like nails against the floor, drew my attention. Then two sharp, assertive barks.

Stormy?

Her yelps went wild when she saw me, and she darted down the hall to the left—toward a trace of cold—the sensation of death rippled through my feathers, pulling me, needing me. *No. No.* I zoomed left and soared out into the dark hallway.

Does she know where Adele is?

One hallway led to another that was tunnel-like. Stormy gained speed, and I matched her. We ducked through a doorway into a cavernous space, where her barks bounced hard off the marble floors. We'd entered the church from a side entrance near the altar. *Where is Adele?* I flew straight up, pumping my wings, and circled high above, avoiding the chains that hung from the gold-painted ceiling suspending the light fixtures.

Observe.

I swooped long. The alcove behind the altar was painted with clouds carrying horn-blowing angels through a bright-blue sky. The walls glittered gold with gilded crucifixes and other Catholic paraphernalia. On the far opposite end was the street entrance, over which was a mezzanine choir loft—it was dark and empty except for the huge pipe organ. On the long walls in between, moonlight glowed through tall stained-glass windows onto statues of saints.

Stormy's barks continued to echo up to the ceiling along with voices . . . tiny voices, and faint clapping. Shining through an enormous circular stained-glass window above the choir loft, a moonbeam spotlight illuminated two little girls who were sitting on the marble floor in the center aisle. *What the hell are kids doing here?* The girls were slapping their hands together in a singsong game. Their voices drifted up to me.

See, see my playmate,
Come out and play with me

I swooped lower, getting a better look at the girl leading the song, and answered my own question. Celestina. Her black curls spilled down her baby-blue dress all the way to the floor, and the words floated sweetly out of her thin lips, to a smaller girl in a yellow dress who giggled with delight as they slapped their hands in time with the rhyme.

There was something about her giggle that made me circle to see her face. I nearly lost bird form midflap.

Jade.

It was as if she'd stepped out of my dreams—a smaller version of Rosalyn, her two tiny puffs of hair tied up with yellow ribbons that matched her dress. She appeared no less real than Celestina.

Stormy circled them, eyes on Celestina, a low growl grumbling from her throat.

Adapt.

I swooped down and dropped to my feet a few yards away, stunned.

It's not Jade, Isaac. Jade is dead.

The little girl looked at me, giggling, and then repeated the words back to Celestina:

And we'll be jolly friends
Forever evermore

I stepped closer. "She's not your friend, Jade."

"Hi, Isaac," Celestina said, looking up at me, her blue eyes as piercing and bright as her voice. "Do you want to play too? I can teach you. We can all play." Nothing in her tone indicated anything other than sweetness and purity. Nothing was mocking. Nothing sinister. Yet chills pricked up my spine.

They began slapping their hands together again.

I had an overwhelming urge to get both of them out of there, away from the vampires and whatever the hell else might be lurking in this place. "What are you doing, Celestina?" I asked, unable to keep my eyes off Jade.

The last time I'd seen her, I was handing her limp, waterlogged body off to a marine. I reached out and touched her shoulder, my hand pressing into her skin and bone.

Again, she turned to me and giggled.

"This can't be real. Jade is dead."

"Of course Jade is dead, silly! But she's still my friend. Callis says I can't drink her. He'll be mad if I do. He said I had to wait until you got here." Celestina gazed at me. "Are you going to drink her?"

Drink her? What the fuck?

"Are you going to share?" she asked. "Sharing is nice. I love you, Isaac."

"Y-you do?"

"My brother says you're our hero. We were starving before we met you because spirits are hard to find, but you can see all the ghosts, and you bring us straight to them. Are we going to drink her now?"

"*No.* No one is going to drink Jade."

Her sweet little doll face morphed into the scowl of a rabid animal. "I'm *hungry!*" she screamed, and then let out a shriek that made me take a couple steps back.

Footsteps pounded closer from the back hallway. "Celestina!" Callis yelled frantically, bursting in from the doorway near the altar.

His worry turned to a smile when he saw me. "Very good job, Stina. You've found Isaac."

"Now can I have dinner?"

"Not yet, darling, but soon."

She squealed with delight, stood up, and skipped in a circle around Jade, singing the song again.

> *My dollies have the flu.*
> *Boo hoo boo hoo*

Stormy crouched low to the ground, snarling.

In between singing the phrases, Celestina took deep breaths—unnaturally deep breaths.

Jade began to flicker away, her head pulling toward Celestina like she was being plunged.

"No!" I yelled, throwing my hand toward them. A gust of wind lifted Jade up and carried her across the room and into the arms of a statue high on a pedestal—a woman holding a book and a skull.

"No!" Celestina screamed, chasing after her, with Stormy nipping at her heels.

Jade wrapped her arms around the statue's purple-robed shoulders and stared back at us, looking both scared and delighted. Celestina reached the statue and jumped up trying to grab Jade's feet, but Jade climbed higher and sat on the statue's shoulders.

I looked back to Callis, who was now sitting on the long altar table, keenly watching me.

"It's fascinating," he said. "Celestina can see Jade, but no other spirits. It must be some kind of child connection. If I could only get it to extend to full-grown ghosts, I wouldn't need you."

"What the hell does she mean *drink Jade*?"

"She's a growing witchling, Isaac; she needs sustenance."

My gaze flicked back and forth between him and the girls. "What did you do to Julie? And Alessandro?"

"We did nothing more than what's natural for witches with the right Spektral powers—well, supernatural, if you will." He smiled at his own joke.

"There's nothing natural about witches drinking ghosts. It's *subnatural.*"

He leaned forward, gripping the table. "You can choose to see it that way, or you could just call it evolution. The natural pecking order. Ghosts are food for the Animarum Praedators."

I charged the altar, ready to knock the smug smile from his face. "You sound just like one of *them.* The vampires! No regard for life!"

"We live off ghosts! Ghosts are *not living.*"

"They have souls!"

"*Pfft.* Witches of this generation are *so* sensitive. I don't know who's worse, you or Adele. Ghosts are dead, and vampires are monsters!"

"Where is Adele?" I yelled, grabbing him at the collar. I twisted and threw him down the altar steps.

"Have you already given up on Jade's soul?" he said, smiling and propping himself up. "That's not very heroic of you." He laughed, his gaze moving over my shoulder.

I quickly looked back. Celestina was climbing the statue as if it were a tree.

My boot went to his chest, slamming him back down, and with my right hand, I directed a stream of air, pinning him to the floor.

"*Air witch,*" he said. "I've always wanted Air powers. The whole flying thing."

As he struggled to get out from under the current of wind, rambling about my powers, I concentrated on the street outside: the trees rustling, and the flag blowing in the breeze. I yanked my free hand, and an enormous gust of wind slammed open the church doors as I pulled it in. My arm whipped to the statue, and the air ripped the ceramic skull from the saint's hand and shot it straight into my palm.

I let that little girl die once already—I would not let this deranged witch drink her ghost and turn her soul into a parasite. I bobbed the skull in my palm a couple times, immediately grabbing Stormy's attention. It wasn't a tennis ball, but it would have to do.

With one swoop of air, I brought Jade to the ground in the center aisle and hurled the ceramic skull past her out the door. Stormy tore after it, and Jade ran after her furry friend, and they both blinked out before they crossed the threshold. Back to the spirit world? The Ninth Ward? I didn't know, but anywhere was better than here for a ghost currently.

Enraged, Celestina knocked over a collections box. I dragged Callis to his feet and shoved him up against the wall. "I hope you have backup dinner plans."

"I'm curious, Isaac," he said, his tone still light considering how tight I was holding him. "How do *you* think those vampires got free? Did Adele's death break the curse, or did she open the attic for her beloved Niccolò? If she's alive, where do you think they are now? Run off together under the stars?"

My fist smashed into his mouth so hard I lost my grip and staggered back a couple steps.

His teeth lined with blood as he adjusted his jaw and spat on the floor. "And that's why you should join my coven—to fight with me against them. I know your hatred for Niccolò Medici runs as deep as mine. I made a very sensible offer to Adele, but she just doesn't seem to understand that witches and vampires *don't mix.*"

I grabbed him again and shook him hard. "You're not *drinking* Jade, and you're not taking Adele."

"Too late." A flame rose out of his palm. Celestina's tantrum stopped at the sight of the fire, and all went silent as I stared at the flame. "I already took her magic."

I dropped him to the floor, startled by the sight of his Fire. *Her Fire.* "If you hurt her . . ."

The flame extinguished. "Again, Callis! Again!" Celestina yelled, clapping.

He took his time standing up, brushing off his clothes, lamenting a torn sleeve. I knew he was purposefully trying to set me off.

"Where is she?" I said through gritted teeth. "You got what you wanted: the Medici!"

He carefully rolled the cuff of his shirt. He had about five more seconds before I pounded him. "Screw this." I turned to leave. I was wasting seconds that for all I knew were precious.

"And now I want something else," he said, his voice steady. "I've recently gotten into collecting old books, and I hear you have a rather rare one from the Norwood family collection. One of the occult variety."

"You will never get anything of my family's." I turned back, swinging, but this time his knee launched into my stomach. I stumbled back, breathless.

"Then I guess we're going to have to do this the hard way, Isaac."

His hand flung out, like when Adele was throwing a fireball, but instead of unleashing fire, he yanked his hand back again—and I felt a tug at my chest. I tried to back away, but it was like an invisible fist was clenching my insides.

"I told you, I always wanted Air power."

The invisible fist clinched tighter. He wasn't throwing magic.

He was pulling my Air.

Celestina squealed, skipping up the center aisle as the siphon dragged me a step forward. I clutched at my chest, grinding my heels into the marble floor. "There is no chance in *hell* you are taking my magic, Callis."

"And how are you going to stop me?"

Without thinking, my hand shot toward Celestina. She erupted with giggles as a twist of wind took her up through the dark shadows to the cavernous ceiling.

Callis kept tugging at my chest, pulling away my magic.

"If you take my power," I yelled over the wind, "your sister drops to her death. She may be an Animarum Praedator, but she's still made of blood and bone like the rest of us!"

Fear flicked in his eyes before he managed to play it cool.

"Where the hell is Adele!"

"Adele's a traitor!" Celestina yelled from the moonlit twister. "She helped the witch slayers! She should be burned!"

I turned back to Callis. "Keep siphoning if you want to see your sister splattered all over the marble floor!"

"You'll never do it! You're too much of a hero to kill a little girl, or to kill anything!"

A loud crash caused us both to turn—a woman's limp body spilled over the balcony from the choir loft, a freestanding candle rack impaling her as she smashed onto the marble floor.

"But *I'm not*," Emilio said. He leaped off the balcony and landed next to the corpse, crouched over like an animal, fingertips to the ground. The stained-glass moonlight speckled across his face like a kaleidoscope. His jaw was covered in blood.

He was there and then he wasn't.

In a blink, he pummeled into me, sending me crashing into the gilded tabernacle. Chalices of communion wafers, a cross, and a Bible fell on top of me.

"Stina!" Callis screamed as his sister plummeted.

Knocking off the Catholic props, I flung up another gust to catch her. She shot back up and into the choir loft.

Her eruption of giggles echoed down to us. "Again! Again!"

Emilio looked to me and then Callis, licking his lips. "It's like Christmas and my birthday in one."

I scrambled to my feet as he stalked straight to me. I'd fantasized about the day Callis and I would take Emilio down together as fellow witches, but instead, just as Emilio neared—a killer's glint shining in his eyes—I yanked a gust of wind and jerked Callis in front of me. Blood sprayed across my face as Emilio tore savagely into his neck instead of mine.

Fireballs rose from Callis's palms, and he slapped them into both sides of Emilio's face. Emilio's eyes tightened with pain, and his throat filled with grunts as his skin singed, but his jaw only clamped down harder on Callis's neck, blood oozing from his lips.

Psycho.

Celestina's shrieks echoed throughout the church, and she spewed words at Emilio that even I wouldn't utter as she ran down the metal spiral stairs.

As Emilio sucked Callis's life away, his glare told me that I better start running. I backed away, not wanting to take bird form so close to Emilio that he could snatch me.

"Isaac," Callis choked. "Help me, witch."

"Help yourself," I spat. "It's just the natural pecking order, right? The food chain."

Through the cacophony of Emilio's grunts, Celestina's shrieks, and Callis's dying words, a girl's screams sliced through the musty air. Adele.

Dominate.

I tore back through the hallway and into the convent toward her voice, arms pumping.

Hold on. I'm coming. Hold on.

CHAPTER 46

Ma mère

The walls rumbled, like cyclopses were stomping around the building, but that was all I could feel. Darkness and cyclops footsteps and the cool stone floor against my cheek. I couldn't move.

Chaos hummed in the distance, echoing down the halls, through the window from the gardens—from everywhere.

I wondered if my phone was in my pocket. As I forced my eyes open, they felt unnaturally heavy, but then a glimpse of feet in the hallway made them pop open: someone walking past the doorway paused in the moonbeam that cut across the dungeon-like room. I knew from the Burberry print on the shoes that the feet belonged to Annabelle.

My heart rate accelerated against the stone floor.

Get up, Adele! If she finds you like this, you're toast. I forced myself onto my elbow, but the small motion spun my head like a drunken ride on the Tilt-A-Whirl; I collapsed back down, and I lay there, paralyzed with fear that she'd heard me stir.

Would Annabelle really try to kill me?

Another girl stepped into view, mumbling in French—long, flowing waves of shimmering white-blond hair. Lisette.

Shit. My heart pounded harder. *Lisette definitely would.*

"*Tu est Annabelle?*" she asked her great-something-grandniece.

"*Oui.*"

Hearing the fear in Annabelle's voice made my pulse flick, though I wasn't sure whether it was out of fear for her, or rather a hint of glee. A part of me hoped she survived all of this just so I could take her down myself.

Lisette's bloodstained hand moved to Annabelle's face, touching her as if to confirm she was real and not an apparition. Annabelle's voice softened and I couldn't hear whatever she said over the ringing in my ears, but Lisette laughed.

"You're going to have to try much harder than that to control me, *ma fifille.*" Her hand slid down Annabelle's throat. "You're not touching my heart. Not even close."

The muscles in Lisette's arm went taut, and she lifted Annabelle in the air until the tips of her toes barely touched the floor.

Lisette must have been out-of-her-mind starving if she'd really bite Cosette's descendant—her own family's magical heir.

Get up, Adele, do something. You have to help her. No one deserved to have their life sucked out of them. *Besides, it's your fault the curse was broken in the first place.* But I couldn't even feel my fingers, much less get magic to rise out of them. I simply lay there on the floor, listening to Annabelle Lee Drake begging her own vampire-witch ancestor to spare her life.

Her pathetic life.

Maybe you should have joined your mixed-magic ancestral coven, Annabelle, instead of turning your back on us?

She hadn't just turned her back on us; she'd served us up on a silver platter to the first witch who came calling with empty promises. Maybe I didn't care if she died at the hand of a vampire.

But then Lisette set her back on the floor, and Annabelle pulled her into a tight hug, whispering something about "helping our family." Keeping hold of Lisette's hand, Annabelle turned away and screamed.

Seconds later a new set of footprints thunked down the hallway. "Annabelle?" a man's voice echoed. "Where are you?"

"In the hallway! Philippe! Hurry!"

So long, Philippe. Right into the spider's web.

And just like that, Annabelle served up one of her own coven members to Lisette in exchange for her own life.

Blood splattered across the shadowy threshold. I could feel my own consciousness slipping away once again, and that terrified me more than anything—the idea of lying here lifeless. As blood gurgled into Lisette's throat, I used my last bout of strength to shove myself across the floor, out of sight from the entranceway and into the dark corner across from Codi.

Codi.

He was still lying in the shadows beneath the window where I'd set him, slumped over, eyes closed. I tried to hang on to the sight of him. *He's sleeping,* I told myself. *Sleeping.* I tried to focus on the muffled screams outside, on the smell of smoldered grass wafting in, and on the chill in the air, but little by little it all slipped away no matter how hard I fought.

As I drifted away, all I could imagine was Isaac finding me here in the convent, dead, after releasing Nicco. My heart ached with regret over not telling him everything.

Who would he think was the bigger traitor: Annabelle . . . or me?

A sense of panic jarred me awake. Voices in the darkness.

"Mrs. Le M-Moyne—?" Codi trembled.

Panic exploded in my chest. He was still catty-corner to me, but now a woman towered over him, her skin silvery in the pale moonlight. She was breathing heavily, her shoulders heaving, as if she were fighting herself.

"Mrs. Le Moyne, it's me! Codi Daure! Remember, I lived down the street? Adele's friend from the tearoom. You used to visit with her when she was a little girl and drink chamomile tea."

She was barefoot, and blood dripped from her fingertips. I hoped it was from her last victim and not Codi.

Get up, Adele. Get the hell up. This isn't Annabelle!

"Mom?" The word barely rasped out of my throat.

Codi's eyes caught mine, and he vigorously shook his head. My mother leaned over him, and his eyes watered as he looked back up to her. I couldn't see her face, but I knew her fangs were out by the way Codi coiled. She knelt down—

"No!" I flung myself up, screaming, "Mom! Please!"

She didn't so much as look my way. I tore the silver feather from the thin chain around my neck. The medallion slipped off and spun away.

I pressed the sharp edge of the feather against the inside of my arm. *She's my mom; she won't kill me.* But Codi was not so safe.

"No, Adele!" Codi yelled. "No!"

"Get away from him!" I ripped the metal feather into my skin, expelling a scream from my throat. It slipped from my hand and clanked to the floor as blood welled from the wound.

"Cover it up, Adele!" Codi smacked his hand against the ground.

I squeezed my arm, spattering droplets of red.

Brigitte whipped around, the silhouette of her hair glimmering in moonlight.

My eyes welled. "Mom . . . ?"

The word sounded unrecognizable from my voice. It felt so strange to see her, I didn't know what else to say. She looked like a slightly taller, vampiric version of me, and it was terrifying.

Blood, so dark it looked black on her shadowy face, was smeared across her chin like she'd tried to wipe it off.

"Mom . . ."

A tear dripped down her cheek into the blood—it was the most emotion my mother had ever shown me, as far as I could remember.

She stepped closer. I held my arms out to her, tears pouring down my face. *I can survive a vampire bite if it comes to that. Adeline did. Morning Star did.*

That's what I told myself as I caught the look in her eyes—the begging for forgiveness—just before they glossed over like Nicco's predatory stare.

And that's what I kept telling myself when she didn't go for my arm—when my head slammed back against the wall and her fangs plunged into my neck. When my scream didn't faze her in the slightest, and she instantly began pulling on my blood. Paralysis overcame me as her venom spidered into veins.

In the distance I heard my name echoing down the hallway.

Isaac.

He was too far away. He was going to be too late, and then he'd hate himself forever. I didn't want him to hate himself. I hoped he'd move on and be happy, without me.

My fingernails clawed into her shoulder, and her nails clawed into mine. I wanted to beg her to stop, but the only words that came out of my lips were, "It's okay, Mom. It's okay."

The sound of my name came closer.

Nicco?

Still not close enough.

I trembled, and she trembled, and my skin was slippery with my blood and her tears, but still she didn't stop drinking. As I sank to the floor underneath her, the pain faded into numbness, and my arms went limp.

She didn't stop when Isaac burst through the door, nor when Nicco rushed in at his heels, screaming her name.

Isaac dove straight for her, but Nicco leaped at him and wrestled him to the ground. Isaac got an arm free and pulled out a stake.

"No!" I croaked.

He released it, using a gust of wind to whip it straight toward my mother's back.

I barely saw it, just felt her fangs push deeper into my neck as the stake plunged into her.

No, Isaac. No.

Her grip tightened, and her bite tightened, and then she froze.

No.

She leaned into me, lifeless.

No.

Nicco and Isaac rolled over each other, grappling, and slammed into the wall near Codi. They jumped apart, whirling back to me.

Nicco's eyes went wide.

Isaac rushed past him, screaming my name. He pulled my mother off, letting her body fall to the stone floor without even a glance, and he ripped open my collar, but my gaze didn't leave my mom. "Adele!" His hands cupped my face as he repeated my name over and over.

Nicco lifted her up and carried her into the beam of moonlight. He gently set her down on her side and slid the stake from her back. My chest tightened as he took her pulse.

Italian words slipped from his lips as he draped his fingers over her eyes.

No. No. No.

She can't be dead. She's a vampire.

Watching her eyes slip shut, I felt like I was watching my own death in some out-of-body experience.

"Adele, you're going to be okay," Isaac said, reaching his arms under my back to pick me up.

A man's voice cried out from the hallway. "Brigitte!" Emilio burst through the door, a look of total panic on his face.

"Isaac," I choked. "Behind you."

It was just enough time for him to glance over his shoulder, change form, then flap up and away, out the window, out of Emilio's reach.

As Emilio fell next to Brigitte, hysterical, Nicco dashed to me, scooped me into his arms, and whipped out the door, cradling me against his chest.

CHAPTER 47

The Fifth Element

I pounded my wings, soaring over the back gardens, the wind zipping through my feathers as I caught the air current, rising higher into the starry night, flapping faster and faster as my thoughts ping-ponged back and forth between two images: the stake releasing from my fingertips, and Adele's bloody bite mark.

When I was far enough away, I looked down. No one was chasing me. I'd expected full-on retaliation after staking one of their own.

I killed a vampire . . .

I *killed* a vampire.

A Medici sister. And no one was chasing me . . . yet. That left me more freaked out than if I'd seen all three of Giovanna's brothers at my heels.

I need to get back to Adele.

I tipped to the side and soared a wide circle around the gardens.

The sight below sickened me. Total carnage. Trails of blood led to drained bodies—one strewn across a hedge, another crumpled against the concrete wall perimeter, and another facedown in the fountain, turning the water crimson. The arc of statues in the middle of the yard still gleamed white under the stars, but two were now covered in smears of red. A circle had been burned into the patch of grass around them, and tiny piles of burning embers glowed here and there on the lawn. Blackened lemon trees and bushes still smoldered. It smelled like a campfire, but looked like a campsite that had been attacked by wild beasts.

As I swooped over the roof, the sound of cracking glass rippled overhead. I craned my neck to look up toward the moon just in time to see the glimmering invisibility shield shatter into a million twinkling pieces. They rained down around me, vaping out before hitting the ground.

Annabelle had broken the spell . . . or someone had broken Annabelle.

And then, as if the spell being broken had tripped some kind of silent alarm, witches and vampires began scattering from the school grounds, running away from the now-unprotected site of the massacre. If the witches headed straight past Esplanade, they'd be safe from most of the vamps—from all but Nicco and Emilio—but in that moment I didn't care about warning them. All I cared about was getting back to Adele.

I dove down to Chartres Street and through the front doors of the church. The dead witch was still impaled on the candle rack, but there was no sign of Callis's dead body, just a splotch of blood in the spot where Emilio had attacked him. Celestina was gone too. I zoomed through the door into the dark hallway and dropped to the floor, taking human form as I landed. Panting, I pounded across the wooden floorboards and burst into the room where I'd left Adele.

"Isaac!" a girl yelled from the shadows. "Thank God!"

She leaned into the glow shining up from her phone, which was resting on the floor.

"Désirée?" I stepped closer.

She was hunched over a guy who looked bad off: his white T-shirt was completely sweat-soaked through, his breathing was rapid and shallow, and his lips were turning blue. Désirée's arm glistened with fresh blood. His, I think.

"Are you okay?" I spun around looking for Adele.

There was more blood on the floor, but no one else in the room, not even a body. No dead vampire. No Adele.

"Where's Adele?" I yelled.

"How would I know—I just got here! What the hell happened? Did Adele open the attic? Where's Annabelle?"

"Adele was right here two minutes ago. Come on, we have to find her!"

Désirée took off her jacket and pressed it into the guy's leg. "Isaac, we can't just leave him."

I paced back and forth. "I don't care about helping any of Callis's coven members right now. We have to find Adele!"

"This isn't one of Callis's coven members!" Her voice lowered. "This is Codi Daure."

I paused, peering down at him.

"And from what I'm guessing . . . he's our fifth."

The guy on the floor stirred. "She saved me. Adele saved me from the vampire."

Of course she did. "Dammit!" I lowered down to pick him up. "Come on. Let's get him out of here."

"No!" Désirée shouted, quickly moving her hands so I could see the wound: a bone stuck out of his thigh. "He's going to bleed out if we move him."

"Jesus!" I unhooked my belt and ripped it through the loops.

He howled as I lifted his leg just enough to slip the band of leather underneath it; I tightened it, and he really howled, followed by a slew of profanity.

"I didn't know southerners knew words like those," I said, seeing the fear in his eyes.

His mouth twitched into a half smile. He looked up at me, his whole body trembling as he spoke. "It wasn't your fault. There was nothing else you could have done."

What the hell is he talking about?

"You had to stake her," he continued. "She was going to kill Adele."

Clearly, Codi Daure and I were going to have a lot of bonding to do if he thought I gave a shit about taking out Giovanna Medici, especially when she was attacking Adele.

I pulled out my phone and activated the flashlight so I could get a better look. *"Désirée,"* I said, seeing that his lip color was turning from periwinkle to cornflower. "He's going into hypovolemic shock! He needs an emergency room, now. He needs blood!"

Désirée didn't answer. She didn't even look up. Her head was bent over him, her hands clutching her blood-soaked jacket over his wound as if she were hanging on for dear life.

"What's wrong?" I asked as her knuckles clenched even tighter. "Dee!"

She rocked back and forth, and then she screamed as if in great pain.

"Désirée!" I hustled around to her side, ripping my hoodie over my head, ready to replace her blood-soaked jacket. I pushed away her hands, but when I peered down at the wound, there was no longer a splintered bone, just a severe cut deep into his thigh.

"Dee, what the hell?"

Codi's fingers moved. He pulled her hands back over the wound, barely coherent as he mumbled, "Please don't stop."

Her eyes slipped shut, and she began again. Color drained from her face, making her look even paler by the glow of our phones, and tears poured from her eyes in steady streams. Her brow scrunched, as if she was trying not to scream in pain.

"Dee, stop. Just stop." I shook her shoulder. "Whatever you're doing! Stop!"

Codi sucked in a giant gasp of air, and she collapsed into my arms. Her eyes rolled back in her head until I saw nothing but the whites of her eyes.

"Désirée!" I shook her harder than I should have. "Answer me!"

"What the?" Her eyes fluttered open. "G-get off me."

Fuck.

"What's going on?" She slowly sat up, and gasped, looking down at her left arm. "Oh, my Goddess . . ." A mark on her left arm was glowing lime green. "My Maleficium," she said despondently.

Codi hoisted himself into a sitting position, sucking in air and patting his ripped jeans where the broken bone had been. "What the hell, Borges?" he said in wonder. "You have the power to heal?"

"Where's Adele?" I asked him, flashing my phone around the room. There were red spatter marks everywhere.

A glint on the stone floor across the room caught my attention.

With a sinking feeling, I strode over and picked it up: the feather, sticky in blood. *"No."* I twisted around and saw the medallion.

I scooped it up along with the broken chain.

Codi picked himself up as if he hadn't just had a near-death experience. His gaze hardened as he walked over to me. "He took her."

My fingers curled around the feather.

"I'm coming with you," he cried, but I was already flying out the window, higher and higher, caws ripping from my throat.

CHAPTER 48

The Maleficiums

I faded in and out of consciousness along the way.

I didn't know where we were going, but I was eager to get there with Nicco.

By the time he climbed the narrow, winding stairs to the bell tower, I could feel his strength ebbing, how he strained to lower me to the cold stone floor.

The starlit sky poured in through the broken shutters, and even in the dark Nicco's Medici-green eyes twinkled like points on a constellation. His face was pale and gaunt, and I wondered if it was the filter of moonlight or because he hadn't fed. That question didn't scare me as much as the fear that flickered in his eyes.

He propped me up against the stone wall.

Feverish waves shook my entire being. I could smell my burned hair and clothes.

He ripped off his hoodie, bunched it up, and cradled my head, slipping it underneath. My eyes grazed over the mark on his left arm as he sat back. It was just as Isaac had described the thin black line work.

Wait. What?

"Nicc—?"

His left hand covered my lips tightly, his eyes glazed over, and his nostrils flared. He leaned in, his other hand pushing away the flannel from my collarbone. As I began to protest, his mouth went straight to my neck. It all happened so fast: his breath against my skin, the slither of his tongue—and then his teeth.

My eyes pinched shut, and I screamed into his hand, clutching his wrist as his fangs sunk into me, reopening the wound. His grip tightened, and his bell tower fantasy of killing me replayed in my head.

But he quickly pulled out and began to suck.

The venom seared as he siphoned it out through the bite. He spit the poison over his shoulder and came back to my neck again. As he sucked and sucked, all I could think of was Callis siphoning my fire. All I could do was scream.

The bells in the tower began to clang, drowning out my voice. As he pulled out the venom, I pulled the bells, and it was the only thing that gave me hope. Hope that all of my magic wasn't gone forever, that Emilio had been able to rescue my mother in time . . . that somehow she was still alive.

But I couldn't feel the magic. All I could feel was the burning, and the poison, and my voice turning raw, and Nicco's energy draining. All I could feel was Nicco.

Each time he came back to my neck, his grip was looser and his pull more gentle, and I knew it wasn't because he was finished. I knew it was because he was fading too.

Nicco can't be fading.

Then he stopped. With his forehead against the side of my head, he inhaled deeply through his nose.

And then he propped himself against the stone wall next to me and pulled me into his lap so my back was resting against his chest. His silence scared me.

I craned my neck, trying to look up at him—that fear in his eyes hadn't gone away.

His right arm slipped around my waist, gripping me. Tight.

Then I realized why.

No.

He drew his wrist to his mouth, bit down, and before I could even squirm, blood drizzled on my cheek and he was wedging his wrist against my mouth.

I gagged as the blood trickled down my throat. He held me tighter. And then suddenly I was trying not to think about it—any of it. I tried not to think at all. I just sank back against him, watching the colors spin in front of my eyes, and inhaled his leather-and-soap scent.

When he pulled his wrist out of my mouth, it was *crushing.*

I felt completely drained.

Of blood.

Of venom.

Of magic.

I tilted my head up to his because I wanted more. I wanted more of him.

He smiled his not-so-innocent smile, and my heart swelled.

"No more, *bella.*"

I smiled back at him and let my head fall against his chest. His arms circled me tighter. My eyes slipped shut, and somehow I knew his did too.

I heard the thump-thump-thumping of his heart, but this time not through a door, not through a dream.

"You have to survive this, Adele," he said softly, the only words he'd spoken all night. His hand circled my wrist, two fingers placed over my pulse. "You have to survive this for us."

Thump-thump.

Thump-thump.

    Thump-thump.

        Thump-thump.

CHAPTER 49
Brooklyn Girl

I flew and I flew and I flew, searching for her. Up every street, down every block of the French Quarter. I flew to her house. To Mac's bar. To HQ. The Voodoo shop, the tearoom, the café. Over and over.

I circled the Carter brothers' compound on St. Ann and Royal until I no longer trusted myself not to go inside. I wanted to chimney-dive in. It was beyond reckless—I shouldn't have been on the streets, not even above the rooftops, after killing a Medici.

I killed a vampire, but all I could think about was whether a vampire was killing the girl that I loved.

There was no sign of Nicco or Adele. I wanted to drive a stake through him for taking her. I should never have given her that note. I should never have trusted Callis. I should never have left her side at the convent.

I soared through Jackson Square to the Moonwalk. There was no one. No vampires or witches or drunk gutter-punks or kids making out after curfew. Just the moonlight shimmering down on the waves as they crashed up the cement steps.

I circled back.

Where are you, Adele?

I couldn't stop searching, because as long as Mother Nature's silent black sky was wrapped around me, I could believe she was still alive. As long as I was in the air, swooping and diving beneath the crystal-dripped stars, I could keep it together. But back on solid ground I wasn't so sure.

In the sky it was easy to imagine what I'd do when I found her. I'd take her out of this town, back to New York, away from the vampires, away from the coven, even away from the magic.

Fuck all of this. I just want her.

In New York, she'd drag me around for hours looking at hundreds of fabrics in the garment district for fashion-school projects, and I'd sketch her naked body as she slept in our bed in the morning light. She'd hang fairy lights all year-round, and she'd wear that perfectly thin shirt while making coffee in the mornings, and we'd fight over who forgot to water the plants, and it would all be magical.

So I flew.

I flew until dawn broke.

I flew until I fell out of the sky.

CHAPTER 50
Family Matters

January 22nd

I awoke on the cold stone floor, my teeth chattering. The slice of light shining onto my face felt like it was piercing my brain, and the ringing in my ears was nauseating. The bells were perfectly silent.

I was alone in the bell tower.

No bag. No phone.

No Nicco.

Just me and the bells and his hoodie folded into a perfect square under my head. My ears were freezing. So were my hands. I slipped the hoodie on, over Nicco's flannel shirt, and hugged myself into it. I tried to ignite my hand, just for the warmth.

Nothing.

I sucked in a sharp breath as it all came back.

I wasn't quite ready to relive it. I wasn't sure I'd ever be. My hand went to my neck, where Brigitte had bitten me. The skin was sensitive. Fresh. It stung a little bit, but there were no puncture wounds, not even a scab.

With a foggy head, I pulled myself up.

As I descended the spiral staircase, I paused twice to lean against the wall, taken with dizziness. I made it to a door that said **ALARM WILL SOUND IF OPENED**, but it didn't.

I walked at a slug's pace, overwhelmed with exhaustion and with the memory of my mother's death. That little moment of pressure when the stake pierced through her chest touching mine, and how she instantly stopped drinking from me. It was all I could think about on the walk home. That, and seeing Nicco's fingers brush her eyes closed.

She was dead.

Isaac had killed my mom.

And now I was going to have to tell my father. But what was I supposed to tell him? My eyes welled.

I passed my house and walked around the block twice, trying to mentally string words into sentences. Each step became a series of breathing exercises, blinking back tears, and repeating the first sentence over and over until I didn't recognize the words.

When I opened the kitchen door, my father was sitting at the table, staring at the moon mug in his hands. The room smelled of fresh coffee, and there was an open bottle of whiskey in front of him. The pungent smell of booze hung in the air with the french roast. He didn't look up.

I pulled out a chair and gripped the back of it, holding myself up. My voice shook. "Dad . . . ?"

"Where have you been?" he asked, staring at the crescent handle.

"I—I was with Isaac."

"You never were a good liar . . . just like your mother. She didn't have the heart for it."

He picked up the bottle, poured another glug into the mug, and took a sip.

"Dad, what's wrong?"

"Is Emilio Medici in New Orleans?"

"What?" I choked.

He didn't look up, but I knew the one little question had implicated me.

"Dad, how do you—?"

"Tell me the truth, Adele." He finally looked at me, his eyes more bloodshot than usual, even after a graveyard shift. "I remember. I remember everything."

I sat in the chair next to him. "Remember what, Dad?"

He paused, and I fought the avalanche shaking inside my chest. He took another sip from the mug, and I wondered if there was any coffee in it at all.

"My last trip to Paris . . . ," he finally said. "You were little. I left you with Sabine and Bertrand because I couldn't *not* go after her. I didn't understand why she left. I knew if I could just talk to her, I could fix whatever was wrong."

"I remember." My words were no more than a whisper. What I wanted to say was, *There was nothing you could have done, Dad.*

"A week went by before she'd see me, and even then it was in secret. One night she stayed at my hotel room and told me everything . . . that they—" His fists clenched. "That he'd killed her."

I clutched my hands together and sat perfectly still, waiting for him to continue. I didn't understand. *How is it possible that my father's known for twelve years?*

"She told me what happened. How this Emilio Medici brought her back to life, and how she killed those students. She told me she'd never forgive herself for walking down the street that night when I'd always told her not to walk through the Quarter after dark by herself."

The tears in my eyes welled so huge he became nothing but a blur as he continued.

"I should have been with her that night. I should have been with her every night."

I took his hand from the mug. "What would you have done, Dad? What could you have done against a vampire?"

Tears dripped out of his eyes, and I felt my chest caving in. I breathed slow, shallow breaths.

"After she told me everything, we had one last night together, and then in the morning she *bit* me. She bit me and told me to forget everything she'd told me. She told me to forget about her. To go home and raise our daughter for the both of us. To find someone else, and to be happy without her. She kissed me good-bye . . . and I got on the plane and forgot that she ever came and met me."

Suddenly it all made sense. My mother had used her vampiric thrall to make him forget, and now his memories had come back because . . .

"I forgot about the visit until this morning," he said quietly. "The memories started coming back, one by one, and I came home and you weren't here and weren't answering your phone, and ever since, I've just had this feeling like I've lost everything."

"Because she's dead." My voice was soft. "Your memories are coming back because . . . she died, Dad." My throat closed up, threatening to smother my words. "But I'm here." And with that I reached my threshold. I couldn't talk anymore because I couldn't breathe. All I could do was climb onto my father's lap, wrap my arms around his neck, and cry.

He hugged me tight. "I could never forget her."

Feeling his chest shudder shattered me. "I know, Dad. I know," I choked. "And you haven't lost everything. You have me. You'll always have me." I hugged him tighter.

"And you'll always have me. Come hell or high water."

"I think we've already been through both," I said, trying to smile.

Somehow through the tears and the shudders and the swollen lungs, I felt better. Better than I had since before the Storm. Better than I had since before my mom left, because finally my father and I didn't need to have any secrets.

I told him about Adeline Saint-Germain's diary, and the Count, and her medallion—and our Fire magic. Even though I couldn't produce a flame to show him, he didn't act like I was having some kind of psychotic break. He just quietly listened, scratching his scruffy face. Maybe magic wasn't so weird after grappling with the reality of vampires.

I told him about Adeline's coven, and about our coven. Everything but what Isaac did, because I just couldn't get his name out of my mouth. I couldn't tell my father that Isaac had killed his love . . . his ballerina.

I poured us both coffee, and he asked questions, trying to hide how overwhelming it all was. I wondered if, when he was my age, he was a Fire witch who didn't receive his mark and whose memories faded out along with the magic.

I wanted him to be magical.

Eventually I even told him about Nicco.

But every time we got close to how Brigitte had died, permanently this time, he backed off and stopped asking questions. I don't know if it was because he couldn't bear to think of her being gone, or because he was my dad, and he knew talking about it was going to send me into an asthma-induced coma.

We'd finished our coffees, so I got up to make more. Just as I poured the boiling water into the french press, the door slammed open. Someone blew into the room so fast, every cup on the counter flew across the room with him, showering the kitchen with broken glass.

When I unshielded my face, Emilio had my dad by the neck, up against the wall. "What do you remember?" he yelled. "What did she tell you?"

"Everything," my father squeezed out, his face turning plum.

I lifted the carafe of coffee, ready to smash it against Emilio's head, but then another flash whipped into the room and knocked him away. *Nicco.* The two brothers fell backward and smashed into the table, breaking it in half like it was made of toast.

They twisted around and Emilio slammed Nicco to the floor. "Mac knows about me, so he *dies.* End of story, *fratellino.*"

In that moment, Nicco seemed frailer than his brother, and I wondered how much more blood Emilio had consumed since their release.

My father aggressively stepped toward them. "Get ou—"

But I pulled him away until we were both backed up against the sink, me realizing just how vulnerable we were without my Fire.

"I'll take care of it," Nicco said under his breath. He shoved Emilio up to his feet and jumped up himself.

Emilio looked at us.

Nicco grabbed him by the shoulder before he could make another move. *"I'll take care of it,"* he said again through locked jaw.

"Fine," Emilio spat, turning to leave. But then he spun around and grabbed Nicco by the collar. "You have *one* chance. Do you hear me?"

"Sì."

"What the hell is that supposed to mean?" I muttered.

Nicco rattled off more aggressive-sounding Italian words, and Emilio stalked to the door, shooting a cold glance back as he crossed the threshold. "I have another thing to take care of anyway." He snickered. "One that I know even you'll approve of, baby brother."

And then he was gone, and the entire room felt like it exhaled.

Nicco watched the door for a long moment before he turned around to face us.

I extended my arm protectively over my father, just like he always did with me. "What the hell do you think you're going to do?" I shouted.

"Mr. Le Moyne, can I have a word with your daughter?"

"Absolutely not." My father pushed my arm away, stepping toward him. "You need to leave. Now."

"I'm afraid I really do need to speak with Adele. It will only take a minute, I promise."

"No."

Nicco sucked in a long breath through his nose. "I apologize in advance for this."

I wasn't sure if he was talking to me or Mac, but then he stepped close to my father and looked him straight in the eye. "Mac, I need to talk to Adele. You're going to take your coffee into the sitting room and wait for me. Do not fret; no harm will come to her."

"It's okay, Dad," I said, but it didn't matter because he was already nodding.

He walked over to the pot of coffee I'd almost thrown at Emilio's head and topped off his mug.

Nicco and I watched him leave the room.

He turned to me, stepping close. His hands slid over my neck. "What are you do—?" I started to ask. "It's fine." His touch made me shiver.

But he didn't let go until I complied, angling my neck slightly so he could inspect the wound. He brushed away my hair, and I imagined him in Florence, treating people of their seventeenth-century ailments, in the life he never got to have.

His hands rested at the base of my neck, and he inhaled. I could sense his relief.

"You'll be okay, *bella*."

"*Grazie,*" I said, a near whisper.

Our eyes locked, and it felt like the last three months hadn't happened. Like no time had passed at all.

"Are you okay?" I asked. He didn't look as gaunt as last night, but he still looked paler than I remembered him being. Then again, maybe I was used to the human Nicco from my dreams. From his dreams.

He smiled lightly.

"What?"

"I knew you would get me out."

His smile was impossible not to return, even if only slightly. I nodded, fighting the urge to touch him back. "I'm sorry it took so long. I didn't kn—"

"*No, è colpa mia.* I'm sorry, Adele. If I'd thought for a second Callisto might arrive in town, I would have never left you." His fingers slid through my hair. "I would have found another way."

I nodded again, my hand slipping over his wrist. It all felt like a dream. Him being here in my kitchen. His cool touch on my skin and how much I wanted to pull him closer.

He tensed. It was slight, but I felt it. The look in his glassy green eyes changed too. Sadness.

"Adele, I have to do it." His voice was drenched with sympathy.

Which made mine sharpen. "You have to do *what?*"

"Your father cannot know about my family—or about you. Your magical side. The entire witching world is held together by secrets. The mundane cannot know." He took my left arm and pushed up my sleeve.

I gasped.

"My Maleficium," I whispered. A memory from last night flashed through my head. *Only a witch who has a mark can see the mark of others.* "You." I grabbed his left arm and pushed his black sweater up his taut forearm.

But he stopped me. "I'm a vampire, Adele."

"*No,* I saw it last night. *I saw it,* Nicco. I saw your mark."

He pushed my chin up so my gaze was on him. "I'm a vampire. And that's why I'm going into the sitting room to alter your father's memories."

He turned and walked away.

"No!" I grabbed his arm, like a child begging. "Nicco, please don't!"

"There's no other way." He pulled his arm back.

"Nicco!" I followed him into the dark hallway. "I'm not going to let you do this!"

He quickly spun around, and I shrunk back into the wall. "Which would you prefer? For me to go in there and harmlessly erase the same memories your mother already wiped away, or for your father to have to run from Emilio for the *rest of his life?*"

"I can't lose him, Nicco. I—I can't do this alone."

"You're not alone. You have your coven."

"Not anymore." My head shook. "Not after I opened the attic. Not after I let you out."

He lightly touched my jaw, and his eyes caught mine. I didn't think he would actually say it, but he did. His voice softened. "You have me."

"You're a vampire, remember?"

"*Sì.*"

His hand cupped my cheek, and my welling tears shook out.

As he wiped them away, his own eyes darkened with pain, but I was unable to look at him anymore—my gaze shifted over his shoulder—which I knew hurt him deeper.

"Just stay right here," he said. "It will only take a minute."

"No. If you're going to do it, I'm going in too."

"I have to *bite* him, Adele. If I don't drink from him, the memory loss won't be permanent."

"And?"

"Absolutely not. I am not biting your father in front of you. I am not biting anyone in front of you. Ever."

My fingers rapped against my leg like hummingbird wings. "Then I have one condition." I quickly explained my request.

"No." He shook his head. "I understand why you're asking me to do it, but I promise you don't want me to. You're just upset with him right now. *Rightfully* upset."

"Do it, or I'm coming in."

"Adele. It cannot be undone."

"That's the point."

He sighed and walked through the door, leaving me alone in the hallway.

The seconds felt like minutes, and the minutes felt like hours, but I didn't pace. I didn't fidget or twirl my hair. I just stood there, staring at the closed door, heart racing.

I shouldn't have asked him to do it. But in those moments in the hallway, the pain had flooded in and I hadn't felt anything but loss.

The loss of my mother. The loss of my magic. And now the loss of my father.

With every inhale, anger poured into me, taking up all the space that magic used to fill. My jaw clenched, and my fists tightened. Heat surged through my limbs, making me want to kick and punch things until I couldn't move.

The door gently opened, and Nicco looked at me.

"Did you do it?" I asked.

He nodded.

I peered behind him. My father was sitting on the couch, rubbing his eyes like he'd just woken up. When I turned back to Nicco, a rush of tears came with it.

"Get out," I spat.

He moved toward me, but I raised my hand and stopped him. "Get out!"

I pushed him down the hallway toward the kitchen.

"Adele, I—"

But I wouldn't let him speak. I just kept pushing him, through the kitchen and toward the door, repeating the words until I was screaming. "Get out, get out. Get out of my head!"

He stumbled out, and I slammed the door, falling against it, sobbing.

"Adele, what's wrong?" my father said, running into the room.

I sucked a giant breath through my nose, swallowed back the tears, and turned around.

He didn't seem to notice that he was standing on broken glass.

"Dad, sit down . . . I need to tell you something. It's about Mom."

Obediently, he sat down at the broken table, his face pale.

"Dad, there's been an accident . . ."

I sat down next to him and burst into tears again, but this time feeling like I'd lost both of my parents.

CHAPTER 51

The Romeo Catcher

Despite all the horrors that had unfolded last night, there were no nightmares when I slept. Just warmth from a fire and air that smelled like cinnamon and soft cushions and plush blankets.

And pressure against my back, I realized as consciousness folded back—my eyes popped open, and I twisted around, but it wasn't Adele lying against me. It was Jade. One of her arms rested over Stormy as tiny coos slipped from her lips.

It took me a moment to figure out where I was. *HQ.* In Cosette's secret room, in the invisible bed under an invisible blanket. With a child and a dog who were only visible to me. I couldn't remember how I got here, but I knew Désirée had drugged me, because I felt completely drowsy and completely rested at the same time.

"You saved her, Isaac," a female voice said.

I blinked, and she came into focus. Julie was sitting at the foot of the bed, watching over us.

"You saved her soul. And souls are forever."

"You're aliv—I mean, you're okay," I said, feeling a momentary flicker of happiness.

She wasn't completely back to her opaque self, but she was barely fluttering in and out. "I told you I would never let him get me."

"Is Ade—"

She shook her head. "Codi and the Earth witch have just gone back out to look for her."

"Nicco has her," I said, getting out of the bed, looking for my sneakers. I grabbed them from the corner chair, along with my jacket. "I'm going over there."

"The Earth witch said that you need to stay here. It's the only place you're safe. A dangerous vampire is looking for you."

"I'll take my chances," I said, lacing them up. "I'm going to find Adele, and then I'm going to find Callis and make sure he can never hurt another ghost again—"

Stormy shot up and sprang out of bed, growling, her teeth bared.

I turned. Emilio was standing in the threshold, leaning against the doorway.

Stormy barked.

"Where is she?" I yelled.

Stormy crouched low, growling again. Emilio walked straight up to her, bent down, and rubbed her head. He looked in perfect vampiric health, making me wonder how many people he'd drained.

"You can see her?"

"An advantage of once having died."

"Julie, get out of here!" I said without taking my eyes off him.

He stood, looking at the unmade bed and back to me. "Well, I see it's not just Adele who's moved on so quickly." He nodded at Julie. "She's beautiful."

"Fuck off."

He took another step closer, and Julie blinked out, taking Jade and Stormy with her.

"Did you kill Annabelle?" I asked. "How did you see this place through the invisibility shield?

"You're the only person I'm concerned with killing."

"Where's Nicco?" I don't know if it was adrenaline or sleep deprivation or desperation, but I wasn't scared of him.

He smirked. "Adele should be the least of your concerns right now."

"Where is she?" I yelled, stepping toward him.

"She's at home. With her father. And *my little brother*. He's only been out a few hours and they're like a little cozy family."

"She's alive—" I choked.

"Of course she's alive, unlike her *mother*." His fist slammed into my chest, sending me sliding across the floor. I crashed into a vanity. Heavy silver hairbrushes and perfume bottles clanked to the floor around me.

I turned to the open window, getting ready to change form, but froze as his comment registered. "What do you mean unlike her mother?" I stealthily reached for the stake strapped to my ankle as I stood.

He looked at me, equally perplexed. "Did someone cast a memory spell on you last night? You *staked* her." He moved toward me, crazy flickering in his eyes.

"I staked your sister."

He stopped short. "*What?*"

"I killed your sister, just like I'm going to kill you!" I hurled the stake directly at his chest, but his hand whipped out and the weapon came flying back toward my head. It grazed my ear, drawing blood, before it smashed straight through the window behind me like a bullet. I was sure he missed on purpose, which only amplified the tension in the air. He was taking pleasure in dragging this out.

Neither of us moved as he just stood there, staring at me. Then he started laughing. "You think you killed my sister? *You?* Now that's a farce worthy of the stage. Giovanna hasn't been seen in three hundred years. The idea that she is even alive is ridiculous!"

"Liar! You wept over her body last night as I flew out the window!"

Again he paused, looking at me. Then he burst into laughter and held up his palms. "Oh gods, thank you for letting me be the messenger!" He looked straight at me. "*Grazie mille* for letting me be the one to tell you right before you die that you did not kill my sister, *witch*. You *murdered* my love—my child—Brigitte Dupré Le Moyne!"

"You're insane. Adele's mother is in France."

"*Non, elle n'y a pas été.* She's been in the attic with me for months, exactly where you trapped her on Halloween night with your Air."

"Bullshit."

A new voice floated into the room: "I guess you aren't as close to Adele as you thought, Isaac."

We both looked toward the entrance. Nicco was leaning in the doorway just as his brother had moments ago. They looked strikingly similar in the room's dim light. My pulse hammered as I wondered if Adele had told him about me hiding his note from her.

Emilio smirked. "I knew you'd come. I knew you'd want to kill him yourself. I bet you've been dreaming of this moment for the last three months."

"You have no idea what I dream about, Emilio." Nicco's eyes never lifted from me.

"Brother, I have a pretty good idea of *who* you dream about. We all do."

An image of Nicco slumbering in the attic and dreaming about Adele made my pulse hammer double time. "She's never going to love you," I said, my voice even. "She's never going to be with a monster."

I eyed the nearest window, a path out over the balcony. Emilio's gaze followed mine.

This time Nicco was the one who smirked. "I might be the monster, but I'll never be the one who killed her mother."

This time the words stunned me. There was something about Nicco delivering the message that made my breath short.

There's no way I killed Adele's mother.

I was too stunned to move, too stunned to think, or to turn when Emilio lunged at me. His hands hit my chest, and then he hurled me through the window. In a shower of glass, my side hit the rail, and I flipped over the iron bar, feeling my ribs cracking and what felt like my insides ripping apart. It was so fast and the pain so intense, I was unable to take bird form. All I could do was grasp the balcony railing, but it was slick with morning dew and my hands immediately began to slide off. I looked down to the bricked courtyard, three long stories below.

It was over.

Everything.

Yet all I could think about was Adele. *It can't be true. They're just fucking with me.*

My right hand slipped off the rail entirely. I strained to hold on solely with my left, grunting with effort to pull myself up. But I couldn't hold on any longer. As my left hand slipped, and I began to drop, the balcony shook and a hand gripped mine, nearly jerking my arm out of the socket, catching me.

I howled in pain, dangling over empty space, and looked up.

Nicco didn't pull me over or offer his other hand. He just held on, his eyes fixed on something just below my chest.

My gaze followed his, and then I saw it: mere inches from my gut, on the inset pole that supported the gallery, a cluster of spikes jutted out like the petals of a lethal flower. Panic rushed me, and I looked back into his eyes—I could see how much he wanted to slam me into the spike.

He tightened his grip, and I knew he wasn't going to.

"Why?" I asked as his crystalline green eyes stared down at me.

"Because Adele's had enough loss for one day." He paused. "And if I let you die, she'll never trust me again. And she'll never forgive herself for opening the attic."

I didn't know which killed me more: that Nicco was so concerned with winning Adele's trust, or that she opened the attic to save him.

Emilio's footsteps stomped onto the balcony, and Nicco swung me, dangerously close to the Romeo catcher. On the upswing he flung me into the air and let go.

I soared over the brothel grounds.

The airtime was all I needed to take crow form and fly away.

EPILOGUE

Dead Mothers Club

I was only able to fly for three blocks before I felt my magic blinking out. I don't know if I was still weak from Callis's siphoning, or if it was the several cracked ribs, or the news about Adele's mother, but I began to lose altitude. I flapped frantically into the nearest alleyway and landed.

Leaning against the brick wall, I sucked in a sharp breath. The pain in my ribs was incomparable to the pain I might have caused Adele. It couldn't be true. I killed a vampire—*she was feeding off Adele.* The ache of losing my own mother rushed me.

I ran nonstop to Adele's house, staggering and clutching my side. *It can't be true.*

I knocked on the kitchen door, sucking in air, hoping Mac wasn't home. I didn't know how I could look him in the face.

He answered the door. "Can I help you?"

"Mr. Le Moyne, I need to—"

"Son, this really isn't a good time." He started to close the door. "We're having a family emergency."

I caught the door in my palm. "I know. I just need to talk to Adele. For a minute." My throat swelled shut. "I have to," I croaked.

He opened the door a couple feet, so I could see her sitting at the kitchen table.

"Adele!" I shouted.

He turned to her. "Sweetheart, do you know this boy?"

She looked straight at me. Her eyes glistened.

No. It can't be true. I can't have killed her mother.

"Adele . . ."

Tears slid down her cheeks. "No, Dad. I've never seen him before."

And for the first time, I was telling myself to breathe rather than telling her.

ACKNOWLEDGMENTS

So many stars have been added to the TCG constellation since the last book was published, my heart palpitates thinking that I may have forgotten someone. So many amazing people have given me latitude as a writer to make this book something I love. We love. I don't take a single one of you for granted. The trust. The faith. The hard work as I washed the pages clean when new ideas sprouted from the depths of my mind. Finding a place to start with the thank-yous is disorienting. I'll start at the beginning.

I want to thank all of the people who have taken a trip to New Orleans through Adele's eyes. To the readers who have stuck with me through glitter and grit as this sequel moved through all of the various nontraditional and traditional phases of publishing. Thank you to all of the fans who read the original five chapters on Wattpad and encouraged me to keep going, even when I flung the story back into seventeenth-century Italy.

Thank you to my agents extraordinaire at ICM Partners, Alexandra Machinist and Zoë Sandler, who sold the book. And who don't look at me like I'm crazy when my ideas slip from my lips.

Thank you to my sister and my parents for letting me continue to be crazy.

Thank you to all of my friends who welcome me back after long bouts of escaping into the clouds and off the grid. Thank you to every barista in the French Quarter who has kicked out a gutter-punk for trying to touch my hair. Thank you to the psychics and the witches and ghost storytellers. To the Mambos and the Second Liners and the Katrina first responders. And to everyone else in New Orleans who inspired this story. To the Florentines. To the ghosts of the Medici, who are hopefully not turning over in their graves. And if they are, see you on the flip side.

Thank you to everyone in cyberspace. To the bloggers and the BookTubers and the late-night Tweeters. To the Instagram book collectors and the hashtag generators. I <3 u. To Casey Ann Davoren! To the mermaids and unicorns and Goth kids and cheerleaders and mommies and teachers who all want to get swept away into stories. To all of the amazing librarians and booksellers I've met over the last few years. Thank you. The conference organizers and magazine editors. Podcast creators. And early reviewers. Thank you.

I wrote the very first chapter of *The Romeo Catchers* in Los Angeles, so that means I need to thank by best friend, Jennifer, who has supported me since the very first words were written, no matter how loony they were. To Lucas for being my human whiteboard every morning for months when I awoke having to work out the plotlines I dreamt about the night before. To Marissa Van Uden for not thinking I was a loser when I finally broke down and cried while editing. Thank you Marita Crandle, proprietress of Boutique du Vampyre, who I now consider to be Nicco's godmother. Beaming gratitude for Emilie Gagnet Leumas, archivist of the Archdiocese of New Orleans, for sharing your knowledge and for your friendship.

To Charlotte Ashley, Laura Perry, and Francesca Testaguzza, whose fingerprints have left marks on the manuscript. And special thanks to Ben Tague for sharing your maritime insights.

And to all of these amazing people who continue to support me on my journey: Sue Quiroz of the Vampire Lestat Fan Club. Monica S. Kuebler of *Rue Morgue Magazine*. Russell Desmond, proprietor of Arcadian. Amy Lowery of Garden District Book Shop. Candice Detillier Huber of Tubby and Coo's Mid-City Book Shop and Veronica Brooks-Sigler at Octavia Books. Lucy Silag.

To Alex Rosa and Melissa Lucas for being there during the early days of drafting. Amanda de Leon for encouraging me to always explore the dark side. To Jackie Garlick and Stormy Smith for reading *all* the different versions. Emma Leech, Lindsey Clarke, Hellvis, and ALL of my beta readers! To Heather Graham, and Viktor and Lynda Salazar.

And last but certainly not least, to the amazing team at Skyscape, whose list of names has grown tremendously since TCG: my editor, Courtney Miller, who ensures the books meet their greatest potential. Thank you. Thank you. Thank you. And to Adrienne Procaccini! Many heart-eyed emojis to Kimberly Cowser! And to Britt Rogers! Marianne Baer. Miriam Juskowicz and Robin Benjamin. To Matt Patin, Karen Parkin, and Nicole Burns-Ascue of Girl Friday Productions. To Katie Kurtzman. A *massive* thank-you to Galen Dara for another cover that drips beauty.

Special love for all the people in Louisiana who have been flooded out of house and home last year. We are #LouisianaStrong. You inspire me every single day.

And I would be remiss to not thank Julie, Otis, and everyone at Bottom of the Cup for filling my childhood with memories I continue to ponder to this day. Thank you to all of the ghosts of the French Quarter.

Merci beaucoup.

ABOUT THE AUTHOR

Alys Arden was raised by the street performers, tea-leaf readers, and glittering drag queens of the New Orleans French Quarter. She cut her teeth on the streets of New York and has worked all around the world since. She still dreams of running away with the circus one star-swept night. Follow her adventures on Twitter or Instagram at @alysarden.